# TUESDAY'S GONE

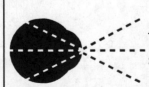

This Large Print Book carries the
Seal of Approval of N.A.V.H.

A FRIEDA KLEIN NOVEL

# TUESDAY'S GONE

## NICCI FRENCH

**THORNDIKE PRESS**
*A part of Gale, Cengage Learning*

Detroit • New York • San Francisco • New Haven, Conn • Waterville, Maine • London

GALE
CENGAGE Learning·

Copyright © Nicci Gerrard and Sean French, 2012.
A Frieda Klein Novel Series.
Map illustration of the River Tyburn by Michael Hill, Maps Illustrated.
Thorndike Press, a part of Gale, Cengage Learning.

Thorndike Press® Large Print Mystery.
The text of this Large Print edition is unabridged.
Other aspects of the book may vary from the original edition.
Set in 16 pt. Plantin.

**LIBRARY OF CONGRESS CATALOGING-IN-PUBLICATION DATA**

French, Nicci.
    Tuesday's gone / by Nicci French.
        pages ; cm. — (Thorndike Press large print mystery) (A Frieda Klein novel series)
    ISBN-13: 978-1-4104-5863-6 (hardcover)
    ISBN-10: 1-4104-5863-6 (hardcover)
    1. Women psychotherapists—Fiction. 2. Swindlers and swindling—Fiction. 3. Murder—Investigation—Fiction. 4. London (England)—Fiction. 5. Psychological fiction. 6. Large type books. I. Title.
    PR6056.R456T84 2013
    823'.914—dc23                                      2013008094

Published in 2013 by arrangement with Viking, a member of Penguin Group (USA) Inc.

LT-M

Printed in the United States of America
1 2 3 4 5 6 7 17 16 15 14 13

To Francis and Julia

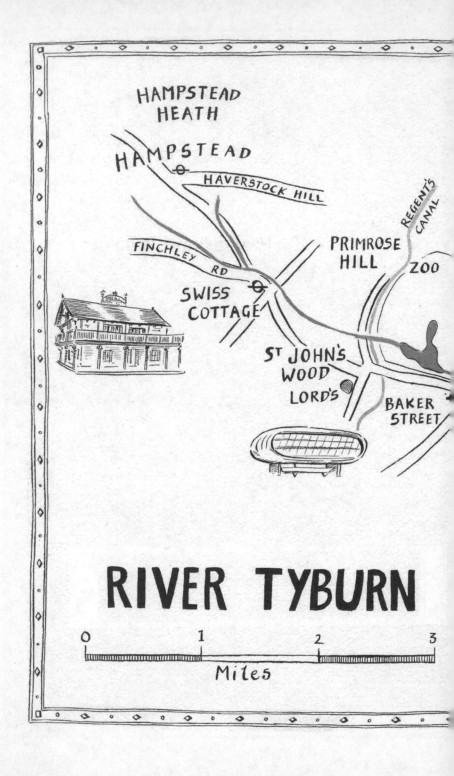

HAMPSTEAD
HEATH

HAMPSTEAD

HAVERSTOCK HILL

REGENT'S
CANAL

FINCHLEY RD

PRIMROSE
HILL

ZOO

SWISS
COTTAGE

St JOHN'S
WOOD

LORD'S

BAKER
STREET

# RIVER TYBURN

0        1        2        3

Miles

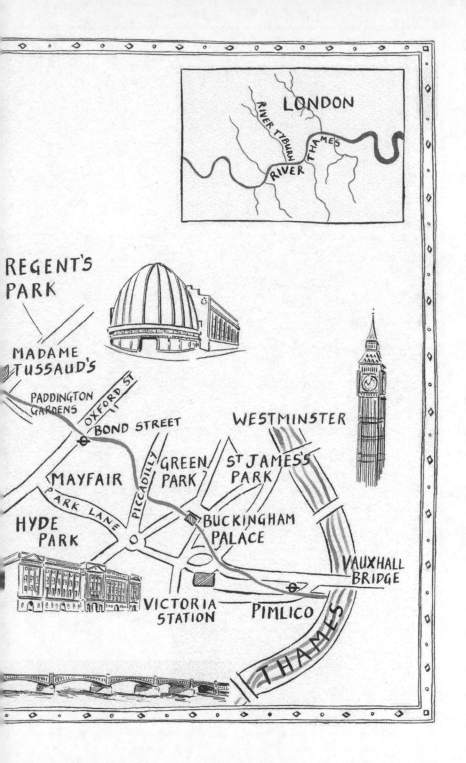

# 1

Maggie Brennan half walked, half ran along Deptford Church Street. She was talking on the phone and reading a file and looking for the address in the *A–Z*. It was the second day of the week, and she was already two days behind schedule. This didn't include the caseload she had inherited from a colleague who was now on permanent sick leave.

"No," said Maggie, into the phone. She looked at her watch. "I'll try to get to the meeting before you finish."

She put the mobile into her pocket. She was thinking of the case she'd just come from. A three-year-old with bruises. Suspicious bruises, the doctor in A&E had said. Maggie had talked to the mother, looked at the child, checked out the flat where they lived. It was horrible, damp, cold, but not obviously dangerous. The mother said she didn't have a boyfriend, and Maggie had

9

checked the bathroom and there was no razor. She had insisted that the child had fallen down the stairs. That's what people said when they hit their children, but even so, three-year-olds really did fall downstairs. She'd only spent ten minutes there, but ten hours wouldn't have made much difference. If she removed the child, the prosecution would probably fail and she would be disciplined. If she didn't remove the child and he was found dead, there would be an inquiry; she would be fired and maybe prosecuted. So she'd signed off on it. No immediate cause for concern. Probably nothing much would happen.

She looked more closely at the *A–Z*. Her hands were cold because she'd forgotten her gloves; her feet were wet in their cheap boots. She'd been to this hostel before, but she could never remember where it was. Howard Street was a little dead end, tucked away somewhere toward the river. She had to put her reading glasses on and move her finger around on the map before she found it. Yes, that was it, just a couple of minutes away. She turned off the main street and found herself unexpectedly next to a churchyard.

She leaned on the wall and looked at the file on the woman she was going to see.

10

There wasn't much at all. Michelle Doyce. Born 1959. A hospital discharge paper, copied to the Social Services department. A placement form, a request for an evaluation. Maggie flicked through the forms: no next of kin. It wasn't even clear why she had been in the hospital, although from the name of it, she could see that it was something psychological. She could guess the results of the evaluation in advance: just sheer general hopelessness, a pathetic middle-aged woman who needed somewhere to stay and someone to drop in just to keep her from wandering the streets. Maggie looked at her watch. There wasn't time for a full evaluation today. She could manage a basic checkup to make sure that Michelle was not in imminent danger, that she was feeding herself — the standard checklist.

She closed the file and walked away from the church along a housing estate. Some of the flats were sealed up, with metal sheets bolted on to the doors and windows, but most were occupied. From the second level, a teenage boy emerged from a doorway and walked along the balcony, his hands stuffed into the pockets of his bulky jacket. Maggie looked around. It was probably all right. It was a Tuesday morning, and the dangerous people were mostly still in bed. She turned the corner and checked the address she'd written in her notebook. Room One, 3 Howard Street. Yes, she remembered it now. It was a strange house that looked as if it had been built out of the same materials as the housing estate and then had decayed at the same rate. This hostel wasn't a proper hostel at all. It was a house rented cheaply from a private landlord. People could be put there while the services made up their minds about what to do with them. Usually they just moved on or were forgotten about. There were some places Maggie visited only with a chaperone, but she hadn't heard anything particular about this one. These people were mainly a danger to themselves.

She looked up at the house. On the second floor a broken window was blocked up with brown cardboard. There was a tiny paved front garden and an alley that went along the left side of the house. Beside the front door a bin bag had burst, but it had only added to the rubbish that was strewn everywhere. Maggie wrote a one-word note. There were five buzzers next to the front door. They didn't have labels next to them, but she pressed the bottom one, then pressed it again. She couldn't tell whether it was working. She was wondering whether

12

to knock on the door with her fist or look through the window when she heard a voice. Looking round, she saw a man right behind her. He was gaunt with wiry ginger hair tied back in a ponytail and piercings right across his face. She stepped to one side when she saw the man's dog, a small breed that was technically illegal, though it was the third she'd seen since she'd left Deptford station.

"No, he's a good one," the man said. "Aren't you, Buzz?"

"Do you live here?" Maggie said.

The man looked suspicious. One of his cheeks was quivering. Maggie took a laminated card from her pocket and showed it to him. "I'm from Social Services," she said. "I'm here to see Michelle Doyce."

"The one downstairs?" the man said. "Haven't seen her." He leaned past Maggie and unlocked the front door. "You coming in?"

"Yes, please."

The man just shrugged.

"Go on, Buzz," he said. Maggie heard the clatter of the dog's paws inside and up the stairs, and the man disappeared after him.

As soon as she stepped inside, Maggie was hit by an odor of damp and rubbish and fried food and dog shit and other smells she couldn't place. It almost made her eyes water. She closed the front door behind her. This must once have been the hallway of a family house. Now it was piled with pallets, tins of paint, a couple of gaping plastic bags, an old bike with no tires. The stairs were directly ahead. To the left, what would have been a door to the front room was blocked up. She walked past the side of the stairs to a door further along. She rapped on it hard and listened. She heard something inside, then nothing. She knocked again, several times, and waited. There was a rattling sound, and then the door opened inwards. Maggie held out her laminated card once more.

"Michelle Doyce?" she said.

"Yes," said the woman.

It was difficult for Maggie to define even to herself exactly what was strange about her. She was clean and her hair was brushed, but perhaps almost too brushed, like that of a small child who had wetted her hair and then combed it so that it lay flat over her head, thin enough to show the pale scalp beneath. Her face was smooth and pink, with a dusting of fuzzy hair. Her bright red lipstick extended just a little too far off her lips. She wore a baggy, faded, flowery dress.

Maggie identified herself and held out the card.

"I just wanted to check up on you, Michelle," she said. "See how you are. Are you all right? All right in yourself?"

The woman nodded.

"Can I come in?" said Maggie. "Can I check everything's OK?"

She stepped inside and took out her notebook. As far as she could tell from a glance, Michelle seemed to be keeping herself clean. She looked as if she was eating. She was responsive. Still, something felt odd. She peered around in the shabby little anteroom of the flat. The contrast with the hallway of the house was impressive. Shoes were arranged in a row, a coat hung from a hook. There was a bucket with a mop leaning against the wall in the corner.

"How long have you been here, Michelle?"

The woman frowned. "Here?" she said. "A few days."

The discharge form had said the fifth of January and today was the first day of February. Still, that sort of vagueness wasn't really surprising. As the two women stood there, Maggie became aware of a sound she couldn't quite place. It might be the hum of traffic, or a vacuum cleaner on the floor above, or a plane. It depended on how far away it was. There was a smell also, like food that had been left out too long. She looked up: the electricity was working. She should check whether Michelle had a fridge. But, by the look of her, she'd be all right for the time being.

"Can I have a look round, Michelle?" she said. "Make sure everything's OK?"

"You want to meet him?" said Michelle.

Maggie was puzzled. There hadn't been anything on the form. "Have you got a friend?" she said. "I'd be happy to meet him."

Michelle stepped forward and opened the door to what would have been the house's main back room, away from the street. Maggie followed her and immediately felt something on her face. At first, she thought it was dust. She thought of an Underground train coming, blowing the warm grit into her face. At the same time, the sound got louder, and she realized it wasn't dust but flies, a thick cloud of flies blowing against her face.

For a few moments she was confused by the man sitting on the sofa. Her perceptions had slowed and become skewed, as if she were deep underwater or in a dream. Crazily, she wondered if he were wearing some sort of diving suit, a blue, marbled, slightly ruptured and torn diving suit, and she wondered why his eyes were yellow and cloudy. And then she started to fumble for her phone and she dropped it, and suddenly she couldn't make her fingers work, couldn't get them to pick the phone up from the grimy carpet, as she saw that it wasn't any kind of suit but his naked, swollen, rupturing flesh, and that he was dead. Long dead.

# 2

"February," said Sasha, sidestepping a puddle, "should be abolished."

She was walking with Frieda along a street lined with modern office blocks, whose height blocked out the sky and made the dark day seem darker. Everything was black and gray and white, like an old photograph: the buildings were monochrome, the sky chilly and blank; all the men and women — but they were mostly men — walking past them, with their slim laptop cases and umbrellas at the ready, wore sober suits and coats. Only the red scarf around Frieda's neck added a splash of color to the scene.

Frieda was walking swiftly, and Sasha, although she was the taller, had to make an effort to keep up.

"And Tuesdays," she went on. "February is the worst month of the year, much worse than January, and Tuesday is the worst day of the week."

"I thought that was supposed to be Monday."

"Tuesdays are worse. It's like . . ." Sasha paused, trying to think what it was like. "Monday's like jumping into ice-cold water, but you get a shock of excitement. On Tuesday you're still in the water but the shock has worn off and you're just cold."

Frieda looked round at her, noticing the winter pallor that made her seem frailer than usual, although there was no hiding her unusual beauty, even bundled up in a heavy coat, with her dark blonde hair tied severely back.

"Bad morning?"

They turned past a wine bar and briefly out on to Cannon Street, into the blur of red buses and taxis. Rain started to spit.

"Not really. Just a meeting that went on longer than necessary because some people love the sound of their own voices." Sasha suddenly stopped and looked around. "I hate this part of London," she said, not angrily, but as if she'd only just realized where she was. "When you suggested a walk, I thought you were going to take me along by the river or to a park. This is just unreal."

Frieda slowed. They were walking past a tiny patch of fenced-in green, untended and full of nettles and overgrown shrubs.

"There was a church here," she said. "It's long gone, of course, and the graveyard as well. But this tiny bit survived, got forgotten about somehow, among all the offices. It's a fragment of something."

Sasha peered over the railings at the litter. "And now it's where people come for a cigarette."

"When I was little, seven or eight, my father took me to London."

Sasha looked at Frieda attentively: this was the first time she had ever mentioned any member of her family or brought up a memory from her childhood. In the year or so since they had known each other, she had told Frieda almost everything about her own life — her relationship with her parents and her feckless younger brother, her love affairs, her friendships, things she kept hidden from view suddenly exposed — but Frieda's life remained a mystery to her.

The two of them had met just over a year ago. Sasha had gone to Frieda as a patient and she still remembered their single session, when she had told Frieda, in a whisper and barely lifting her eyes to meet Frieda's steady gaze, how she had slept with her therapist. Her therapist had slept with her. It had been an act of confession: her dirty secret filling the quiet room and Frieda, leaning forward slightly in her red chair, taking away the sting and shame by the quality of her attention. Sasha had left the room feeling drained but cleansed. Only later had she learned that afterward Frieda had gone straight from their session to the restaurant where the therapist was sitting with his wife and punched him, creating havoc, smashing glasses and plates. She had ended up in a police cell with a bandaged hand, but the therapist had declined to press charges and insisted on paying for all the damage at the restaurant. Later, Sasha — who was a geneticist by profession — had repaid the debt by surreptitiously arranging a DNA test on a piece of evidence Frieda had lifted from the police station. They had become friends, yet it was a friendship unlike any that Sasha had ever known. Frieda didn't talk about feelings; she had never once mentioned her ex, Sandy, since he had gone to work in America, and the only time Sasha had asked her about it, Frieda had told her with terrifying politeness that she didn't want to discuss it. Instead, Frieda talked about a piece of architecture, or a strange fact she had unearthed about London. Every so often she would invite Sasha to an exhibi-

tion, and sometimes she would call and ask
her if she was free for a walk. Sasha would
always say yes. She would break a date or
leave work in order to follow Frieda through
the London streets. She felt that this was
Frieda's way of confiding in her, and that
by accompanying her on her rambles, she
was perhaps taking some of the edge off her
friend's solitude.

Now she waited for Frieda to continue,
knowing better than to press her.

"We went to Spitalfields Market and he
suddenly said we were standing on top of a
plague pit, that hundreds of people who had
died from the Black Death were lying under
our feet. They had done tests on the teeth
of some of the corpses that had been exca-
vated."

"Couldn't he have taken you to the zoo?"
said Sasha.

Frieda shook her head. "I hate these
buildings as well. We could be anywhere.
But there are the tiny bits they've forgotten
to get rid of, the odd space here and there,
and the names of the roads: Threadneedle
Street, Wardrobe Terrace, Cowcross Street.
Memories and ghosts."

"It sounds just like therapy."

Frieda smiled at her. "Doesn't it? Here,
there's something I want to show you."

They retraced their route to Cannon Street and stopped opposite the station, in front of an iron grid set into the wall.

"What's this?"

"The London Stone."

Sasha looked at it dubiously: it was an unprepossessing lump of limestone, dull and pockmarked, and reminded her of the kind of uncomfortable rock you perched on at the beach when you were rubbing sand off your feet before pulling your shoes back on. "What's it for?"

"It's protecting us."

Sasha gave a puzzled smile. "In what sense?"

Frieda indicated a small plaque beside it. " 'So long as the Stone of Brutus is safe, so long shall London flourish.' It's supposed to be the heart of the city, the point from which the Romans measured the scope of their empire. Some people think it has occult powers. Nobody really knows where it came from — the Druids, the Romans. Maybe it's an old altar, a sacrificial stone, a mystical center point."

"You believe that?"

"What I like," said Frieda, "is that it's in the side of a shop and that most people walk past without noticing it, and that if it got mislaid, it would never be found because it looks like a completely ordinary piece of rock. And it means what we want it to mean."

They were silent for a few moments, and then Sasha put a gloved hand on Frieda's shoulder. "Tell me, if you were ever in distress, would you confide in anyone?"

"I don't know."

"Would you confide in me?"

"Perhaps."

"Well. You could, that's all." She felt constrained, embarrassed by the emotion in her voice. "I just wanted you to know."

"Thank you." Frieda's voice was neutral.

Sasha dropped her hand, and they turned from the grille. The air had become notably colder, the sky blanker, as if it might snow.

"I have a patient in half an hour," Frieda said.

"One thing."

"Yes?"

"Tomorrow. You must be worried. I hope it goes all right. Will you let me know?"

Frieda gave a shrug. Sasha watched as she walked away, slim and upright, into the swallowing crowds.

# 3

Detective Constable Yvette Long arrived a few moments before Karlsson. She had got the phone call just fifteen minutes previously, but already a small crowd was gathering in the street: children who ought to be at school, young mothers with babies in buggies, men who seemed in no hurry to get anywhere. It was bitingly cold, but many of them were not wearing overcoats or gloves. They looked excited, bright eyed with curiosity. Two police cars were parked in front of number 3, and a barrier had been put up. Just behind it, a thin stringy man with a ginger ponytail was pacing up and down, up and down, with his barrel-chested dog. Every so often it sat down and yawned, saliva drooling from its jaws. There was another man, enormously fat, ripples of flesh encased in his T-shirt, behind the barrier. He was standing quite still, mopping his shiny forehead, as if it were high summer, not icy February. Yvette parked and, as she opened the door, DC Chris Munster came out of the house, holding a handkerchief to his mouth.

"Where's the woman who found him?"

Munster took the handkerchief from his mouth and put it into his pocket. He made a visible effort to control the working of his face. "Sorry. It got to me for a bit. She's there." He nodded toward a middle-aged African woman sitting on the pavement with her face in her hands. "She's waiting to talk to us. She's shocked. The other woman — the one who was with him — she's in the car with Melanie. She keeps talking about tea. Forensics are on the way."

"Karlsson's on his way too."

"Good." Munster lowered his voice. "How can they live like this?"

Yvette and Karlsson pulled on paper overshoes. He gave her a reassuring nod and, for a moment, put his hand on the small of her back, steadying her. She took a deep breath.

Later, Karlsson would try to separate all his impressions, put them in order, but now it was a jumble of sights and smells and a nausea that made him sweat. They walked through the rubbish, the dog shit, the smell,

26

half sweet and so thick it caught in the back of the throat. He and Yvette made their way to the door that wasn't blocked off. They stepped inside, into a different universe of order: it was like being in a library, where everything was meticulously catalogued and stored in its allotted space. Three pairs of ancient shoes, on top of each other; a shelf of round stones; another shelf of bird bones, some of which still had matted feathers stuck to them; a tub of cigarette butts lying side by side; another plastic container with what looked like hair balls. He had time to think, as he passed into the next room, that the woman who lived here must be crazy. And then, for a while, he stared at the thing on the sofa, the naked man sitting upright, in a halo of slow, fat flies.

He was quite slender, and although it was hard to tell, didn't seem old. His hands were in his lap, as if in modesty, and in one of them was an iced bun; his head was propped up with a pillow so that his open, sulfurous eyes stared straight at them and his lopsided, stiffened mouth leered. His skin was a mottled blue, like a cheese left out for too long. Karlsson thought of the acid-washed jeans his little daughter had made him buy for her. He pushed the thought away. He didn't want to bring her into this setting,

27

even in his mind. Leaning forward, he saw vertical marks striping the man's torso. He must have been dead for some time, judging not just from the way his skin had darkened where the blood had puddled on the underside of his thighs and buttocks, but also from the smell that was making Yvette Long, standing behind Karlsson, breathe in shallow, hoarse gasps. There were two full cups of tea by his left foot, which was curled upward at an unnatural angle, the toes splayed. He had a comb stuck into his light brown hair, and lipstick on his mouth.

"Obviously he's been here some time." Karlsson's voice sounded calmer than he had expected. "It's warm in the room. That hasn't helped."

Yvette made a noise that might have been agreement.

Karlsson forced himself to look more closely at the mottled, puffy flesh. He waved Yvette over. "Look," he said.

"What?"

"At his left hand."

The tip of the middle finger was missing from above the knuckle.

"It could be a deformity."

"It looks to me like it's been cut off and the wound hasn't healed properly," said

Karlsson.

Yvette swallowed before she spoke. She absolutely wasn't going to be sick. "I don't know," she said. "It's hard to tell. It looks a bit mushy, but it could be . . ."

"General decomposition," said Karlsson.

"Yes."

"Which is happening at an advanced rate because of the heat."

"Chris said the heater was on when they arrived."

"The autopsy should tell us. They'll need to get a move on."

Karlsson looked at the cracked window and its rotting sill, the thin orange curtains. There were things that Michelle Doyce had collected and ordered: a cardboard box of balled-up, obviously soiled tissues; a drawer full of bottle-tops, color-coded; a jam jar containing nail clippings, small yellowing crescents. "Let's get out of here," he said. "Talk to her and the woman who found her. We can come back later, when he's been taken away."

As they left, the forensic team arrived, with their lights and cameras, face masks, chemicals, and general air of professional competence. Karlsson felt relieved. They would take away the horror, turn the ghastly room boiling with flies into a well-lit laboratory where the objects would become data and be classified.

"What a way to go," he said, as they went back outside.

"Who the hell is he?"

"That's where we start."

Karlsson left Yvette talking to Maggie Brennan and went to sit in the car with Michelle Doyce. All he knew about her was that she was fifty-one years old, that she had recently been discharged from the hospital after a psychological evaluation that had come to no real conclusions about her mental health, and that she had been living in Howard Street for a month, with no complaints from neighbors. This was the first time Maggie Brennan had visited her: she was standing in for someone else, who wouldn't have paid a visit because she had been on sick leave since last October.

"Michelle Doyce?"

She looked at him with eyes that were very pale, almost like the eyes of a blind person, but didn't reply.

"I'm Detective Chief Inspector Malcolm Karlsson." He waited. She blinked. "A police officer," he added.

"Have you come a long way?"

"No, I haven't. But I need to ask you some

questions."

"I have come a very long way. You may well ask."

"This is important."

"Yes. I know it."

"The man in your flat."

"I've been entertaining him."

"He's dead, Michelle."

"I cleaned his teeth for him. Not many friends can say that about their guests. And he sang for me. Like the sounds of the river at night, when the dog has stopped barking and the shouting and crying dies down."

"Michelle, he's dead. The man in your flat is dead. We need to find out how he died. Can you tell me his name?"

"Name?"

"Yes. Who is he? Was he."

She looked puzzled. "Why do you need a name? You can ask him."

"This is a serious matter. Who is he?"

She stared at him: a strong, pale woman with uncanny eyes and large reddened hands that floated in vague gestures when she spoke.

"Did he die in your flat, Michelle? Was it an accident?"

"One of your teeth is chipped. I am quite fond of teeth, you know. I have all my old teeth under my pillow, just in case they

31

come, and a few of other people's, but that's rare. You don't find them so often."

"Can you understand what I'm asking you?"

"Does he want to leave me?"

"He's dead." Karlsson wanted to shout it, to use the word like a stone that would shatter her incomprehension, but he kept his voice calm.

"Everyone goes in the end. Though I work so hard."

"How did he die?"

She started to mumble words he couldn't make out.

Chris Munster was making a preliminary assessment of the rest of the house. It repulsed him. It didn't feel like a criminal investigation at all; it was about people who were hopeless, who had slipped through the cracks. This upstairs room was full of needles — hundreds, no, thousands of used needles covering the floor, so at first he'd thought it was some kind of pattern. Dog shit here too, most of it old and hardened. Bloodstained rags. One thin mattress with nasty stains near the middle. Right now, he didn't care who'd killed the man downstairs. He just wanted to empty everyone out of this house, torch it, and get out, breathe some clean air, the colder the better. He felt dirty all over, outside and in. How could people live like this? That fat man with the red-veined eyes and the livid skin of the drunk, hardly able to speak, hardly able to balance his bulk on his small feet. Or the skinny dog-owning one, with his punctured arms and scabby face, who grinned and scratched himself and bobbed around: was this his room and were these his needles? Or maybe it was the dead man's room. That was probably it. The dead man would turn out to be part of this household from Hell. Fucking landlord. They'd been pushed in here, the hopeless misfits, the ones society didn't know how to deal with, had no money to treat, and abandoned so that now the police had to clear up the mess. If the public knew, he thought, his feet in their heavy boots sliding among the syringes, if they knew how some people lived and how they died.

# 4

Karlsson was on his way into the case meeting when he met Commissioner Crawford in the corridor. He was in conversation with a tall young man who was wearing a shiny blue suit and brightly patterned orange and green tie. He had slightly oversized black-framed glasses. Everything about him, from his strictly parted hair to his pointy green leather shoes, seemed to signal a degree of irony.

"Mal," said the commissioner, "have you got a moment?"

Karlsson held up the file he was carrying.

"Is it that body in Deptford?"

"Yes."

"Are you sure it's a murder?"

"No, I'm not."

"Then why are *you* handling it?"

"Nobody can make any sense of it," said Karlsson. "We're trying to decide what to do."

The commissioner gave a nervous laugh and turned to the other man. "He's not always like this," he said.

The commissioner was expecting some sort of joshing retort from Karlsson, but he didn't get one and there was an awkward silence.

"This is Jacob Newton," said the commissioner. "And this is DCI Karlsson, the man I was telling you about. He's the one who got the Faraday boy back."

The two men shook hands.

"Call me Jake," said the man.

"Jake's going to be around for a few days, looking at procedures, structures, that sort of thing."

Karlsson was puzzled. "Are you from the Met?"

The man smiled, as if Karlsson had said something unintentionally amusing.

"No, no," said the commissioner. "Jake's from Mangold Hutton. You know, the management consultancy."

"I didn't," said Karlsson.

"It's always useful to have a fresh pair of eyes. We can all learn lessons, especially in these days of budget reorientation."

"You mean 'cuts'?"

"We're all in this together, Mal."

There was another silence that lasted just

a little too long.

"They're waiting for me," said Karlsson.

"Mind if I come along?" said Newton.

Karlsson looked quizzically at the commissioner.

"He's got a free hand," said Crawford. "Go anywhere, see anything." He clapped Karlsson on the back. "It's not as if we've got anything to hide, is it? You can show Jake what a lean team you run."

Karlsson looked at Newton. "All right," he said. "Join the tour."

Yvette Long and Chris Munster were sitting at a desk drinking coffee. Karlsson introduced Newton, who told them to pretend he wasn't there. They immediately looked ill at ease and self-conscious.

"Anyone else coming?" Karlsson asked, and Yvette shook her head.

"Autopsy's this afternoon," said Karlsson. "Wouldn't it be good if it was a heart attack?"

"You thought he might have been strangled," said Yvette.

"I can hope, can't I?" said Karlsson.

"It's the dog I feel sorry for," said Munster. "These guys, they live in shit, they can't hold down a job, but they've always got a bloody dog."

"From the fact that I haven't heard any-

36

thing," said Karlsson, "I'm assuming that the deceased has not been identified as one of the other residents."

"All accounted for," said Munster. He picked up his notebook. "Lisa Bolianis. Aged about forty, I think. Apparent drink problem. I talked to her. Not very coherent. She said she'd seen Michelle Doyce once or twice. Never with anyone else." He pulled a face. "I don't get the impression that these housemates are meeting much around the barbecue. Michael Reilly — our dog owner. Got out of prison in November. Three and a half years for possession and distribution of a class-A substance. He said he'd nodded to her in the hall. She didn't care much for his dog. He didn't see her with anyone either." He looked down at his notebook. "She collected things. She'd come back with bagfuls of stuff she'd bought or found or whatever."

"We saw that in the flat."

"Anyone else?"

Munster looked back at his notebook. "Metesky. Tony Metesky. I could hardly get him to talk at all. Wouldn't look at me. He's clearly got some kind of mental problem. I've rung Social Services about him and someone's meant to ring me back. His room was in a real state, even by the prevailing standards. There are needles on the floor, hundreds of them."

Karlsson frowned. "His?"

Munster shook his head. "Cuckooing, I reckon."

"What's that?" asked Newton. The three officers all glanced at him and he looked embarrassed.

"Cuckooing," said Munster, "is when a dealer identifies a vulnerable person and uses his accommodation as a base for activity."

"I suppose that Mr. Whatever-his-name-is didn't give you any information about the deceased?"

"I could hardly get any sense out of him at all."

"What kind of place is this?" asked Yvette.

Munster shut his notebook. "I think it's where they put people when they can't think what else to do with them."

"Who owns the house?" asked Karlsson. "Maybe the dead body is the landlord."

"The owner is a woman," said Munster. "She lives in Spain. I'm going to call her, check she's actually there. She owns several houses and uses an agent. I'm getting the details."

"Where are they all now?" asked Karlsson.

Munster nodded across at Yvette.

"Michelle Doyce is back in the hospital," she said. "The others are still there, as far as I know."

"Still there?" said Karlsson. "It's a crime scene."

"Not strictly speaking. Until we get the autopsy result, it may just be a matter of failing to register a death, and I don't suppose any court will find Michelle Doyce fit to plead. As for the rest of them, where are they supposed to go? We've been ringing the council and we can't even find a person to talk to about it."

"Do they not care that one of their own hostels might be being used as a center for drug dealing?" asked Karlsson.

There was a pause.

"Well," said Yvette, "if we could find someone in Social Services and get them down here, what they would probably say is that if we suspect a crime, then it's a matter for us to investigate. Which we probably won't do."

Karlsson tried not to catch the eye of Jake Newton. This might not have been the best introduction to police work. "So what we've got," he said, "is a woman serving tea and buns to an unidentified naked rotting man, whose only distinguishing feature is the missing finger on his left hand. Could the finger have been removed to get a ring off?"

"It was the middle finger," said Munster. "Not the ring finger."

"You can have a ring on your middle finger," said Karlsson. "Who the hell is this guy?"

"Don got prints off him," said Munster. "It wasn't much fun, but they got them. And they didn't get a match."

"So what do we think?" said Karlsson. "Where do we start?"

Munster and Yvette looked at each other. They didn't say anything.

"I don't know what I think," said Karlsson, "but I know what I hope."

"What?"

"I hope he had a simple heart attack and this crazy woman panicked and didn't know what to do."

"But he was naked," said Yvette. "And we don't know who he is."

"If he died of a heart attack, it'll be someone else's problem." He frowned. "I wish someone could make sense of what Michelle Doyce is saying."

As he spoke, a face came into his mind, unsmiling and dark-eyed: Frieda Klein.

# 5

"Please take a seat, Dr. Klein."

Frieda had been in the room several times before. She had come to seminars here as a trainee; she had led seminars here as a qualified analyst; once, she had even sat where Professor Jonathan Krull was now, with a sixty-year-old therapist, whose name had since been removed from the British Psychoanalytic Council's register, in the seat she occupied today.

She took a deep, steadying breath and sat, folding her hands in her lap. She knew Krull by reputation and Dr. Jasmine Barber as a fellow practitioner. They were on friendly terms, and Dr. Barber now looked awkward, finding it hard to meet Frieda's eyes. The third member of the team was a squat, gray-haired woman in a violently pink jumper who was wearing a neck brace. Above it, her wrinkled face was shrewd and her gray eyes bright. Frieda thought she looked like an intelligent frog. She introduced herself as Thelma Scott. Frieda felt a tremor of interest; she had heard of Thelma Scott as a specialist in memory and trauma but had never before met her. The only other person in the room sat at the far end of the table; she was there to take notes of the proceedings.

"As you know, Dr. Klein," said Professor Krull, glancing down at the sheets of paper in front of him, "this is a preliminary investigation into a complaint we have received." Frieda nodded. "We have a code of ethics and a complaints procedure to which as a registrant you have subscribed. We are here today to investigate the complaint against you and to make sure that one of your patients has not been a victim of poor professional practice, and that you have behaved in a safe and appropriate manner. Before we begin, I need to make clear that none of our decisions or findings have the force of law." He was reading from the paper in front of him now. "Moreover, whatever we decide does not affect the right of the individual making the complaint to take legal proceedings against you, should they choose to do so. Do you understand?"

"Yes, I do," said Frieda.

"Also, this screening committee is made

up of three psychotherapists who are here to give impartial professional consideration to the case. Have you any reason for doubting the impartiality of any of us, Dr. Klein?"

"No."

"You have chosen to have no representation."

"That's right."

"Then we can begin. The complaint has been made by Mrs. Caroline Dekker, on behalf of her husband, Alan Dekker. You can confirm that Alan Dekker was your patient?"

"Yes. I saw him in November and December 2009. I've written the dates of each session down." She brought out a typed sheet and slid it across the table.

"Mrs. Dekker claims that her husband came to see you in a state of acute distress."

"He was experiencing severe panic attacks."

"She also claims that, far from helping him, you used him as a" — Krull looked down at his notes — "pawn in a police investigation. That you acted like a detective, not a therapist, casting suspicion on him, and indeed reported him to the police, making him a suspect in a case of child abduction, that you violated your pledge of patient confidentiality and furthered your own career at the expense of his peace of mind and future happiness."

"Would you like to give us your version of events, Dr. Klein?" Thelma Scott, the elderly woman in the neck brace and ugly jumper, fixed Frieda with her sharp eyes.

Now that this moment, which she had long dreaded, had at last arrived she felt calm. "Alan Dekker came to me in November because he was tormented by fantasies of having a child. He was childless himself, although he and his wife had been trying for some time to have a baby. So we talked about why his childlessness should cause not just grief but severe dysfunction. At the same time, an actual child, Matthew Faraday, had disappeared. The child that Alan described — the one he had never had — was so like the boy who had disappeared that I felt I had to report it to the police. And then I told Alan what I'd done."

"Was he angry?" asked Jasmine Barber.

Frieda thought for a moment. "He seemed understanding, maybe even too much so. He found it hard to express anger. I found him to be a gentle, self-doubting kind of man. Carrie — Mrs. Dekker — was angry on his behalf. She was very protective of him. It doesn't surprise me that she's the one complaining for Alan."

"But that wasn't the only time you crossed a boundary, was it?" said Krull.

Frieda met his eyes. "The case turned out to be complicated. Alan was adopted. He discovered — no, I discovered and told him — that he was an identical twin. He had a brother, whom he knew nothing about, and yet they had an extraordinary psychological similarity and also a kind of connection, an affinity if you will. They saw things in the same way, to some extent. Not surprisingly, this discovery was disturbing to Alan. It was this brother who had taken Matthew: Dean Reeve — a household name now, the nation's favorite bogeyman."

"Who killed himself."

"He hanged himself under a bridge by a canal over in Hackney when he knew he couldn't escape us. However much Alan hated the thought of his brother, he loved him as well. At least, he felt he had lost part of himself when he died. He must have suffered a great deal. But that's not what Carrie means when she talks about me using him." Frieda looked at the three of them with her large, dark eyes. "On one occasion," she continued, "I talked to him as a way of entering his brother's mind, of trying to find out what his brother was thinking. Without telling him. If I'd told him, it

45

wouldn't have worked."

"So you did use him?"

"Yes," said Frieda. They were all struck by her voice, which sounded angry rather than conciliatory.

"Do you think that was wrong?"

Frieda was silent for several moments, frowning. She let herself slide back into the darkness of the case, among its shadows and its inky dread. Her patient Alan had turned out to be the identical twin of Dean, a psychopath who had abducted not only Matthew but, twenty years previously, a little girl. And that little girl Joanna, once skinny and gap-toothed and shy, mourned without cease by her family, had turned out to be the fat, lethargic wife of Dean, hiding in plain sight, a victim turned perpetrator. It was Sasha's DNA test that had proved the obese, chain-smoking Terry was knock-kneed Joanna, that Dean's willing collaborator was also his victim. What was more — and this was what Frieda still thought about when she stalked the London streets at night until she was so tired she could sleep, and what she still dreamed about — Frieda's discovery of the freakish similarity between the twins had led to the abduction of a young research student, whose body had never been found. She thought of Kathy

Ripon's clever, likable face and the future she would not have. Perhaps her parents were still waiting for her to return, their hearts turning at every knock on the door. These people, her judges, asked her if what she had done was wrong, as if there were a simple answer, a truth that was not slippery and treacherous. She lifted her eyes and faced them again.

"Yes," she said, very clearly. "I wronged Alan Dekker, as my patient. But I don't know if I was wrong. Or, at least, I think I was both wrong and right in what I did. What Alan said to me on that day led directly to Matthew. He saved a little boy's life, there's no doubt about that. I thought he was glad he had helped. I know that time alters the way one thinks about things, and I have no idea what he's been through since then, but I don't understand why now, a year and a bit later, he would want to complain about something that at the time he accepted. Can I say one more thing?"

"Please." Professor Krull made a courtly gesture with his thin, blue-veined hands.

"Carrie talks about me putting my career before her husband's peace of mind and happiness. I did not further my career. I do not work for the police and have no interest in being a detective. A young woman dis-

47

appeared because of my actions, and I live with that. But that is a separate issue, not what we're talking about now. As a therapist, I believe in self-knowledge, in autonomy. What people discover about themselves during therapy may not lead to peace or to happiness. Indeed, it often doesn't. But it can lead to the possibility of turning what is unbearable into what is bearable, of taking responsibility for yourself and having a degree of control over your own life. That is what I do, as far as I can. Happiness . . ." Frieda raised both hands in an expressive gesture and fell silent.

"So if you were asked to apologize . . ."

"Apologize? For what? To whom? I'd like to know what Alan has to say in all of this. He shouldn't be letting his wife be his mouthpiece."

There was an awkward silence, and then Thelma Scott said in a dry voice: "As far as I know, Mr. Dekker has nothing to say."

"I don't understand."

"I imagine you don't. The complaint appears to come from Mrs. Dekker."

"On his behalf."

"Well. So one would assume."

"Wait. Are you telling me that Alan has nothing to do with this?"

"I'm not sure." Professor Krull looked

embarrassed.

"What's this for?" Frieda made a gesture at the long oval table, the woman taking the minutes at the far end, the portraits of august members of the council hanging on the walls. "I thought it was to investigate a complaint made, however indirectly, by a patient. Since when are we responsible for dissatisfaction felt by the partner of a patient? What am I doing here? What are *you* all doing here?"

Professor Krull cleared his throat. "We want to head off any possibility of litigation. Smooth things over."

Frieda stood up abruptly, her chair scraping over the wooden boards. Her voice was quivering with suppressed fury as she said, "*Smooth things over?* You want me to apologize for something I believe to be justified, or at least not unjustified, to someone who wasn't involved anyway?"

"Dr. Klein," said Krull.

"Frieda," said Jasmine Barber. "Please wait."

Thelma Scott said nothing; her gray eyes followed Frieda.

"I've got better things to do with my time."

She took her coat from the back of the chair and walked out, making sure not to bang the door behind her. As she went along the corridor toward the front entrance, she caught a glimpse of a woman going down the stairs on her left and stopped. Something about the sturdy frame, the short brown hair, was familiar. She shook her head, continued toward the exit, but then changed her mind and turned back, taking the stairs to the canteen. And she was right: it was Carrie Dekker, Alan's wife, the woman who had just made her sit through the charade upstairs. In the year since she had seen her, she seemed to have grown shorter, stockier, older, more tired. Her brown hair was shaggy. Frieda waited while Carrie got herself a mug of coffee and took a seat in the corner, next to a radiator, then approached her.

"Can I join you for a moment?"

Carrie stared at her, her face tightening with hostility. "You've got a nerve," she said.

Frieda took the chair opposite her. "I thought we should talk face-to-face."

"Why aren't you still being interviewed? You've only been in there for a short while."

"I wanted to ask you something."

"What?"

"Alan was my patient. Why are you, rather than him directly, making the complaint against me?"

Carrie looked startled. "Don't you know?"

"Know what?"

"You've really got no idea? You came into our lives. You talked about safety. You told Alan he could trust you. You fed him with ideas about knowledge, about being true to himself. You told him not to be ashamed of anything he felt. You gave him permission."

"And?"

"I just wanted him cured." For a moment her voice wavered. "He was *ill* and I just wanted him to get better. That's what you were for. Is that what you mean by cured? You find yourself and leave your wife."

"What?"

"You changed him."

"Carrie, stop a moment. Are you telling me that Alan left you?"

"Didn't you know?"

"No. I haven't seen or talked to Alan since the December before last, when his brother was found dead."

"Well. Now you know."

"When did he leave?"

"When?" Carrie lifted her head. Her eyes met Frieda's. "Christmas Day, that's when."

"That's hard," said Frieda, softly. She was beginning to understand why Carrie had complained. "So it's been just over a month."

51

"Not this Christmas. Last Christmas."

"Oh," said Frieda. For a moment, the room around her seemed to lose its definite shape. "You mean straight after his brother killed himself?"

"As if he was just waiting. You really didn't know? I assumed he'd talked to you — I assumed you'd *encouraged* him."

"Why did he go?"

"Because he felt better. He didn't need me any more. He's always needed me. I looked after him. But after you'd got to him, he was different."

"Is that what he said?"

"Not in so many words. But that was how he behaved. For a few days after Dean killed himself, he was — I can't describe it. He was cheerful, full of energy, decisive. It was the best few days of my life. That was what made it so hard. I thought everything was going to be all right. I'd been so scared for so long, and suddenly there he was, the old Alan. Or, rather, a new Alan. And he was so — so affectionate. I was happy."

She turned her head so that Frieda wouldn't see the tears in her eyes, and sniffed angrily.

"He must have given some explanation."

"No. He just said it had been good but now it was over. When I think of what I gave up for him, how I looked after him, how I made him safe in the world . . . I loved him and I knew he loved me. Whatever else happened, we had each other. Then he just left without a backward glance — and what have I got now? He took everything — my love, my trust, my child-bearing years. And I'll never forgive you for that. Never."

Frieda nodded. Her anger with Carrie had long gone.

"You know, Alan went through a terrible trauma," she said. "Perhaps he just couldn't bear to be in his old life for a bit, so he ran away from it, but it doesn't mean it's permanent. The important thing is to keep communicating with him, keep doors open."

"And how am I supposed to do that?"

"Won't he talk to you?"

"He's gone. Disappeared."

Frieda felt suddenly cold in spite of the radiator blasting out heat beside her. She spoke slowly and carefully. "Do you mean you don't know even where he is?"

"I've no idea."

"He didn't leave a forwarding address?"

"He just walked out with a few clothes and that bag of tools his psychopath brother left him just before he killed himself. Oh, and almost all of the money in his bank account. I opened his statements. I've tried to find him but he obviously doesn't want to be found."

"I see," said Frieda.

"So that's why I made a complaint. You stole my life from me. You might have found that little boy and rescued Dean's wife, who didn't seem to want rescuing, but you lost my Alan."

Carrie stood up and buttoned her jacket; a skin was forming on the surface of her untouched coffee. Frieda watched her as she left but didn't move for several minutes. She sat quite still, her hands on the table in front of her, her face without expression.

# 6

As Frieda walked away from the Institute, she was thinking so hard that she scarcely knew where she was. When she felt a nudge on her shoulder, she thought she had bumped into someone.

"Sorry," she began, and then gave a start. "What the hell are *you* doing here?"

Karlsson laughed, feeling his grim mood lift at the sight of her grumpy face. "It's good to see you too, after all these months," he said. "I came to find you."

"This isn't a good time," said Frieda.

"I can imagine," said Karlsson. "I saw Carrie Dekker leave a few minutes before you came out."

"But why are you here at all?"

"Charming. After all we went through together."

"Karlsson," Frieda said warningly. He had never persuaded her to call him by his first name.

"I had trouble reaching you. Why don't you ever switch your mobile on?"

"I only check it about once a week."

"At least you got round to buying one. I talked to your friend Paz, up at the clinic. She told me what was up. Why didn't you call me?" He looked around. "Can we go for a coffee somewhere?"

"I was just in the canteen with Carrie. Alan's left her. Did you know that?"

"No," said Karlsson. "I didn't stay in touch."

"And when I say 'left,' I mean really left. He's just gone. Don't you think that's strange, for someone who was so utterly dependent on her, and adoring?"

"He'd been under a lot of pressure. Sometimes people just need to escape." He gave a small wince that Frieda noticed, as she noticed the new lines in his thin face, the silver threads flecking his dark hair, and the patch of stubble that he'd missed while shaving.

She shook her head. "It doesn't feel right. Something's happened."

"You haven't answered my question," he said.

"Which one?"

"The one about why you didn't call me about the hearing. I'd like to have helped.

56

You got a kidnapped child back. You got kidnapped *children* back. The idea that you should be hauled in front of some bureaucrat is fucking ridiculous."

Frieda looked at Karlsson with the sharp expression that always made him feel wary. "It's not ridiculous," she said. "I've got to answer for what I do, and Alan is free to complain about me."

"I'd have spoken up for you," said Karlsson. "So would the police commissioner. I could probably have got the home secretary."

"That's not the issue. The question was whether I betrayed my duty to my patient."

"Which you didn't."

"I had different duties," Frieda said. "I tried to balance them. I'd like to talk to Alan about it but it looks like that won't be happening."

Karlsson started to speak but gave up. "As it happens, this isn't really what I was here about. Look, if you don't want a coffee, can we go for a walk? You like walking, don't you?"

"Don't you have a car?"

"With a driver," said Karlsson. "We can walk and then he can pick me up."

Frieda's expression turned suspicious.

57

"This isn't something to do with work, is it?"

"It's nothing big," said Karlsson, hastily. "It's something I thought might intrigue you. Professionally. You'd be paid for your time. There's someone I'd like you to have a word with. Five minutes. Ten minutes. Have a chat with her, tell me what you think. That's all."

"Who is she?"

"Which way?" said Karlsson.

Frieda pointed behind him. "Through Primrose Hill."

"All right. Just give me a moment."

After he'd given instructions to the driver, Karlsson and Frieda walked along the street and turned into a cul-de-sac that ended at the park. In silence they walked up a hill, then looked down at the zoo and the city beyond it. It was a cold day, and through a break in the clouds, Karlsson could see the Surrey hills, far to the south.

"You know all about this," he said. "Tell me something interesting."

"Not long ago some foxes got into the penguin enclosure," she said. "They killed about a dozen of them."

"That wasn't really what I meant."

"It's what came into my mind," said Frieda.

"They should have jumped into the water."

"You don't know what you're going to do in a crisis," said Frieda. "Until it happens. So what was it you wanted to talk to me about?"

As they walked down the slope and the view flattened out, Karlsson told Frieda about Michelle Doyce, the house in Deptford, and the decaying body that had been found propped up on her sofa, with a comb in his hair and lipstick on his mouth.

"We thought it might have been natural causes or an accident, but there's a bone in the neck that only breaks when you're strangled."

"The hyoid bone," said Frieda.

"I thought you were a psychotherapist."

"I studied medicine before. As you know."

"Anyway, you're right. Sometimes you're strangled and the hyoid bone doesn't break. But if the hyoid bone does break, you've been strangled. I think I've got it the right way round. The point is, the man was murdered."

"Where is this woman?" said Frieda.

"She's back in a psychiatric hospital, which she should never have left. As far as I can make out, she was living with a dead body for five days or more. From the look of it, she was serving him fucking tea and iced buns. Now, she could be the most brilliant actor in the world, but I think she's insane and she's not making any sense at all. She probably still killed this man somehow and she's probably going to spend the rest of her life in the bin but . . ." Karlsson paused. "I'd like to see what you make of her."

"I'm not the right person," said Frieda, without even looking round.

"Aren't you intrigued?"

"Not especially. Nor am I properly qualified. I've never done abnormal psychiatry. My area is the unhappiness of ordinary people. There are plenty of experts. I could probably dig up some names for you, but there must be people you use."

"It's not about examining her," said Karlsson. "They're probably doing that at the moment. I want someone to talk to her. We can't do that. Well, we can do it. It's just that we don't know what to say, and we don't understand what she says back to us. That's what you do."

"I don't know," said Frieda, doubtfully.

"You talk about unhappiness," said Karlsson. "You know what Yvette said? I mean, DC Long. You remember her, don't you? She said she thought Michelle was the unhappiest person she'd ever met in her life. I didn't completely see it myself, but that's what she said. She may not be ordinary but she's unhappy."

When Frieda turned to Karlsson this time, it was with a look almost of alarm. "What do you think I am? Some kind of misery junkie?"

"Only in a good way," said Karlsson.

"Tell me something."

"What?"

"Are you all right?"

"What do you mean, all right?"

"You seem troubled." She hesitated, then added, "More than usually so, I mean."

For a moment Karlsson thought of confiding in her. It would be a relief to tell someone and hear their words of sympathy and advice. But then he felt a flash of irritation: Frieda was a professional listener and he didn't want to talk to someone whose job it was to listen. He wanted someone who would be on his side, an intimate. He simply smiled and shrugged and said, "So, will you do it?"

Frieda entered the cobbled mews and approached her home — a narrow house squashed between a flat and a garage — with a familiar feeling of relief. She found

61

the key and opened the door, taking off her coat to hang it on the hook in the hall, removing her boots, and sliding her feet into the slippers that waited. Every morning when she left she would lay a fire ready for her return, and now she went into the living room, turned on the standard lamp, and knelt down by the hearth. She struck a match and held it against the balled newspaper, watching the flames curl up and gradually catch the kindling. It was a matter of pride to her to use only one match, and she waited to make sure the fire had caught before going into the kitchen and filling the kettle. The light on the answering machine was winking and she pressed the "play" button, then turned to take down a mug from the cupboard.

"Hello, Frieda," said a voice, and she stood ambushed and absolutely still, her hand pressed hard against her stomach. "You haven't answered my e-mails so I thought I'd ring. I need to say . . ."

Frieda pressed the "off" button. The voice ceased mid-sentence and she stared at the machine as if it might suddenly come to life again. After a few moments, she went to the sink and ran the water cold, then splashed her face. She made a pot of tea, waited for it to brew, then poured herself a large mug and took it to the living room where she sat in her chair by the fire, which was burning steadily but not yet giving out true heat. Outside, the drizzle strengthened to steady rain. Sandy: the man she had allowed herself to love and who had gone away a year and a month ago. Sometimes there were days, even weeks, when she didn't think of him at all, but still the sound of his voice made her stomach churn and her heart beat faster. Yet she hadn't answered his e-mails. Mostly she hadn't even read them. She had deleted them as soon as they appeared and then made sure she emptied the Trash folder on her computer so she wouldn't be tempted to retrieve them. He had asked her to go to America with him, and she had refused; she had asked him to stay, and he had said he couldn't. What was there left to discuss?

Eventually she went back into the kitchen and listened to the rest of the message. It wasn't long; Sandy simply said he needed to talk to her and wanted to see her again. He didn't tell her he loved her or missed her or wanted her back, but he said there was "unfinished business" between them, and his voice sounded strained and hesitant. Frieda imagined him speaking the words — the way he frowned when he concentrated, the furrow between his eyes, the shape of his mouth. Then she erased the message and went back to the fire.

Later that day Karlsson also listened to a message on his voice mail that sent a sharp pain through him. He had to sit down and wait to recover.

He had just come back to his ground-floor Highbury flat after having dinner with a friend from the university and his wife. They saw each other rarely, perhaps once a year, and each time the gap between them seemed to grow wider. Like Karlsson, Alec had studied law at Cambridge, but where Karlsson had joined the Met, Alec had kept on track and was now a senior partner in a law firm. His wife, Maria, was a lecturer in politics; she was tiny, sardonic, and endlessly energetic. They had three children who had been up when Karlsson arrived, bearing a bottle of wine and a tired bunch of flowers. He had sat in the living room with this apparently perfect family, the children in their pajamas, the youngest still in diapers, and had felt melancholy wash over him: he was an underpaid and overworked detective. His wife had left him and now lived with another man. His two children were growing up without him to tuck them into their beds at night or teach them how to ride a bike, kick a ball, swim their first length of the local pool with their faces almost submerged under the turquoise water.

Now he listened to the message his wife had left on his mobile.

"Mal? It's Julie. We need to talk." He could tell from her slightly slurred words that she'd been drinking. "You can't just think this will go away if you ignore it and it's not fair on me. Call when you get this. It doesn't matter what time."

Karlsson went into his kitchen and pulled out a bottle of whisky. He'd drunk several glasses of wine already but felt clearheaded. He poured himself a generous slug and added a splash of water. Then he picked up the phone again.

"Hello?" She had definitely had several drinks: there was a wobble to her voice.

"I got your message. Can't this conversation wait until morning? It's nearly midnight, we're both tired . . ."

"Speak for yourself."

He swallowed his anger. "*I*'m tired. And I don't want us to have an argument about this. We should think about what's best for Mikey and Bella and not rush into things."

"You know what, Mal? I'm sick to death

65

of thinking about what's best for Mikey and Bella. I've spent my adult life thinking about what's best for you, what's best for them, being understanding about your work, your shifts, putting everyone first. It's my turn."

"You mean it's Bob's turn." Bob was his wife's partner. They lived together in Brighton, and when the divorce came through, they planned to marry, so Karlsson supposed he was really Bella and Mikey's stepfather. He took them to school each morning on his way to work, and he read stories to them each evening. Karlsson had seen photographs of Bella beaming on his solid shoulders, and Mikey had told him how Bob had taught him to play French cricket on the beach. Apparently he might buy them a dog. Now Bob had been offered a job in Madrid, and Julie wanted to move the family out there — "just for a couple of years."

"Madrid's not Australia," she was saying. "You can fly there in a couple of hours."

"It's not the same."

"And think what a wonderful experience it would be for them."

"Children need their father," Karlsson said, wincing at the platitude.

"They'd still have you. That won't change. And they could have holidays with you. It won't be for a few months anyway — you can spend lots of time with them until they go."

I'm losing them, thought Karlsson, staring at the phone he clutched in his hand. First they moved to Brighton, now they'll go all the way to Spain. I'll be a stranger. They'll hang back when they see me, hide behind Julie, get homesick when they're in my home. "I can refuse," he said. "I still have joint custody."

"You can stop us going. Or try to. Is that what you want?"

"Of course not. But do you want me to barely see them?"

"No." Julie sighed heavily. He heard her suppress a yawn. "But tell me what we're going to do, Mal. We can't really compromise on this."

"I don't know." Karlsson, however, was already sure that he was going to agree. He felt trapped in the sort of argument they'd had when they were together. He felt defeated and lonely.

The knife had its own special drawer, where it lay wrapped in plastic, with the whetstone. Sometimes she lifted it out and laid it on the table in front of her, studying the dull gleam of its long blade, perhaps touching its edge cautiously to feel the fresh sharpness. It sent a shiver of excitement and dread through her, something almost sexual. She never used it for cooking: she had a blunt kitchen knife for that. She kept it ready. One day it would have its use.

Now she lifted the hatch cautiously; it used to creak, but she had poured a few drops of cooking oil on to its hinges so it levered open quietly. The wind blew directly into her face, cold and carrying a few drops of rain. It was very dark on the river. There was no moon tonight and no stars. The lamps on the barges that lined the bank, those that were occupied, had been extinguished and only a few lights in the distance glimmered. She pulled herself out and stared around. On the marshes, a long way off, someone had lit a fire. The orange flames flickered against the sky. She squinted but could not make out any figures beside it, black cutout shapes. She was alone. Water slapped very gently against the side of the boat. When she had first come here, she had been unsettled by the sound and the slight, occasional motion, but now she was used to it. It was like the blood inside her body. She was used to the night sounds as well — the wind in the trees and in the thick rushes that sounded sometimes like a moan, the rustle of rodents from the bank, the sudden shriek of the owls. There were foxes here, and fat rats with long, thick tails. Herons and white swans that looked at her with their wicked eyes. Mangy cats. She had had a cat once, with a white tip to its tail and silky ears; it used to wash itself so fastidiously and purr like a steady motor. But that was a long time ago, in another life, and she was another person now.

Very cautiously, she stepped into the cockpit of the boat and from there on to the path. She was wearing dark clothes — navy tracksuit trousers and a thick gray hoodie — so even if someone was looking, they probably wouldn't see her. She was always careful. The important thing was never to let your guard down or think you were safe. She walked slowly along the track, feeling her body limber up. She had to keep fit and strong, but it was hard when you were cooped up all day. She did push-ups inside sometimes, and two or three times a day she did twenty chin-ups, using the rim of the slightly open hatch as a bar and counting out loud so that she didn't cheat. Her arms were strong, but she didn't think she would be able to run far or fast. Sometimes when she woke at night, her chest felt tight and it was hard to breathe. She wanted to call out for help but she knew she mustn't.

She walked past the other boats moored to the side by thick ropes. Most of them were empty from one week to the next, and some were falling apart, their paint blistering and wood rotting. Some had people on board; they had plants on their flat roofs and bikes that lay on their sides with the spokes whirring when the wind blew. Even in the dark, she knew which boats were inhabited. It was her job to be vigilant. When they had first come here, it had been exciting, a mixture of hiding and setting up home. It was their safe place, he had said; no one else would know they were there, and whatever happened, they could retreat here and wait until danger had passed. But then he had left, returning only for a few days every month. At first she had wondered how she would pass her days when she was alone, but it was surprising how much there was to do. The boat had to be kept clean, for a start, and that wasn't easy because it was old and had been long abandoned before they'd found it. There were damp patches on its sides, and water leaked in through the floor, round the sides of the shower and toilet, and up through the boards in the kitchen area. The windows were narrow rectangles that no one could

70

see through from the outside. The doorway was always kept closed, and when she washed her clothes in the tiny sink with the tablets of soap he bought her, then laid them out over chairs and the table to dry, the air smelled thick and slightly festering.

Once there had been space, comfort, light flooding in through large windows, and roses on the lawn. She remembered as in a dream clean sheets and soft clothes. Now she lived with the dark, enclosed space; the long winter nights, when it was so cold her breath smoked and ice formed on the inside of the little windows; the candles guttering secretly when she didn't even dare use the dynamo torch he had given her; the fear, an ache in her stomach. Yes, you could even get used to fear. You could turn fear into something that was strong and useful and dangerous.

She turned back. The drops of rain were increasing and she didn't want to get too wet. The winter had been so cold and so long. For weeks, the paths had been hard with ice or covered with thick snow. She had felt like an animal in its burrow, watching flakes fall outside the windows. Waiting, always waiting.

Sliding back down the hatch, she pulled it shut after her and locked it. She filled the little tin kettle with just enough water for one teabag and put it on the stove, turning the knob on and lighting the ring with one match. But she could tell that they were running out of gas: the flame was weak and blue. Soon she wouldn't be able to cook the potatoes that were in the basket under the outside seat, or fill a hot-water bottle to take the edge off the cold that seemed to enter her bones. Perhaps he would bring another canister when he came. And surely he would come soon. She had faith.

# 7

"You're joking." Reuben sat back in his chair, looking delighted.

Frieda scowled. "I'm just going to spend a few minutes with her."

"It's the thin end of the wedge."

"I don't think so. Karlsson said he wanted me to see if I could make sense of what she was saying."

"You told me you were never going to get involved with police work again, under any circumstances."

"I know. And I'm not going to. Don't look at me like that."

"Like what?"

"As if you know me better than I know myself. It's irritating. I hope you don't look at your patients like that."

"I know you're intrigued."

Frieda was about to protest, but stopped herself because, of course, Reuben was right. "Perhaps I should just have said no," she said slowly. "I thought I was going to, and then I heard myself agreeing."

They were sitting in Reuben's office at the clinic, where Frieda worked part-time and on whose board she sat. The Warehouse had been Reuben's creation and had made him famous as a therapist. Frieda still hadn't got used to the changed appearance of his room. For years — ever since she had known him when he was her mentor and she a young student — Reuben had worked in chaos, papers strewn everywhere, piles of books collapsing around his chair, ashtrays and plant pots overflowing with half-smoked cigarettes. Now everything was in a state of determined order: there was an in-tray with a few papers in it, the books were on their shelves, there wasn't a cigarette stub in sight. And Reuben himself had changed as well. Gone was the look of an aging rock star. Now he was wearing a plain navy suit over a white shirt, his face was shaved, his graying hair was no longer down to his collar. He looked trim; a few months ago he had shocked everyone by joining a gym. Worse still, he went there every morning before work. Frieda had noticed that his suit trousers had to be held up with a belt. What was more, he ate green salads at lunch and carried a bottle of water around with him

from which every so often he would ostenta-
tiously drink. She couldn't help feeling he
was playing a part and that he was pleased
with the impression he was creating.

"There's another thing," she said.

"Go on."

"I had a strange idea — no, to call it an
idea is to make it sound more definite than
it actually was. A sensation, perhaps. When
Carrie told me how Alan had changed, and
then disappeared out of her life."

"And?" Reuben spoke after a long pause.

Frieda frowned. "It was as though I'd
walked into a shadow. You know, when
you're suddenly cold, even on a hot day. It's
probably nothing. Forget I said anything.
When's Josef back?"

Josef was their friend, a builder from
Ukraine who had quite literally fallen into
Frieda's life just over a year ago when he
had crashed through the ceiling into her
consulting room. He had ended up living
with Reuben, when Reuben was going
through what he now called, rather proudly,
his depressive breakdown. Josef had become
the tenant who paid no rent but mended
the boiler and fitted a new kitchen, made
endless pots of tea and poured shots of
vodka whenever there was a crisis. He had
never left, until a few weeks ago, when he

had returned to his homeland to see his wife and children for Christmas.

"He's probably snowed in. I looked up Kiev online the other day. It was about minus thirty. The real answer is, I don't know. Maybe never."

"Never?" She was surprised by the dismay she felt.

"He said he was coming back. His things — not that he owns much — are still in his room. His van's parked in my drive, with a flat battery so I can't even move it to make way for my own car. A couple of young women have knocked at my door asking for him, so they must think he's coming back. But he's been gone for six weeks now. It's where his family are, after all. He misses them, in his own way."

"I know."

"I thought you would have heard from him."

"I did get a postcard recently, but he sent it weeks ago. He hadn't put the postcode on."

"What did he say?"

Frieda smiled. "It said, 'Remember your friend Josef.'" She stood up. "I should go. They're sending a car to collect me."

"Be careful."

"She's not dangerous. She's just disturbed."

"I'm not worried about her. I'm worried about you. Beware of slippery slopes."

"Thin ends of wedges, slippery slopes — you'll be warning me to look before I leap next."

"I'll remind you of this conversation."

Frieda and Karlsson walked together up the long corridor. An artist had been brought in to brighten up the forbidding stretch of windowless wall. Every so often they passed a mini-landscape in primary colors, a painting of a bridge over a blue river, or a green hill with miniature figures at its domed summit. At a picture of an oversized bird with feverishly bright feathers and a cruel turquoise eye, which Frieda thought would disturb the calmest patient, they went through double doors into another, broader corridor. Although it was the middle of the day, it was eerily quiet. An orderly walked past, and his shoes creaked in the silence. Trolleys and wheelchairs stood by the walls. An old woman came toward them on a Zimmer frame. She was tiny, like a weak child, and moved with infinite slowness, rocking back and forward on the rubber-tipped legs of the frame, going almost nowhere. They stood to one side and let her pass, but she didn't look up. They could see her lips moving.

"It's just to the left here." Karlsson's voice sounded too loud and he winced.

Pushing open the door, they entered a ward of eight beds. The windows looked out on to a patch of garden, which was in need of tending. The damp uncut grass and the weeds in the borders gave the place an abandoned air. Several of the patients in the ward seemed to be asleep, just motionless blanketed humps in their beds, but one was sitting in her chair and crying steadily in a high pitch, rubbing her small dry hands together. She looked young and would have been pretty but for the burn marks all over her face. Another, with a homely gray bun and wearing a Victorian nightdress buttoned up to her neat chin, was doing a jigsaw puzzle. She looked up and smiled at them coyly. There was a smell of fish and urine in the air. The nurse at the desk recognized Karlsson and gave him a nod.

"How is she today?" he asked.

"She's on her new drug regime and she had a quieter night. But she wants her things back. She keeps looking for them."

The striped curtain had been drawn around Michelle Doyce's bed. Karlsson drew it back slightly and gestured for Frieda to step inside. Michelle was sitting up in her bed, very straight. She was wearing a beige hospital gown, and her hair was brushed and tied into two pigtails, like a schoolgirl. Frieda, looking at her, thought that her face was strangely indeterminate, as if it lacked a clear outline: she was like a watercolor of diluted layers — her skin was pink but had a faint tinge of yellow; her hair was neither gray nor brown; her eyes had a curious opacity; even her gestures were vague, like those of a blind woman who feared she might knock against something.

"Hello, Michelle. My name's Frieda Klein. Is it all right if I sit here?" She gestured to the metal-framed chair by the side of the bed.

"That's for my friend." Her voice was soft and hoarse, as though it had gone rusty through lack of use.

"That's all right, then. I can stand."

"The bed is empty."

"Can I sit on it? I don't want to crowd you."

"Am I in bed?"

"Yes, you're in bed. You're in a hospital."

"Yes," said Michelle. "I can't get home."

"Where is your home, Michelle?"

"Never."

"You don't have a home?"

"I try to make it nice. All my things. Then maybe he won't go away again. He'll stay."

Frieda remembered what Karlsson had told her about Michelle's compulsive collecting — her bottles and nail clippings, all neatly ordered. Perhaps she had been trying to make the drab room in a run-down house in Deptford into a home, filling it with the only possessions she could lay her hands on — all the detritus of other people's lives. Maybe she had been trying to fill the emptiness of her days with the comfort of things.

"Who is it that you want to stay?" she asked.

Michelle looked at Frieda blindly, then abruptly lay down flat in the bed.

"Sit beside me," she said. Her eyes stared up at the ceiling, where strip lights flickered.

Frieda sat. "Do you remember why you're here, Michelle, what happened?"

"I'm going to the sea."

"She keeps going on about the sea, and the river," said Karlsson.

Frieda looked round at him. "Don't talk about Michelle as if she weren't here," she said. "Sorry, Michelle, you were saying about the sea."

The woman who was wailing in the ward gave a sudden shriek, and then another.

"Lonely lonely lonely," said Michelle.

"Not for them, though."

"For who?"

"They come to be near again. Like he did. Admirable." The unexpected syllables came out of her mouth like stones. She looked surprised. "That isn't the right word. Not a patch on it."

"The man who was on your sofa . . ."

"Did you meet him?"

"How did you know him?"

She looked puzzled. "Drakes on the river," she said, in her rusty voice. "He never left me. Not like the others."

She held out her roughened hand; Frieda hesitated, then took it. Outside the curtains, a nurse was talking in a brisk voice to the weeping woman.

"Never left," repeated Michelle.

"Did he have a name?"

Michelle stared at her, then down at their two clasped hands, Frieda's clean and smooth, the hands of a professional woman, Michelle's calloused and scarred, with broken nails.

"Did you notice his hands?" Frieda asked, following Michelle's gaze.

"I kissed it where it hurt."

"His finger?"

"I said, 'There there, there there.'"

"Did he talk to you?"

"I gave him tea. I welcomed him. I said to him, 'My home is your home,' and then I asked him not to go away, I said 'please' at the start of the sentence and at the end as well. Everyone leaves because they're not really here. That's the secret no one else understands. The world goes on and on with nothing to get in its way, just the empty world and then the empty sea. You can feel the wind that comes all the way from the beginning, and then there's the moon looking at you and it takes a hundred hundred years to see. You want a final resting place. Like him."

"You mean like the man on your sofa?"

"He just needs feeding up. I can do that."

"Was there an accident?"

"I cleared that away. I told him it didn't matter at all and he mustn't be embarrassed. It happens to the best of us. I like to help people and give them things so they might want to stay. Wash their clothes and comb their hair. Sharing is caring. A problem halved. I could even give him some of my things, if he wanted to stay."

"Did something happen when he was with you, Michelle?"

"He rested and I tended him."

"His neck was hurt."

"Poor love. He was so uncomfortable until

I cleaned him up and made him better."

"Where did you meet him?"

"Well, now. Dreaming all the while and then catching fish and then, of course, it was the one who never came home alive."

"This is getting us nowhere," Karlsson said, from the end of the bed.

"Michelle." Frieda's voice was quiet. "I know that the world is a scary and a lonely place. But you can speak to me. Sometimes talking makes things a little bit better."

"Words," said Michelle.

"Yes. Words."

"Sticks and stones. I pick them up." Michelle stroked the back of Frieda's hand. "You've got a nice face and so I'm going to tell you. His name was Ducks. His name was My Dear. You see?"

"Thank you." Frieda waited a few seconds, then stood up and tried to pull away her hand. "I must go now."

"Will you come again?"

"I don't think that's a good idea," said Karlsson.

"Yes," said Frieda.

# 8

Frieda guessed it was he as soon as he appeared at the bottom of the road. He ran up the steep hill, his long, loping stride speeding up as he approached her, pushing himself harder and harder. He stopped beside her and bent over, panting heavily. The morning was bright and sunny and cold, but the man was wearing only an old T-shirt, sweatpants, and running shoes.

"Are you Dr. Andrew Berryman?"

The man removed a pair of green earphones. "Who are you?"

"I was put in touch with someone who passed me on to your boss and he told me to contact you. I need to talk to someone about extreme psychological syndromes."

"Why?" said Berryman. "Have you got one?"

"It's about someone I've met. My name's Frieda Klein. I'm a psychotherapist and I'm doing some work with the police. There's a woman who's involved with a murder and I'd like to talk to you about her. Can I come in?"

"It's my Friday off," said Berryman. "Couldn't you have phoned?"

"It's urgent. It would only take a few minutes."

He paused for a moment, weighing it up. "All right."

He unlocked the front door and led Frieda up several flights of stairs and then unlocked another door to his flat on the top floor. Frieda stepped into a large bright room. It had almost nothing in it. There was a sofa, a pale rug on the bare boards, an upright piano against the wall, and a large picture window overlooking Hampstead Heath.

"I'm going to have a shower," Berryman said, and walked through a door to the left.

"Shall I make coffee or tea?" Frieda said.

"Don't touch anything," he shouted from the next room.

Frieda heard the sound of the shower and walked slowly around the room. She looked at the music on the piano: a Chopin nocturne. Then she stared out of the window. It was so cold that it was mainly only people with dogs who had braced themselves to go out in it. There were a few small children in the playground, wrapped up so they looked like little bears waddling around. Berryman reappeared. He was wearing a checked shirt, dark brown trousers, and bare feet. He walked with a stoop as if he were apologizing for his tallness. He went through to the kitchen, switched on a kettle, and heaped coffee grounds into a jug.

"So you're playing Chopin?" said Frieda. "Nice."

"It's not nice," said Berryman. "It's like a neurological experiment. There's a theory that if you do ten thousand hours of practice in some particular skill, you attain proficiency at it. Constant practice stimulates myelin, which improves neural signaling."

"How's it going?"

"I'm about seven thousand hours in and it's not happening," said Berryman. "The problem is, I'm not clear how the myelin is supposed to distinguish between good piano playing and crap piano playing."

"And when you're not playing Chopin, you're treating people with unusual mental illnesses?" said Frieda.

"Not if I can help it."

"I thought you were a doctor."

"I am technically," said Berryman, "but it was really just a mistake. I started studying medicine, but I didn't want to deal with actual people. I was interested in the way the brain works. These neural disorders are useful because they settle disputes about the way we perceive the world. People didn't realize we had a bit of our brain that recognizes faces until patients had a headache and suddenly couldn't recognize their own children. I'm not particularly interested in treating them, though. I'm not saying they shouldn't be treated. It's just that I don't want to be the one to do it." He handed a mug of coffee to Frieda and suddenly smiled. "Of course, you're an analyst. You'll be thinking that my wish to turn medicine into a philosophical subject is an evasion."

"Thank you," said Frieda, taking the mug. "I wasn't thinking that at all. I know lots of doctors who think everything would be fine if it weren't for the patients."

"So, are you going to tell me about your patient?"

Frieda shook her head. "I want you to come and see her."

"What do you mean?" he said. "When?"

"Now."

"Now? Where is she?"

"She's in a hospital in Lewisham."

"Why on earth would I do that?"

Frieda drained her coffee mug. "I think you'll find her philosophically interesting."

"Are we allowed to do this?" asked Berryman.

"They know me there," said Frieda. "And, anyway, we're both doctors. Doctors can go anywhere."

When Berryman first saw Michelle Doyce, he seemed slightly disappointed. She was sitting reading *Hello!* magazine with great concentration. She looked utterly normal. He and Frieda pulled over two chairs and sat down. Berryman took his heavy brown suede jacket off and draped it over the back of his chair. Outside the small window there was a gray wall. It was starting to rain heavily from a blank, low sky.

"Remember me?" said Frieda.

"Yes," said Michelle. "Yes."

"This is Andrew. We'd both like to have a chat with you."

Berryman looked at Frieda with a puzzled expression. She had been almost silent as he had driven her across London and had said nothing about the case. Now she leaned across to Michelle. "Could you tell Andrew about the man who was staying with you?"

Michelle seemed puzzled as well, as if she was being forced to state the obvious. "He was just staying with me," she said.

"How did you meet him?" asked Frieda.

"Drakes and . . . and . . ."

"What? What do you mean?"

"And . . . and . . . boats."

Frieda looked at Andrew, then asked, "And what did you do for him?"

"I looked after him," said Michelle.

"Because he was in a bit of a state," said Frieda.

"He was," said Michelle. "He was in a state."

"He needed looking after."

"I made him tea," said Michelle. "He needed tidying up. He was messy." She paused. "Where is he? Where's he gone?"

"He had to go away," said Frieda. She looked at Andrew. He gave a cough and stood up. "Well," he said, "it's been nice meeting you both but I'm afraid . . ."

"Hang on," said Frieda. She turned to Michelle. "Can you excuse us for a moment?"

She took Berryman's arm and led him a few yards away.

"What do you make of her?" she asked.

He shrugged. "Seems lucid enough to me," he said. "Mildly dissociative. But not worth coming to Lewisham for."

"That man she was talking about," said Frieda.

"Yes?"

"When a social worker called on her, the

89

man was sitting on her sofa. He was naked and he was dead and in an early state of decay. She had been living with him during that time. So?"

Berryman was silent. Then a slow smile spread across his face. "All right," he said. "All right."

"My first question," said Frieda, "is that this is so weird, so completely off the wall, that maybe she's faking. She could have killed the man. She probably did kill him. And now she's pretending to be crazy."

"She's not faking." Berryman's tone was almost one of admiration. "Nobody could fake that."

"We still don't know the identity of the man, whether he was a friend or relative of hers, or whether she even knew him."

"Who cares about that?" Berryman wandered up the ward to where some people were sitting, watching TV. Frieda saw him leaning over a bed. When he came back, he was carrying a small brown teddy bear.

"Did you ask if you could borrow that?"

Berryman shook his head. "The woman was asleep. I'll put it back later."

He walked over and sat down in front of Michelle. He put the bear on his lap. "This is a bear," he said. She looked puzzled. "Where do you think he lives?"

"I don't know," she said. "I don't know about them."

"If you had to guess," he said. "Do you think he lives in a forest or a desert?"

"Don't be stupid," she said. "He lives here."

"And if you had to guess, what do you think he eats? Little animals? Fish?"

"I don't know. Just what people give him, I suppose."

"I think that's a good guess."

"Is he hungry?"

"I don't know — what do you think?"

"He doesn't look hungry, but sometimes it's hard to tell."

"You're right, it is." He smiled at her in delight. "Thanks very much."

Then he got up and walked along the ward, tossing the bear from one hand to the other.

"Excellent," he said, as he returned to Frieda. "What I'll need to do is pop her into the MRI, but I think I can guess what I'll find. There'll be lesions of some kind in the inferior temporal cortex and the amygdala and —"

"Sorry," Frieda interrupted. "What's this about?"

Berryman looked around, almost as if he'd forgotten Frieda was there.

"She's terrific," he announced firmly. "We just need to get her into a laboratory."

"No," said Frieda. "What we need to do is to cure her, then find out who the man is and who killed him."

Berryman shook his head. "It won't be curable. Steroids may relieve some cranial pressure."

"But why is she behaving like that?" Frieda asked.

"That's the interesting bit. Have you heard of Capgras Syndrome?"

"I'm not sure."

"It's brilliant," he said. "I mean, unless you get it. People start believing someone close to them, like their wife or husband, has been replaced by an impostor. Did you ever see that movie *Invasion of the Body Snatchers*? Like that. The point is, when we look at someone we know, our brain does two things. One bit recognizes the face, and another bit tells us that we have an emotional bond to that person. If that second bit doesn't work, the brain decides there must be something wrong with the person because we're not feeling anything for them."

"But that's not what Michelle Doyce is doing."

"No, no," said Berryman, gesturing toward Michelle as if she were a wonderful exhibit. "She's better. There's an even rarer syndrome that Alzheimer's patients some- times — well, hardly ever — get, in which there's an emergence of delusional compan- ions. It means they invest objects with life, just as Michelle Doyce did with that teddy bear. But she's even more interesting than that. You know how toddlers, all toddlers, start out as animists —"

"Which means?"

"That they don't make a distinction between their sister or their doll or even the wind blowing or a stone rolling down a hill. For them a leaf is falling because it wants to fall. As they grow up, the brain develops, and we can only interact with the world by making constant subconscious decisions about what in our environment is like us and is responsible and makes decisions, and what isn't. If I twisted your ear, you'd make a screaming sound, and if I scrape my foot on the floor, it'll make a screaming sound. You and I know that there's a difference. I'd guess that when someone gets Michelle into a lab . . ."

"I'm not sure that will be possible."

"It would be a crime not to," said Berry- man. "And when she's investigated, I'd bet that she's either been a chronic drinker or drug addict, or that she's suffered a severe head injury, or, most likely, she's got a brain tumor. So whoever's investigating her probably needs to get a move on."

"She's a person. A suffering person."

"A very interesting suffering person," said Berryman. "Which is more than you can say for most people."

"So her evidence, all the statements she's made, are just gibberish."

Berryman thought for a moment. "I wouldn't say that. She doesn't see the world the way we do. There's probably not much point in asking whether she killed that man because she doesn't know the difference between being dead and being alive, but she felt to me like someone who was trying to tell the truth as she saw it. I'd guess it's pretty frightening. It must feel like she's been born into a different, very strange kind of world. You could try paying attention to what she says about it. And that's what you do, isn't it?"

"And you don't?" said Frieda.

Berryman's expression hardened. "I sometimes feel like carrying around a little card, which I'd give to people like you. It would say that a lot of the science that ends up helping people is undertaken by men and women who are doing it for its own sake, and that going around weeping for those who suffer doesn't mean you're actually doing anything to help them. Except that that's a bit too much to fit on a little card, but you know what I mean."

"I'm sorry," said Frieda. "You came all this way with a strange woman on your day off. That was a good thing."

His expression relaxed. "She should be moved to a ward by herself."

"Do you think so?"

"Certainly. Being surrounded by people will not help her one bit. She needs quiet."

"I'll ask," said Frieda, doubtfully.

Berryman waved his hand. "Leave it to me. I'll see to it," he said airily.

"Really?"

Yes." He considered Frieda for a moment. "You're working with the police?"

"At arm's length."

"How did that come about?"

"Some other time," said Frieda. "It really is a long story." She turned to look at Michelle Doyce, who hadn't picked up her magazine and was staring in front of her. Then Frieda thought of something quite different. "That syndrome," she said.

"Which one?"

"The one where they think someone they love has been replaced."

"Capgras Syndrome."

"It must be terrifying," said Frieda. "I mean, so terrifying that we can't really imagine how terrifying."

As they entered the lobby, she stopped him. "Can you wait for me for just a couple of moments?"

"Do I have a choice?"

"Thanks."

Frieda went into the hospital shop. There were racks of magazines, shelves of crisps, sweets, and unhealthful-looking drinks, a paltry collection of shriveled apples and dried-out oranges, books of sudoku, and, in the corner, a basket of toys. Frieda went over and started rummaging through them.

"Can I help you?" asked the woman at the desk. "Are you looking for anything in particular?"

"A teddy bear."

The woman's face softened. "You've a child in there," she said. Frieda didn't contradict her. "I'm not sure we have actual teddies, though. There's a very popular doll that cries when you sit it up."

"I don't think so."

Frieda pulled out a green velvet frog with protuberant eyes, then a rag doll, with long, spindly legs, and a small, shabby-looking snake. Near the bottom of the basket was a squashy dog, with soft floppy ears and button eyes. "This will do."

She ran up the stairs to the ward and stopped at the desk.

"Do you think you can give this to Michelle Doyce in bed six?"

"Don't you want to give it to her yourself?"

"No."

The nurse shrugged. "All right."

Frieda turned to go, but at the double doors she stopped. Out of sight, she saw the nurse hand the dog to Michelle. Frieda watched intently: Michelle sat the dog beside her on the pillow and nodded at it respectfully. Then she put out one finger and touched its nose, smiling shyly; she picked up her glass of water and held it under its snout. Her face wore an expression of tender solicitousness and anxious happiness; it had taken that little. Frieda pushed the doors and slipped through them.

Some days she slept. It was wrong, she knew, but torpor would settle on her, and she would curl herself up into a ball of body and thick clothes and damp hair and close her sticky eyes and let herself go, drifting down through murky dreams, green weeds, and silky, shifting mud. She was half aware that she was asleep: her dreams would get tangled up with what was going on around her. The footsteps on the towpath, the rise and fall of voices, shouted instructions coming from the rowing boats that passed her boat.

When she woke, she would feel thick and stale with sleep. And guilty. If he could see her, he would be angry. No, not angry. He would be disappointed. Let down. She hated that. She remembered her mother's slumped shoulders, the brave smile that wavered and disappeared. Anything was better than disappointing people.

On this day, she had let herself sleep, and when she jerked awake, she couldn't remember where she was — saliva on her chin, her hair itchy and her cheek sore from the rough fabric of the seat where she lay. She couldn't remember who she was. She was nobody, just a lumpy shape without a name, without a self. She waited. She let herself know herself again. She pressed her forehead against the narrow window and stared outside at the shifting river. Two grand swans sailed past. Vicious, vicious stares.

# 9

"This case." Commissioner Crawford spoke with barely concealed irritation. "Are you winding it up?"

"Well," began Karlsson, "there are several —"

"I looked at the preliminary report. It seems pretty straightforward. The woman's not all there." The commissioner tapped the side of his forehead with a finger. "So the outcome doesn't matter much. The victim was killed in a frenzy. She's already in a psychiatric hospital anyway, out of harm's way."

"We don't even know who the victim is yet."

"Drug dealer?"

"There's no evidence for that."

"You've done a search through missing people?"

"Nothing there. I'm about to interview the other residents of the house to see if they can move us forward."

"I'm not convinced this is a good use of your time."

"He was still murdered."

"This isn't like your missing children, Mal."

"You mean people don't care?"

"It's all about priorities," said Crawford, frowning. "Take Jake Newton with you, at least. Show him the crap we have to deal with."

Karlsson started to speak but Crawford interrupted him. "For God's sake, wrap this one up for me."

Today Jake's trousers were thin, striped corduroys and his shoes were a pale tan, highly polished with yellow laces. He put up an umbrella as he got out of the car, for it was now pouring with a rain that was thickening toward snow, and walked into the house with care, holding his buttonless jacket closed with one hand. The barriers had been taken down, the crowds had long since gone, and there was no sign that a crime had ever been committed here, except for the tape across Michelle Doyce's door. There was the same rubbish in the hall, the same smell of shit and decay that coated the back of Karlsson's throat and made Jake

Newton wince. He pulled a large white handkerchief out of his pocket and blew his nose several times, unnecessarily. "A bit close in here, isn't it?"

"I don't think they have a cleaner," said Karlsson, leading the way upstairs, taking care where he stood.

Later, talking to Yvette, he wasn't sure which of the three interviews had made him feel the most depressed. Lisa Bolianis was the loneliest. With her creased and reddened face, her thin arms and legs but drinker's pot belly, she looked as though she was in her forties but turned out to be only thirty-two. She was an alcoholic, who had lost her children and her home. She reeked of cheap spirits as she spoke in flat, mumbling sentences. Karlsson could see bottles under her bed and several dirty blankets stacked on top of it, along with a torn pink eiderdown. Her clothes were in two black bin bags in a corner. She said that Michelle Doyce was "nice enough" but knew nothing about her and nothing about the man who had been found in her room. She said lots of strange men came to the house, but she didn't mix with them, and she wouldn't be able to recognize anybody if they showed her a picture. She'd had enough of men: they'd never done her any good from her stepfather onwards. She had cold sores at the corners of her mouth; when she tried to smile at Karlsson, he could see them cracking. He had his notebook in his hand but didn't write anything in it. He didn't really know why he was there — Yvette and Chris Munster had already talked to her: what had he been expecting? All the while, Jake stood by the door, twitching uncomfortably and picking imaginary pieces of lint off the sleeve of his jacket.

If she was the loneliest of the inmates, Tony Metesky was the one who seemed furthest from the reaches of society — a vast, scared ruin of a man, who wouldn't meet Karlsson's eye, and who rocked back and forth and talked without making sense in disconnected words and fragments of sentences. The needles had been cleared away. A team from the council had come in their special uniforms, like police divers, and it had taken them a whole day to clean the room. Karlsson tried to ask him about the dealers who had taken over his room, but Metesky wrung his dimpled hands together and his blubbery face screwed up in terror.

"You're not in trouble, Tony," Karlsson said. "We need your help."

"Not me."

"Did you see anyone go into Michelle Doyce's room — any of the people who came here?"

"Like a big baby, that's me. Won't tell nobody. Fat smelly baby." He laughed anxiously, looking into Karlsson's face for an answering smile.

"The men who came here, they threatened you, didn't they?"

"It's all right."

Karlsson gave up.

Jake didn't accompany him into Michael Reilly's room, but chose to wait in the car. He'd been warned about Reilly's dog. It was chained to the radiator but kept lunging forward to snarl at Karlsson, who was starting to think the radiator was in danger of coming away from the wall. The air was thick with the smell of dog hair and dog shit, and of the dog food in the plastic bowl on the floor. But Michael Reilly was the most voluble of the three remaining residents. He paced round and round the room, jabbing his forefinger in the air. Metesky was a freak, and that Lisa Bolianis couldn't see what was going on under her own nose, but he, Michael, could tell him a thing or two. He wanted to cooperate fully with any investigation. Did they know, for instance,

that kids came to get their drugs here —
and that means *kids,* no more than fourteen?
It wasn't right. He knew he wasn't one to
talk, but those days were in the past for him;
he'd served his time and cleaned up his act
and was going straight now; he just wanted
to help.

"I see that," said Karlsson, gravely. He'd
spent enough time in the Met to recognize
a crack addict. "Can you tell us anything
about Michelle Doyce?"

"Her? She avoided me. I try to be friendly
— but with this lot, it's hard going. The first
time I saw her she wanted to give me tea,
but she changed her mind. I think it was
Buzz. She didn't like you, did she, Buzz?"
Buzz growled and saliva poured from his
open jaws. The radiator trembled. "She
wasn't here much, always out looking for
stuff. I once saw her down on the riverbank
when the tide was out, picking things up
from the mud."

"Did you ever see her with anyone?"

He shook his head. "I never heard her
speak much either."

"The men who used Mr. Metesky's room,
did they ever go into the rest of the house?"

"I know what you're getting at."

"Then answer it."

"No. They didn't."

"Not into Michelle Doyce's room?"

"She kept herself to herself. Quite a sad kind of lady, if you ask me. Why else would she end up in this dump? You wouldn't be here if you had anywhere else to go, would you? Except I've got my dog, eh, Buzz? We keep each other company."

An unearthly sound came from Buzz's barrel chest, and Karlsson could see the whites of his rolling eyes.

Frieda walked over Blackfriars Bridge, stopping in the middle to look west toward the London Eye and Big Ben, then east at the smooth dome of St. Paul's, everything flickering and dissolving in the falling snow, which was turning to slush on the pavements. Then she moved swiftly, trying to throw off a feeling of dread and dejection, not pausing at Smithfield Market or in St. John Street, and at last she was in Islington, standing in front of Chloë and Olivia's house, five minutes early for her niece's chemistry lesson. She knocked and heard feet running to the door. Chloë had grown taller and thinner over the past few months, and her hair was cut dramatically short; it stood up in uneven tufts, and Frieda wondered if she'd done it herself. She had kohl smudged round her eyes, and there was a new piercing in her nose. She had a fading love bite on her neck.

"Thank goodness you're here," Chloë said dramatically.

"Why?"

"Mum's in the kitchen with a *man.*"

"Is that such a crisis?"

"She found him on the Internet."

"Is that a problem?"

"I thought at least you'd be on my side."

"I didn't know there were sides."

"I'm not a patient, Frieda."

Frieda wiped her feet on the mat and hung her coat on the hook. She stepped into the wild disorder of the living room and looked around for somewhere to sit. "Chemistry?" she asked.

Chloë rolled her eyes. "It's Friday. What else would I be doing with my fucking life?"

The snow turned back to rain. It rained for the rest of the day and through the night, so heavily that the roads ran with water and in the parks puddles formed and spread into each other. Drains overflowed. Cars sent up blinding arcs of dirty spray. Canals bubbled. In the streets people ran between shops under umbrellas that barely protected them. The drenched world shrank. In the sheets of cold, driving rain, it was barely possible to see to the end of a road or the top of a tree. The brown Thames surged. It rained through the evening and into the night. In houses and in flats, alone or in pairs, people lay in their beds and listened to it hammering against their windows. The wind ripped through the trees, and dustbin lids clattered along streets in the teeming darkness.

In a small road in Poplar that led through boarded-up estates toward the Lea River, a storm drain flooded. At just after three in the morning, the drain cover was dislodged. About ten minutes later, a clump of hair floated to the surface. Beneath it, something glimmered faintly.

But it wasn't until eight twenty-five the next morning, when the rain had eased to an icy drizzle, that a teenage boy walking his terrier came across the remains of a body that was unmistakably human. Unmistakably that of a woman.

Frieda had woken at five. She liked being in her small, orderly house when the weather outside was wild. Everything was battened down against the rain that flew in bullets against her windows; the gusts of wind sounded like a stormy sea, the foamy rush of an incoming tide. She lay for a while, not thinking, simply listening, but gradually thoughts clarified and pushed their way into her consciousness. The thoughts were people and she could see their faces: Sandy, who was far away but whose fingers touched her when she was asleep, whose arms wrapped around her at last; Alan, with his brown spaniel eyes, who had left his wife and disappeared; his identical twin, Dean, dead for more than a year but who stalked her dreams again, always with that nasty smile; Dean's wife, Terry; Terry's sad and careful sister, Rose. And then there was Michelle Doyce, with her fading face and her strong, blistered hands, who talked to dead men and stuffed dogs, as if they could understand everything she said. Frieda turned toward the window, waiting for the first light to appear through the curtains. Words and phrases flickered through her mind, tiny lights in the darkness. She tried to separate her anxieties and give them a proper name.

Just before six, she got up, pulled on a dressing gown, and went downstairs to light the fire in the living room and make herself a pot of coffee. It was Sunday; she had no patients to see, no conferences to attend, no duties to attend to. She had planned to go for a walk through the watery streets, visit the flower market, buy provisions, pop in at her friend's café, Number 9, for a bowl of porridge or a cinnamon bagel, perhaps spend an hour or so making a drawing in her study, which was like an aerie at the top of her narrow house. Instead, she sat by the fire, occasionally crouching to blow strength into the flames, drank mug after mug of coffee, and attempted to sort through the events of her week and the murky emotions that had been stirred up by the hearing and by Karlsson's surprise reappearance in her life.

Then the doorbell rang.

# 10

Karlsson looked strange on Frieda's doorstep, as if he were in fancy dress. He was
wearing black jeans, a sweater, and a leather
jacket, and was damp from the rain. His
hair was wet and clung to his skull, making
him look older and thinner.

"You gave me a shock," she said. Anxiety
curled through her: he was not bringing
good news. "You're not wearing a suit."

"It's Sunday," he said.

"Can I get you a coffee?"

"I don't think so. Another time perhaps."

"Are you going to come in?"

"Just for a minute." He stepped over the
threshold. "I wanted to tell you that we're
having a meeting about the case tomorrow
morning. We're probably winding it up. I'd
like it if you were there. You've probably got
a patient, though."

"What time?"

"Nine thirty."

"I've got a gap. I could come for an hour."

"Good. Someone you probably know is going to be there. Dr. Hal Bradshaw."

"I've heard of him."

"He does some profiling for us. He's pricey but the commissioner's keen on him."

"I don't want to get into a turf war."

"We'll be deciding whether to send the case to the CPS. Will you come?"

"All right," said Frieda. "But you didn't arrive at my house early on a Sunday morning to tell me about a meeting."

"No."

Now that the moment had come, he felt unwilling to speak the words.

She looked at him with concern. "Come through to the kitchen. I'll make us that coffee — I'm having some myself anyway, and you look like you could do with it."

He followed her, and she pulled a packet of coffee beans from the fridge. She took a white poppy-seed roll from a bag and put it on a plate for him. He stood by the window and watched her, not speaking. Only when the mug of coffee was in front of him and he had taken off his jacket did she sit down opposite him.

"Tell me, then."

"With all the rain," he said, "there've been floods." He stopped.

"Floods," Frieda prompted him.

"Yesterday morning, someone's dog came across some bodily remains floating in a storm drain in Bromley. In the next couple of days, they're doing the full identity check. Dental records, probably. But I know what they're going to find."

Frieda was quite still. She gazed at him with her dark eyes. He put out a hand and laid it across hers for a second. She didn't respond, but neither did she pull away.

"Kathy Ripon," she said at last.

Kathy Ripon, the young research student whom Professor Seth Boundy, specialist in identical twins and their genetic implications, had sent to Dean Reeve's house last December, following information that Frieda had given him. Kathy Ripon, who had never been seen since but whose parents still waited for. Kathy Ripon, who lay across Frieda's conscience like an unyielding boulder, and whose narrow, intelligent face appeared to her in dreams and in waking hours.

"There was a locket," said Karlsson, quietly, removing his hand and picking up his mug of coffee.

Frieda had known that Kathy Ripon was dead. She'd known it a hundred percent. But, even so, she felt as if she had been punched in the stomach. Speaking was a great effort. "Do the parents know?"

"They were told yesterday afternoon. I wanted you to know before you saw it in the papers."

"Thank you," said Frieda.

"It was different from the children," said Karlsson. "Dean didn't need her. He didn't want her. He just had to get her out of the way. She was probably dead by the time we heard she was missing."

"Probably. Maybe." She made a great effort to look at Karlsson. "Thank you," she said.

"What? For being the bringer of bad news?"

"Yes. You didn't need to."

"Yes, I did. There are some things —" He was interrupted by a harsh electronic version of "The March of the Toreadors." He took his phone from his pocket and looked at it.

She saw his face become grim. "Work?"

"Family."

"You should go."

"Yeah. Sorry."

"That's fine," said Frieda.

After she had let him out, she scarcely moved, just leaned her head against the inside of the door. She tried to stop herself thinking about what it must have been like. That sort of empathy is no good to anybody, she told herself. But still. There had been all the celebrations about the children being found, triumphant press conferences, and all the time Kathy Ripon had been under the ground with nobody coming for her: a clever young woman, hard-working, anxious to please her boss, standing eagerly with her notebook and her researcher's questions on the rim of the black hole of Dean Reeve's life — and then being sucked into it.

Frieda hoped so much that Karlsson was right and that Kathy Ripon had died quickly, had not been toyed with or buried alive. You heard of such things: victims knowing their would-be rescuers were above them but unable to make them hear. She shuddered. For a moment, her little house — huddled in the mews and surrounded by tall buildings, its rooms dim and painted with rich dark colors — felt like a vault rather than a refuge, and she like an underground creature hiding from the bright world.

And then, like a body rising to the surface of a murky lake, the thought came to her of Carrie Dekker talking about Alan, her husband, Dean's identical twin. How he'd disappeared. She pressed her head harder against the door, feeling her brain working, her thoughts hissing. She couldn't stop herself: the past was seeping into the present and there were things she needed to know. She wondered why she was doing this. Why was she going back?

On Monday morning, she had an eight a.m. session with a man — he seemed more like a boy — in his mid-twenties, who sat crouched over in his chair, his bulky body shaken by sobs for the first ten minutes, and then, stumbling from his seat and sinking down beside her, tried to get her to hug and hold him. He so badly wanted reassurance, a mothering presence to tell him that everything would be all right, that she would take the burden of it all for him. He was lonely and loveless and lost, and he wanted someone to care for him. He thought that Frieda could become his mother figure, his friend, his rescuer. She took him by the chapped hand and led him back to his seat. She handed him a box of tissues and told him to take his time, then waited in her red chair while he wept and mopped his streaming face, all the while sobbing out apologies. She watched him in silence until his weeping subsided when she asked, "Why did you keep saying sorry?"

"I don't know. I felt stupid."

"Why stupid? You felt sad."

"I don't know." He stared at her helplessly. "I don't know. I don't know. I don't know where to begin. Where shall I begin?"

After he had left and she had written up her notes, Frieda walked to Warren Street station and caught the tube. The train stopped in a tunnel for fifteen minutes. A crackly voice had talked about a "body under a train at Earl's Court" and there had been a murmur of discontent. "It's not even on the same line," a woman next to her had muttered, to nobody in particular. Frieda got out at the next station, looked for a taxi in the cold rain and didn't find one, then just walked. Even so, she was only a few minutes late for the meeting. There were five people sitting around a table: Karlsson, Commissioner Crawford (whom she had never met but had seen on television the year before, talking about the tremendous police work that had been done to recover Matthew and how he didn't want to take all the credit), and Yvette Long (who gave her a puzzled look, as if she wondered what she was doing there). There were also two men she didn't recognize — someone the commissioner introduced as Jacob Newton, who peered at

116

her as if she were some interesting speci-
men in a museum of curiosities, and a Dr.
Hal Bradshaw. He looked as though he was
in his early fifties, his curly dark hair
streaked with gray. He was wearing a pin-
striped suit, but the stripes were in a shade
of green. When Karlsson described Frieda's
part in the Dean Reeve case to him, Bradshaw frowned at her.

"I don't quite see the need," he said, to
Commissioner Crawford. "Just my opinion,
of course."

"I want her here," said Karlsson, firmly.
He turned to Frieda. "Dr. Bradshaw was
about to give us his assessment of the
murder scene and of Michelle Doyce's state
of mind. Dr. Bradshaw?"

Hal Bradshaw coughed. "You all probably
know my methods," he said. "It's my view
that murderers are like artists, like storytell-
ers." Crawford nodded approvingly and sat
back in his chair, as if at last he felt on safe
ground. "The scene of a murder is like the
murderer's work of art."

As Bradshaw got into his stride, Frieda
leaned back in her chair and stared up at
the ceiling. It was made of polystyrene tiles
with a rough gray pattern, which gave them
the appearance of paving stones.

"When I saw the photographs, I felt like I

117

was looking at a chapter from one of my own books. I feel like I'm giving away the punch line at the beginning of the joke, but it was instantly clear to me that Michelle Doyce was a highly organized psychopath. Now, when I use a phrase like that, most of you think of a man cutting up women. But I'm using the term strictly. It was clear to me that she entirely lacked empathy and thus she was able to plan the murder, carry it out, arrange the crime scene, then continue to lead a normal life."

"Did you decide all this before you talked to her?" Karlsson asked.

Bradshaw turned to him with an expression of tolerant amusement. "I've been doing this job for twenty-five years. You get a sixth sense for these things, the way an art expert can instantly spot a fake Vermeer. Of course, I then interviewed Michelle Doyce, to the extent that it's possible to interview her."

Frieda was still staring at the polystyrene tiles. She was trying to establish whether the streaked pattern repeated itself or whether it was truly random.

"Did she confess?" asked Karlsson.

Bradshaw snorted. "The crime scene was her confession," he said, addressing most of his remarks to the commissioner. "I've looked at her file. She has led a life of utter failure and powerlessness. This crime and this crime scene were her final belated assertion of some kind of control of her life, some assertion of sexual power. 'Here is a naked man,' she was saying. 'This is what I can do to him.' Men have rejected her all her life. Finally, she decided to fight back."

"That makes sense," said Commissioner Crawford. "You agree, Mal?"

"But did she say anything," Karlsson said, "when you asked her about the body?"

"She wouldn't answer directly," said Bradshaw. "She just babbled about the river and about ships and fleets. But if the story I'm telling is right, which I'm sure it is, then this isn't just nonsense. This is her way of explaining herself. Obviously, she lives near the river. She could almost see it from her house. But the way I read it, the river is the great symbol of the woman. The fluvial woman." Frieda looked down from the tiles just in time to see Bradshaw make a flowing gesture with his hands to accompany his words. "And the ships and the fleet," he continued, "are symbols of the man. I think what she is telling us is that the river, with its feminine tides and currents, is sweeping the male boat out to sea. Which is a form of death."

"I wish she could just tell us," said Yvette. "It sounds a bit abstract to me."

"She is telling us," said Bradshaw. "You just have to listen — with all due respect."

Commissioner Crawford nodded. Frieda looked across at the young woman and saw her flush crimson and her fists clench on the table for a moment, before she let them uncurl again.

"Did you see Dr. Klein's notes?" asked Karlsson.

Bradshaw gave another snort. "Since Dr. Klein is present, I'm not sure I should comment," he said. "But I really don't think it's necessary to chase up incredibly rare fantasy psychological syndromes. No offense, but I thought the notes displayed a certain naïveté." He turned to Frieda and smiled at her. "I heard from the nursing staff that you bought a teddy bear for Michelle."

"It was a stuffed dog."

"Was that part of your examination or part of your treatment?" said Bradshaw.

"It was something for her to talk to."

"Well, that's very touching. But, anyway, to business." He tapped a cardboard file that lay on the desk in front of him and directed his remarks once more to the commissioner. "It's all in here. It's my conclusion that this is a slam dunk. She clearly fits the profile.

Obviously, she won't be fit to plead, but you can close your case."

"What about the missing finger?" asked Frieda.

"It's all in here." Bradshaw picked up the file. "You're an analyst, aren't you? It all fits. What do you think cutting off a finger symbolizes?"

Frieda took a deep breath. "Your argument," she said, "is that Michelle Doyce, having killed this man and stripped him naked, wanted to symbolize cutting off his penis by cutting off his finger. Why didn't she cut off his penis?"

Bradshaw smiled again. "You need to read my report. She's a psychopath. She arranges the world in terms of symbols."

Karlsson looked at his deputy.

Yvette shrugged. "It just seems too vague to me, too theoretical," she said. "You don't convict someone based on symbols."

"But she's mad," said the commissioner, harshly. "It won't matter anyway."

"What about you?" Karlsson turned to Frieda, as if Crawford hadn't spoken. Frieda could sense his anger, rather than see it. A vein ticked in his temple.

"I'm not an expert on this," she replied. "Not like Dr. Bradshaw. I don't know. I mean, I *really* don't know."

"But what do you *think*?" said Karlsson.

Frieda looked back up at the ceiling tiles. Definitely random, she decided.

"I just can't believe that Michelle Doyce committed that murder. I've been trying to construct scenarios in my mind in which she does it and none of them makes sense."

"I've just provided a scenario," said Bradshaw.

"Yes. That's what I mean."

"But the body was in her flat," said Commissioner Crawford, impatiently. She turned, and he leaned toward her, banging his hand on the table to make his point. She could see spittle at the corners of his mouth. "Of course she must have killed him. Did someone else come in and leave it there? If we don't believe she did it, what the hell do we do?"

"What I wrote in my notes is that we should listen to her."

"But all she's doing is rambling about boats."

"Yes," said Frieda. "I wonder what she means by that."

"Well." Frieda almost thought Karlsson was trying not to smile. "There's Dr. Bradshaw's theory about rivers and women and all that."

Frieda thought for a moment. "That's the

big thing I have trouble with," she said. "I mean, I have trouble with all of it, but especially with that. The thing about Michelle is that I don't think she talks in symbols. I think she lives in a world where everything is real. That's her curse."

Karlsson looked across at Bradshaw. "Well?"

"I saw a woman in the corridor with a tea trolley," Bradshaw said. "Do you want her opinion as well?"

Karlsson looked back at Frieda, raising his eyebrows. There was a long silence that she didn't see any reason to break.

"I agree with Dr. Klein," he said finally.

"Fuck it, Mal."

"Michelle Doyce might have killed this man, but since when is 'might' enough for us?"

"I want this case closed."

"Indeed. We're trying to do just that, but —"

"No! You're not listening. I'm beginning to think you're taking your eye off the ball. I mean that I want this case closed right now. I agree with Dr. Bradshaw. This Doyce woman did it. I'm overruling you, Mal. Send the file to the CPS."

"Sorry for wasting your time, Frieda."

"It wasn't your fault. What are you going to do now?"

"What do you mean?"

"About the case."

"You heard. I'm sending the file to the CPS. She'll be unfit to plead. Case done and dusted, commissioner satisfied, Michelle Doyce safe in a psychiatric hospital for the rest of her life."

"But if you think she didn't do it?"

Karlsson shrugged. "Welcome to my life."

## 11

Jack Dargan looked around. "This is different," he said. "Not necessarily in a good way. I preferred it when we had our meetings at Number 9. I could do with a cappuccino and one of Marcus's brownies."

They were walking down Howard Street in the sleety drizzle. Jack's face looked raw, where it was visible. He was wearing a green bobble hat with side flaps and a checked brown and orange scarf wrapped several times round his neck. Whenever he wasn't speaking, he pulled it up over his mouth. He'd also put on an ancient bright blue anorak with a broken zip. He'd forgotten to wear gloves, though, and kept blowing on his hands. Frieda was Jack's mentor and Jack her trainee, but today he looked more like her truculent nephew.

"In ten years' time, five, this area will be all done up. Houses like this will have been pulled down to make way for offices," said

Frieda, stopping in front of number three.

"Good."

"They'll still have to find a place to dump all the misfits and the rejects, all the hopeless, forgotten people."

"Is it where your man was found?"

"He's not exactly my man, but yes."

"So why are we here? You told me the case was closed."

"It is closed. They've decided Michelle Doyce did it and she's unfit to plead. I just wanted to see where she lived. I thought you and I could talk better while we walk."

She turned and led Jack back up Howard Street toward Deptford Church Street.

"I don't know that I've got anything worth telling you," muttered Jack.

"I've been your supervisor for nearly two years."

"That's the bright spot in my week. Other than that . . ." He looked away so she couldn't see his face.

"Other than that?"

"I like talking about people's problems — just not to them. I'm interested in it all in theory, but sitting in that little room hearing someone tell me about what their stepfather said to them when they were six — it feels pointless. Or maybe I'm no good at it. I try to listen and then I catch myself thinking about what I want to eat for lunch or what film to go and see. People's lives are mostly so *dreary*."

Frieda looked at him attentively. "What's *your* life like?"

"I tell you what was good — last year, that time with Alan and Dean, being involved with all that, even on the edge of it. When it seemed relevant and there was some kind of answer — like a key fitting into a lock and the door swinging open. Most of the time, it's just me and them in a room saying stuff."

"Stuff," said Frieda. "Is that all it is?"

"You know what I think, Frieda? I think I'm only still doing it because of you. Because I want to be like you. Because when I'm with you it all seems to make sense. Most of the time I think what we do might be a great con, a joke played on people who feel heroic because they suffer and that's all they want to talk about."

"You sound resentful. You almost sound as though you're saying, 'And what about me?' "

"They give me a nasty mess and I pat it into some kind of shape. It could be any kind of shape, it doesn't really matter. I want to tell them to look outside themselves at the real world. There's proper suffering out there. Rape and violence and sheer, grinding poverty."

Frieda touched him on the shoulder. They had turned off Deptford Church Street and come to a small church, set back from the road, with an old tower. A skull and crossbones was set on one of its gate posts, a charnel house to the right.

"St. Nicholas was the patron saint of sailors," said Frieda, as they went through the gates and into a small graveyard. "It's what you'd expect in a church by the docks."

"I haven't been into a church since my grandma's funeral," said Jack.

"This one used to be in the countryside. It was all orchards and market gardens and small boats tied up at the wharves. Pilgrims to Canterbury would pass through it. Christopher Marlowe was killed in a brawl in a house nearby. They carried the body here."

"Which is his grave, then?"

"It's unmarked. He could be anywhere."

Jack shivered and stamped his feet and looked around at the flats that surrounded the church. "It's gone down a bit in the world since then."

"It'll come up again."

They made their way back to the road that ran along the river. On the other side they could see the towers of Canary Wharf, lights glittering in the February gloom, but here it felt deserted. A tiny primary school seemed to be closed, even though it was a Tuesday in February. They walked past a breaker's yard, piles of twisted rusting metal visible through the iron gates, nettles and brambles erupting over the wall, which was topped with coils of barbed wire. There were several boarded-up houses with smashed windows, and then an ancient industrial unit with cracking walls, whose fence bore the faded legend "Guard Dogs on Patrol." Jack walked further up the tiny street and pressed his face against some railings. He could see a deep, muddy pit where a building had stood, and on the far side of it the façade of a warehouse, through whose ruined arches he could see, over the muddy waters, the gleaming skyscrapers of Docklands.

"All ready for the developers," said Frieda, pointing at the notice to keep out.

"I prefer it as it is."

They continued along the river, past a rotting wooden pier. The low tide had exposed plastic crates and old bottles on the shore. Frieda thought about Jack's heavy, oppressive discontent, and waited for him to speak again. At the same time, she pictured Michelle Doyce here, picking up all those things Karlsson had told her about — tin cans, round stones, dead birds, forked sticks — and carrying them back to her room to arrange. Making a shape out of mess, as Jack put it; the instinct in us all, something deeply human and fearful.

Glancing across at Frieda's smooth profile, her chin held up in spite of the icy wind, Jack felt the familiar grip of his adoration for her. He wanted her to look him in the eye and tell him that everything would be all right, that he would be all right, there was no need to worry, and that she was going to help him. She would never do that. If there was one thing he had learned from her, over all the time they had spent together, it was that you had to take responsibility for your own life.

He took a deep breath and cleared his throat. "There's something I should tell you," he said. Now that he'd come to it, it was hard to say it out loud; his chest felt tight. "I've been slipping a bit."

"Slipping?"

"I've missed a few sessions."

"With your patients?"

"Yes. Not many," he hastened to add. "Just occasionally — and a few I've arrived late for. And I've kind of stopped seeing my own therapist so regularly. I'm not sure she's right for me."

"How long has this been going on?"

"A couple of months. Maybe more."

"What do you do when you don't go or when you arrive late?"

"Sleep."

"You pull the covers over your head."

"Yes," Jack said. "And it's not a metaphor. An actual cover over my actual head."

"You know, don't you, that for the people who come to you this may be the most important fifty minutes of their week — and that they might have screwed up all their courage to come?"

"It's really, really bad. I'm not making excuses."

"This doesn't sound like just a problem with therapy. You sound a bit depressed to me."

They kept walking. Jack seemed to be looking at something in the river. Frieda waited.

"I don't know what that word means," he said eventually. "Does it mean down in the dumps or does it mean something more?"

"It means you're lying in bed with the covers over your head, letting your patients down and yourself, worrying that you've made the wrong career choice, and you don't seem to want to change."

"What should I change?" They were walking past sparkling new gabled houses with front gardens and balconies. It felt a long way from Deptford.

"I think that the first thing you need to do is stop lying in bed, letting down people who badly need you. You get up however you feel, and you go to work."

Jack looked at her, his cheeks flushed in the cold. "I thought you dealt with feelings."

"You can think about that. We can talk about it. In the meantime, you do your job."

"Why?" asked Jack.

"Because that's what we do." Frieda stopped and nudged him. "On a normal day I'd show you the *Cutty Sark,* but it's still being mended so you can't see a thing." It was true: the ship was completely hidden from view by boards.

"It's better this way," said Jack. "It's all a fake anyway."

"How do you mean?"

"There was a fire, remember? What I heard is that there was nothing left. When it's rebuilt, it'll be like a Madame Tussaud's replica of the real *Cutty Sark.* It'll be another fake bit of London for the tourists to look at."

"Does it matter?"

"Don't you care if people mistake a crappy

heritage museum for real life?"

Frieda glanced at Jack's wretched face. Maybe breakfast at her local coffee shop would have been a better idea. "Real life is an overrated idea," she said.

"Is that supposed to comfort me?"

"Comfort? No, Jack. We're going down here."

They walked through a doorway in a small domed building by the river and entered a battered, creaky lift operated by a man wearing headphones, singing along to a song that only he could hear. Jack didn't speak as it descended. The doors opened, and he saw the tunnel stretching ahead of them in a long gentle curve.

"What is this?" Jack said.

"The tunnel under the river."

"Who uses it?"

"It used to be for the dockers to walk to work on the Isle of Dogs. It's mostly empty now."

"Where are we headed?"

"I thought I'd buy you lunch."

Jack was surprised. They'd never eaten lunch together before. "Aren't you working?"

"A patient canceled. Anyway, I need to think things through. Walking helps me think."

"Even when I'm here moaning about my problems."

"Even then."

Jack listened to the echoes of their steps in the tunnel and tried not to think of the weight of the water above. "You mean, think about this dead man?"

"I'm thinking about the woman they found him with. The one who was looking after him."

They entered the lift at the other end. The operator was reading a magazine. Jack looked at Frieda. "I guess that some jobs are worse than mine."

They came out into the wind and rain on the north side of the river.

"Don't do that again," Frieda said.

"What?"

"Talk about someone like him as if he's deaf, as if he's too stupid to understand." She walked swiftly, in long, smooth strides, looking suddenly stern.

"Sorry," he said humbly. "You're right. But what can you do about the woman?"

"She clearly didn't kill him," said Frieda.

"She's in an institution now, right? And that's where she'll stay, whatever happens. So . . ."

"You sound like a policeman," said Frieda. "Like the commissioner."

■ ■ ■ ■

Frieda led them on a path along the bank of the Isle of Dogs. On the left side there were flats, converted warehouses, compact modern houses. On the right was the widening river and beyond, on the other side, scrubby wasteland. They walked briefly along a busier road, then Frieda turned off into a smaller street and suddenly they were in an old inn: a warm, oak-beamed room, the chink of wine glasses, the rise and fall of conversation, the crackle of an open fire, young women in white aprons sailing past with dishes held high on one hand.

They sat at a table with a view across the water. Frieda looked out. "You can understand why all those old sea captains came back here when they retired. It was the nearest they could get to being at sea."

"I noticed all those names in Deptford." Jack took his seat opposite her. He picked up a menu and looked at it intently, concealing his nervousness. What was he going to eat? It depended on Frieda. Did she expect them to have a full meal, like beef pie or salmon *en croûte,* or should he have a bar snack?

"What names?"

"The street names. They reminded me of studying the Spanish Armada at school. Fisher Road, Drake Road, or whatever. There's probably a Nelson Road somewhere, or is that too late?"

"Say that again."

"Sorry?"

"The names."

Jack repeated them. A young woman put a basket of bread rolls on the table, and he tore a large piece off one and stuffed it into his mouth, realizing how hungry he was.

"Are you ready to order?" asked a waitress.

Frieda paused. Jack waited for her to go first.

"No," said Frieda, slowly. "We've got to go."

"What do you mean?"

Frieda stood up and pulled a crisp five-pound note from her wallet, which she laid on the table under the basket of bread rolls.

"Come on."

"That was quick," he said, but she was already on her way out. He had to run to keep up with her.

# 12

"You remember Jack Dargan?" said Frieda to Karlsson, after he'd got out of the car. "A colleague of mine."

Karlsson nodded at Jack. "Funny to meet in Deptford. What are you even doing over here?"

"Jack and I had things to discuss," said Frieda. "I thought it would be a good place for a walk. It's an interesting area."

"So I've heard." Karlsson looked through some railings at the remains of a warehouse. "But mainly it's a dump." He pushed his hands into the pockets of his jacket. "Before you say anything, I'd like to point out the reality of the situation. What is probably going to happen is that the CPS will read the file and decide that Michelle Doyce is unfit to plead, which I'm sure you agree with. At that point, the British taxpayer will be saved the cost of a trial as well as any further police investigation. Michelle Doyce will finally get the medical attention she should have received in the first place and you can get back to your patients." He paused. "We'll probably never know exactly what happened."

"I think I know what Michelle Doyce was saying," said Frieda.

"I hope it was a confession," said Karlsson. He looked at her, then at Jack, whose face showed the faint trace of a smile that quickly vanished. "Well? What was it?"

"Follow me." Frieda set off along the street toward the house, the two men walking quickly to keep up. "I was talking to Jack about the history of this area. Did you know that it was somewhere along here that Queen Elizabeth knighted Francis Drake?"

"No, I didn't," said Karlsson. "I visited the *Cutty Sark* when I was at school."

"It's all a fake, apparently," said Frieda.

Now they had turned into Howard Street and Frieda stopped. They looked at the house. Number three.

"Look at this," she said. "There's nothing left. Four, five hundred years ago there were orchards here and shipyards, and it's where Francis Drake came and moored his boat after he had sailed round the world, and it's all gone. They just built warehouses on top of it, and then it all got bombed in the war, and then they built the housing estates."

"Frieda," said Karlsson, with a slight edge to his voice, "I'm really hoping that this is leading somewhere —"

"It was Jack," Frieda cut in.

Karlsson looked across at Jack, who turned red and seemed both pleased and baffled.

"He reminded me that the names of the streets survive, even when the buildings have been knocked down. The shipyards and docks are gone but not the streets that were named after them." She pointed up at the street sign. "Look. Howard Street. Wasn't he the admiral of the Armada?"

"I don't know," said Karlsson.

Frieda walked toward the house and stood in front of it. She turned to Karlsson. "Andrew Berryman said I should try listening to Michelle Doyce. When we asked her where she had met the man, she kept talking about Drake and the river."

"Fluvial," said Karlsson. "Isn't that what Dr. Bradshaw said?"

"Fluvial?" echoed Jack.

"Well, that was a load of crap," said Frieda.

"He's a leading authority," said Karlsson.

"Michelle was just trying to answer the question."

"Then why didn't she answer it more

clearly?" said Karlsson.

"She doesn't see the world the way we do. But she did her best." Frieda led them along the front of the house to where a walkway passed along the side. It was blocked off at the far end. "Drake's Alley," she announced.

"And?" said Karlsson.

"Michelle Doyce collects things," she said, "brings them back to her flat, and arranges them."

"Are you saying she collected a dead body?"

"I think that's what she told us."

There was a long silence while Karlsson thought hard.

"You think Michelle Doyce found a dead body here and carried it back to her flat?"

"She wouldn't need to carry it," said Frieda. "It's — what? — fifteen, twenty feet from here to her front door. And it was an emergency. She must have thought she was helping him."

Karlsson nodded slowly. His face wore a look of concentration. And almost, Frieda thought, a kind of rueful amusement.

"OK," he said. "Good. Stand back now. This might be a crime scene. I don't think we should blunder in."

"What about your commissioner?"

"I'll inform him," said Karlsson. "In due

course."

The three of them stood and gazed into the alley. It was a muddy, gravelly path, littered with pieces of paper and shopping bags; used needles were strewn around. A bin bag had been dumped in the far corner.

"Bradshaw might still be right," said Frieda. "Michelle might have been talking about men and women. You know, boats and rivers."

"Someone needs to go through all that stuff," said Karlsson, as if she hadn't spoken. He took out his phone. "Fortunately, there are people who do this for us."

In February, the days are still short. She knew it was February, and she even knew the date because she had made herself a calendar. She had been good at art in school; it had been her favorite subject. Even now, if she closed her eyes, she could make herself remember the feeling, when she was very little, of dipping the thick brush into the pot of paint, then running it across the blank page, seeing the bright, steady line following it.

The pictures in this calendar had been of trees. A tree for each month. When she was a girl, she had had a sketch pad, which she kept in the top drawer of her desk. In it, she

141

had made a painting of each of the trees in her garden: ash, oak, beech, hornbeam, false acacia; apple tree and plum tree and walnut tree. She had spent hours shading in the trunks, trying to get the leaves right. She never painted towns, houses, people — all those eyes staring at you, faces peering out of windows when you didn't know you were being looked at. Strangers behind you, or in corners, in shadows. She preferred empty landscapes. She liked the desert and the sea and wide lakes.

He had brought her the paper, several pencils, and colored crayons. He hadn't brought a sharpener, though, so she'd had to use the knife she pared potatoes with. There was a page for the tree, and a page that she divided into a grid for all the days. Thirty days have September, April, June, and November . . . It had taken ages, but she had time. That was one thing she did have, while she was waiting. She had sat at the little table and, instead of a ruler, she had used a book about gardening that he had left behind on one of his visits. She couldn't write down the days that each date fell on — that would have been too complicated and, anyway, she had made the calendar in September and now it was the following year, 2011: February 2011.

In each square she wrote down what she had done during the day. It wouldn't give anything away; she never put down things that were important. She wrote: "20 push-ups," "2 cups of tea," or "bad migraine," things like that. She had run out of migraine tablets, but he would bring them when he came. She only put a small star in the top right-hand corner of each square on the days that he was with her. That was how she knew that it was three weeks and three days since he had been there. He had never been away that long, not even when he was on a mission.

The tree for February was a beech, al-though few except her would recognize that because its branches were bare. She liked the smooth gray bark of a beech tree and the fluted column of its trunk. At the trunk's fork, she had put in the tiny initials of her name and his. Nobody would ever see it, but she knew it was there — like a lover's carving. She did it with each tree, in a different place. It was a secret code. She hadn't even told him because perhaps he wouldn't like it, but after this was over, she would tell him and he would wrap his arm around her shoulders and kiss her on the top of her head or on the side of her jaw just beneath her ear and tell her how proud he was of her and of what she had endured for his sake. He needed her. Nobody had ever needed her before. It was because of this that she had given up everything: her home, her family, her comfort, her safety, herself.

She put her face to the window and looked out at the gray sky that was darkening toward night. Days were short and nights were long, and it was cold and she wanted him to come.

# 13

At just past seven on the following morning, Frieda was standing at the door of a well-lit basement room in the police station. It was windowless and cold, and there was even an underground smell, a tinge of decay and dirt. The odor was from the detritus in the alley that had been laid out on the surfaces with evident care, each item in its own space.

"You wanted to see it," said Karlsson.

"Is there anything?"

"Judge for yourself." He entered the room and Frieda followed him. "Obviously we were looking for things like traces of human blood, bodily fluid, but even if there had been anything like that, the rain and melted snow would have washed it all away. If the body had been in that alley, it would have been about two weeks ago. Of course, it would have been nice to find his missing finger."

"There was nothing else?"

"What? Like a wallet full of cards or a set of keys with an address tag on them? No. We have a list of items." He waved a sheet. "The boys were very diligent. They even sorted things into categories." He glanced down at the paper. "Things like tinfoil cartons containing the remains of sweet and sour chicken, that kind of thing. Here. A souvenir for you. They'll start putting it in bin bags at nine — all that effort just to repackage rubbish."

Frieda glanced at the list: remains of one dead cat minus its tail, forty-eight syringes, two dirty nappies, seven condoms . . . She looked around the room, oddly compelled by what was clearly a forensic examination of everyday litter. She turned to Karlsson. "Is that it, then?"

"As far as Crawford is concerned, the case is closed. I'm now investigating a nasty case of domestic abuse," Karlsson said, by way of answer. "Sixty-three stitches in the poor woman's face from being repeatedly hit with a broken bottle, four fractured ribs, and a badly bruised kidney. It's the third time she's been injured in the last eighteen months, and each time so far she's withdrawn the complaint and gone back to her charming husband. I'm trying to persuade her to press charges this time."

"I don't want to hold you up any more. Maybe you can just leave me here for a few minutes to look around."

"So you can find something we've missed?"

"Now that I'm here."

"Be my guest. Get them to buzz me from Reception when you're done."

Karlsson left and Frieda closed the door. She took off her coat and laid it with her scarf and shoulder bag on a metal chair but kept her gloves on. The first category was the largest: rotten food. There were chicken bones with shreds of flesh hanging off them, apple cores, the remains of bread rolls with the toothmarks still visible in some, foil containers full of different kinds of unspeakable greasy glop, a small heap of rotten pulpy tomatoes, a few knobs of chocolate, lots of flabby gray chips smeared with tomato, pieces of what Frieda took to be battered fish, fragments of pies in different states of decay. She looked at them all swiftly and moved on to the next category, which was packaging: crisps packets, cigarette packets, sweet wrappers, old plastic bags, beer cans, Coke cans, cider cans, empty vodka and wine bottles, polystyrene cups. Then came clothing: one child's flip-flop, two sneakers with their soles peeled back, a woman's once-white shirt from M&S missing an entire sleeve, a woolen scarf covered with what smelled like dog shit, a graying bra, size 36B, men's running socks with balding heels.

Frieda moved on: nappies and condoms; syringes; dead tailless cat; unidentifiable very dead rodent with innards spilling on to the counter; newspapers and magazines, dating back as far as January 23; flyers for various gigs and takeaways; fragments of broken pottery, including one nearly complete bowl with an Indian-tree pattern on it that reminded Frieda of her grandmother; batteries; the rusting casing of a mobile phone and three plastic lighters; coins in mostly one- and two-penny denominations, though there were a few euros as well.

The final space on the surface had been reserved for all that couldn't be categorized: a small, dusty heap of cigarette stubs, matches, tiny scraps of paper and cardboard, hair grips, metal tabs from cans.

Frieda sighed. She put on her coat and scarf and slung her bag over her shoulder. But she didn't leave at once. She stood in the middle of the room, looking from one section to the next, frowning. Then she walked over to the flyers and picked through them again. She extracted one and, holding it between her thumb and forefinger, she left the room, shutting the door behind her.

"Is that it?" said Karlsson. He was sitting behind a desk piled high with paper. On the shelf behind him Frieda saw the photographs of his two little children, a flaxen-haired girl with a cleft in her chin, like his, and an older boy with big, anxious eyes. She had met them once, when she had visited his flat in Highbury, but couldn't remember their names.

"It's not local." Frieda pushed the torn, crumpled, grubby flyer under Karlsson's nose. "All the others were from nearby. This one's got a Brixton area code. Look."

"And?"

"So why was it there?"

Karlsson leaned back, his hands behind his head. "Amazing how people get about these days," he said companionably. "Look at me. I traveled all the way in to work from Highbury, and this evening I'm actually going to visit someone in Kensal Rise. That's nothing compared to Yvette. She comes in from Harrow."

"This is from a little alleyway. It's not a place for passers-by."

"There were people buying drugs in the

house. People shooting up in the alleyway."

"With receipts?"

"Even heroin addicts buy things."

"Have you noticed the writing on the back?"

Karlsson turned it over and smoothed out the paper. " 'String,' " he read out loud. " 'Straw. Cord. Stone.' "

"Do you make anything of it?"

"I presume it's a shopping list. Maybe whoever wrote it is a DIY enthusiast. There are a lot around nowadays. If I had to guess, judging from my own experiences last year, I'd say that someone's planning to grow strawberries in their garden."

"What about the letters?"

"C, SB, WL. I don't know, Frieda. You tell me."

"I can't."

"Let's see, Cabbage, Salted Butter, Waxed Lemon. Or Cointreau, sesame bagels, and washing liquid. Fun as this is, I don't really have the time."

"I can see that."

Karlsson pushed the flyer back at her. "Listen, I know I persuaded you to get involved. I know you've put a lot into this. I know you think we're wrong about Michelle Doyce. I know Hal Bradshaw is a jerk and his theories are hot air dressed up in pompous language. What's more, I even know it's possible, even likely, that Michelle Doyce wasn't the actual murderer. But I've got a crime nobody gives a toss about, I've got a corpse with no name, I've got a single witness who makes no sense and is in a psychiatric hospital where she belongs. I've got a management consultant with pointy shoes looking over my shoulder, and I've got a commissioner who's already moved on. What would you do?"

Frieda held up the flyer. "Follow this up."

"Sorry."

Frieda was about to leave when she thought of something. "Is there a photo of the body?" she said. "Just the face."

"Of course," said Karlsson, suspiciously. "Why?"

"Could I have a copy?"

"You can't show it to anyone, you know," he said. "It's not in a good way."

"Even so," said Frieda.

"All right," said Karlsson. "But it had better not end up on your Facebook page."

"Can I get it on my way out?"

"As long as you promise to go."

As she left, she remembered his children's names. Mikey and Bella, that was it.

# 14

Frieda sat down at her desk. She opened her drawing pad and stroked the grainy page gently, the way she always did, almost as a superstition. She took the photograph out of its buff envelope and laid it on the desk. The creamy eyes of the dead man stared up at her. Except they weren't staring up at her. When you look at a face, you concentrate on the eyes because you feel you're looking in at a person who can look back at you. But these eyes were just a clouded vacancy. The whole head was puffy and swollen. The flesh had cracked on the temple and in the right cheek.

She picked up a soft lead pencil. She never drew faces or figures, only objects: bridges, bricks, iron railings, old doorways, broken pottery, and lopsided chimneys. And normally, when making a drawing, she would be looking at the details, the flaws, the cracks, the discolorations. This time she wanted to see beneath them. What had he been like before? She started with what hadn't changed: the eyebrows, the hair. The cheekbones were prominent, even with all the swelling and the decay. He had a firm chin. The lips were thin, the ears flat against the skull. What about the nose? She reduced it slightly. She could only guess the contours of the face and jaw line. Narrower but not gaunt, she decided. The hair was dark brown, so she made the eyes dark as well. She sat back and looked at it from a distance. It was a face, certainly. Was it *the* face? She folded it in half and put it in her shoulder bag.

In the computer forensics lab in the City, Yvette Long was standing at the shoulder of a young man with straggly hair and a ginger mustache. He was a forensic anthropologist, and he was seated at a computer, pressing buttons and typing in information from a sheet of paper at his side. All the while, he hummed a tune, over and over again, that she supposed was from an opera, but she didn't know anything about opera.

"I'm using three-D graphics for this," he said, breaking off mid-hum.

Yvette nodded. She knew — he told her every time she came down here.

"Tcl/Tk scripting," he added. "Very smart stuff."

"Mm," said Yvette. She didn't know what it meant, but she knew that a face was growing on the screen in front of them on the interlocking mesh of lines.

"You understand it's quite a generic image we're producing. You could have a three-dimensional reconstruction made up from this."

"I don't think we'll be needing that."

The face was quite thin, with a straight nose and ears that lay flat against the head. A high forehead. Brown hair. Brown eyes. A prominent Adam's apple.

Although they couldn't know it, it wasn't so different from the face that Frieda had drawn, though the eyes were more vacant and the mouth less curved.

"That'll do," said Yvette. "That'll do nicely."

By eight forty, Frieda was in her consulting room. She had twenty minutes before her first patient, so she made herself a cup of tea and stood by the window that looked out on to the vast construction site. When she had first come there, that space had been a row of Victorian houses. She had seen families moved out, windows and

154

doors boarded up. Then the squatters had arrived and they, too, had been ejected. A fence had been put up round the area, with large signs warning the public to keep clear. Bulldozers and cranes had appeared; a wrecking ball had swung through the roof-tops and walls, and whole houses had toppled as if made from matchsticks. Men in hard hats had drunk their tea on top of the rubble; Portakabins had been erected. A year ago, this site had been cleared of every last standing stone and had become an empty wasteland, waiting for the brand new development to begin. It was still waiting. There was one lonely crane still parked in the center, and a Portakabin remained, though its windows were smashed, but all the diggers had gone, the workers had gone. The plan had been put on hold, like so many plans in this city, at this time. And meanwhile, kids had found their way in through gaps in the fence to reclaim the area; they stood about in gaggles in the evening, smoking cigarettes or drinking, and sometimes in the morning they would gather there before school.

Today, eight or nine of them were playing football. Frieda watched them as they tore over the muddy, churned-up ground, yelling to each other to pass. Their school

155

clothes were beginning to look the worse for wear. Perhaps nothing would ever get built here, she thought. Perhaps it would turn back to a kind of natural wilderness in the center of the urban density where children could play, gangs could fight each other, and homeless people could retreat from shop fronts.

She heard footsteps outside. Putting down her mug, she stood for a while, clearing her thoughts and readying herself, then went toward her door and opened it into the waiting area. Joe Franklin sat on the sofa, his head tipped to one side as if he was listening to some sound only he could hear. Frieda had a chance to examine him before he noticed she was there; she had been seeing Joe for two and a half years now, twice a week if he managed to turn up, which he frequently didn't. Today he was early, which was a good sign, and she saw that he was properly dressed: his buttons matched up, his shoelaces were tied, his jeans were held up with a belt, not sliding off his wasted frame, his hair was quite clean. She saw that his fingernails weren't dirty and that he had shaved recently. What was more, as he turned toward her, his eyes were clear and he stood up in one smooth gesture, no longer toppling upward like an old drunk.

There were weeks and months when he could barely make it through the day, when all his efforts were a blind stumble through a slow-motion nightmare, and then there were times like this, when he emerged from the shadows.

"Joe." She smiled at him reassuringly and held the door open. "Good to see you. Come in, sit down. Let's begin."

At ten to two, Frieda had finished for the day. Four patients, four stories in her head. She sat for a few minutes, making her notes from the final session in her notebook with her old fountain pen that Reuben always mocked her for, calling her old-fashioned. She checked her mobile for messages, reminded herself that she had to call her niece Chloë later that day, and washed her mug in the little kitchen off her room. She had eaten nothing that day, but she wasn't going home just yet. She pulled on her long black coat and wrapped her red scarf twice round her neck, then set off briskly for Warren Street and the Victoria Line.

A little later, walking up Brixton Road, she found Andy's Pizzas within a few minutes. It was easy. She had the flyer. She looked at the brightly colored exterior. Andy didn't just offer pizzas. He offered hamburgers and chips as well. There were livid photographs of them on display. They suddenly made Frieda think of the photographs of the body, and once she had thought of it she couldn't stop herself. She walked inside. There were a couple of plastic tables at the front by the window. At one, a woman was sitting with a small child and a baby in a buggy. Frieda went up to the counter. A man was taking an order over the phone. He was balding with a black beard and he wore a red polo shirt with "Andy's" printed over the left breast. He put the phone down and handed the order through a gap in the wall behind him. A hand took it. Frieda could hear frying and clattering pans. The man looked inquiringly at her.

"Yes," said Frieda, looking beyond him at the list of food and prices on the wall. "Can I have a green salad? And a bottle of water."

"Salad," the man shouted. He leaned down and took a plastic bottle from a fridge. He placed it on the counter. "Anything else?"

"That's fine," said Frieda, handing over a five-pound note.

The man slid the change across the counter. "The salad'll be a minute," he said.

Frieda took the flyer and put it on the counter. "I got your flyer," she said.

"Yeah?" said the man.

Frieda had worried about this. All it would take was one wrong question, one that made it sound as if she was from the council or the VAT office and they'd clam up and that would be that.

"I wanted to ask you," she said. "I was going to get some flyers done myself. I've got a little business. I thought I could print some up like you've done, get some publicity."

The phone rang. The man picked it up and took another order.

"What I was saying," Frieda continued, when he was done, "was that I was interested in getting flyers like that. I wondered where you got them done."

"There's a printer along the road," said the man. "They done us a few hundred."

"And then what happens? Do they deliver them for you?"

"They just print them up. My cousin dropped them off."

"You mean he pushed them through doors?"

"Something like that."

"Do you know where he did it?" asked Frieda.

The man shrugged. Frieda felt a sense of hopelessness, as if she were trying to grab something and it was slipping through her fingers.

"I'm just curious," she said. She took the A–Z from her bag and fumbled for the right page. "You see, I'd probably end up delivering them myself, so I wanted to know how big an area you could cover. Could you just show me on the map where he went? Or did he just wander wherever he wanted?"

She pushed the map across the counter toward him. A sound came from behind him and a polystyrene container appeared in the gap. The man took the salad and gave it to Frieda. There was chopped cabbage and carrot and onion and a slice of tomato, with a swirl of pink liquid across it. "Thank you," she said. "About this map."

The man sighed. He leaned down and put his forefinger on the page. "I told him to go along Acre Lane and do all the streets along it on that side."

"Which streets?"

The man swirled his finger around. "All those," he said. "Until he ran out."

It looked like a lot of streets.

"And there were three hundred?"

"Five, I think. We've got a pile in the shop."

"And this was about a fortnight ago?"

The man looked puzzled. "What do you mean?"

"I wondered how well it worked," said Frieda. "Whether it made lots of people ring up for pizza."

"I don't know," said the man. "A few, maybe."

"All right. Thanks for your help." She turned to go.

"Hang on. You forgot your salad."

"Yes, right."

She walked out of the shop and, feeling guilty, waited until she was thirty or forty yards away, well out of sight, before she crammed the salad container into an over-flowing bin.

As she sat on the underground train, returning north, she looked at the back of the flyer once more, though she knew the words by heart. It was laid out like a shopping list. String. Straw. Cord. Stone. Why would you buy those? What would you use them for? Why would you need to buy both string and cord? Were they actually different in some technical DIY sense that she didn't recognize? Was there a job that string couldn't do for which you needed cord? It sounded like something outdoors, unless this had a medieval theme. Weren't Elizabethan taverns scattered with straw? Or per-

161

haps it was a drinking straw. Frieda stared at the list until her head hurt. When she came out of Warren Street station she kept going over and over it. Was she missing an obvious connection? She played mental games. You could tie straw with string. Or a cord. What about the stone? She thought of David and Goliath, except that that was a sling and a stone.

What would you do with those four things? Who might know? One name came straight into her mind. She couldn't meet him but she could phone him; in fact, she should have phoned him long ago, just so that he knew she was thinking of him. As soon as she came into her house, she flicked through the leather-bound notebook she kept by the phone. She found the number and dialed. It rang and rang, and she was preparing to leave a message when there was a click.

"Frieda," said the voice.

"Yes, Josef. Hello! It's good to hear your voice after all this time. How are you? Are you doing all right there? We miss you."

"How am I?" he said. "That is a big question. I don't know the answer."

"Has something happened, Josef?"

"Oh, I don't know. Frieda, how are you? How are things with you?"

"Just the same," she said. "On the whole.

But I want to hear about you. I should have called. I'm sorry I didn't."

"That is OK," he said. "Life is busy for all. Many things happen, things that do not do well on the phone."

"I keep looking at the weather," Frieda said. "Whenever I get the chance, I check the weather in Kiev. That's you, isn't it? The last time I saw, it was minus twenty-nine. I hope you're wrapping up warm."

There was a long silence, followed by a strange sort of moan.

"Are you all right?" asked Frieda. "Are you still there?"

"Frieda, I am not in Kiev at the moment."

"Oh. Where are you?"

He said something she couldn't make out.

"Sorry? Is that somewhere in the country-side?"

He said the name again.

"Can you speak more slowly?"

He said the three syllables one by one.

"Summertown?" said Frieda. "You mean, like Summertown in London?"

"Yes," said Josef. "Not like. The Summer-town in London. That one."

It was several seconds before Frieda could speak coherently. "You're . . . you're only about five hundred yards away."

"It is possible."

"What the hell are you doing here?"

"I have been in complications."

"I need to see you."

"No good."

"I'm your friend, remember?" Frieda said. "Come to my house. Right now."

# 15

Frieda hadn't seen Josef for nearly two months. The last occasion had been shortly before Christmas, when, in memory of the previous Christmas they had spent together, he had made some traditional Ukrainian food and carried it to her house, wrapped in white linen and placed inside a ribboned box, as a parting gift: little cakes made of wheat, honey, and poppy seeds. She remembered him as he had been then, beaming with pride, expansive with generosity, and full of solemn excitement. After many months of absence, he was returning to his country to visit his wife, Vera, and his two sons. His usually shaggy hair was cut short and he wore a new quilted jacket for the cold Ukrainian winter. He had bought his sons T-shirts saying "I love London," small Union flags, and snow domes with miniature London scenes inside.

It was a very different Josef who came to

her door now. His hair was long, dirty, and full of dust; he had the beginnings of a beard that looked like the unintended result of not bothering to shave. He was wearing an old pair of canvas trousers, held up with a plastic belt, and a thick jersey. Over it was that quilted jacket, but it was torn and filthy. His boots were cracked. His hands were chapped and blistered. There was a fading bruise on his neck and a plaster across his grimy forehead. Above all, his face was slack, his eyes were dull, and he wouldn't meet Frieda's gaze; he stood in the doorway, twisting his woolen hat between his hands and shifting from foot to foot.

Frieda took his hand and pulled him into the hall, shutting the door behind them. She caught a thick whiff of body odor, tobacco, and alcohol. She pulled off his jacket and hung it next to her coat. There were holes in the elbows of his jersey.

"Do you want to take your shoes off," she said. "Then we can go through and sit down."

"I not stay."

His English seemed to have deteriorated in the short time that he had been away.

"I'll make you tea."

"No tea."

"How long have you been back, Josef?"

He held up his palms in a familiar gesture. "Some weeks."

"Why didn't you say?"

Josef's eyes lifted to her face, then dropped again.

"All your things are at Reuben's. Your van's there. Where have you been staying?"

"Now? On site. In house that must be built. Is cold. But is roof."

Frieda considered him. His entire body spoke of misery and defeat. "I want you to tell me what happened," she said gently. "But don't worry — you don't have to do it all at once. Whenever you're ready, I'm here. I'm glad you're back. So will Reuben be. His house needs you. And I need you."

"You only say."

"No, it's true."

"I have no uses."

"Here's the plan. I'm going to call Reuben and you're staying there tonight. He has things wrong in his house. You can mend them. When you feel like it, you can tell me — or him — what's happened. In the meantime, you're going to sit in my kitchen, drink tea, and I have a question for you."

Josef's brown eyes stared at her for a moment. "Why?"

"Why what?"

"Why you help me? I am bad man, Frieda. Bad, sad man."

Frieda put a hand under his elbow and steered him into the kitchen. She pulled out a chair and he lowered his body into it. She boiled the kettle and, while the tea was brewing, toasted two pieces of bread for him, which she spread with butter and honey. "There. Get that down you."

He took a hot gulp of tea and his eyes watered. He picked up a piece of toast, and she saw how his hand trembled.

"Now. I need you to help me." She put the flyer in front of him, facedown, and pointed to the letters. "If you had to guess, what do those letters mean?"

Josef put his toast back on the plate, dragged his sleeve across his mouth, and peered at the words. "String, straw, cord, stone."

"They're things you could use in building. But why string and cord together? Karlsson said strawberry planting, but I don't think so. He wasn't giving it serious attention."

"Is easy."

"What?"

"Is easy," repeated Josef. For the first time, his eyes looked brighter.

"So?"

"Is paint."

"Paint?"

"Names of paint. Gloom colors — like colors in your working room. Pale, dim colors. String, straw, cord, and stone. So."

"Oh," said Frieda. "Josef, you're brilliant."

"I?"

"What about those letters: C, SB, WL."

"Is easy," Josef said again. For a brief moment he sounded almost happy. He pointed a finger upward: "C is ceiling." His finger moved like the hand on a clock. "WL is left wall. And . . ." His finger moved down.

"Skirting board," supplied Frieda. "Why didn't I think of that?"

"You are doctor, not builder."

"So someone was having their house painted." She looked at her watch. It was nearly half past four. "If we go now, we might get there before five. Will you come with me on an errand?" He didn't reply at once, so she added, "I *need* you to help me, Josef. Like you did before."

It was beginning to get dark and the rain was turning to hail. Frieda thought that Josef looked like a large, helpless child as he trudged along the streets, his hat pulled low over his head and his hands thrust deep into the pockets of his shabby trousers. She had called Reuben and told him that she and Josef would be there in the evening, and he should make up the bed and perhaps put some baked potatoes into the oven.

"Why we look?" Josef asked now.

"I'm trying to find someone. It's a bit of a long story and I'll tell you later."

"So how we look for walls of stone and straw?"

"We can't knock at every door of every house. But I thought if we see any external signs of building work we can knock at that door."

"So you take this road and I take that." Josef held up his phone. "I call you, you call me."

Frieda was glad of these signs of engagement. She nodded, and they set off in different directions, met at the top of the streets without progress, and separated once more down another pair of parallel streets that led off from the high street and that Andy's Pizzas flyers had apparently been delivered to.

Frieda was two thirds of the way along Tully Road when her mobile rang. "Josef?"

" 'Painting and Decorating, No Job Too Small.' Van here by me now, one tire looks flat. Outside thirty-three Owens Close."

"Don't move. I'll be there."

But there were no lights on in Owens Close and no one answered when Frieda rang the bell. She tried thirty-one, stood back from the door, and waited. She heard footsteps and the door opened. A young man with a shaved scalp stuck his head out. She saw he was wearing a suit, and had a phone in his hand. "Yes?"

"I'm sorry for bothering you," she said, conscious of Josef hovering on the street behind her, "but I was hoping you could help me. Do you happen to have decorators with you?"

"Yeah. Hang on, let me just finish this call. Sorry, Cas, I'll call back, OK? There. Sorry, decorators. Yes. Doing us top to bottom. They're in the front room at the moment, I think they're just finishing up for the day. But why do you want to know? Do you live nearby? Want a bit of painting done, maybe, because if so I can't honestly say I'd recommend —"

"No. It's hard to explain. I'm looking for someone and I think you can perhaps help me."

"Me? I don't get it. Do you want to come into the hall? It's getting a bit chilly out here. And, um, your friend."

"It's OK. I won't take long." Frieda stepped into the hall, which still smelled of

171

fresh paint. She pulled the flyer out of her bag. "Do you recognize this?"

"Well." The young man looked at her warily, as if she might turn out to be a nutcase. "It's a flyer. Obviously. Andy's Pizzas."

"Do you get them delivered here? The flyers, I mean, not the pizzas."

"Yeah. I think so — all sorts of junk comes through our letterbox."

Frieda turned the leaflet. "And this."

He squinted, frowned. "I don't think it's my writing. Or Cas's. My wife. What is this?"

"Are you using Straw, String, Cord, and Stone on your walls?"

"Yeah. Yeah. I think so. I'm sure, actually. This is beginning to spook me out, if you don't mind me saying so."

"Sorry. There's a drawing I've got here. Can you tell me if it reminds you of anyone?"

She took her drawing out of the envelope she'd put it in and handed it to him. He stared at it. "Maybe."

"Maybe?"

"It bears a resemblance. There was a guy — he was going to do our decorating. Really keen, as a matter of fact. Nice guy. Very helpful. This looks a bit like him. And he wrote down the paints, now I come to think of it. But we never used him, if that's what you're going to ask. He just disappeared. Didn't answer his phone or anything. Left us in the lurch. That's why we got this lot to come."

Frieda tried to keep her expression steady. "When did he disappear?"

"Well — maybe two weeks ago, something like that. I don't know exactly. Cas could probably be more accurate. Is there a problem? Has he done something?"

"What was his name?" She heard her own use of the past tense, but the young man didn't notice.

"Rob. Rob Poole."

"Do you have his address?"

"No. Nothing. Just his mobile number." He scrolled down on his phone and found it, jotted it on the back of Andy's worse-for-wear flyer. "He's not answering it, though — I must have left him half a dozen messages."

"Thanks."

"Do you know him?"

"Not exactly. Could I have your name as well, please, and your phone number?"

"Why on earth?"

"I think the police might want to talk to you about him."

Reuben hadn't put potatoes in the oven: he'd made a greasy, rich lasagne, garlic bread, and a green salad. The smell greeted them when he opened the door, wearing an apron and his half-moon spectacles balanced on the end of his nose. With one swift glance, he took in the state of Josef, then stepped forward and clapped him on the shoulders.

"Thank goodness you're back," he said. "I was beginning to think I was actually going to have to pay someone to mend my roof and assemble my bloody easy-self-assembly chest."

"I not stay," Josef mumbled. "I just give hello and take my things."

"Can we come in?" said Frieda. "It's too cold to be standing out here."

So, they bundled him inside, peeled off his jacket and shoes, and Reuben pushed a bottle of beer into his hands and took him to see where the leak came from, and somehow, ten minutes later, Josef was immersed in a scalding hot bath. From where they sat in the warm, fugged-up kitchen, Frieda and Reuben could hear him splashing and moaning.

"What the fuck's happened?" Reuben asked.

Both of them instinctively looked across at the dog-eared photo stuck to Reuben's fridge that Josef had put there more than a year ago, when he'd first moved into Reuben's house: his dark-haired wife and his two dark-haired sons.

"He was in Summertown, living on a building site."

"Why didn't he say?"

"He's ashamed."

"Of what?"

"I don't know yet."

"It's lucky I really do have a leaking roof."

"Yes."

"Well done for rescuing him."

"I didn't. I called him up for advice on something."

"He's here now, anyway."

Frieda nodded, then said, "By the way, I'm going to Kathy Ripon's funeral at the end of the week. I've been thinking a lot about her death, and about Dean Reeve. I have these disturbing dreams about him and they don't go away when I wake."

"So he's haunting you from beyond the grave?"

"I wish."

■ ■ ■ ■

That night she was sick. It started with beads of sweat on her forehead and a horrible breathlessness, a taste in her mouth that wouldn't go away, and even when she lay down, she felt dizzy, her stomach churning.

She managed to get to the toilet in time and knelt beside it, her eyes stinging, her body cold and sweating, vomiting, half sobbing and choking as she did so. She felt poisoned, every bit of her. But she had barely eaten anything, not for days and days, and soon there was nothing left to vomit, so she just retched and gasped, occasionally laying her forehead against the rim of the toilet, her knees sore on the hard floor and her hair sticky, her mouth foul, every bit of her unclean. She thought of hot baths, fresh sheets, lemon barley water, a cool hand against her hot cheek, and retched again. Wanting to die. She mustn't die. He would come. That was all she knew or needed to know.

# 16

Frieda sat in the corner of the pub and waited for Karlsson. He came across, balancing two whiskies and two packets of crisps. He took a seat at the table and ripped open both packets.

"I got salt and vinegar," he said, "and cheese and onion. I didn't know which you liked."

"Neither, really."

"You probably don't like pubs either," said Karlsson.

"It's better than the police station."

"At least it's an escape from that guy Newton, following me around like a ghost."

"What's he there for?"

"Time and motion," said Karlsson. "Blue-sky thinking. A fresh eye, that's what the boss calls it. He's looking at our procedures, our management style. But I think I know what he's going to find."

"What's that?"

"The word is that there are going to be budget cuts. Ten percent, maybe even twenty or twenty-five. If young Jake draws some diagrams to show we can catch more criminals with fewer officers, I think he'll find a receptive audience."

They sipped their drinks and looked at each other.

"I'm sorry if I've made your work more difficult."

"We got the file back," said Karlsson. "Charges have been put on hold while investigations continue. That's roughly what I've said in the memo." He took a sip of his drink and rubbed his face. Frieda thought he looked more tired than ever. "I know why the commissioner did what he did," Karlsson continued. "Nobody cares much about a case like this. And I know why *I* did what I did. But what I don't understand is why *you* did what you did. Michelle Doyce was never going to prison. She was going to get the medical help she needed. It was all going to be sorted out. Don't you have enough to do with your own work?"

Frieda looked at him speculatively. "What does it matter why I did it? Maybe I don't like untidy stories with bits left over. There was a patient I had once, a young woman. You know that feeling when you've left the house and you wonder if you've left the stove on? For her it wasn't just the stove. Perhaps she'd left a window open or the tap running or shut her cat in her bedroom. She'd try and check them all before she left, but there was no way she could check everything, and then there was the thought that while she was checking she might have opened another door or switched something on by mistake. In the end, she couldn't leave home."

"How did you cure her?"

"I wasn't right for her. I sent her to a behavioral therapist. But that's not my point. What I'm saying is that I'm a bit like that with stories. I couldn't have left it like that, knowing the body had been found outside in the alley but not knowing why, or who he was, or whom he had left behind. It was like going out knowing the gas was on."

Karlsson shook his head. "You wouldn't enjoy my job. I spend most of my life knowing that the gas is on and the bath is overflowing and the window's open."

"What makes you think I enjoy life as a therapist?" Frieda said. "So, what happens next?"

"I've sent a couple of officers down to talk to your couple in Brixton. Robert Poole is a pretty common name and, at the moment, there's nothing else. He's as much a mystery as he ever was."

"You mean, you know his name but you've still no idea who he actually was?"

"Exactly."

"What about his mobile number? Surely that gives you a lead. Can't you track him from that?"

"His number was from a pay-as-you-go phone, but we'll see if we can do anything with it. We've got a facial reconstruction done and we'll distribute that — you know, 'Have you seen this man?' That, with his name, might do the trick, though usually the people who get in touch are not what you'd call reliable witnesses. We've got one old man who's always seen every single person on the posters. Anyway, it's worth a try. And we'll have another look at Michelle Doyce's room. It is — I should point out — not totally, completely, a hundred percent certain that the body in the room is this painter and decorator."

"They recognized the sketch I showed them."

"Yes. I saw your sketch, and possibly you should have talked to me before flashing it around, but all right, I accept that. Actually, it's not far off our own visual."

Frieda drained her glass. "Thanks for telling me," she said. "I won't get involved like that again."

Karlsson gave a cough, as if he was preparing to deliver a speech.

"There was something else, Frieda. I wanted to say, quite clearly, that, despite occasional differences of opinion, you've been a great help and —"

"This sounds like the sort of speech you give when you're firing someone," said Frieda.

"No," said Karlsson. "Quite the opposite. We need to get on a proper footing. If you're going to do work with us, or with me, from time to time, you should be a consultant, with a contract and appropriate fees and agreed responsibilities. What do you feel about that?"

"Hang on." Frieda stood up and went over to the bar, returning with two more whiskies.

"Well?" said Karlsson.

"I'm not sure I'm comfortable with the idea."

"Why ever not? It would just be making it official."

"I'll consider it," said Frieda. "But at the moment all I can think of is reasons why not. I don't feel I've got anything more to contribute to this case. Once you find out properly who Robert Poole is, you'll find who did it. That's the way it usually works, isn't it?"

"A jealous lover," said Karlsson. "That's what it'll be."

"Except for the finger." Frieda frowned. "That looks more calculating."

Karlsson gave a triumphant smile. "You can't stop yourself. You're interested. She could have cut off the finger to take back the wedding ring. For the gold. Or an extreme form of divorce. My wife would have done that to me, if she could."

"It was the wrong finger," said Frieda. "Anyway, the idea of a contract worries me. Then I'd have duties and I'd have to be responsible. I helped you because I felt I needed to, and I didn't have to worry about justifying my expenses or ticking a box."

"Don't say no," said Karlsson. "I mean, don't say no straight away without thinking it through. Give it a few days. You see, I'm going to be the therapist for a moment —"

"Oh, please —"

"No, honestly. I think you rather like the idea of getting involved when you aren't meant to, when you're telling people things they don't want to hear. You have difficulty with being invited in. Wasn't there the old joke about not wanting to join a club that would accept you as a member? That's you."

"There's something else," she said.

"About the case?"

"Not this one. Remember I took that neurologist Andrew Berryman along to see Michelle Doyce? That, incidentally, is the kind of thing I wouldn't be able to do if I was under contract."

"You'd have to ask in advance," said Karlsson. "Which I know you don't like doing."

"And I'd have to justify it and fill out a form and it would get turned down, but that's not the point. There's something he told me that I can't get out of my mind. While we were talking about Michelle Doyce's perceptual problem, he told me about a neurological disease called Capgras Syndrome. Certain, very rare, cases of neural damage result in the patient suffering the delusion that a close family member or friend has somehow been replaced by an impostor."

"Sounds uncomfortable," said Karlsson. He paused. "Well?"

"The idea of it obsessed me. And I didn't know why. Then I thought about Carrie Dekker."

"What on earth for?"

"She said that after Dean died, her hus-

183

band's behavior changed. Then, quite suddenly, he left her and disappeared. I thought of Carrie with a husband who seemed to have been replaced by an impostor."

Karlsson's face took on a bemused expression, and when he spoke it was as if his brain was working slowly. "I don't get this," he said. "Are you saying that Caroline Dekker was suffering from an incredibly rare brain disease?"

"No," said Frieda. "The opposite, in a way. What kind of person could have the symptoms of Capgras Syndrome but not the disease?"

"I don't know what you're talking about."

"If it wasn't a delusion."

"What do you mean?" said Karlsson. "Do you . . . ?" And then he stopped. "Oh, God. You can't be serious. We found Dean's body. I met Alan afterward. He was with her."

"I was fooled by Dean. I was as close to him as you are to me. I talked to him. I didn't see a difference."

"But we had the body."

"What does that prove?" said Frieda. "Dean and Alan were identical twins. They even shared the same DNA."

Now Karlsson frowned. "What's your evidence for this?" he asked.

"It's just a feeling," said Frieda. "Because

of what happened to Alan. Or Dean. I always felt strange about it but I couldn't pin it down."

"That's ridiculous," said Karlsson. "He couldn't fool his own wife. He wouldn't know about their life, he wouldn't know who their friends were."

"He was only there for a matter of days. He refused to do anything, see anyone. It was a perfect way of escaping — in full view of everyone. It gave him the opportunity to really escape — to escape without anyone realizing he'd got away."

"So where is he?" said Karlsson. "According to your theory."

"I've no idea."

"There's no evidence."

"No, there isn't," said Frieda. "And there won't be."

"Just your feeling."

"You see, that's why you should think twice about giving me a contract. And I should think twice about signing one. I'm not like a policeman, and I don't want to be."

The desk sergeant knew the type. They'd come into the station as if they'd wandered in out of the rain. They'd glance at the desk, then look around at the posters on the wall, maybe even start reading them. Sometimes they'd lose their nerve and just leave. Otherwise they would make their way across, casually, as if it didn't matter. This woman was in her late forties, she thought, perhaps older. Smartly but unshowily dressed, professional, as if she'd come on her way home from work. Old workaday shoes, but polished. She didn't look like the victim of a crime. It took her several minutes to approach the desk and peer through the security grille.

"Can I help you?" the sergeant asked.

"It's my neighbor," she said. "He lives in the flat upstairs."

"What's he done?"

"He's disappeared."

The sergeant assumed her most comforting expression and embarked on the explanation she gave every week or two, about how common it was for people to go away and, unless there was a particular reason, there was almost certainly no cause for concern.

"No," said the woman. "I've got a key. I feed the cat when he's away and water his plants. I went to check. The mail was just piled up on the doormat. The food in the fridge had gone off. There was no food in the cat's bowl. The cat wasn't there, thank

186

God. He comes in and out on the sill, and there's a sort of shelf he walks along to get down on the roof of the bike shelter in the next door's front garden. Something's happened."

The desk sergeant sighed. "This is an adult male?" she asked.

"Yes," said the woman. "It's completely out of character. What can you do?"

The desk sergeant walked across to a filing cabinet and, after trying one drawer and then another, returned with the form.

"We fill out this form," she said. "Then we'll put the details on the computer, and if his name comes up anywhere, it'll pop up on the screen."

"Aren't you going to look for him?"

"This is the normal procedure," said the sergeant. "Unless it's an emergency."

"I think this is an emergency."

"They usually turn up," the sergeant said. "But let's start with the form. What's his name?"

"Bob," said the woman. "I mean Robert. Robert Poole."

# 17

Frieda walked from Gloucester station. Tiny flakes of snow were catching in her hair and melting on the streets. She had thought all the snow was over, that the bitter cold of the winter was lifting at last. Perhaps this was the end of it, like a reminder of what they were leaving.

She arrived at the church early, walking quickly past the photographers and journalists already gathered at the entrance, and took a seat at the back, next to the wall. Gradually, other people started to slide into the pews, pulling off hats and gloves, removing their thick coats, glancing around and nodding at people they knew in a blend of conviviality and self-conscious seriousness. A group of young people arrived together, and Frieda guessed they were Kathy's fellow students, with cheeks flushed from the cold. She picked up the order of service and looked through the hymns they were to sing.

The church filled and people had to squeeze into pews or stand at the back. An elderly couple walked slowly up the aisle, the woman leaning on the man's arm as they made their way to the front. Kathy's grandparents, she guessed. A man in a long camel coat passed her pew and she recognized Seth Boundy. Kathy Ripon had been his student and researcher, and he had sent her to her death. He and Frieda.

His hasty shuffle was very different from the stately stride she associated with him; his head was down and his collar pulled up, as if he didn't want to be noticed. But perhaps he felt Frieda's gaze upon him, for he turned, briefly glanced at her, then dropped his eyes and moved on. At last Kathy's family arrived: her parents, hand in hand, and behind them two young men, awkward in unaccustomed black suits, hair brushed, faces shaved raw.

The coffin was carried by the undertakers' assistants, young men with professionally sad expressions. Frieda pictured the swollen remains that lay inside, then the young woman's shrewd, pleasant face. As the congregation sang "The Lord Is My Shepherd," she thought, as she had thought every day for the last fourteen months, that if it hadn't been for her, Kathy would still

189

be alive, and her parents wouldn't be sitting with hunched shoulders in their pew, pale and old. A child would be dead, but Kathy would be alive. A young woman with a long, sad face went to the front and played the flute. One of Kathy's brothers read a poem, but couldn't reach the end. He stood in front of them, his face working furiously, and everyone leaned forward, willing him on, tears rolling down cheeks. The vicar stood and said a few words about a life cruelly cut short, about how at last her parents could bury their daughter. He mentioned a merciful God and the triumph of good over evil, of love over hate. Frieda closed her eyes but she didn't pray.

At last it was over. The coffin was carried slowly out into the feathery snowfall and Kathy's family followed. Frieda waited until most of the mourners had left. Then she slipped out of her pew and stood in front of Seth Boundy. "It was good of you to be here," she said.

"She was my student." His eyes flickered from her face to the stone floor.

Snow was now starting to settle on the gravestones and the roofs of cars that were parked outside. People milled about, hugging each other. Frieda had no intention of staying for the wake. As she reached the gate, she brushed against a tall man.

"Hello, Frieda," said Karlsson.

"You didn't say you were coming."

"Neither did you."

"I had to. She died because of me."

"She died because of Dean."

"Are you getting the train back?"

"There's a car waiting. Would you like a lift?"

Frieda considered for a moment. "I'd rather go home alone."

"Of course. You might like to know that a Robert Poole has been reported missing."

Frieda looked startled and Karlsson smiled, his stiff face softening for a moment. "Who by?" she asked.

"A neighbor. A woman in the flat below. It's in a house down in Tooting."

"Then what the hell are you doing here?" she asked. "Why aren't you in Tooting, tearing the place apart?"

"Yvette's down there today. She can handle it."

"Of course."

"But are you available?"

Frieda hesitated. "Perhaps."

"Is that a yes?"

"It's a perhaps. This . . ." She gestured behind her at the church and the mourners. "This doesn't make me want to be involved again. Ever."

"It doesn't get better," Karlsson said. "Unless you stop caring. I'll call you."

The journey to London took two hours, and Frieda would have been able to get back in time for her afternoon session with Gerald Mayhew, an elderly and wealthy American banker who had woken up one morning to find himself inexplicably stricken with grief for his long-dead parents. But she had canceled all her patients that day, and when she arrived at Paddington, she took the Bakerloo Line to Elephant and Castle, and walked through the slush and sleet toward a block of council flats on the New Kent Road. They were gray and unprepossessing, with metal grilles over the ground-floor windows, and a treeless courtyard where a single toddler rode round and round on his tricycle, his body bulked out by quilted layers and his nose dribbling in the icy wind.

Frieda took the stairs and went up to the fourth floor, then along the concrete corridor to a brown door with a knocker and a spy hole. She knocked and waited. A chain pulled back, an eye peered out.

"Yes? Who is this?" It wasn't the voice she had been expecting.

"I've come to see —" She nearly said,

"Terry," but caught herself in time. "Joanna Teale. She's not expecting me. My name is Frieda Klein."

"The doctor?"

Frieda had been the one who realized that Dean Reeve's wife, Terry, was actually the little schoolgirl, Joanna Teale, who had been snatched more than twenty years previously. She had also insisted to Karlsson that Joanna be treated like a victim, abducted and brainwashed for decades, rather than a perpetrator — although sometimes Joanna had made it hard for others to take her side. She was self-righteous, aggrieved, and unapologetic. She treated her parents — who were almost as derailed by her reappearance as they had been wrecked by her going — with a kind of angry indifference and her elder sister, Rose, with contempt. It had been a shocking reunion for them all. Frieda, after the first few weeks, had kept out of everyone's way, until now.

The chain pulled back and the door opened. On the doormat stood a young woman with a tight bright ponytail and over-shapely eyebrows. She was wearing a short skirt and leg warmers and had a striped cotton scarf wrapped round her neck, though it felt warm inside to Frieda. She held out a hand. "I'm Janine," she said.

"Come in."

"Is Joanna here?"

"She's in there with Rick."

"Rick?"

"Rick Costello. Joanna, you've a visitor."

"Who is it?" Hoarse and slightly slurred — that was the voice Frieda had been expecting.

"You'll never guess. Talk of the devil. Shall I take your coat?"

"Can you tell me who you are first?" asked Frieda. "You seem to know me but I certainly don't know you."

"I'm working with Joanna."

"In what way?"

"I'm helping her tell her story."

"Her story?" said Frieda, cautiously. "Are you a writer?"

"Me? No. I'm just the PR her publisher has hired to make sure she reaches the largest possible audience. It's such a terrible story — and the strength it's taken her to survive. Tragedy and redemption. With a real-life monster, as well. But you don't need me to tell you." Janine looked at Frieda with a knowing smile. "I've heard about your role."

Frieda took off her coat. All of a sudden she had a headache, like a band wrapped around her skull. "So she's writing a book?"

"It's all done. We've been working on it for days. I'm just privileged that I've been chosen to help her. But you're a counselor so you know all about enabling people, don't you? She's through here."

Janine led Frieda into a small room, hardly big enough for the large leather sofa and the deep, bulky armchair. The room was thick with smoke — and sitting in the thickest part of the cloud was Joanna, curled up at one end of the sofa with her bare feet tucked under her. Last time Frieda had seen her, her dark hair had been dyed blonde; now it was a metallic chestnut. But she had the same slumped posture and the same heavyset face. It was pale, overlaid with tan makeup. A cigarette hung from her lower lip and an overflowing ashtray stood on the small table at her elbow. Her large body was squeezed into a pair of skinny jeans and a leopard-print top. The folds of her white stomach showed, and Frieda glimpsed the Oriental tattoo there. A young man with a pink baby face, spots on his forehead, was in the armchair. He was looking at Frieda suspiciously. His trousers had ridden up his legs, exposing yellow socks and shiny white shins.

"Hello, Joanna," said Frieda.

"You didn't say you were coming."

"No."

"Why are you here, after all this time?"

"I came to see how you were getting on."

Joanna sucked on her cigarette. "It's not just coincidence?"

"What do you mean?"

"Now that I'm setting the record straight."

"I didn't know about this."

"This," said Joanna, complacently, nodding toward the young man and jerking more ash from her cigarette, "is Rick."

Frieda nodded to Rick, who held out a limp pink hand.

"He's my editor."

"Of your book?" He didn't look like Frieda's idea of a publisher.

"From the *Sketch*."

"I thought you were writing a book."

"It's being serialized," said Rick.

"I see."

Janine bobbed her head so that her ponytail swung. "Can I get you coffee?"

"No, thanks."

"So you didn't know?" Joanna asked again. "You haven't been sent to spy?"

"To spy on what?"

"On me, on all of this."

"It's too late for that," said Rick. "We're pretty much done and dusted. It's being lawyered as we speak."

Frieda perched herself on the sofa and looked at Joanna, trying to ignore the two others. "You've written a book?"

"That's right."

"About what happened?"

"What else would I write a bleeding book about?" She stubbed her cigarette out and lit another. "What do you think of that?"

"It depends on what you've said and why you've done it."

"It's my story," said Joanna. "Everything I've gone through in my life. Snatched away, hidden, abused, beaten, raped, brain-washed." Her voice rose. "No one rescued me. And I don't hold back. I don't duck it. I looked after Matthew, you know. I saved him. There was a hidden core of strength in me. How else could I have survived every-thing? A core of strength," she repeated. Then: "You want to know *why* I've written it? To give hope to others. That's why."

"I see."

"I need the money as well. I didn't get compensation. Not a penny, after everything I endured. I lived in Hell," she said, "with a monster, for twenty-two years. You can never get back those years."

"Have you seen your family, Joanna? Have they read this book?"

"They don't understand. Rose comes

round, but she just sits and stares at me with those big eyes of hers. She wants me to talk to someone about what happened. Someone like you, I mean." She took another drag on her cigarette, inhaling deeply. "It's much better talking to someone like Janine or Rick. Anyway, she didn't take care of me. She was supposed to be looking after me that day I was got."

Frieda thought of Rose Teale's stricken face, her enduring guilt: a good woman who'd been almost as much a victim of Dean Reeve as her younger sister. "She was nine, Joanna."

"My big sister. They all let me down. That's what they can't cope with." Joanna dropped the cigarette end on to the pile of dead stubs. "But I forgive them."

"You forgive them?"

"Yeah."

Frieda forced herself to think of why she had come here. "When Dean died," she said, "were you surprised that he took his own life?"

Joanna's eyes flicked from Janine, then back to Frieda. "It showed he loved me, that he knew he'd abused me. It was his last spark of human decency, that's what it was."

Gobbets of the book flew past Frieda, phrases about strength, evil, goodness, survival, victims. She steadied herself. "So you never thought it was out of character?"

Joanna gazed at her, off script at last. She gave a shrug. "He'd reached the end of the line."

"Have you seen Alan?" asked Frieda.

"Who's he?"

"Dean's brother, his twin."

"Why would I see him?"

"So you haven't, not even once?"

"No."

"What about June, Dean's mother?"

Joanna pulled a face. "She's gone demented. She wouldn't know me if I did go and see her, which I wouldn't anyway." She paused, then found her lines again. "The curse that's passed down generations," she said. "I'm going to be on TV, you know. Rick says. He's setting it up. And I'm in the paper next week."

"A major serialization," said Janine. "Over four days. You should read it yourself. *An Innocent in Hell.* You wouldn't believe some of the things that are in it."

"I probably would."

"I don't want to see you again, though," said Joanna. "I don't like the way you look at me."

# 18

For Yvette, it was mainly a matter of bureaucracy and logistics, like most of her job. Early in the day she obtained confirmation in writing that, since Flat 2, 14 Waverley Street, was associated with an indictable offense, no search warrant was required. She contacted the police station in Balham where the disappearance had been reported. From there she got a number for the woman who had reported Poole missing. She phoned Janet Ferris, and when she told her that a body had been found, the woman started to cry. From her, Yvette got the number of the landlord, a Mr. Michnik. She arranged to meet Janet Ferris at the address, then phoned Mr. Michnik and asked to meet him there as well. She had just booked the scene-of-crime team when her phone rang and she picked it up. A female voice told her that she had Commissioner Crawford for her. Yvette took a deep breath.

"Is that DC Long?"

"Yes, sir."

"Where's Karlsson?"

"He's in Gloucester. At a funeral."

"Family?"

"No," said Yvette. "It's Katherine Ripon." There was a pause. "The woman Dean Reeve snatched."

"Oh, her."

"The one we didn't find," said Yvette.

There was a pause. She stared out of the window and waited.

"All right," he said at last. "What's happened with that murder charge? The Deptford lunatic case."

"We've got the file back, sir. From the CPS."

"I thought that one was finished," he said, his voice deepening ominously. "I made it quite clear."

"There was new evidence. It's turned out to be a bit more complicated."

"Really?"

"We know who he is."

Crawford sighed.

She could hear a pen tap-tapping and knew the grim expression on his face. "Do you want me to tell you the details?" Yvette asked.

"Anything I need to know? Anything operational?"

"No."

"Just get on with it, then."

Before she had a chance to say yes, the line had gone dead. She was left with the feeling she had done something wrong, but she wasn't sure what it was.

Her car was late picking her up, and they got stuck in traffic on Balham High Street. By the time she arrived at the house, she saw that the scene-of-crime van was already there. It was an ordinary pebbledash house on a residential street. A man wearing an anorak was standing outside.

"Mr. Michnik?" she said.

"I am the owner of the house." He had an accent she couldn't place exactly. Something Eastern European. "I let the people in already." Yvette looked up. The window on the first floor was illuminated by the lights they'd set up inside. "Is he dead?"

"We've found a body," she said. "We think it may be Mr. Poole's. Did you know him?"

"He is my tenant. I meet him."

She took a notebook. "At some point we'll need a proper statement from you," she said, "but, first, can I ask when you last saw him?"

"Two months," Michnik said. "Maybe three. I don't know. I meet him just a few

202

time. He pays the rent regular. He's not trouble, so I don't see him."

"When did he move in?"

"I check that when you ring. He come here in May last year. The beginning."

"Do you know what his job was?"

Michnik thought for a moment. "A businessman, maybe. He wears a suit."

"What kind of person was he?"

"He pays the deposit, he pays the rent. He's not trouble. He's polite. He's good."

"How many people live in this house?"

"There are three flats."

"I talked to Janet Ferris."

"Yes, she is on the ground floor, and there is a German on the top floor. He is a student but he is a good student. He is an older student."

"Are the flats furnished?"

"Not the ground, not Miss Ferris. But the others. All the chairs and tables and pictures, they are all mine." He seemed to remember something. "What is happening to the flat?"

"We'll be sealing it," said Yvette. "We're treating it as a crime scene for the moment. You shouldn't go in there, and I should warn you that it is an offense to take anything away or move things around."

"How long is this for?"

"It shouldn't be too long. Is Janet Ferris here?"

Michnik frowned. "I will take you inside." Janet Ferris answered the knock at the door so quickly that Yvette suspected she'd been standing inside, waiting. She was a middle-aged woman, red hair streaked with gray, a thin, anxious face. "Is it really true?" she said. "He's dead?"

"We need to confirm it," said Yvette. "But we think so."

"Oh, God." She pressed her ringless left hand to her chest. "That's terrible."

"When did you last see him?"

"It must have been about the twentieth, twenty-first of January. I remember because I met him when we were both going out, and I said something about posting a card to my niece for her birthday, which is on the twenty-fourth."

"Did he seem worried about something?"

"No, he was completely normal. His usual friendly self, always so helpful." Her voice wavered slightly. "I was on holiday. I went to see my sister and her family in France. I always go at this time of year. He was supposed to look after my flat while I was away, water the plants, pick up the mail, things like that. It was our arrangement: he would look after mine and I would look after his. I always fed his cat for him. When I came back, I saw at once he hadn't been in. All my mail was piled up, and when I went into the flat, my plants were shriveled. It wasn't like him to forget. He was very thoughtful. Then I noticed his mail was piled up too." She pointed to a bundle of letters in the corner. Yvette knelt down and picked through them. It was all junk mail.

"I went and knocked at his door," Janet Ferris continued, "but, of course, he didn't reply. I let myself in, and I knew at once something was wrong. That's why I went straight to the police."

"Did people come to visit him here?" she asked.

"I never saw anyone," said Janet Ferris. "But he was out at work a lot, and I work in the day. He was away sometimes."

"Were *you* friendly with him?"

"He came in for coffee several times. We used to talk."

"Did he say anything about himself?"

"He wasn't like that," Janet Ferris said. "He seemed interested in my life, my work, where I came from, why I moved to London. He didn't talk about himself at all."

Yvette arranged for Janet Ferris to give a full statement, then walked up the stairs. She was met at the door by Martin Carlisle from the scene-of-crime team. Gawky, with untidy dark curly hair, he looked as if he belonged in a sixth-form chemistry lab. "There's nothing to see here," he said. "No stains, no signs of a struggle. And it looks like a place where he perched, rather than lived, if you see what I mean. Too neat. We've got a toothbrush and a hairbrush for DNA."

Yvette pulled the little cloth bags over her shoes, put on a pair of plastic gloves.

"I'm not finished," said Carlisle. He handed her a notebook. "I had a peek inside. There's some names. And, even better," he brandished some printed papers, "we found some bank statements. How much do you think he had in the bank?"

"I'm not going to guess," said Yvette.

"Whatever you guess, it'll be less than he had," said Carlisle. "He was rich, your Mr. Poole."

Yvette stepped inside. She moved cautiously: her feet felt too big in the cloth bags, and her hands sweated inside the gloves. She remembered her mother — a petite, flirtatious creature — telling her she was clumsy. "Look at you," she'd say, but Yvette never wanted to look at herself. She didn't like what she saw in the mirror: someone big-boned, brown-haired, noticeable only when she dropped things or spoke abruptly and out of turn, which she often did. She would hear herself saying words she hadn't known she was going to utter, especially when she was with Karlsson.

Carlisle was right: Robert Poole's flat was too neat, nothing like the mess she lived in. There was nothing homely about it. She stood in the doorway and looked around, trying to imitate Karlsson when he entered a crime scene. He would stand very still and alert, his eyes moving from object to object as if he had become a camera. "Don't make up your mind," he'd say. "Just look." She saw a sofa, a chair, a table, some pictures, a shelf with a few books ranged in order of size, a rug. It was like a hotel room.

The kitchen was the same — matching mugs on a hook, a saucepan and a small milk pan on the side, an electric kettle. She opened the fridge and saw half a packet of butter; a piece of cheddar cheese, shrink wrapped; two chicken drumsticks, with a green tinge; a plastic bottle of tomato ketchup and a jar of low-fat mayonnaise. That was all.

After she had walked round his bedroom, opened every drawer and every cupboard, looked under the bed, then stood for a while in the clean, empty bathroom (toothbrush, razor, shaving foam, spray deodorant, liquid aloe vera soap, paracetamol, Band-Aids, nail clippers), she returned to the sitting room and sat down.

First of all, she thought about what there was not: there was no passport, there was no wallet, there were no keys, no phone, no driving license, no birth certificate, no certificates of qualifications, no National Insurance number, no photographs, no letters, no computer, no address book, no condoms, no drawer stuffed full of the odd bits and pieces of a person's life.

She opened the notebook Carlisle had given her. Robert Poole's writing was neat and pleasing, easy to read. She turned the pages. There were lists, perhaps shopping lists, but more specific than the usual shopping lists she drew up. One, for instance, was made up of names of plants — though she recognized only a few. Another looked like book titles, or maybe they were films.

Then there were names, spaced apart with doodles and exclamations and asterisks next to some. A few had addresses or partial addresses beside them — that was useful. She flicked through the notebook to the end. There were a few sums and, on one page, what looked like a sketched plan of a house.

There were numbers that might have been phone numbers without the area code.

Then she looked into the A4 brown envelope Carlisle had handed her and drew out the wad of bank statements. She looked at the top one, which was the most recent, dated January 15. She squinted at the number, blinked, then slid it carefully back into the envelope and stood up. It was going to be a long day.

# 19

The last thing Frieda wanted that evening, after the funeral and her unsettling visit to Joanna, was to go out. She needed time alone, in the cocoon of her house, where she could draw down the blinds, light a fire, and shut out the world. Yet after her chemistry lesson with a bad-tempered Chloë, she stayed on. She had been invited — or, rather, ordered — to come for dinner. And not just any dinner: this was a dinner to introduce her to Olivia's new boyfriend, Kieran. Chloë described him as her mum's eBay find. A few days before, Olivia had asked Frieda to bring someone else along too, so Frieda had asked Sasha if she was free.

"Not a *woman*! God, Frieda, what planet are you living on? I meant, bring another man along or it might seem odd."

"Odd in what way?"

"I don't know. Too intense — kind of meet

the family."

"The ex-sister-in-law."

"Whatever. You know what I mean. But if you bring someone, it'll seem more casual. Two couples."

"I'm not a couple."

"You know what I mean."

"And isn't Chloë going to be there?"

"Oh, God, probably. She'll sit there glaring at him all evening. You know the way she can glare. I've never seen such a brow. It's a Klein brow — she gets it from her father. I hope she goes out." In the end, Frieda had reluctantly invited Reuben to accompany her. He asked if he could bring Paz as well, because she had just broken up with her boyfriend and needed cheering up. And then they had to ask Josef too, didn't they? Josef couldn't be left alone at the moment, not in his present state. Reuben was worried about him: he sang sad songs in the shower and had grown a straggly mustache but still wouldn't talk about what had happened. And with three new guests, Olivia announced it didn't make sense to disinvite Sasha after all; she just had to be kept away from Kieran. So the simple supper turned into an elaborate meal of overcooked salmon fillets rolled in pastry and a pudding made from meringues that stuck to the teeth. Reuben arrived in his favorite waistcoat that glistened like a jeweled breastplate. He drank water all evening (except when he was taking sips from other people's glasses) and glowed with his new virtue. Josef came with him, wearing a strange jacket that looked as if it had been made from a potato sack. He carried a large bunch of wilting flowers that Frieda was willing to bet he had lifted from the house whose boiler he was mending. Sasha arrived straight from work, dressed severely, no makeup on her beautiful face, and was placed at the far end of the room, safely in the shadows. Olivia had put on a red gown and dangling gold earrings. Her eyes were kohl lined and her lips scarlet. She walked like a crane in her high-heeled shoes and laughed in the wrong places. And then Chloë decided she wouldn't go out after all, but her Goth friend Sammy would be joining them and no one was to stare at the way she had shaved one side of her head.

Chloë had told Frieda that Olivia's new friend Kieran was a creep. She rolled her eyes whenever she talked about him. But Kieran turned out to be a shy, crumpled man, who stooped to hide his height, blushed easily, and seemed baffled but delighted by the lavish attentions of Olivia. She popped olives into his mouth with her long, painted fingernails, ruffled his hair, and called him "honey," while he gazed at her with a heartfelt gratitude that everyone found touching except Chloë, who found it gross. Frieda saw that Kieran was terrified of Chloë, and she felt a lurch of pity for him. Her niece was a formidable enemy: she had no sense of restraint, and she wouldn't mind making a scene in public.

"What do you do, Kieran?" she asked him, and Chloë gave a snort of derision.

"Guess," she said. "Just try and guess."

"I'd prefer to be told."

"Twenty questions."

"I work for a firm of funeral directors."

"See?"

"That's a good job," said Frieda. "An important one."

Kieran smiled warily at her to check she wasn't being ironic. "I work in the office," he added. "Doing the accounts."

"He doesn't carry a coffin," said Olivia, "and pretend to be sad."

The evening lurched by. Olivia got tipsy, took off her shoes, and let down her hair, leaning her flushed face on Kieran's bony shoulder. Reuben, absentmindedly taking hold of Sasha's wine glass, told Chloë and Sasha a long story involving snow geese. It sounded like a parable but without a final moral: the snow geese simply disappeared at the end of the winter. Josef taught Sammy and Paz a drinking song about wood alcohol and dubious country pleasures. Frieda stacked plates, filled glasses, and passed cups of coffee round the table. She heard about Kieran's two sons, now grown-up, one in the army and the other living in Australia, and about Sammy's elder brother, who had joined a gang and had a knife that he hid in his shoe. She thought about Kathy Ripon, once more buried but this time with love, and about Joanna telling her story to the world, with all the uncomfortable bits rendered anodyne and harmless. She looked at Olivia's smeared and happy face and thought that there were many worse ways to find men than on the Internet.

That evening, Karlsson bought a packet of ten Silk Cut and a small box of matches on his way home. He used to smoke Marlboros, twenty a day and more on bad days, but when his wife had got pregnant he had given up and never smoked since. Even when she'd left him and taken the kids to Brighton, he'd resisted. He didn't want Mikey and Bella coming to a flat that smelled of tobacco.

Now he went straight out into his small

garden at the back of his ground-floor flat, put a cigarette into his mouth, lit a match, and cupped his hand around it. The first drag made him feel dizzy and slightly sick. The tip glowed in the darkness, brightening, then fading. In the garden next door, a woman was calling her cat and banging a fork against the side of its bowl. "Here, Skit, Skit, Skit. Here, Skit, Skit, Skit." On and on. She didn't see him over the fence, hunched inside his coat. It wasn't snowing as it had been in Gloucester, but there was a stillness to the air, as if it might at any moment.

He smoked two cigarettes in a row, then went inside. He brushed his teeth, as if she might be able to smell him over the phone and use his weakness against him, then made the call.

"It's me, Mal."

"Yes?"

"I've been thinking about what you said."

"About Madrid?"

"Yes."

"And?"

"Of course I can't stop Mikey and Bella going, you all going, if that's what you want and feel is best for them."

"Oh, Mal, if you only knew how —"

"But I want to see more of them before

you go. Mid-April, you say?"

"Yes. And of course you can see as much of them as you want."

"And I want to see them regularly when they're away. We'll have to work something out. Have a system, a structure."

Even as he spoke, he felt the hopelessness of it. They would get swept up into their new life and he would be just a memory, a figure from the past, receding from them. Loneliness washed over him, a wave that almost took his breath away.

"I appreciate this."

"OK."

"I know this isn't easy for you."

"No."

"But you won't regret it."

After he had put the phone back into its holster, he went and poured himself a stiff whisky. It was a drink he associated with Frieda. He pictured her watching eyes and the way she held her chin high, as if she was waiting for battle. He pressed the tumbler against his forehead. If he'd been a weeping man, he would have wept.

Soon he would come. He had said he would come and she had to believe him. Unless something had happened. But, no, he would come. She would hear him rap out their code on the hatch, and she would lift it up and see him silently swing his way down into the boat. He would hold her by the shoulders and look into her eyes and she wouldn't even have to tell him — he would know she had done well, that she had kept faith, that she had never wavered. He called her his soldier, his loyal one. She wouldn't let him down.

She was running out of basic things. Not water, which was the most important, because there was a tap down the path near the rowing club, and she could go there at night with her two plastic containers. She had a bucket that she filled from the river, as well, when she wanted to scrub the decks or flush the toilet. But her food supplies were almost gone, and candles, toilet rolls, soap. She had no deodorant left, and she didn't like that, and her razor was blunt now. She should make a list to give him when he came. Nothing expensive: matches, washing-up liquid, more milk powder, toothpaste, and Band-Aids because there were cuts that kept opening up on her legs. And perhaps some cordial.

Elderflower cordial. She got so thirsty; her mouth was dry, and it had a nasty taste in it that she couldn't get rid of. Water on its own doesn't really quench your thirst. She allowed herself to think about freshly squeezed orange juice, in a tall tumbler; sitting on a lawn with bare feet and the sun on the back of her neck.

Because the gas was nearly gone, she decided to cook all the remaining potatoes. She could eat them cold over the next few days. There were tins of tuna and sardines she could add to them, and she had stock cubes as well. Sometimes she just added boiling water to a cube for a meal. She put the potatoes in the sink, which had a crack running down one side so it didn't hold water, and found the knife. The potatoes were large, knobbly and grimy; some of them were beginning to sprout. When she was younger, she used to dislike potatoes, but he had shown her you couldn't be fussy. It was like being in a war, in the trenches or hiding behind enemy lines. You had to remember why you were there, your purpose and your solemn mission. He had held her very tight when he'd said that and his eyes had shone.

She peeled the potatoes with slow precision and cut them into small chunks so that they would boil more quickly and use less gas. She put them in the pan and added salt. She must put salt on the list. There was so little left. Everything was running out. She thought of sand trickling through an hourglass, the way it seemed to speed up at the end. That was how it felt now. There were lights behind her eyes and her heart was beating like a drum; sometimes she couldn't tell if it was inside her or out, like distant thunder gathering and coming nearer. Time running out.

# 20

Although she had gone to bed late, Frieda got up early the next morning, vacuumed the house, washed the kitchen floor, laid a fire in the living room for when she returned, showered, and left the house shortly after nine. She had been to River View Nursing Home twice before, but both times by car. This time she took the overland train and got out at Gallions Reach, then walked past lines of apartment blocks, light industrial units, and a down-at-heel shopping mall until she arrived at the nursing home, which was far from the river. Its windows were covered with metal grilles. She pushed open the front door, went past the Zimmer frames and wheelchairs that seemed as though they hadn't been moved since her last visit, and went to Reception, where a young woman in a uniform was thumbing through a magazine.

"Is Daisy here?" asked Frieda, remembering the woman who had accompanied her last time.

"Left."

"I wondered if I could see June Reeve."

"Why?"

"I'm a doctor," said Frieda. "I visited her last year. I'd like to talk to her."

The young woman looked up and Frieda saw a flicker of interest animate her features. But she shook her head. "She's on a ventilator."

"What's wrong with her?"

"Pneumonia."

"Will she recover?"

"I'm not the one to ask," said the young woman.

"Could I talk to someone about her? The manager, perhaps?"

"Mrs. Lowe's around," said the young woman. "You could talk to her."

Mrs. Lowe was about fifty, and she had a bright, high voice, a merry face, a brisk and bouncy style of walking. Everything about her was designed to lift the spirits. Frieda found it difficult to stand close to her or even to look at her. But, then, how else did you get through day after day, working somewhere like this?

"Do you want to pop your head round her door?" she asked. "Poor dear. Come along with me." She tucked a friendly arm into Frieda's. "It's just down here."

She led the way along the corridor that Frieda remembered so well, past an old man in slipping-down pajamas, and stopped at a door.

"She's not her usual self," announced Mrs. Lowe, and pushed open the door onto a small, bare room: same bars over the window, same picture of the Bridge of Sighs on the wall, same bookshelf holding only a leather-bound Bible, same vase empty of flowers. Frieda looked for the framed photograph of Dean and saw it had been removed. June Reeve was no longer sitting in the armchair but lying in bed with an oxygen mask over her mouth. Her skin had a leathery look to it and was the color of tobacco leaves. Her chest rose and fell unevenly. Her eyes were closed.

"Not long for this world," said Mrs. Lowe. She had strong white teeth.

"Does she ever speak?"

"Not now."

Frieda looked at Dean and Alan's mother, her small mean mouth and her folds of dying flesh. She had abandoned Alan when he was a baby without caring whether he lived or died; she had helped Dean snatch Joanna and turn her into Terry; and she had never exhibited anything but self-righteousness and self-pity. But she was beyond any kind of reproach now, or hatred. Frieda wondered what she was dreaming of behind her collapsed face.

"Thank you." She turned from the door and waited while Mrs. Lowe pulled it shut. "Does she ever have visitors?"

"Not a soul." Mrs. Lowe beamed.

"Never?"

"Not that I know of."

"Her son never visits?"

"You mean the other son? Dean's twin?"

"Alan. Yes."

"Never. Not once. You can't quite blame him, can you? After all, she wasn't a mother to him, was she? She picked the wrong one to keep, is what I always say."

"So she's been quite alone since Dean killed himself?"

"Not that she minded. She's not what I'd call a sociable lady. Never did join in with our fun and games, even before her memory got as bad as it did. Always kept herself to herself. Perhaps it's just as well. I have to admit that some of our old dears here didn't take very kindly to having the mother of an evil monster . . ." Mrs. Lowe's mouth lost its fixed smile and momentarily twisted in a grimace. "Now it's too late for things like that. Too late for anything. She never did make her peace with the world."

"Thank you for your help."

"Someone did come once, but they didn't even go and visit her. They just left her a bag of doughnuts at the front desk."

"Doughnuts," said Frieda, softly, to herself more than to Mrs. Lowe.

"She was always very partial to doughnuts."

"Yes," muttered Frieda. "I know. Her son Dean used to bring them to her."

"It must have been someone else, then."

Frieda waited until she was several streets away from River View Nursing Home before pulling out her mobile and calling the number she had copied on to it that morning. She then walked to Gallions Reach, but traveled only as far as Canning Town, where she changed trains for Stratford. It was a foggy day, and in the wet, cold air, the half-built Olympic Village took on a ghostly appearance — scaffolded buildings and segments of domes and towers surfaced from the dank mist, below which Frieda could make out vans and diggers and crowds of men in hard hats.

It took her fifteen minutes to walk to Leytonstone, where she turned up the long, straight road of Victorian terraced houses shrouded in the gray light to number 108. Frieda didn't hurry; she was trying to order her thoughts and to prepare what she was going to say. That she must say it she finally had no doubt. She rang at the dark green door, hearing its double chime in the distance, and had the eerie sense of being back in a previous life. She almost expected Alan to answer, standing before her with his sad brown eyes and his apologetic smile.

It was Carrie who came to the door, in a yellow jersey that made her pallor more obvious, and she wasn't smiling. "You'd better come in," she said.

Frieda stepped inside, wiping her boots carefully on the doormat and hanging her coat up. "Thank you for agreeing to see me."

"You didn't give me much choice. Shall we go through to the kitchen?"

It was the same as it had always been, neat and pleasing, with one half given over to domestic appliances and the other to Alan's tools. On dozens of shelves, divided into small compartments, were his screws and nuts and bolts, his fuses and washers and keys. Carrie noticed Frieda's glance and smiled wryly. "He didn't take any of his stuff. I kept thinking he would come back, so I didn't clear it out. Stupid, isn't it, when he's obviously not coming back? Only I don't know how to begin."

"There is something you should know."

"About Alan? I knew it. You *do* know where he is."

"It's about Alan, yes. You should sit down."

Carrie obeyed, looking wary, as if anticipating a blow.

"This is going to be a shock, and perhaps you won't believe me, but I am certain that Alan is dead."

Carrie's hands flew to her mouth. Her gray eyes stared at Frieda. "Dead?" she whispered. "Dead? Alan? My Alan? But . . . when? When did he die?"

"On the twenty-fourth of December 2009."

Carrie's hands slid away from her mouth, which was working uselessly, mouthing words she couldn't utter. She leaned forward slightly in her chair and her head lolled to one side. "What are you . . . ?" she said thickly, in a voice that was scarcely recognizable as her own. "I was with him after that. I was with him at Christmas. I told you."

"I believe that Dean killed Alan on the day your husband went to meet him."

Frieda paused for a moment, so that Carrie could begin to see the implication of what she was saying. "He swapped clothes, strung him up, wrote a suicide note for himself, came home to you, as Alan, and you called the police. You know the rest."

Carrie said something that Frieda couldn't make out. The voice came from her belly, low and guttural. Then she sprang up and flung the table over; it caught Frieda on the shin and crashed to the floor in a scream of breaking china and screeching wood on tile.

"You *fuck*."

"Carrie."

Frieda grasped Carrie by her wrists and tried to hold her steady, but, although she was smaller than Frieda, rage made her strong. Frieda could see the spittle on her chin and the white patches on her cheeks, as if someone had pressed a thumb deep into them.

"Get off me. Don't touch me. Don't come near me. Do you hear?"

Frieda wrapped both arms around Carrie's body from behind, gripping her fiercely. "Carrie," she repeated.

Carrie surged in her arms. The back of her head was against Frieda's mouth. She kicked at Frieda's leg and, wrenching her head round, tried to bite Frieda's shoulder. "It's not true," she yelled, low and hoarse.

"It's a lie. You're lying to me. It's not true. Alan's not dead."

Frieda felt Carrie's body tense and then go limp. She made a gagging noise and then, as Frieda relaxed her hold, bent forward and vomited on her kitchen floor. Frieda put a hand on her forehead and held her, then eased her onto the chair that was still standing. Carrie crumpled onto it like a rag doll. Frieda found some kitchen towel and wiped Carrie's mouth, pushed her hair back from her sweaty face. Then she picked up the fallen table and Carrie laid her head on it and wept in retching sobs that sounded as though she might weep up her organs and her heart, turn herself inside out.

Frieda picked up the other chair, then used several squares of kitchen roll to wipe up the vomit and flush it down the next-door lavatory. Returning, she filled a washing-up bowl with hot, soapy water and scrubbed the floor. She boiled the kettle and made a pot of strong tea. She heaped four teaspoons of sugar into a mug and added a big splash of milk. She pushed it in front of Carrie, who lifted her face, swollen with weeping.

"Just a bit," said Frieda. "Are you cold?"

Carrie nodded. Frieda ran upstairs and came back with a quilt she'd removed from

228

the bed. "Wrap this round you and drink your tea."

Carrie sat up. She tried to hold the mug, but her hands were shaking so badly that Frieda took it from her and held it to her lips, tipping it carefully until Carrie could take small gulps.

At last, Frieda said, "Have you understood?"

Carrie wrapped the quilt more tightly around her body so that only her face was showing. She looked like a beaten animal.

"Carrie?"

She nodded. "I've understood," she whispered.

"Do you believe me?"

"Alan had this habit." Carrie's voice was hoarse from her weeping. "He always used to take bits of my food, or drink half of my tea, even when he had his own. I'd be eating a biscuit and he'd lean over and pop it into his mouth, or pick up my sandwich and take a large bite out of the middle of it, the best bit, very casually, as if he didn't even know he was doing it. I'd turn my head, and when I turned back, there'd be his toothmarks in my Jaffa cake or something. It irritated me but it was like a running joke between us. Even when things were at their very worst, even when he'd lost his appetite for anything, he went on nicking my food. I often think that's what makes a marriage work, not the big obvious things, like sex and children, but all those habits and routines and funny tics, the little things that drive you mad but bring you close." She wasn't looking at Frieda anymore but down at the table, and speaking in a voice so quiet that Frieda had to lean forward to hear it. "He took my food because my food was his food. My life and his life hadn't got any boundaries. We'd kind of merged. The day he left . . ." She gulped. Her blotchy face twitched. "The day the man I thought was Alan left, we were sitting on the sofa and I'd warmed up two mince pies. We never had Christmas pudding at Christmas. We liked our luxury mince pies from M&S, with cream, it was one of our traditions — and for once he didn't take any of mine. I made a joke out of it. I held it up to his lips and said, 'What's mine is yours and what's yours is yours,' or something stupid like that. But he just smiled and said he'd got his own. Later, once he'd gone away, I thought it was a demonstration of his separateness — he wasn't eating my food because he no longer wanted me. Do you see?"

Frieda nodded but said nothing. She stood up and refilled Carrie's mug, adding more sugar.

"He made me one cup of tea," Carrie continued, in a dreary voice. "That same day. Usually I made the tea, but I'd done all the cooking and I asked him to get me a cup. He made a song and dance of it. He put the mug on a tray, with milk in a little jug and sugar in a china bowl, even though I don't take sugar. I thought he was being funny and romantic. I didn't get it. He just didn't know, did he? He didn't know how I took my tea."

"I'm so very sorry, Carrie," said Frieda.

"I *slept* with him," cried Carrie. "I had sex with him. For the first time in months and months, because Alan — he couldn't. It was good." Her face contorted as if she would throw up again. "It was the best it had ever been. *Ever.* Do you understand? Do you?"

Frieda nodded again.

"And it wasn't Alan. It wasn't my darling, darling, hopeless Alan. Alan was dead, strung up like some criminal. And I didn't know and I didn't grieve and I fucked his foul, murdering brother and I was *happy*. I was so happy, lying tangled up in the dark with the man who killed Alan and then had sex with me and listened to me crying out in pleasure, oh, and then heard me telling

231

him how it had never been this good before. Argh! This is — I can't —"

She stood up, her face chalky, and rushed from the room. Frieda could hear her being sick again, then the lavatory flushing and water running. Carrie returned, sat down again, and fixed her red-rimmed eyes on Frieda.

"You are sure?" she said.

"Yes, I am. But I don't have evidence. Not the sort the police would accept."

"Can't you do a DNA test? I've got his toothbrush. His comb."

"Their DNA was the same," said Frieda. "Anyway. What matters is what you think."

"I believe you." She seemed flatly calm now.

"Carrie, you must hold on to the fact that Alan did not leave you and he always loved you. You loved him and were loyal to him. You've got nothing to reproach yourself for."

"How could I not know, not feel it? And now I can never make it right. I can never take Alan in my arms again and hold him and comfort him and hug him to me until he feels safe again. I can never be forgiven by him. This is what it will be like until the day I die. Oh, my poor sweet Alan. Nothing ever went right for him, did it? Of course, he wouldn't have left me — how did I not know that?"

Through that dark, wet day, Frieda sat in the kitchen and listened as Carrie talked about Alan, about Dean, about her loneliness and childlessness, about grief and anger, hostility and self-disgust. She heard her talk of hatred — for Dean, of course, but also for her, Frieda, who had sucked Alan into a vortex from which he had never returned, for the police who hadn't stopped him, for herself — and of her desire for revenge. She heard of Carrie's early days with Alan, and how she had known on their first date that she would marry him because of the way he had said her name — with flushed shyness, and as if he were uttering some solemn and precious oath. Frieda made numerous cups of tea and, later, a boiled egg that Carrie listlessly poked pieces of toast into. Only when Carrie had called her friend and asked her to come over did she leave, promising to call her the following day, and even then, she didn't go straight home by cab or train but walked there through the London streets, winding her way westward as the day turned to evening and the fog became sleety darkness. Her mind was crowded with thoughts and ghosts: Carrie's staring white face, Alan's eyes, which had always reminded her of a spaniel's, timid and pleading, and the jeering smile of Dean, who had been dead but was now alive again. Somewhere in the world.

# 21

"So," said Karlsson to Yvette Long and Chris Munster, "this is what we have, and stop me if I get it wrong." He ticked items off his fingers as he spoke. "One, a murder victim, confirmed by DNA to be the Robert Poole who lived in the flat, whose body was found naked in a disturbed woman's room, having been collected from an adjacent alley, whose job we don't know, whose friends haven't missed him, and whose neighbor says that he was charming, helpful, kind, and would always water her plants for her."

Karlsson stopped and took a sip of water, then continued. "Two, Mr. Poole's bank statements." He picked them up and waved them. "The most recent of which show that he had just under three hundred and ninety thousand pounds in his current account. I don't know what that's about. We're checking with the bank as we speak." He looked at his watch. "They should have phoned by now. Anyway, three, a flat of which Yvette made a preliminary search, as well as the scene-of-crime team. No passport, no wallet; in fact, no personal documents of any kind. Nor is he on Facebook or Twitter or any of the other social networks. But there's a notebook, with several pages ripped out, in which there are a handful of names, some addresses, scrawls, and doodles. Correct, Yvette?"

"Including the name of the couple in Brixton, whom your old friend found."

"You mean Frieda Klein? She's not an old friend; she's someone who helped us. And now that you mention her, I should say that I want to use her on a more permanent basis."

Yvette frowned. "What for?"

"She can be useful to us."

"Fine."

"By which you mean not fine."

"It's your decision," said Yvette, hating how her voice sounded. Her cheeks burned scarlet. She was sure that Frieda Klein didn't turn an unbecoming red whenever she was embarrassed — but perhaps Dr. Klein never felt embarrassed.

"That's right, and I've made it, and now we can concentrate on Robert Poole. How far have you got with the names in the notebook?"

Chris Munster picked up a pad of paper. "We're going to work our way through them. A few will be easy to find and others may take longer. We've already made an appointment to see a Mary Orton. We're going straight after this meeting. She sounded rather flustered on the phone — she's an elderly lady, lives alone. Apparently, Robert Poole had been helping her repair her house in some way. We're going to start distributing that visual we've had drawn up. That might flush out a few more people who knew him."

"Right, it should be —" Karlsson was interrupted by the phone ringing. He picked it up, listened, frowned, jotted something on his notepad. Putting it down, he said, "They've talked to the bank." He tore the page off his notepad and handed it to Yvette. "We've got a next of kin, a brother in Saint Albans. Go and see him. And about that money in his account. It's gone. It was transferred out of the account on the twenty-third of January. I want the two of you to go and break the news to the brother and find out anything you can about Robert Poole — photos, documents, whatever." He looked at his watch, then, picking up the notebook, stood up, pushing back his chair. "Right. With a bit of luck, we'll find someone who's suddenly acquired three hundred and ninety grand, and we can wrap this up quickly."

Karlsson had to ring several times before he got through to Frieda. "I left a message," he said. "Two messages."

"I was going to ring," she said. "I've been with patients all morning."

He gave her an account of the way the case was developing, about the notebook. Frieda didn't say much in reply.

"We've found a member of Poole's family," he said. "A brother. Yvette's on her way to see him."

"It seems things are progressing," said Frieda.

She sounded detached, and Karlsson caught himself feeling resentful, as if he wanted Frieda's full attention and knew he wasn't getting it. There was a long pause.

"Some of the team have been checking through the names in Poole's notebook," Karlsson said finally. "One of them is an old woman called Mary Orton who lives in Putney. Poole was organizing building work for her. It wasn't finished when he disappeared."

"Yes?"

Karlsson took a deep breath. "That friend of yours you brought round to me once, Josef. He's a builder, no?"

Karlsson could almost hear her soften over the phone.

"That's right."

"Is he good? And trustworthy?"

"Yes, he is."

"I thought you could go and talk to her and bring your builder friend with you, suss out what Poole actually did. He might even get some work out of it. What with the job not having been finished. According to Chris, she's an old woman whose husband has died and sons live away. I think she's a bit lonely." There was another pause. "Unless, of course, you're only interested in doing things when you do them without telling me."

"I think he's available for work," Frieda said. "But I'll need to check with him."

"That would be kind of you," said Karlsson, and gave her the Putney address.

"Did she say anything about Robert Poole?" asked Frieda.

"She said he was nice and polite," said Karlsson. "That's what they all say. Nice and polite."

■ ■ ■ ■

"Have you ever done this before?" asked Yvette Long.

Chris Munster was driving and didn't look round. "In my first year," he said. "A kid had been knocked over and I went along with a sergeant to tell the parents. The mother answered the door and I just stood in the background while he told her. We were talking to her and then the father came home from work and we stood there while she told him. The bit I remember was my sergeant hovering around like someone who was about to leave a party. Those parents partly wanted us to go and leave them to it. At the same time, they couldn't let us go. They kept talking about him and asking if we wanted tea. I've done it a few times since then, but that's the one I remember. What about you?"

"A few times," said Yvette. "More than a few. I always feel nervous in advance. I look at the front door and feel guilty about what I'm going to do to them. They open the door and sometimes you can tell that they know even before you say anything." She looked at him. "It's the next exit."

They drove off the motorway, and there

was no voice except for the satnav, directing them this way and that through residential streets in Saint Albans.

"Ever been here before?" asked Munster.

"I think there are some Roman ruins," said Yvette. "I came on a school trip once. I can't remember anything about it. I'd probably enjoy it if I went now."

The satnav told them they'd reached their destination. They sat for a moment. Yvette checked the printed sheet on her lap to make sure this was the right address. It was.

Munster looked at her. "So are you nervous now?" he said.

"If I did it every day," she said, "I'd get used to it."

"Are you going to say it or do you want me to?"

"I'm in charge," Yvette said.

They got out of the car, opened the gate to the miniature front garden, and took the three steps that brought them into the little Georgian portico. Yvette pressed the bell, which set off a tinkling chime. A man answered the door. He was thick-set, with short blond hair, shaved at the sides of his head, dressed in jeans and a short-sleeved football shirt. He looked at them inquiringly.

"Are you Dennis Poole?" said Yvette.

"That's right."

She introduced herself and Chris Munster. "Are you the brother of Robert Poole?"

"What?" he said, looking surprised. "Why do you want to know?"

"You *are* his brother?" said Yvette.

"Well, yeah," said Poole. "But —"

"Can we step inside?" said Yvette.

They walked into the front room, where the TV was on with a game show Yvette didn't recognize. She asked Poole to switch it off. Instead, he turned the sound down.

"I'm afraid I have to tell you that your brother's dead," she said.

"What?"

"I'm very sorry," she continued. "We found his body on the first of February, but it took some time to identify it."

"What do you mean, his body?"

"His body was found in a house in south London. We've begun a murder investigation, and we're currently interviewing witnesses and taking statements. I know this must be a shock."

"What do you mean, south London?"

Yvette was used to this. In shock, people lose the ability to process information. You have to take things slowly. "I'm sorry," she said. "I know how difficult this must be for you. Are you surprised that your brother

242

should have been in that area?"

"What the hell are you talking about?" said Poole. "Rob died six years ago. Seven almost. You've made some mistake."

For a moment Yvette couldn't speak. She looked at Munster. He was the one who'd tracked down the birth certificate. What kind of disastrous error had he made? She took the sheet from the bag she was carrying.

"We're talking about Robert Anthony Poole," she said. "Born on the third of May 1981. Huntingdon. Father James Poole."

"That's right," said Poole. "That's my dad. But Rob died in 2004. Work accident. Some scaffolding collapsed. The company put all the blame on him. He got fuck-all compensation. That's what you should be investigating."

"I'm so sorry," said Yvette. "There's clearly some kind of . . ." She paused, at a loss. "Problem," she finished lamely.

"I'll say there's been a bloody problem."

She took a deep breath. "I'm extremely sorry about all this," she said. "I promise you that we're going to investigate and find out what's happened." She hesitated. "Do you have any details about your late brother? Papers?"

"Up in the attic somewhere. It might take

some time to dig out."

"We can wait," said Yvette.

# 22

Josef was suspicious at first. "This thing," he said. "Is for charity?"

"For you or for her?" said Frieda.

"For both."

"Karlsson rang me because he thought you could help. I think she's been left in the lurch. But if she wants any work done, she'll pay for it."

Frieda thought he seemed a bit better. At least he smelled clean and he had dressed himself properly; his face was less gaunt, too. Reuben had told her that he was only working from day to day. Building work was still slow. He drove her in Reuben's car. His old van was still sitting, with its dead battery and its flat tire, outside the house. The traffic was bad and the journey took almost an hour.

"The old joke is that it used to be quicker in London when people traveled on horseback," said Frieda.

Josef didn't reply.

"Except that it's not really a joke," she said. "It's true, I think."

Josef just looked ahead.

"If you're doing a job in a London garden," she said, "and you cut yourself, you need a tetanus shot. It's because of the horse shit. In Victorian times, people filled their gardens with it, and the bacteria are still active."

Silence from Josef. Frieda looked across at him. He seemed like someone who'd had the fight knocked out of him. Frieda knew that he hadn't told Reuben anything about what had happened. When she had first seen him, after his secret return, she had said she was ready to talk to him whenever he felt like it. But perhaps she was going to have to make the first move.

"Josef," she said, "something bad happened at home, didn't it?"

He stared straight ahead, but she saw his hands tighten on the steering wheel.

"Do you want to tell me?"

"No."

"Because you believe that I'll think the worse of you?"

"I know you think the worse."

"Is that why you never told us you were here?"

"You are good woman. Is easy for you. I am bad man."

"Josef, everyone's good and bad. Everyone makes mistakes."

"Not you."

"That's not true," Frieda said energetically. She hesitated, then said, "Last Friday, do you know where I was?"

"Friday? When we all have dinner with Olivia?"

"Before then. I was at the funeral of Kathy Ripon. You know, the young woman who was snatched by Dean Reeve and whose body was finally found in the storm drain." Josef, negotiating a mini-roundabout, nodded. "I was to blame for her death. No, don't interrupt. I was. I acted hastily; I didn't think about what I was doing, and she died because of it. So. That's me. What about you?"

He asked abruptly, "You think I am good father?"

"What does that mean? I think you love your sons and miss them. I think you'd do anything for them. I'm sure you've made mistakes. But they're lucky to have you."

He braked, turned his heavy face to her. "They do not have me now. They have him."

"Him?"

"Him. She have new man, they have new

papa. They look at him like hero. Suit and tie and cakes on weekend wrapped up in box with ribbons. They look at me like something on bottom of shoe. Shit," he supplied. "Like shit."

"Why?"

Cars backed up behind them and started sounding their horns. Josef moved off again. "Because I am shit."

"What happened?"

"She knew about straying."

"Straying? You mean, other women?"

Frieda had also known about the other women. Josef loved his wife with a sentimental, unwavering attachment, but she'd been in Kiev and he'd been in London, and for him it had been as if the two worlds were entirely separate — in one, he had a wife whom he loved; in the other, he didn't.

"She knew," Josef repeated. "I go home with my presents and my tender heart, all gladness, and my loneliness gone at last, and she shut the door. Just shut the door, Frieda. My boys see me turned like a dog away."

"Did you ever manage to talk about it?"

He shook his head from side to side, slowly. "I try. I meet new man. Good job. Toys for my boys. Cars that move with radio. Computer games with shooting and bombs. They not want my cheap little presents, not want me. Is over. All over. Life turned dust. I come back here again."

"So you never actually had a proper conversation about it?"

"What to say, Frieda, what to do? Everything is over. Gone."

"To tell her what you feel, to hear what she feels, to work out if things really are over."

"I am nothing," said Josef. "I have no money. I live in faraway land. I am wicked when her back is turned. Why she want me as husband? Why you want me as friend?"

"I like you," said Frieda, simply. "And I trust you."

"Trust? Me?"

"Why else would I ask you for help?"

His eyes filled with tears. "Truth?"

"Yes. Listen, we're going to talk about this more, Josef. But now we're here. Turn left. This is where Mary Orton lives."

Josef found a place to park, and they both got out.

"Are you all right?" she asked, as they walked down Brittany Road.

He stopped. "I thank you," he said, and put his hand on his heart, making his curious little bow.

They looked up at Mary Orton's large

detached house.

"Is big house for one woman," said Josef.

"Her husband's dead," said Frieda. "Her children left home a long time ago. She probably doesn't want to leave. Maybe she wants somewhere for the grandchildren to stay."

Josef looked up at the house and Frieda looked away from it at Josef's face. She liked that expression, the expression of someone engrossed in something she couldn't see. "What do you think?" she said.

He pointed up to a window on the second floor.

"You see a crack there," he said. It was like a dark thread running down from the sill. "The house move a bit. Not so much."

"Is it bad?" she said.

"Not so bad," said Josef. "Is London." He held out his flat hands and shifted them about horizontally. "Is on clay. You have no rain and then much rain and the houses moved and you know . . ." He mimed something, like a tired person flopping down.

"Settle," said Frieda.

"Settle," said Josef. "But not so bad."

The front door opened before they had even approached it. Mary Orton must have noticed the two strangers staring up at her house. Frieda wondered how much time she spent gazing out of the window. She was wearing dark blue corduroy slacks and a checked shirt. Frieda saw that she must once have been beautiful. She was still beautiful, in a way, but her face was more than wrinkled. The flesh looked like brown paper that had been folded and folded and folded again, then flattened out. Frieda introduced herself and Josef.

"Did the detective tell you that we were coming?" she said, catching herself talking a bit loudly, as if Mary Orton was slightly deaf and slightly stupid.

She bustled them into the house and through the hall into a large kitchen that looked out on a shockingly large garden. There were two substantial trees at the end, and more gardens on either side and opposite. It was like looking at parkland. While Josef and Frieda were gazing at it through the French windows, Mary Orton busied herself behind them, making tea and getting out two cakes, putting them on plates and cutting slices.

"A very small piece, please," said Frieda. "Half that."

Josef took Frieda's and ate it as well as his, drank tea, and had a slice of the other cake. Mary Orton turned a grateful look on him.

"If Josef has quite finished," said Frieda, "he can have a look at what needs doing. He's very good."

Josef put his plate into the sink. "That is a very nice cake, both of them."

"Have some more," said Mary Orton. "It's just going to waste."

"I will have some more later," said Josef, "but first, what things was the man doing for you?"

"It's so terrible what happened," she said. "So very awful." She passed a hand over her face, seeming dazed. "And the detective, the woman, said that he was killed. Is that really possible?"

"I think so," said Frieda. "I'm not a policeman. I'm just a . . ." She stopped for a moment. What was she? "Just a colleague."

"He was so helpful," she continued. "So reassuring. He made me feel in safe hands. I haven't felt that since my husband died, and that was a long time ago. He said the house needed a lot of work. He was right, of course. I've let it go dreadfully." She reached over for a packet of cigarettes and an ashtray. "Do you mind?" Frieda shook her head. She lit a cigarette. "There were all sorts of things that needed doing, and he and a couple of men who worked for him patched things up here and there. But the main thing was the roof. He said that other things could wait, but once the roof starts going and water gets in . . ."

"Is true," said Josef. "The roof is important. But outside no scaffolding. Is gone?"

"No," said Mary Orton. "They worked at it from the inside."

"What?" Josef wrinkled his face.

"How long was he here?" asked Frieda.

"A long time," said Mary Orton, with a smile. "I can't remember. Of course, they weren't here all the time. They sometimes had to go and do other jobs. But I was flexible about it."

"And now it's still leaking," said Frieda. "At least, that's what I heard."

"He hadn't finished," said Mary Orton. "Suddenly he didn't come any more. I missed him — not just for the repairs. Now we know why. It's so terrible." Her old face seemed to crumple even more. She turned her head away to hide her expression.

"Is it all right if Josef takes a look?"

"Of course," said Mary Orton. "Shall I show you?"

Josef smiled. It was one of the few times Frieda had seen him smile since his return.

"I know the way to the roof," he said.

When Josef had gone, Frieda looked around the kitchen. There were snapshots of children on the dresser, all in little frames. "Are they your grandchildren?"

"Yes. They're more grown-up now, of course."

"Do you see much of them?"

"My two sons don't live in London. They come to see me when they can on holidays. I have friends, of course."

She sounded almost defensive. Frieda picked up one of the pictures. It was a primary school photograph dated 2008. Three years ago, a long time in a child's life, she thought.

"It must have been quite nice just to have Robert Poole around," she said.

"Oh, well, he was a kind young man," said Mary Orton, seeming embarrassed. "He asked me about my life, took an interest. When you get old, people usually stop seeing you. You become invisible. But he wasn't like that."

"Attentive," Frieda said.

"Yes, I suppose he was. It's hard to believe he's dead."

There was a thump on the stairs and both women turned as Josef came into the kitchen.

"Mrs. Orton." He stood solidly in front of her. "There is a small leak. I fetch my bag from the car and in just five minutes I stop the water. Then maybe just one day's work, or two days. I fix it for you. All fine."

"That would be wonderful. Can you do that?"

"No problem. I go to the car. Frieda?" He nodded at her. "Mrs. Orton, you excuse us one moment?"

Frieda followed him out into the hall. "Everything all right?"

Josef pulled a contemptuous face. "The roof. That all bullshit. I know it when I don't see scaffolding. He did nothing."

"What do you mean?"

"I mean, he did nothing up there. Bit of banging maybe, no new roof."

Frieda was baffled. "Maybe you just didn't see what he'd done."

"Frieda," said Josef, "I show you if you want. I go there, I climb up ladder in top bedroom and I shine torch. I look at roof boards, rafters. There is some new boards, some" — he waved his hands around, searching for the word — "felt, but is nothing. And the water is coming in." He tapped his head. "Maybe she's . . ."

"All right," said Frieda. "You should go ahead and fix the hole." She put out a hand

255

and touched his shoulder. "And thanks, Josef."

He shrugged and went outside. Frieda thought hard for a couple of minutes, then walked back into the kitchen. She sat down next to Mary Orton at the kitchen table and pulled her chair even closer, so they could talk in low voices.

"Mary, I want to ask you something. Can you tell me how much you paid Robert Poole?"

Mary Orton blushed red. "I don't really know," she said. "I just paid him in bits, from time to time. I didn't really think of the amount."

Frieda leaned closer, put her hand on the woman's forearm. "I wouldn't ask this if it wasn't important, but could you show me your bank statements?"

"Well, really . . ."

"You don't have to show me," said Frieda, "but if you don't, I'm afraid the police will come and look anyway."

"All right." Mary Orton nodded. "But it feels a bit strange."

She left the room. Frieda heard sounds on the stairs, going up and then coming down. Mary Orton came back into the kitchen and put a bundle of papers on the table. "They're in a complete mess," she said. "My husband used to do all that sort of thing."

Frieda found the current-account statements and arranged them in order of date, then started to scan them. After just a few seconds, she felt her heart beating faster. She could feel it pulsing in her neck. She put the last sheet down and turned to Mary Orton.

"I was only making a rough count. Maybe I missed a couple of payments. But I make it about a hundred and sixty thousand pounds you paid him. Does that seem right?"

Mary Orton took another cigarette from her packet and lit it. Her hands were trembling, and it took two matches to get it alight. "Yes, it could be. But roofs are horribly expensive, aren't they?"

"Yes," said Frieda. "That's what I've heard."

# 23

There had been eight names or pairs of names in Robert Poole's notebook. Yvette read them out. "One: Mrs. Mary Orton."

"We've talked to her. She definitely knew Robert Poole — probably best of anyone we've come across so far."

"Two: Frank and Aisling Wyatt."

"Who also knew him, though not so well."

"Three: Caroline Mallory and David Lewis, the couple in Brixton who were our initial lead and say that they met him just the once. Then four, there's a name you'll know: Jasmine Shreeve." Yvette paused, as if expecting a reaction.

"Am I meant to know who she is?" said Karlsson.

"She presented a makeover show a few years ago. I think it was mainly broadcast in the day."

"When did you get the time to watch daytime TV?"

"I never actually saw it. She told me about it. She said she had met Poole. She had no idea why anyone would want to kill him."

"We'll need to interview these people in more detail," said Karlsson. "What about the rest?"

"Those are the only ones who actually met him." Yvette looked down at her notes. "After that, there's the Coles, out in Haywards Heath, a retired couple who have no idea who he is or any memory of meeting him; Graham Rudge, single, a head teacher of a private school, who lives up near Notting Hill, and also says he's never met anyone called Robert Poole, although he wonders if someone of that name called him once — can't remember where, can't remember when. A young couple in Chelsea, Andrea and Lawrence Bingham, just back from their honeymoon, both something in the City. And someone called Sally Lea. We have no idea who she is."

"Is that the lot?" asked Karlsson.

"Yes."

"These people, do they have anything in common?"

"Chris and I talked about that. They all live in completely different parts of London, and a couple of them are outside the city. Mary Orton and Jasmine Shreeve live fairly near where he lived. The Wyatts live near where the body was found. They all have different occupations. They're different ages, different social types. Some of them said they knew him, others didn't. None of them know each other. There doesn't seem to be any link, as far as we can see."

"So we have eight names and absolutely nothing to link them, not even knowledge of the victim."

"They're all well-off," said Chris Munster, hesitantly.

"Some are well-off and some are very well-off," agreed Yvette. "You should see where the Wyatts live. It's like something in a magazine."

"I'll pay them a visit."

"So." An hour later, Karlsson leaned forward across his desk. "What do you say? Are you in or out?"

"I'm still not sure this should be on a formal basis."

"You know, Frieda, I think we're doing a strange sort of dance. What you like is when I ask you not to do something and then you do it anyway, or when you go ahead and do something that you're not meant to do, then tell me afterward. You know what? If you were going to be your own therapist, you

might decide that you have trouble committing yourself."

"You want me to sign an oath and fill out
all the right forms?"

"It's not like that."

"I'm not really a team player, especially in
a team that isn't sure it wants me."

"What the hell do you mean?"

"What about Yvette Long?"

"Yvette? What about her?"

"She dislikes and disapproves of me."

"Nonsense."

"Are you blind?"

"She's just protective of me."

"She thinks I'll get you into trouble. She
may be right."

"That's my problem. But if you don't
want to work with me, fine. Just say so, once
and for all, and I'll not bother you again.
But we can't carry on in this half-arsed way
with you popping in and out and nobody
knowing quite what you're up to. It's decision time: yes or no?"

Frieda looked at him and he looked back
at her. At last, she nodded. "I'll give it a
try."

"Good," said Karlsson, seeming almost
surprised by her decision. "That's good.
There'll be some paperwork. You'll need to
sign a contract."

"Is this all to do with health and safety?"

"No, it's about police work, which mainly consists of filling out forms. And now you can come with me and visit the people on Robert Poole's list who actually knew him. This nice young man doesn't seem to have been so nice after all — and he doesn't seem to have been Robert Poole after all, either."

"Can I ask you a favor before we go?"

"Go on."

"Alan Dekker."

Karlsson's expression became wary. He put his chin on his steepled hands and looked at Frieda. "We've been through this before . . ."

"I know."

"You've nothing to go on, Frieda. A feeling."

"I know Dean is alive."

"You don't know. You believe."

"I firmly believe. If Alan's out there, there must be obvious ways of tracking him down. That's what you do, isn't it?"

Karlsson sighed heavily. "Tell me, Frieda," he said. "If we find something, what then?"

"It's simple. If you find Alan, we'll know Dean is dead, and I'll admit I'm wrong."

"That'll be a first."

"So will you do it?"

"I'll see. It's sometimes difficult to find

262

people who don't want to be found."

In the car, Karlsson told Frieda what they knew so far of the man known as Robert Poole: that he had taken the identity of a man who had died six years ago. His real identity was still unknown. They'd found no evidence of any settled job or fixed income, yet he had had a large amount of money in his bank shortly before his death. His account had been emptied around the time of his murder. People spoke warmly of him, but no one seemed to know much about him. They had found a notebook in his flat with several names in it, including those of Frieda's couple in Brixton, and of Mary Orton.

"Who are we seeing first?" asked Frieda.

"Frank and Aisling Wyatt. They live in Greenwich. We've rung ahead and they'll both be in this time. Last time it was just her."

"What do you know about them?"

"He's an accountant in the City. She's an interior designer. Part-time, probably a hobby. They have a couple of young kids at primary school."

The car drew up at a row of gleaming apartment blocks that looked out across the widening river; now the tide was low, the

Thames a thinning flow of brown water between two banks of silt and sand.

"They're not badly off," said Karlsson.

They took the paved river walkway that led to the Wyatts' home. It was on two floors, with a wrought-iron balcony on the first, and the ground floor giving on to a small garden that was filled with a profusion of pots, some terra-cotta, others pewter and brass. Even on a gray, windy February day, Frieda could see that in the spring and summer it would be a riot of color and scent. Today the only flowers visible were droopy white snowdrops and blue chionodoxa.

Karlsson rapped on the door, which was quickly opened by a dark-haired, powerfully built man in his thirties, with a blue chin, gray eyes, and beetling brows. He was wearing a beautifully cut dark suit, a flawlessly ironed white shirt, and a red tie. He looked distrustful as Karlsson introduced himself but almost amused when Karlsson introduced Frieda.

"Aisling's through here. Can I ask you how long it will take? This is a working day." He looked at his watch, a flash of dials and shimmering metal.

"We'll be as quick as we can."

Frank Wyatt led them through a door into

the main room, which took up the ground floor, an expanse of stripped wooden boards, throw rugs, pillowed sofas, soft pale curtains, vivid plants, a low table, and at the far end a gleaming kitchen with stainless steel cooktop and surfaces winking in the light thrown from the river-view window. For a moment, Frieda thought of Michelle Doyce rooting through Dumpsters and bins just a little upriver. Then she turned her attention to the woman, who rose from the sofa to greet them. Aisling Wyatt was tall and thin and aquiline, rich brown hair tied back from a face that was bare of makeup. She was wearing jogging pants and a cream cashmere jumper, and her feet, which were long and thin like the rest of her, were bare. She had an air of self-assurance that seemed to go with the furniture.

"Can I get either of you something? Tea or coffee?"

They both declined. Karlsson stood with his back to the window. Frieda noted his air of never quite fitting in, whatever the setting, never being won over.

"Aisling's already talked to a police officer, you know. I'm not sure what more we can add."

"We just wanted to check a few things. As you know, Robert Poole was murdered."

"Awful," murmured Aisling. Frieda saw that there were little smudges under her eyes and her lips were bloodless.

"We're trying to build up a picture of him," continued Karlsson. "Can you tell us how you both met him?"

"That was Aisling." Frank nodded at his wife.

"Mrs. Wyatt?"

"It was because of the garden," said Aisling.

"We saw it on the way in," Frieda said. "It's beautiful."

"I love it." Aisling turned to her and smiled for the first time, her thin face losing its haughtiness, its air of weary disdain. "It's my passion. Frank works very long hours, and it's what I do when the children are at school. I have a job of sorts but, to be honest, people don't want to spend their money on interior design at the moment."

"Hard times for everyone, even the better off," said Frank, pacing to a chair and studying it as if undecided whether it was worth his while to sit down.

"So." Frieda concentrated her attention on Aisling. "You met Robert Poole through your interest in gardens?"

"It's funny to hear him called Robert. We knew him as Bertie," said Aisling. "He was walking past one day and saw me planting a particular rose I love. I've grown it along the wall where it sort of folds over it. He stopped and we got talking. He said he worked quite a lot with garden design. He was interested in what I'd done in such a small space. He noticed even the smallest touches." Her eyes slid to Frank, who was now sitting in the chair opposite but had perched on its edge, as if to demonstrate his impatience to be out of there and back to work.

"He passed again a day or two after," said Aisling. "He said he often walked this way to visit local clients. But he had time to chat. After that, we often talked. He had coffee a couple of times and showed me plant catalogues. He was just setting up in business himself. He even suggested that we join up, so I could be the interior and he could be the exterior designer. It was a joke, of course. But it was nice to have someone take me seriously."

"Did you meet him as well?" Karlsson turned to Frank.

"A couple of times," said Frank. "Nice guy."

"What did you talk about?" asked Frieda.

"Nothing important."

"Tell us anyway."

Frank suddenly seemed embarrassed. "The only time I was actually on my own with him, we talked about going to boarding school when we were very little. I've put it behind me, so I don't normally talk about it. He knew what it was like because he'd been to one himself. Don't know which."

"So he was easy to talk to," said Frieda.

"I suppose so."

"Did he talk about his job?"

"No," said Frank.

Aisling shook her head. "Not really," she agreed.

"So you were both friends of his."

"I wouldn't say *friends,*" Frank said.

"Mrs. Wyatt?"

"No-o." She drew the word out so it seemed like a tired sigh. "Not a friend. A friendly acquaintance."

"How many times did you meet him?"

"Why do you want to know all of this?" Frank asked, his voice suddenly harsh and his nostrils flaring. "He's dead. We're shocked and sorry, of course, but we barely knew him. There must be dozens — hundreds — of people who knew him better than us."

"Not many times," Aisling said, ignoring her husband's outburst. "Six, seven. He just passed by every so often, on his way."

"On his way where?"

She shrugged.

"From where?"

"I told you, from where he lived."

"Tooting," said Karlsson. "Which isn't exactly round the corner."

"He never said he lived nearby."

"There seem to be a lot of things he didn't say," said Karlsson. "We know almost nothing about him. But he had your name in his notebook. That's why we're talking to you."

"Why would he have our names?"

"Did he ever work for you?" asked Frieda.

"He helped with the garden a bit," said Aisling.

"Did you pay him?"

The Wyatts said no at the same time.

"And there's nothing you can tell us about him?"

"We barely knew him," said Frank, standing up. "And we've told you what we know."

"When did you last see him?"

"I couldn't tell you," said Frank. "He just used to drop by."

"You can't remember, then?"

"No idea."

"The twenty-first of January," said Aisling Wyatt.

"That's very precise."

"It was the day I had to take my son to

269

the hospital. I talked to him about it."

"The twenty-first of January."

"Yes. A Friday."

"Good," said Karlsson. "That's very helpful. If you think of anything else . . ."

"Yes, yes." Frank Wyatt was impatient for them to be gone. "We'll be in touch. Of course."

"What did you think of them?" asked Karlsson, once they were in the car.

"Rich."

"That goes without saying."

"She's lonely."

"You think?"

"Yes. And they never looked at each other. Not once."

That evening, when Frieda returned from a meal with friends, she opened the door of her house to the sound of the phone ringing. She hadn't left the answering machine on, and she didn't get to it in time, but even before she was able to do a last-number recall, it rang again.

"Yes? Frieda here."

"God, at last! Where have you been? I've been trying and trying to get hold of you. At home, your mobile, e-mail."

"Hello, Olivia."

"I even tried that number you gave me at work."

"That's for emergencies."

"Well, this is a fucking emergency. I'm going to be out on the streets. So is Chloë."

Frieda sat down and shifted the phone to her other ear. She eased off her boots and rubbed her feet: she had walked several miles home.

"What's wrong?"

"What's wrong? Your brother is what's wrong."

"David."

"Do you have other brothers I was married to who are trying to ruin my life? Isn't it enough he leaves me for some bimbo, humiliates me, abandons me to loneliness, dumps his only child, without this?"

"Tell me what's happened."

"He said he's talked to some lawyer and that he's going to reduce what he pays me." Olivia was talking fast now, between tearful gulps. Frieda imagined she was also knocking back the wine. "Can he do that, Frieda?"

"Don't you have a legal agreement?"

"I *thought* so. Oh, I don't know. I was such a mess at the time. I didn't think. He says he'll continue to pay toward Chloë's upkeep, but that it isn't fair to expect him to pay for me. He says I should get full-time

271

work. Doesn't he think I'm trying? Doesn't he know there's a recession? What am I supposed to do? I'm forty-one, I don't have a profession, I'm a single mother. Honestly, Frieda, it's a brutal world out there. Who'd choose me when they could have a twenty-something graduate doing it for half the price — or for nothing but the good of their CV?"

"I know it's hard," said Frieda. "Did you tell this to David?"

"Do you think that bastard *cares*? He's got his new life now."

"Do you have letters from solicitors, bank statements, things like that?"

There was silence at the other end.

"Olivia?"

"I just wanted to get rid of everything. I might have some of it — but I've no idea where. I don't exactly have a filing cabinet. Things just get, you know, put down. Can't you ring him?"

"I haven't spoken to David for years."

"He'll listen to you. They're all scared of you."

"I'll think about it," said Frieda, grimly.

She thought about it. She paced around the living room in her bare feet, frowning. She picked up the phone, rang his number, even heard the ringing tone, and slammed it down. She felt clammy and sick. There had to be another way.

# 24

Jasmine Shreeve treated Karlsson and Frieda as if she were conducting the interview, and she became even more animated when she discovered that Frieda was a psychotherapist.

"You remember when I used to do *House Doctor*?" she asked. She paused and Karlsson mumbled something. She looked at Frieda.

"Was it a medical program?" Frieda asked.

"You really didn't . . ." Shreeve began. "It was some time ago, but it was very important at the time. I was teamed with this famous psychologist called Lenny McMullen. Dr. Mac. You must know him."

There was another pause.

"Miss, er . . ."

"Call me Jasmine."

"I don't think I know him."

"He's very respected in his field," said Jasmine. "And he was a TV natural. He was famous for his sweaters. So you never saw the program?" She looked baffled and thought for a moment. "Well, what we used to do was go to someone's home and, while they were outside, Lenny and I would walk around the house and he would diagnose their psychological problems just by looking at the decorations and the furniture and the pictures on the wall. We would bring the person or the couple or the family back in and Lenny and I would talk to them about their problems and then about how they could solve them."

"By redecorating their house?" said Karlsson.

"Sometimes," said Jasmine. "Don't knock it. The places we live express us. Healing our house is the first step to healing ourselves. That's what Lenny used to say." She looked at Frieda. "I know what you're doing," she said.

"What am I doing?"

"You're studying my house. You're trying to do on me what we used to do on *House Doctor.*"

"I don't think I'd be qualified," said Frieda.

"No need to be modest. I'll tell you what you're seeing. Looking around the room, you're seeing a living room that's surprisingly tasteful for a presenter of downmarket TV. The color of the wall is based on something I saw in Pompeii. There are a couple of photographs of me with well-known personalities, but they were taken a suspiciously long time ago. Did you know that when *House Doctor* went off the air, Channel Four didn't even have a Web site? Well, no, of course you didn't because you hadn't even heard of it, so I'm sure you haven't seen the shows I've done for other companies."

"I mainly watch sports," said Karlsson. "And not much of that."

"What you're seeing," said Jasmine, "is the house of a fifty-one-year-old female TV presenter in an industry that doesn't want fifty-one-year-old female TV presenters. You can see the photograph of one ex-husband, because we're still good friends. You can't see the photograph of the other because we aren't. You might have expected this to be the house of someone who's trying to hold on to the past, someone who is bitter about her fate. Tell me, Dr. Klein —"

"Please, call me Frieda."

"Frieda, is this the room of a bitter woman?"

Suddenly Frieda thought of her grandfather. A friend of his had told her about what he'd do at a party if someone discovered he was a doctor and then, as people so often did, asked him about some ache or pain they had. In a concerned voice, he would ask them to close their eyes and stick out their tongue. Then he would walk away and start talking to someone else. She thought for a moment. "If this was a consultation," she said finally, "I'd be asking you what it is that you want me to tell you. It feels like you're trying to force me to say something about you. But we're not in a session. Sometimes a room is just a room. I think this is nice. I like the color from Pompeii."

"Do you know what I did at university?" said Jasmine. "I went to Oxford. I got a first in English. In fact, I got a *double* first. That's not the kind of thing you expect from a woman who did a TV commercial for incontinence pads. Which, incidentally, paid for about half of this house. But do you know what it means? The double first, not the TV commercial."

"It sounds impressive."

"It means I would be a difficult person for someone like you to analyze. What people like you do is turn people's lives into stories, stories with a moral and a meaning. But I learned that when I was at Oxford. I know how to analyze stories, and I know how to turn things into stories. When I did *House Doctor,* and even when I did low-budget documentaries about people behaving badly on holiday, every one of them was a little story. That's why you can't just come into my house and fit me into the psychological story you might have about a faded TV presenter."

There was another pause. Karlsson looked stunned. He glanced at Frieda; it seemed to be up to her.

"So," she said. "What was your story with Robert Poole?"

"He was a friend," Jasmine replied. "We worked together. In a way."

"Can you expand on that?" said Frieda. "How did you meet?"

Jasmine looked wistful. "It was a bit like something in a film. I go to the gym a couple of times a week, but sometimes I also go for a run. One day, a few months ago, I was in Ruskin Park, behind the hospital. I was doing my stretches and he just struck up a conversation."

"What about?"

"Just about the exercises I was doing. He said what a good thing it was to warm up like that, but then he said that one of the moves I was doing could be straining my back and he suggested other things. We got talking and went for a coffee, and I asked if he could help me with exercise."

"Like a personal trainer?" said Karlsson.

"That's right."

"Why?" said Karlsson.

"What do you mean why?" she said. "Why not?"

"Someone you just met in a park."

"How else do you choose people?" she said. "I've got an instinct for people. He knew what he was talking about. I got on with him. I felt like it would be a good motivation for me."

"How much did you pay him?"

She thought for a moment. "Sixty pounds a session. Does that seem unreasonable?" She looked at Frieda. "What do *you* charge?"

"It varies," said Frieda. "Did he talk about his other clients?"

"No," said Jasmine. "That was part of what I liked about him. When I was with him, he was completely focused on me, on the job in hand."

"Were you emotionally involved?" asked Karlsson.

Briefly she was flustered. "He was just a trainer," she said. "Well, not *just* a trainer. The good thing about Robbie was that he was someone I could talk to."

"What did you talk about?" Frieda asked.

"When you're on TV, people think you're different. He didn't. He was a good listener. That doesn't sound like much, but there aren't many people like that."

"When did you last see him?" said Karlsson.

"About a month ago."

"How was he?"

"Same as ever — warm, interested, attentive. Then we had an appointment for the end of January and he didn't turn up. I called him but he didn't answer. And then all this . . . I wish I could say something that made sense of it all. I've been thinking and thinking about it ever since I heard. I really didn't know anything about it."

"Did he ever talk about friends or family?" said Frieda. "Or anything about his past or any other part of his life?"

"No." Jasmine shook her head with a curious smile. "It was all about me. Maybe that's why I liked him."

"And all you paid him was that sixty pounds a session?" said Karlsson.

"That's right."

There was a pause. Karlsson gave a slight nod to Frieda, and she thought of the secret signals couples send each other when it's time to leave a party. They both stood up. Jasmine held out her hand to Frieda, who took it and said, "You told me I wouldn't be able to understand you by looking at your house and that I wouldn't be able to be your therapist because you'd studied English. What did Robert Poole understand about you?"

Jasmine pulled her hand out of Frieda's grasp. "Now you're just trying to be clever. The thing about Robbie was that he didn't see me the way everybody else sees me. He just saw me for who I am. As simple as that."

As they came out of Jasmine Shreeve's house into the quiet little Camberwell street, Karlsson seemed discontented. "Who the hell is this guy?"

Water seemed to be getting into the boat. She couldn't tell from where, but it was wet on the floor and all her clothes were damp. One morning it was so cold her trousers were stiff as well, like cardboard, and she had to grit her teeth when she pulled them on. Her hands throbbed and they were a bit swollen. She held them up to the window and examined them. She needed to look good for when he came. Not glamorous and simpering, he hated all of that — he liked strong women who could accompany him through a world full of dangers — but clean, fit, ready for whatever he wanted her to do.

She had lost weight. She couldn't see it, but she could feel it from her clothes, which hung off her, and from the new definition of her pelvic bone. Also, she hadn't had a period for — how long? She couldn't remember. She would have to look at the calendar where she'd marked it. It didn't matter. But she was worried that she seemed to be having trouble seeing clearly — little motes floated in front of her eyes, and things seemed out of focus at the edges. She wouldn't tell him that, and she'd make sure it didn't interfere with the task in hand.

Task in hand. What was it? Her hair, yes: she wetted it and combed it straight, and then, standing in front of the little mirror in what had once been the boat's shower room, she tried to cut it, snipping at the ragged ends with the scissors. When she used to go to the hairdresser in town and sit in front of the large mirror, she would close her eyes and let André massage her scalp with lemony oil before she had it washed and conditioned and then, very slowly, cut and caressed and dried into shape. This was different — it was functional, a way of preparing herself, but it was hard to get the hair even in this dim light, and her face seemed to shrink, then loom out at her so she had the horrible feeling she was looking at a stranger, whose skin was the color of mushrooms and whose eyes were too big and cheekbones too sharp. But she liked the feeling of the blades slicing through her wet locks.

Afterward, she washed what was left of her hair over the cracked sink, pouring cupfuls of water on to it and rubbing in the last of her shampoo. Her face felt rubbery with cold but she was hot as well. Hot inside. Her hands gripped the sink. It felt greasy and hard to hold on to, and the boat seemed to be tipping to one side.

She knew she needed to eat, but she felt sick and couldn't face the last of the potatoes with reeking tuna fish stirred into them. Canned peaches: that would do. She couldn't find the can opener; she must have dropped it somewhere but the boat was dim and the batteries on the flashlight had died and where were the matches? Everything seemed to be slipping from her grasp and she mustn't let that happen. She was a soldier. Chin up. She found the kitchen knife and, squatting on the floor, started hitting the top of the can with it, making a little dent that gradually grew bigger until the can split and a teardrop of peach juice oozed onto the surface. She licked it greedily with the tip of her tongue. Sweet, life giving. Her eyes filled with tears. She inserted the knife into the hole and levered it back and forth, gradually making the opening bigger, but then she couldn't wait any longer and lifted the gashed can to her mouth and sucked at the fruit and it was only afterward when she could still taste metal that she realized her lip was cut open and pulpy, her mouth full of blood. She tried to stand up but the floor shrank and the ceiling tilted toward her. She put her head on the wet boards and stared at the hatch, where he would come.

# 25

On Sunday morning Frieda woke with a sickening lurch. There were beads of sweat on her forehead and her heart was pounding. For a few moments, her dream lingered: a man with a round face, blotched with ancient freckles, a soft, mirthless smile. Watching her, always watching her. Dean Reeve. She sat up in bed and made herself breathe calmly, then looked at her watch. It was almost ten to nine and she couldn't remember the last time she had slept so heavily and so late. The doorbell was ringing: that must have been what had woken her. She pulled her dressing gown around her, walked down the stairs, and opened the door.

Standing on the step, filling the whole space, blocking out the light almost, were Reuben, Josef, and Jack. Their expressions were slightly uneasy. Her stomach lurched. Something terrible had happened. Someone had died. She was about to hear bad news. She prepared herself for the blow.

"What is it?" she said. "Just say it."

"We wanted to tell you." Jack's face flushed with emotion.

"Before you hear from anyone else," said Reuben.

"What?" said Frieda.

Reuben held up a tabloid newspaper. "It's Terry Reeve, or whatever her real name is," he said. "It's all rubbish and it's fish-and-chip paper anyway. But they've got her story and — there's no getting around it — she does mention you and it's not especially flattering. And they've got a photo of you from somewhere. In which you look rather good, actually."

Frieda took a deep breath. "Is that all?" she said.

Josef held up a paper bag. "And we have pastries and buns. We will come in and make you strong coffee."

Frieda went back upstairs, showered, and, to the sound of clattering plates and pans from downstairs, pulled on a pair of jeans and a black sweater, then pushed her bare feet into sneakers. As she came down, she saw them arranging a random selection of mugs and plates on the table. Josef had built a fire. Reuben was pouring the coffee. Jack came in from the kitchen with a couple of jars and a packet of butter. An unopened one, when Frieda knew there was an opened one in the door of the fridge. What did it matter? Josef handed her a mug, and just as she raised it to her lips, the bell rang again. She opened the door to find Sasha standing there.

"I don't know if you've heard," said Sasha. "I just wanted to come right round and . . ." Her voice faded as Frieda pushed the door open and she saw the scene inside.

"We've got breakfast," said Frieda.

Sasha held up a bag of her own. "I got some croissants from Number 9," she said. "They're still warm."

Sasha came in and coffee was poured and there was an immediate chorus of voices saying all over again that it really wasn't so bad and that nobody who knew her or, in fact, anyone else would take it seriously and that she could probably sue if she wanted. Frieda held up a hand. "Stop," she said. "I don't want to look at any of this. Someone just tell me in two sentences what it says."

There was a silence.

"Basically she's a victim," said Reuben.

"And it's everybody else's fault," said Jack.

"Including yours," said Sasha. "But the photo's actually rather glamorous. The

287

caption's not very nice."

"It is pile of rubbish, all of it," said Josef.

They were all friends. They had come to see her out of the best of motives, but Frieda felt oppressed by the four pairs of eyes on her, as if they were waiting to see how she would react.

"OK, OK," she said. "What does she say about me?"

They looked at each other nervously.

"Out with it," said Frieda.

"She says you exploited her," said Sasha, in an anxious rush. "Which is ridiculous because you didn't take any of the credit. And, anyway, you were the one who saved her."

"It doesn't feel like that to her," said Frieda. "She'd found a kind of safety. I was the one who pushed her out into the big bad world."

"She says you wanted to be famous," said Reuben.

"Anything else?" said Frieda. More uneasy looks. "Just tell me. If you don't tell me, I'll hear it from people who aren't my friends."

When Jack spoke, his mouth sounded dry. "They mention the victim, Kathy Ripon. They give the impression, you know . . ." He couldn't say any more.

"It's completely unfair," said Reuben.

288

"Everyone knows that. I mean everyone involved. Everyone who matters."

Frieda thought of Kathy Ripon's family, of everyone at the funeral. She swallowed hard. "I haven't been murdered," she said. "It's just my reputation." She pointed a finger at Reuben. "Don't go quoting Shakespeare," she said sharply.

He looked startled. "I wasn't going to."

"I'll have a croissant," she said, although she didn't think she could swallow a mouthful of it.

Josef ripped the photograph of Frieda out of the paper and showed it to her. It was an old picture that had been taken for an appearance at a conference a couple of years earlier. They must have got it online somewhere. She saw one word of the caption: "Reckless." She spread jam on the croissant and cut it up but she didn't eat any. She heard a buzz of voices around her and heard herself responding from time to time and trying to manage a smile. She looked at the little group and thought of them contacting each other early on a Sunday morning and agreeing to come over, and she was touched by that. But when they started to leave, she felt relieved. Then she thought of something. She touched Jack's sleeve. "Could you hang on?" she said. "There's something I want to talk to you about."

"What? Is something wrong?"

He looked apprehensive and ran a hand through his hair, making it stick up in a peak. Frieda tried not to smile — he was in his twenties, qualified as a doctor and training as a therapist, yet here he was, in his horrible orange quilted jacket and his muddy sneakers, looking just like a small boy who'd been caught out in a misdemeanor.

"No. I've a proposal for you." Jack's expression changed from anxious to eager. He bobbed from foot to foot until she pointed to a chair. "Do you want more coffee?"

"I'm okay. What is it?"

"I'd like you to see Carrie Dekker."

"Carrie Dekker? Alan's wife? Why? What's happened now?"

"As her therapist."

"Her therapist?"

"You keep repeating what I've just said."

"Me?"

"Jack, you're a therapist. You have patients. That is your job. I'm asking if you would consider seeing Carrie. She needs help, and I think you could be good for her."

"You're not just saying this to be nice?"

Frieda frowned at him. "Do you really

think I'd recommend you to a woman in distress just to cheer you up? Anyway, she might decide you're not right for her."

"Yes, of course."

"And you might decide, after the initial consultation, that it wouldn't work."

"Right."

"She's in a state of shock. When she thought Alan had left her, that was catastrophic enough, but now after what Dean did to her . . ."

"That's too much for me," said Jack. "I don't know how to deal with it."

"Yes, you do. And you can always talk to me about it. I'll see what she has to say."

Jack stood up, zipping his jacket, pulling a yellow and purple beanie over his disordered hair. "By the way," he said suddenly. "Saul Klein."

Frieda stood quite still. She felt as though someone had hit her hard in the stomach. "What?" Her voice sounded calm enough.

"Dr. Saul Klein. *The* Saul Klein. The one the hospital wing is named after. He's your grandfather."

"And?"

"But that's just fantastic. He's a legend, a pioneer. Why didn't you say?"

"Why would I?"

"Did you know him?"

"No."

"It must be special, though."

"Must it?" Frieda felt very cold, as if she were standing in an icy shadow.

"So it runs in your family?"

Jack was clearly uneasy now. This wasn't going the way he had expected.

"What does?" she asked sharply, and he looked disconcerted.

"Being a doctor."

"My father wasn't a doctor."

"What was he?"

"You'll be late, Jack."

"What for? I'm not expected anywhere."

"Then I'll be late."

"Oh. Right. I'll be on my way, then." He hovered at the open door, his scarf flapping and his face turning blotchy in the raw air.

"Good-bye."

After he had gone, Frieda returned to her chair by the fire and sat for several minutes, staring blindly into its leaping flames. Then she picked up the newspaper and word by word, page by page, read the story. Then she crumpled it into small balls and fed it into the fire.

"How often do you see your sister?" Frieda asked.

She had met Rose Teale first a year and a

bit ago, when Rose still didn't know if she even had a sister any more. Then, she had been an anxious and guilty young woman, still haunted by the little girl she had lost sight of on the way home from school and never seen again. She had felt responsible, not just for the tiny Joanna, disappearing into thin air, but also for her parents and their agony. Her mother had remarried and had two more children, but her father had started drinking, sitting in his poky, grimy flat, surrounded by pictures of his lost daughter, addled with whisky and sorrow.

She had seen her a few times since her sister had been returned, and if anything, Rose Teale was more tormented now than she had been before. Joanna, who had been a tiny, knock-kneed, vulnerable, gap-toothed child when she was taken, had come back unrecognizable. Their reunion had been a failure, and Joanna had a robust, jeering contempt for Rose, for her parents, for the world they represented.

"Not very often," said Rose. "She's not keen to see me. I can understand that," she added hastily, "given everything she's been through."

"Do you want to see her?"

Rose looked at her, biting her lower lip. "Honestly? Not really. I dread it. But I feel

I should."

"Because she's your sister?"

"Because she's my sister. Because of everything she's gone through. Because . . ." She stopped.

"You still think it was your fault?"

"Yes, although I know everything you're going to say."

"Then I won't say it. Have you read her book?"

Rose shook her head. "I will, sometime," she said. "I feel I should know what she has to say."

"Do you have a copy?"

"They sent me an early copy. There was a note with it saying she wanted me to see it."

"Can I have a look?"

Rose appeared nervous. "I know from the paper that she's not very nice about you. I'm sorry."

"It's OK," said Frieda. "That's not why I want to see it."

The cover of *An Innocent in Hell* showed a silhouette of a tiny girl with her arms raised in appeal. In the background, there was a lurid red pattern, suspiciously like flames. Frieda opened it. Under the dedication ("To all of you who have suffered, without hope of rescue") was a scrawled message: "To my sister Rose: with forgiveness and understanding, from your little sister Jo-Jo."

"Oh dear," said Frieda.

"It's all right," said Rose. "She means well."

"You think so?"

"I don't know."

"Can I borrow it?"

"Really? You're going to read it?"

"Yes. I'll bring it back as soon as I have."

"I'm in no hurry."

"Good. She's lucky to have you."

Frieda didn't want to read the book in her house. She needed to be somewhere neutral. She thought of taking it to Number 9, but even that felt too close to home. In the end, she did what she had done a few times before: she walked to Great Portland Street and got on the Circle Line, heading east. She knew that to do the entire loop would take about fifty minutes, maybe an hour. It was early on Sunday evening and the train was almost empty. There was a young woman dressed in a pink tutu and a tartan jersey, who got off at King's Cross, and an elderly man who read the Bible, marking passages with a pencil, and stayed on until Liverpool Street. After that, she was alone in her carriage until she reached Monument, when a family got on for a couple of stops. Frieda made notes as she read *An Innocent in Hell,* looking up occasionally as they reached a station to make sure she didn't miss her stop. The train nosed its way under the City — deserted at the weekend, the streets empty and the tall buildings lit up but abandoned — then Westminster and St. James's Park, the rich enclaves of Kensington, and finally she was heading back toward her stop. She closed the book and emerged into the windy night, deep in thought.

## 26

"He made me feel attended to." The woman made a self-deprecating grimace. Although she had been visiting her sister and her family in Spain so recently, her thin face was pale and weary. "Less alone, I suppose you could say. He was a special kind of person."

It was half past seven on Monday morning, and Frieda was sitting in Janet Ferris's kitchen with a cup of tea in front of her. Outside, it was raining and the sky was a leaden gray. Janet Ferris was the practice manager of a nearby GP surgery and had agreed to meet Frieda before work, although she had said she didn't think there was anything else to add to what she had already told Yvette Long about Robert Poole. He had just been a neighbor, she said, a very nice, very kind neighbor, whom she would miss.

The kitchen was small and had old-fashioned floral wallpaper, red tiles, and mismatched chairs round a brightly polished wooden table. Frieda saw that everything was scrupulously clean. There were herbs on the windowsill and a bowl of oranges on the work surface, next to a blue pot of hyacinths whose fragrance filled the room. A charcoal drawing hung on the wall beside the small white-painted dresser. A page cut out from a magazine was stuck to the fridge, with a list of sustainable fish on it. A small transparent bird feeder filled with seeds was attached to the outside of the large window. Frieda had the sense of a self-sufficient, frugal, virtuous life, where everything was in its place. She also took in Janet Ferris's ringless hands, her sad eyes, the worry lines on her face, which was bare of makeup, the sensible clothes that hung off her slim frame, camouflaging her. She had a voice that was soft, low, and very pleasant to listen to.

Frieda nodded to the small tortoiseshell cat curled up on a wicker chair under the window. "Is that his cat?"

"Yes. I thought it was all right for me to keep him. I don't think there was anybody else to look after him."

"What's his name?"

"I don't even know if he had one. Bob used to call him the Mog. So that's what I

298

call him now: Moggie. It didn't seem right to change it."

"How long had Robert Poole lived here?"

"Mr. Michkin would know exactly. About nine months, I think."

"How did you two meet?"

A faint smile twitched her lips. "We nodded at each other a couple of times, coming in and out of the house. And then one Sunday morning — it must have been a couple of weeks after he moved in — he turned up with a great big bowl of early summer strawberries. He said someone had given them to him but he couldn't eat them all, and would I like some?"

"That was nice."

"Yes. I accepted, and then he said that I could only have them on one condition: that I invited him in to share them. It became a bit of a joke between us. Every so often he would turn up with something — cherries, a tin of biscuits, a big wedge of cheese — and say I had to help him eat it. The last time, it was mince pies."

"So he was a friend, not just a neighbor?"

Bright spots appeared on Janet Ferris's cheeks. "I wouldn't say that. It was just occasionally. But it was nice."

"What did you talk about?" Frieda was trying to keep her voice neutral. She sensed that Janet Ferris wanted to talk to someone, let out the shy and dammed-up feelings inside her, but would only do so if she didn't feel pressed.

"I don't know, really. Odd things." Frieda waited. "I used to tell him what I was reading. I read a lot. Victorian novels mostly. Wilkie Collins and Charles Dickens and Mrs. Gaskell."

"Did he read a lot too?"

"I'm not sure. I got the impression he did — but I can't remember him talking about specific books. I think I used to talk more than him. Which is odd, because I'm not much of a talker."

"So, books."

Janet Ferris looked down at her hands, which were thin, with blue veins and smooth, pearly nails. "He was easy to say things to," she said, in a voice that Frieda had to strain to hear. "I once told him I wished I'd had children. That it was my big regret in life. It was when he brought the mince pies over. Just before Christmas. Christmas is a hard time. I have lots of friends and I'm not alone on the day, but it's not the same as for people with families. I told him I'd always wanted children, and once I was with a man and thought we'd have a family together. But it didn't work out, and then it was somehow too late. You know how it is — time slips by. You can't say when you've crossed the line into becoming a childless woman, but one day you realize that's what you are." She looked at Frieda. "Do you have children?"

"No. What did he say, when you told him this?"

"He didn't try to tell me it didn't matter, which is what most people do. He talked about parallel lives. That we're accompanied by other selves, people we might have been, and how painful that can be."

Frieda felt as though something was shifting in her mind, loosening. She had a sense of the dead man, sitting at this table, listening to a lonely middle-aged woman talk of her regrets. "Did you feel he was also talking about himself?" she asked.

"Maybe. I should have asked him. I can't believe he's dead, someone like him. It hasn't sunk in — though sometimes I think about the empty floor above me, the space he used to be in. It doesn't seem real, though."

"He understood loneliness. Do you think he was lonely?"

"Perhaps. Or an outsider."

"Do you know where he was at Christmas?"

"I was in Brighton, with my cousin's family. I think he said he was going away for a day or so — but I don't know. He was here when I got back."

"Did you ever meet his friends?"

"No." She shook her head. "I never saw anyone else go to his flat at all. He went out quite a lot. He was often away for days at a time."

"So you don't know if he had family, close relationships, love affairs?"

"No. He never said and I didn't ask. We didn't have that kind of relationship."

"And you don't know if he was straight or gay?"

"Oh, I'm sure he liked women. He was . . ." She frowned. "I'm sure he liked women," she repeated.

"Why?"

Janet Ferris blushed. "Just the way he was." She lifted her empty mug to hide her confusion. "He was a bit of a flirt — not in a crass way, just to make you feel special."

"Handsome?"

"Not obviously. But he grew on you."

She looked away and Frieda studied her: a clever, kind, and lonely woman who'd been a bit in love with Robert Poole. And Robert Poole had drawn her out, cheered her up, listened to her, made her feel —

what was her expression? — *attended to.*

"Do you know where he was before he lived here?"

"I've no idea. You've made me realize how little I knew about him. I was selfish."

"I don't think so."

"Do you know what?" She stopped, flushing again.

"What?"

"You remind me of him. The way I can say things to you."

"Is that what he was like?"

"Yes. And now he's gone."

Once Janet Ferris had left for work, Frieda had twenty minutes or so before she needed to leave herself, to be in time for her first patient of the week. And so she went upstairs to Robert Poole's first-floor flat. The tape had been removed from the door and there was no sign that any police officers had been there at all. But Yvette Long had told her, very sternly and as if Frieda had already disobeyed her, not to touch or disturb anything, so she simply walked very slowly and quietly from room to room. In the small hall, one coat and one thick jacket hung from a hook and there was a furled black umbrella in the corner. In the living room, there was a green corduroy sofa and matching armchair, a low coffee table, a beige rug, a medium-sized television, a small chest of drawers, in which, Frieda knew from reading the report, the notebook had been found, and an empty newspaper rack. There were no photographs, no knick-knacks or mess. There were a few pictures on the walls. They looked to Frieda like pictures the landlord had bought as a job lot — a photo of the Eiffel Tower at night, a bland and murky Madonna and Child, a pink sun rising or setting over the sea, and Monet's poppy fields. Only one painting, of two bright and almost abstract orange fish, looked as though it might have been Robert Poole's individual choice, not just a tired cliché occupying a bit of wall space. The books, which were arranged on the set of shelves in order of size, not subject, were a bit more revealing: three large illustrated volumes on town gardens, a thick paperback that looked like a builder's manual, *North and South* by Mrs. Gaskell, *Our Mutual Friend* by Charles Dickens, several books about getting fit, a guide to forensic medicine. Frieda stood for several minutes in front of them, frowning.

Then she moved to the kitchen. There was a teapot and a *cafetière* on the work surface; four identical brown mugs hanging from

304

hooks; six matching tumblers and six matching glasses on the shelf; six white plates, six white bowls, oven gloves, and a tea towel by the side of the cooktop. She took the tea towel and used it to open the cupboard. One bag of flour, one of sugar, a packet of muesli and another of cornflakes, a box of mince pies, a jar of instant coffee, English breakfast tea, quick-boil rice. There was nothing in the fridge. It must have been cleared out once the police had finished their search and taken away anything they considered evidence.

In the bedroom, there was a small double bed, neatly made up with a blue duvet and pillowcase, and a single chair near the window. There were cloth slippers under the chair, a striped dressing gown hanging from the door, an open ironing board with the iron, its cord coiled around it, on top. A lamp stood on the bedside table, plus a packet of paracetamol and a book with a garish cover that turned out to be short stories about the Wild West. When Frieda, using her sleeve to cover her hand, pulled open the wardrobe, the long mirror inside it swung past her and she was momentarily startled by her own reflection. There were rows of ironed shirts, plain and patterned, tailored and loose, several pairs of trousers, two jackets, one in sober tweed, the other a macho leather one with studs. On the wardrobe floor were sturdy leather boots, sneakers, brogues. Frieda pursed her lips, then lifted the piles of T-shirts and jerseys that were stacked on the wardrobe's interior shelves.

"Who are you?" she said out loud, shutting the door and going into the bathroom, which was as clean and bare as if it were in a motel: a bath, a washbasin, a toilet, a gray towel, a small round mirror, shaving foam, a razor blade, a green toothbrush, dental floss, a washcloth, nail clippers . . .

Frieda returned to the living room and sat in the armchair. She thought about her own little house on the cobblestoned mews. She was a private person; there were no photographs on display, letters left out, or postcards pinned to a notice board, yet every room was filled with objects that bore witness to her life. The chess table at which she used to sit with her father, long ago in a different world. The cobalt blue bowl from Venice. The painting above the mantelpiece of a tree in spring. Her grandmother's old silk dressing gown, which Frieda never wore but hung in her wardrobe, its faded greens and reds shimmering. The mugs in her kitchen, each one different and picked up on her wanderings round London. The mobile of paper cranes Chloë had made for her. The piece of driftwood, the old maps of London, the battered pans, the necklace Sandy had given her when they were still together in the glory days it hurt her to remember, the books of photographs . . . And then, of course, in her little study in the garret, all the drawings she had done, in soft pencil on thick paper, doodles and more finished pieces that were like a hidden diary of her days. But here, in Robert Poole's flat, there was almost nothing. It wasn't just that there were no clues; apart from the few books, it was a blank, a void, a space that was expressionless and lifeless. Perhaps it was because the man who used to live here was dead so the flat, too, had lost its animating spirit — but Frieda didn't think so. She felt depressed and disturbed just sitting in the room.

Who was Robert Poole? Rob, Robbie, Bob, Bertie: everyone called him by a different name. His clothes were in different styles — a leather jacket, a tweed one; brogues and boots; a gentleman's fitted shirts and casual sweatshirts. Whenever anyone talked of him, they were talking of themselves — the selves he had recognized in them and drawn out of them. He was a listener, an attender, a Good Samaritan. He had taken old Mary Orton's money but he had listened to her stories; to Janet Ferris he had shown neighborly kindness, to Jasmine Shreeve respectful attention. People liked him, yet he seemed to have no friends; people described him as charming and handsome, yet he seemed to have no relationships. And after he had been murdered and left in a grotty alley, he had been collected by Michelle Doyce and sat in her bedsit in Deptford for days, a naked disintegrating corpse, and no one had noticed he was missing.

Frieda looked at her watch. It was time to go. In forty-five minutes' time she would be sitting in her red chair, listening to Joe Franklin, watching him intently, attending to him, drawing him out. She felt a small shiver go through her. It was as if the people on Robert Poole's lists had been his patients, needing his help.

She had lights behind her eyes and a claw in her stomach, sharp and dragging weals of pain through her. Her head was thundering. It wasn't exactly pain; it was more like a painful sound, a boom of dread that rose and fell, came nearer and then receded but only to gather strength again. She needed to think clearly, but how could she do that when her skull was thick with this loud, savage gale? She used to take pills when she felt like this. One large orange capsule with a tumbler of water to wash it down. Her mother had put it in front of her in the morning and stood there until she was sure she had swallowed it. But she didn't have pills anymore; it had been a long time, she couldn't remember how long. All of that was in the fog of the past she had left behind her. He had shown her that drugs were just another way of keeping her tame and docile, muffling her anger, which was righteous and alive. "You need purpose, not pills." And he had laid a hand on her forehead, like a kind doctor or a father soothing his sick child. "And you have me now," he had said. "Always remember that."

But she didn't have him. He hadn't come and she was here alone in this dampness and cramp and cold, the wind outside as bitter as the wind rushing through her head. Thoughts clamoring and jumbled. Hungry, too. Potatoes eaten. Gas all finished. This morning she had stirred a stock cube into cold water, then drunk its salty undissolved granules. It had made her want to gag. Her lip had healed, more or less, but when she looked in the little mirror the puckered scar looked like a sneer. He wouldn't like that. And she thought she was beginning to smell, though she still tried to rub the hard nub of soap into her skin and into her clothes as well, which hung in sodden trails round the cabin. Nothing dried properly.

How long had it been? She took her calendar of trees and held it up to the narrow window, squinting at it. Most of January, and more than half of February, but she seemed to have stopped crossing off the days. Perhaps it was already March. Perhaps spring was coming, yellow daffodils and opening buds, warmth in the sun. She didn't think so. It didn't feel like spring.

But it was too long, even if it was still February. Twenty-eight clear, twenty-nine in each leap year. Was it a leap year? You could ask a man to marry you. But you couldn't ask if he wasn't there. Alone. Alone in a world full of cruel strangers and people with deceiving smiles. What had he said? "I will always return. If I don't come, you'll know that they've got me." Kissing her forehead, brave. She had to be brave, too. She had to continue without him, and do the things he wanted to do. She was the fuse and he had lit her; she was the bomb and he had set her ticking. That was all that was left now.

# 27

In the last two weeks, Joe Franklin had been in a far better state than he had been in for months, even years: he wore jeans and an ironed shirt; his laces weren't trailing; his fingernails were clean and cut; his hair was brushed; his face was freshly shaved. Usually, he sat forward in his chair, hunched over himself, his head held in his hands and often obscured by them, but today he had sat back, his head lolling against the chair rest, like a convalescent who was weak but with the sense of life trickling back into him. He even smiled twice, once when he spoke of licking out a cake bowl when he was little, and once when he told her that a friend was coming round that evening and they were going to eat sea urchins together: "Did you know you could eat sea urchins?" Frieda hadn't known. She noticed the way his face changed and softened when pain ebbed out of it. He looked years younger.

After Joe came Alison, an actress who two years previously, at the age of forty-three, had found herself at the mercy of acute, disabling stage fright. She had been to a hypnotist, then to a healer, then a cognitive therapist, and now she had landed in Frieda's chair, sitting absolutely tense and white knuckled, trying to work out why she was so terrified.

Her final session of the morning was with a middle-aged man called Gordon, who spoke in whispers through his fingers, as if he were ashamed of himself. He was trapped by his own frantic insecurities, by the knots he'd tied himself into, and Frieda's job was slowly, carefully, to go into his world and bring him back out. Sometimes she felt as if she were building a castle one grain of sand at a time.

When it was over, she went and opened her window for a few minutes and leaned out, inhaling the cold damp air, letting the wind blow through her. There was still no work on the building site, but she saw that some kids had made a den out of the planks they'd collected, and as she watched, three young boys ran across to it and inserted themselves through an opening in the wonky structure. She remembered that it was half-term: Chloë had told her very firmly that they were having no chemistry lessons this week; she was on holiday.

She closed the window again and wrote her notes on the last session, but before she had finished, the phone rang. It was Josef. "Where are you?" she said.

"With the woman," he said. "Mrs. Orton. Doing the house. Fixing here and there."

"Is she all right?"

"Can you come?"

"Is there a problem?"

Josef replied, but the line was bad or he was speaking so quietly Frieda couldn't make out what he was saying.

"Can you speak louder?" she said. "I can't hear what you're saying."

"Better if you come," said Josef. "You can come now?"

"Is something wrong?"

"You can come now?"

Frieda gave up. "Yes," she said. "I can come now."

The door was opened by a man Frieda didn't recognize. He was in his fifties, with thinning short gray hair, and was dressed in gray corduroy trousers and a checked shirt. He looked at her with a frown.

"I'm Robin Orton," he said, and led her through. In the kitchen, Mary was sitting at

313

the table with another man. He was also casually dressed, with black jeans and a navy blue sweater zipped up to the neck. Slightly older, slightly bulkier, slightly balder. To Frieda it looked like dress-down day at an office where the employees would have been happier in their normal suits. "This is my brother, Jeremy," said Robin.

"Please, sit down," said Jeremy.

Frieda sat at the table, now feeling as though she'd arrived at an unexpected job interview.

"Hello, Frieda," said Mary Orton, with a nervous smile. "I've just made some coffee. Would you like some?"

Frieda nodded, and the old woman filled a cup, put it on a saucer, and placed it in front of her.

"And some cake as well? I remember how much you liked it."

"Yes, that'd be lovely," said Frieda. "A small piece. A bit smaller than that." She took a sip of cool coffee, conscious that she was being scrutinized by three pairs of eyes. "Josef Morozov asked me to come," she said.

Jeremy folded his arms. He was evidently the elder brother, the one in charge. "Yes, we talked to him. I'm sorry. Can we go back to basics? Can you explain to us exactly what your involvement with our mother is?"

Frieda paused. That was a surprisingly difficult question. "A man who was working for your mother has been murdered." She looked at Mary Orton. She felt awkward talking about her as if she weren't present. "I was involved in interviewing Mrs. Orton."

"Mary, please," said Mary Orton.

"Are you a police officer?" asked Jeremy.

"No. I'm doing some work with them. As a sort of consultant."

"Do you have some identification?"

"Identifying me as what?"

"As officially working with the police."

Frieda spoke as calmly as she could. "No, I don't. If you have any questions, I can give you a number to call. As it happens, I'm here only because Josef rang me. I assumed there was some sort of problem."

"There's all sorts of problems," said Jeremy. "We'll get on to that. But, first, this man Josef, he's here on your recommendation. Is that right?"

"That's right."

"Is this an official service as part of your police work?"

Frieda frowned. "No," she said. "Your mother had water leaking through the roof. Josef's a friend of mine. He's good and he's trustworthy. If you have a problem with him being here, just tell me or him."

The brothers exchanged looks. Robin had been standing to one side. Now he came across and sat at the table. Suddenly Frieda felt surrounded.

"We've been having a family conference," Robin said. "We're not happy about what's been happening with our mother."

"Hang on." Frieda put down her coffee cup. "I was phoned by Josef. Where is he?"

"He's up in the loft," said Jeremy. "You can go and see him if you want."

"I'll see him in a minute," said Frieda. "But if you've got some problem with him being here, just let us know. As far as I'm concerned, he's doing Mary a favor. If you don't see it that way, say so and we'll go."

"I wasn't saying that."

"Why did he ring me?"

"Well, when I arrived I was surprised to find him here. I asked him about his plans, about costs and estimates. I should tell you, Miss Klein, that I'm a company accountant and I know about this sort of thing."

"When Josef first came here, water was coming through the roof," said Frieda. "You should be grateful that your mother was able to get someone so quickly."

"This is really a side issue," said Jeremy.

"When I found this man here, what I really wanted to know was who had arranged it and in general what's been going on with my mother."

"And what's your view," asked Frieda, "about what's been going on?"

"It's a bloody disgrace," said Jeremy. "I come down from time to time to go through my mother's affairs, to help her with her accounts."

Frieda looked at the photographs on the dresser. She remembered Mary Orton talking about her grandchildren, about how the photographs were old, how the children would be more grown-up now. "When did you last go through your mother's accounts?" she asked.

"Some time ago," said Jeremy. "Six months. Before the summer holidays, I think. I live in Manchester. Robin's in Cardiff. We've both got families. We come when we can."

"So, last July?" She looked at him. "Seven months ago."

"Yes. Or June, maybe. But that's not the point. The point is that my mother has been the victim of a crime and I want to establish whether it's being properly investigated."

"What crime are you talking about?" asked Frieda.

The two brothers glanced at each other again.

"Are you kidding?" said Robin. "This man Robert Poole stole more than a hundred and fifty thousand pounds from her. He also faked the work he was doing."

Frieda looked at their mother. She was reminded of sitting with Michelle Doyce, of her case being discussed as if she weren't there. "I'm not sure that this is the time or the place to be discussing this," she said.

"What do you mean?" Jeremy's voice rose slightly. "We've discovered a theft. You're from the police. We want to know what's being done about it."

"I'm not the person you want," said Frieda. "You need to talk to the police directly."

"Then what are you doing here?" said Jeremy.

"I'm here because I was asked to come."

"My mother said you were the person she talked to, that you were the person who went through her accounts and found out about the theft. What's your involvement?"

"My involvement is that I help out when I can in certain areas of my expertise."

"Which are?"

"I'm a psychotherapist."

Jeremy looked incredulous. "A psychotherapist?"

"Yes."

"Who recommends builders?"

Frieda took another deep breath. She addressed her reply to Mary. "I recommended Josef. If there's been any problem with his work or with him, please just tell me."

"Oh, no, no," said Mary Orton. "He's been awfully good. I like having him in the house. He's been telling me about his family back in Ukraine. He's having a difficult time, poor man."

"Of course," said Robin, "she hasn't exactly been up in the attic checking his work."

"You can go up to the attic," said Frieda. "And if you've any complaints, just tell me about them."

"We'll be checking," said Jeremy.

"Did you ever meet Robert Poole?" asked Frieda.

"No," said Jeremy. "I told you we haven't been down here since before last summer."

"No," said Frieda. "You said you hadn't checked her accounts since then. I thought you might have brought the children for the occasional weekend, half-term in London, something like that."

"We live a long way from London."

"What about you?" Frieda asked Robin.

"I've been occupied." Robin's face had turned red.

"And Christmas?" Frieda said softly. "What happened at Christmas?"

"They have very busy Christmases," Mary Orton said hastily. "Jeremy always goes skiing, don't you, dear? And Robin . . ." Her voice trailed away. She picked at the cuff of her jersey.

There was a small silence. Frieda turned back to the brothers. "So you never happened to bump into him?"

"No."

"Did you know the work was going on?"

"Why should we?"

Frieda gave a little shrug. "I just thought that if your mother was having major building work done, you might have talked about it on the phone."

"Well, we didn't," said Jeremy. "I can tell you that if we had, we'd have both been down here to make sure it was being done properly."

"I'm sure I mentioned it," said Mary Orton, faintly.

"No, you didn't, Ma," said Robin.

Frieda turned to her. "When we talked before, you said your husband died a long time ago. How long have you lived alone?"

"Dad died five years ago," said Jeremy.

"He's over there on the sideboard." He smiled at Frieda's puzzled expression. "In that wooden thing. The thing that looks like a coffee pot. Funny thing to have in the kitchen."

"I talk to him sometimes," said Mary Orton.

"You want to watch what you say with her around." Robin gestured at Frieda. "She may not approve of an old woman talking to a box of ashes."

"Why wouldn't I approve?"

"It probably doesn't give good financial advice either," said Jeremy. "On the subject of which, how are the police dealing with this robbery?"

"You do understand that this is a murder inquiry?" said Frieda.

"And you'll understand," answered Jeremy, "that we're a little more concerned about the small matter of robbery. What we want to hear from you is when our mother will be getting her money back."

Frieda was tempted to tell the two brothers that all the money was gone from Robert Poole's account, and that Robert Poole was a stolen identity, and that it wasn't necessarily certain that their money had been taken anyway. But she stopped herself. "I'm afraid I can't talk about what's happening with the inquiry. I don't know the details myself. You'll have to approach the officer in charge." She felt grim amusement at the idea of Karlsson having to deal with the brothers Orton.

"You don't sound very sympathetic," said Jeremy.

"I'm doing what I can," said Frieda. "This is not a competition, but at least I helped to stop the water coming through the roof."

"What do you think it's like to find that your mother is being cheated of her life savings?" Jeremy actually jabbed his finger at her as he spoke.

"Well . . ."

"It wasn't a real question," he continued. "I have to say that it doesn't feel to me as if you're treating this like a real crime."

"I'm not a detective," said Frieda.

"You seem to be behaving like one. You seem pretty calm about this man taking our mother's money."

"It's not really my —"

"And," he interrupted, his color rising, "that's not all he was doing. Was it, Ma?"

"What do you mean?"

"Please," said Mary Orton. "Please don't."

"He was also trying to get her to change her will, to leave a third of everything to him."

"What?"

"No, Jeremy," said Mary Orton. "I didn't . . . I couldn't . . ." She had gone very red. Tears were running from the corners of her eyes.

"That's all right, Ma." Jeremy patted her hand as if she were an old dog. "It wasn't your fault. The man was controlling you. You didn't know what you were doing."

"Mary," said Frieda, "are you comfortable talking about this?" Mary Orton nodded but didn't speak. Frieda looked at Jeremy. "Please explain. About the will."

"I told you. I was going through Ma's papers. I found letters from a solicitor. They were about drafting a new will. Ma has the house and her portfolio, so it was quite a big deal. Fortunately, she saw the light."

"Mary changed her mind?"

"No," said Jeremy. "The solicitor didn't go through with it. Raised objections. She probably smelled a rat. I wish someone had done that a bit earlier. Now, getting a poor old woman to change a will in favor of someone she barely knows, is that a crime?"

"I don't know," said Frieda. "Have you met her?"

"I read the letters. And I asked Ma about her. She was taken advantage of."

Frieda wanted to say, "Your mother is in

the room." Jeremy Orton was treating the old woman as if she were slightly stupid and didn't understand English properly. But pointing this out would only humiliate her even more. "Can I see the letters?" she asked instead.

She was addressing Mary Orton, but Jeremy nodded at his brother, who took a file from his bag and handed it across to Frieda. She opened it and flicked through the official-looking letters. One was an invoice. She felt someone close to her: Robin was reading the letter over her shoulder.

"Three hundred pounds," he said. "Three hundred pounds for not doing a will. I wonder what they'd charge for actually doing it."

Frieda saw the name at the bottom of the letter. Tessa Welles. She wrote it down and the address. "It sounds like a bargain," she said.

"I know what you mean," agreed Robin. "At least someone was looking out for my mother."

"Have you only just discovered this?"

"What do you mean?"

"Did neither of you know about the will before?"

"No," said Jeremy.

"No," agreed Robin, adding, "Of course not."

The kitchen door opened and Josef came in. He seemed tired, but he smiled when he saw Frieda. "I did not know," he said.

"I was about to come up."

"So, what have you been doing?" said Jeremy.

"The roof is fixed," said Josef. "Not fixed, proper fixed, just a patch to stop the water."

"Did you give my mother an estimate for the work in advance?"

Josef gazed at Jeremy with a puzzled expression.

"Come to that," Jeremy continued, "I'm not sure what you're doing commissioning work in my mother's house."

"There was a hole in the roof," said Frieda, "and you were in Manchester."

"Oh, I see." Jeremy's tone turned harsher. "You mean that you and this man were looking after my mother and I wasn't?"

"Please, Jeremy," said Mary. "They were just —"

"It doesn't matter," he said. "What would you feel like, if someone did that to your mother?"

"What *did* you feel like?" said Frieda.

"What do you think?"

"I am sorry," said Josef. "I am finished."

"Actually," said Mary, "there are some other things I hoped you could look at. The boiler's making a funny noise and there's a window upstairs that won't shut properly."

Josef glanced warily at Robin and Jeremy.

"Don't ask me," said Jeremy. "It's not my house."

"I'll show you."

Mary and Josef left the kitchen together, and Frieda looked down at her notebook, at the solicitor's address. "Princes Road. Is that nearby?"

"It's just round the corner," said Robin. "Poole just took Ma up the road to the nearest person he could find. It must have seemed so simple."

"Can I use your phone?" said Frieda.

"Don't you have a mobile?"

"Not with me."

Robin waved her toward the phone in a holster on the wall.

It took several calls and repeated explanations, then Frieda sat for forty minutes of mostly uncomfortable silence before Yvette arrived in a car and picked her up. She didn't seem happy to see Frieda. "You need to tell us," she said, "if you're going to talk to witnesses."

"I wasn't exactly talking to witnesses,"

said Frieda. "Josef is working on Mary Orton's house and he rang me because there was a problem with her sons. I didn't think it had anything to do with the case."

Yvette was sitting in the passenger seat and Frieda was in the back. She felt like a child being driven somewhere by two disapproving adults.

"You can't just act on your own," said Yvette.

Frieda didn't respond. The car pulled up outside a line of shops. "Should I come with you?" she asked.

"If you want," said Yvette, shrugging.

The two women got out of the car. The location of Tessa Welles's office wasn't immediately obvious. Number fifty-two was a shop selling tiles and vases, jugs and coffee cups. Number fifty-two B was a small green door to the left. Long rang the doorbell and they were buzzed inside. The two of them walked up the narrow stairs. At the top, there was an anteroom with a desk, a computer, neatly stacked piles of papers, and a chair. Beyond it, a door swung open and a woman stepped out. Frieda guessed she was in her late thirties, with thick, reddish-blonde hair, long and tied loosely back, as if to keep it out of her way, and a pale face that was bare of makeup, with faded freckles over the bridge of the nose. Her eyes were gray-blue and shrewd, and she was dressed in a charcoal gray shift dress, thick, patterned tights, and ankle boots. She gave a slightly harassed smile. "I'm Tessa Welles," she said. "Won't you come through? I've just made a pot of coffee, if you'd like some."

She took them into a much messier main office, with a window overlooking the street. Files were piled on her desk and shelves held other box files, legal books. There were certificates on the wall and photographs: Tessa Welles in a group of people at a restaurant, Tessa Welles on a beach somewhere, Tessa Welles on a bike among a group of cyclists with mountains in the background. There were also two paintings that Frieda wouldn't have minded on her own walls at home. Tessa poured them coffee and Yvette introduced herself, then Frieda as a "civilian assistant."

"Do you work alone?" said Yvette, sipping her coffee.

"I've got an assistant, Jenny, who comes in half-time. She's not here today."

"Mrs. Welles," said Yvette.

"Ms."

"Sorry. Ms. In mid-November, you met a woman called Mary Orton and a man called

Robert Poole. It was about drawing up a will for her. Do you remember?"

Tessa gave a very faint smile. "Yes, I remember."

"I'm sorry," said Yvette. "Is something funny?"

"No," said Tessa. "It's not really funny. But is this about some kind of fraud?"

"Why do you say that?"

"I don't know. What I mainly remember is that that man made me uncomfortable. He seemed like a bit of a chancer. What's happened? Is this a fraud inquiry?"

"No, it's a murder inquiry," said Yvette. "Somebody killed him."

Tessa's expression changed to one of shock. "Oh, my God. I'm sorry, I had no idea. I —"

"A chancer, you said."

"No, no." Tessa made a gesture of repudiation. "I didn't mean to be nasty. I don't know anything about him."

"What did you mean?"

Tessa took a deep breath. "When someone alters a will in favor of a beneficiary who is not a family member, it always rings an alarm bell."

"What did you say?"

Tessa frowned with the effort of recollection. "I think I just talked it through with them . . . well, with the woman in particular. I asked for her reasons in making the change, why now, whether she had thought it over, discussed it with her family, and so on."

"And what did Mrs. Orton say?"

"I can't remember exactly," said Tessa. "I got the impression that she felt abandoned by her family. I think this man had taken their place."

"What was Poole saying during the meeting?"

"Not much. He was like an attentive son, in the background, supportive."

"So what was the problem?" said Frieda.

Yvette frowned at her.

"What?" Tessa seemed puzzled.

"You're a solicitor," said Frieda. "If someone wants to change a will and comes to you, isn't your job just to draw it up for them?"

Tessa smiled, then looked thoughtful. "I'm a family solicitor," she said. "I do conveyancing, wills, and divorces. Buying houses and getting married and dying. I remember being told when I was a student that if you like law as a kind of theater you should become a barrister. But if you want to discover people's secrets, their deepest feelings and passions, you should become a solicitor."

"Or a psychotherapist," said Yvette.

"No," said Tessa. "I can really help people."

Yvette glanced at Frieda with a secret smile. Tessa noticed it. "Oh, God, you're not . . ." she began.

"Yes, she is," said Yvette.

"Sorry, it was a cheap thing to say. I didn't mean anything."

"That's all right," said Frieda. "You were talking about helping people."

"Yes. I see couples who are divorcing, and sometimes they talk to me in a way they can't talk to anyone else. Not even each other."

"So why didn't you just draw up the will for Mary Orton?" said Frieda.

"I don't 'just do' things for people," said Tessa. "I always talk to them and find out what it is that they really need."

"And what did Mary Orton really need?" asked Frieda.

"She was lonely, that was clear, and in need of support. I suppose what she really needed was her family. And I suspected that this man had come into the vacuum and was taking advantage of her."

"Why didn't you call the police?"

"She didn't call the police," said Yvette,

331

"because changing your will is not a crime."

"Yes, that's right," said Tessa. "I tried to talk to Mrs. Orton about why she wanted to do this. She seemed to find it embarrassing, distressing, even. I felt sorry for her."

"What did Robert Poole say?" asked Yvette.

"He said it wasn't his idea, that it was something Mrs. Orton wanted to do, and that it was important to her."

"He had a bloody nerve," said Yvette, abruptly, then bit her lower lip. "What else did you say?" she asked more calmly.

"I told Mrs. Orton that she was taking a large step and that it was something she ought to think about. I probably also said that if she left everything away from her family, then the will might be subject to legal challenge."

"And?"

"That was all," said Tessa. "They left, and I didn't hear anything more."

"Were you shocked?" said Yvette.

Tessa pulled a face and shook her head. "I used to be. The first few years of hearing what husbands say about wives and wives say about husbands and what people do to their own families, I lost every illusion I had. Sometimes I feel like I'm faced with huge, dangerous engines that are falling apart, and all I can do is put little pieces of sticky tape on them and hope they hold for a while."

"What did you make of Robert Poole?" asked Yvette.

"I told you. Although he was very polite, and Mary Orton obviously trusted him, I felt there was something wrong about him. I did what I could but, of course, I knew it was possible he'd find someone else to do the will, or even that they'd just draw it up between themselves and find a stray witness. There's a limit to what you can do for people."

"What did you think when you heard he'd been killed?"

"I don't know what you mean," said Tessa. "I'm shocked, of course. I can't believe it."

"Why do you think it happened?"

"God, I don't know. I don't know anything about his life."

"But you saw him in action," Yvette said. "What if he did something like that to the wrong person?"

"Maybe," said Tessa. "But I had one brief encounter with him and then I forgot all about him until now. I can't throw any light on his murder, if that's what you're looking for. What did Mary Orton's family think?"

"They weren't pleased," said Frieda. "They weren't pleased at all."

"I'm not surprised."

"Most people seem to have found him charming," said Frieda. "Were you charmed by him?"

Tessa gave another faint smile. "No. I probably met him in the wrong context to be charmed by him."

Yvette stood up. "Thank you, Ms. Welles," she said. "I think that's everything for the time being."

Frieda remained seated. "I want to ask Ms. Welles something," she said. "It's nothing to do with the inquiry. Is it all right if I join you outside?" Yvette glared at Frieda, who added mildly, "I'll only be a minute."

Yvette turned and walked out. Frieda heard her thumping down the stairs. Tessa looked at her with concern. "Is everything OK?"

"A bit of friction. I've only just been appointed."

"Appointed to what?"

"That's a good question. But I wanted to ask you something completely different. I was interested when you talked about the way you worked. About knowing people's secrets and counseling them . . ."

"I didn't exactly say 'counseling.' "

"Well, anyway, my sister-in-law is on very bad terms with her exhusband, my brother, and she needs to get some advice about dealing with the situation."

Tessa leaned back in her chair and crossed her arms. "Whose side are you on in this dispute?"

"I'm not sure I'm exactly taking sides," said Frieda. "But if I were in a balloon with both of them and I had to throw one of them out, it would be my brother."

Tessa smiled. "I've got a brother. I think I know what you mean."

"But is this the sort of thing you do?"

"It's exactly the sort of thing I do."

"No favors," said Frieda. "We'd pay, just like any other client, but you could talk to her?"

"I could talk to her."

Back on the pavement, Frieda found Yvette and the other officer leaning on the car in conversation. Yvette looked round at Frieda, who could almost feel hostility steaming off her. "You did well," she said, through gritted teeth. "But leave the detective work to us, OK?"

# 28

"I know what you're thinking."

"What's that?"

"You're thinking he must have had some ulterior motive, right?"

"What makes you say so?"

"Look, I'm no fool. I know what I look like to you — an aging has-been, with a string of failed relationships behind me, now alone, surrounded by mementos of her not-so-glorious past. I can see myself through your eyes: my dyed hair, my pathetic attempts to hold on to my youth. Am I right?"

"No, you're not right."

"What, then?"

"Try: a successful woman, who's managed to hold her own in a difficult profession, and who's hung on to her dignity and self-respect."

Jasmine Shreeve's face softened. She sat down opposite Frieda and leaned forward. "Sorry. I get defensive."

"That's all right."

"Do you really think that?"

"I don't know enough about your life, but it's another way of looking at it."

"So you don't just assume that Robbie was out to exploit me?"

"He seems to have specialized in inserting himself into vulnerable people's lives," said Frieda, thinking of Mary Orton as she'd last seen her — a small, shrunken figure with her two tall sons on either side.

"So you do think I'm vulnerable."

"We're all vulnerable, in one way or another. Poole seems to have had a knack for finding people's weak points."

"Well, he was kind to me. He seemed to like me." Frieda didn't say anything, and Jasmine Shreeve stiffened again. "You people think there always has to be something under the surface. That there are meanings beneath the meanings we give things. I say he liked me and I can see your eyes gleam. Every word becomes dangerous."

"Are you angry with therapists because your own therapy didn't help you?"

"What?"

"Perhaps you feel that we promise answers and only give more questions."

"How did you know I had therapy? Who's

been talking about me?"

Jasmine Shreeve seemed not just angry, but properly scared. Her voice quivered, and she put one hand up to her face in a self-protective gesture that Frieda was familiar with from her patients.

"Nobody's been talking about you. It just seemed likely."

"What have I said? I've said nothing! What else do you know? Go on. Tell me. Don't just sit there staring at me like that, as if you can see inside me."

Frieda sat back and paused. "Did the therapy help with your drinking?"

"Not really. I . . ." Jasmine stopped. "Did you read about it in some vicious blog and store it up to use against me? That's bloody contemptible."

Frieda looked at her curiously. "Do you really think I would do something like that to you?"

"It would be a way of getting power over me. How else would you know?"

Frieda thought about that. How did she know? "I just felt it." She looked around. "You're surrounded by so many things, everything you've collected through your life." She gestured at the open-plan room. "These little bowls, photographs in frames, china figurines, that little chest open to

338

show its contents. Everything's on view. But there are no wine glasses, no decanters, no bottles. And it's nearly seven o'clock in the evening and you offered me tea, not a drink. So . . ."

Jasmine covered her face with her hands. Her voice was raw with emotion. "I let you into my house and talk to you openly and all the time you're spying."

"Do you want to tell me about it?"

She raised her face. Her mascara had smudged. She looked older and at the same time more childlike. "You're right. Everything you said. I did something terrible."

"What?"

"I assaulted someone in a shop, a shop assistant, a young woman. Isn't that awful? And pathetic? I was drunk and she was being a bitch. At least, that was what I thought at the time." She stopped. She seemed to have difficulty in getting the words out. "I was . . ." Her face was flushed with shame. "They had me committed for a while. For my own safety. And then I booked into a clinic and dried out. I haven't touched a drop since."

"That's good."

"I was so ashamed of myself."

"Jasmine, why is it so very terrible?"

"What do you mean?"

339

"You had an addiction. You overcame it. Why are you so scared that people will find out?"

"For a start, it would be the end of my career. What's left of it."

"Really? Aren't there lots of people who make a living out of their stories of disgrace and redemption?"

"That's different."

"Why?"

"I was a cozy, flirty, wholesome presenter trying to make people's lives a little bit better. If people knew I was actually an old soak who'd ended up in the bin, screaming and attacking people, how do you think they'd react?"

"I don't know. But I can see it's become an area of dread for you. The dread doesn't shrink, but gets bigger and darker. Maybe it's the secrecy that's the problem."

"That's easy for you to say. I can't risk it."

"Is that what Robert Poole said? That you shouldn't risk it?"

"How do you *know* these things?"

"Because you talked to him the way you talk to me," said Frieda. "So Poole understood you had a secret?"

"He said that nobody must find out. That I could be ruined. He was very sympathetic. He said I could always talk to him about it, though." Jasmine stopped and looked at Frieda. "But you think he was wrong?"

"I think giving advice is always complicated. But perhaps you should consider the power this part of your life has over you."

"You're a therapist," said Jasmine. "Don't you believe that a problem shared is a problem halved?"

"Maybe. And maybe if you share a problem with one person, you're giving that person control over you."

Back at home, Frieda found an e-mail from Tessa Welles. She couldn't schedule a meeting for the next couple of weeks, but she was going to the theater in Islington the following evening and could call in to see Olivia beforehand, around six o'clock. Would that be possible? Frieda rang Olivia, who said it wasn't just possible, it was essential, the sooner the better, or she'd be going round to David's house with a knife. She sent a reply to Tessa, copying it to Olivia, and gave Tessa Olivia's landline and mobile numbers.

There was also a message on her phone from Karlsson, asking her to ring. When she got through to him, he said simply, "There's nothing."

"Nothing?"

"Your favor, remember?"

"Oh. You mean about Alan Dekker."

"Yes."

"But you're with someone and can't talk."

"Yes."

"Because you've stuck your neck out for me."

"Right."

"I'm grateful. So he really has disappeared, like Carrie says."

"It seems so."

"Don't you find that odd?"

"This is as far as I'm going, Frieda."

She put the phone down and went up to her study in the garret, where, from the skylight, she could see the lights of London flickering in the February dark. She sat at her desk and made doodles on her sketch pad with her soft lead pencil. She was thinking about Robert Poole, and the light touch with which he had picked people's secrets from their souls. She was also thinking about what she had said to Jasmine about the insidious power of secrets. You hypocrite, she told herself, hatching in her drawing.

When she finally went downstairs again she found another e-mail on her computer, from Sandy. She sat for a long while and then clicked it open.

I was with someone for a while and now I'm not, because she wasn't you. Please, Frieda, talk to me.

# 29

"Think of it as a day out."

Yvette was driving and Karlsson was sitting beside her. They had left London early that morning, just as it got light, but had got snarled up on the North Circular and were only now on the M1, heading north. It was cold and blustery, and the lowering sky threatened rain.

"A long day," said Yvette, but she didn't really mind. She was glad to be spending all these hours alone with Karlsson, and also slightly self-conscious and nervous. "Manchester and then Cardiff. Eight hours' driving, if we're lucky with the traffic."

"We'll get a pub lunch," said Karlsson. "I thought it was better to see the Orton brothers on the same day. Get a sense of them."

"What do you know already?"

"Let's see. The older one, Jeremy — he's in his mid-fifties — is a company accountant for a large pharmaceutical firm. Must be wealthy. Married, with two daughters. He lives in Didsbury and he doesn't see much of his mother. Once or twice a year, for a day or so. Frieda took against him."

"But she takes against lots of people."

Karlsson glanced at her. "She's got an instinct," he said. "We've enough people following procedure."

Yvette just stared at the road; rain was starting to fall. People like me, boring and awkward and plodding, she wanted to say, but didn't. "What about the younger brother?" she asked instead.

"Robin. He's had a more checkered career and personal life. He ran a small company. Garden landscaping, it says here."

"Ponds?"

"I guess so. That went belly-up in the nineties, and since then he's done all sorts. Now he's a business consultant, whatever that means. He's got a son by his first marriage and another, much younger son by his second. Lives near the bay in Cardiff."

"And did Frieda take against him as well?" asked Yvette.

"He doesn't see much of his old mother either. But Frieda thought he was the weaker of the two. Not such a bully."

When they reached the M6 they stopped for coffee and petrol, and by eleven o'clock the satnav was directing them through the more prosperous suburbs of Manchester. Jeremy and Virginia Orton lived in a large detached house in Didsbury, set back from the tree-lined road, with a gravel driveway and two cars parked at the front of the house, a BMW and a Golf. There was smoke coming from the chimney and, sure enough, when Virginia opened the door and led them to the living room, a fire was burning in the grate.

To Karlsson, the dark furniture, the silver tray on which coffee was served, and the silver-framed photographs of the children in their uniforms that were displayed on top of the baby grand seemed like something from another age.

Virginia Orton was a tiny woman, with a brittle manner and a head of tight, burnished curls. But Jeremy was large: not fat, but tall and solid like a rugby player, a center, with broad shoulders, a large, balding head, big hands and feet. He was wearing a lilac shirt under his jacket and a shiny watch. His gray, slightly protuberant eyes watched them suspiciously.

"I expected you half an hour ago," he said.

"Traffic," said Karlsson. "I'm sorry to have kept you waiting."

"Thanks." Jeremy nodded to his wife in

346

dismissal, and she left the room with a click of heels over bare boards. "What's this about?"

"As you know, I'm leading the murder investigation."

"Yes, yes. But why are you here? I don't see what *I*'ve got to do with any of it. Apart from being fleeced by him, of course."

"We'll take as little of your time as we can. But I thought it was your mother who had been fleeced by Mr. Poole, not you."

"Terrible. An old woman cheated like that."

"But you never met him?"

"Of course not. I'd have seen through him if I had."

"Or even heard of him?"

"No."

"Did she tell you she was having work done on the house?"

"If she had, I'd have told her to get quotes. I know about these cowboys. What about the other men he was working with? Can't you get hold of them?"

"We've tried, of course. There's absolutely no record of them. We've no names, no contact numbers, nothing."

"They were probably Poles."

"Did you know her roof was leaking?" asked Yvette.

"I don't know, I can't remember. What's the point of all of this? He conned her, he's dead, she's had a lucky escape."

"So," said Karlsson, "you had no idea she was having her house repaired?"

"Well, she wasn't, was she? It was a way of getting at our money."

"Her money."

"Our money, her money. We're a family."

"You didn't know about the repairs, and you never met Mr. Poole, correct?"

"Correct." Jeremy Orton looked at his watch.

"Because you hadn't been to visit your mother since the summer?" put in Yvette. Karlsson looked at her warningly.

"That *therapist*" — he said the word with distaste — "has already been on about that to me and Robin. I know what she was trying to say. We're busy people. We do what we can."

"So you had no idea that she wanted to change her will?"

"She didn't want to. She was under this man's influence and in a confused state."

"A will that would have given a third of her estate to him."

"No. I didn't know. I've had words with Ma. She won't be so stupid again."

"We're going to need you to inform us of

your movements during the last week of January," said Yvette.

"I beg your pardon?"

"Just for the record. Can you please let us know where you were during the last ten days of January?"

Jeremy Orton stared at her and then at Karlsson, his face turning crimson. "Are you serious?"

"And any witnesses who can corroborate what you say would be useful, so that we can check them."

"You can't seriously suspect me of having anything to do with this."

"We're just establishing the limits of our inquiry, that's all."

Jeremy Orton rose from his chair. "Virginia!" he barked. "Bring me my diary, will you?"

Four and a half hours later, Karlsson and Yvette were in Cardiff. Robin Orton's house had a view of the sea, but it was more modest than Jeremy's. His car was parked on the road outside. His wife was at work. Tea came in mugs, not cups. There was no grand piano, although there were photographs of his children on the wall.

Robin Orton was smaller than his brother. Karlsson thought he looked like a man who had lost a large amount of weight in a short time: the skin was slack on his face, and his trousers were loose, held up by a black leather belt.

They went through the same questions, and he gave the same answers, more or less. No, he had never met Robert Poole. No, he had not known about the repairs to the house. No, he had been unaware about the change in the will — but if you were to ask his opinion, it was a complete disgrace that people like this man Poole could go about worming their way into old women's houses. No, he hadn't seen his mother very recently. What business was that of theirs? It wasn't as if Mary Orton made much effort to come to Cardiff to see him and, anyway, she'd always been more interested in Jeremy than in him — and if they really wanted to know what he thought, then he thought that some of that money she'd handed over so casually to whatever rogue came knocking at the door could much more usefully have been given to him to help him with his new business. Old people should be more generous — it wasn't as if his mother really needed anything for herself. As for that last week of January, as a matter of fact he had been in bed for most of it with a particularly nasty bout of flu. They could ask his wife —

though she might call it a cold, but that was women for you. And they could see themselves out and remember to shut the door firmly.

"Horrible, horrible, horrible men," said Yvette.

"Yes, but what do you really think?"

They were heading back to London, along the M4, and the rain was now falling steadily from a sodden sky.

"I wish they'd killed him together," she said, "and could be put away for a long time. Their poor bloody mother."

"Does that mean you think they didn't?"

"We have to check what they were doing that week, of course, and go back to Mary Orton to confirm they haven't visited her. But unfortunately I'd bet they hadn't been to see her since the summer. Because they were so *busy.*"

"So," Karlsson said, "they have a motive, but it's a motive that comes too late."

"I need a shower."

"I need a drink." He hesitated. "Do you want one too?"

"Yes!" she said, then tried to mute her enthusiasm. "I guess."

"On one condition."

"What's that?"

"That you don't slag off Frieda." She started to protest, but Karlsson interrupted her. "You two need to work together."

She couldn't remember. She couldn't remember what spring felt like, or summer, or even bright golden autumn, which had always been her favorite season. She could only remember winter, because that was what she was in — frozen into an unchanging coldness. The trees all bare, the ground churned into icy ripples of mud, the grass beaten down, the river brown and slow and sad, the drip-drip-drip of water from the ceiling, the waxiness of her fingers when she woke in the morning, and the spider webs of frost on the little windows that she had to scrape away with her fingernails, which were breaking. One of her teeth was coming loose, as if her gums had softened.

She couldn't remember everything he had said to her. What he had told her to do. They were inside her, his words, but she couldn't find them. She rummaged in the drawers of her mind and found odd things, rags of memory. She didn't need them anymore.

Life had narrowed to this boat, this moment. But she couldn't remember why.

# 30

At half past two on the same day, acting on a feeling that had been growing in her all morning, Frieda returned to Greenwich, to the Wyatts'. She didn't tell Karlsson and neither did she call in advance, even though she knew it was likely that nobody would be there. But when she arrived at their apartment, she saw Aisling through the large downstairs window, sitting at the piano and playing. Even from where she stood, among the spring bulbs and the copper pots carefully planted with herbs, Frieda could tell that her hands moved fluently over the keys. She also saw that her posture was tense. She walked to the front door, rang the bell, and the distant piano music stopped. After a few seconds, the door opened.

"Yes?"

"I'm sorry to arrive unannounced," said Frieda. "We've met before."

"Yes, I remember."

Aisling looked uncertain. Her thin face was strained, and there were small lines around her mouth that Frieda hadn't noticed before. "The children will come back from school soon," she said. But she stood aside and Frieda walked into the wide, clean spaces of the apartment, which felt to her like a showroom rather than a home. It was hard to believe the Wyatts had children, and she wondered how many hours a day the cleaner came. Her feet slid on the polished wood. On the low glass table, bright satsumas were arranged in a pyramid within a carved wooden bowl.

"Can I get you something? Tea, coffee, anything herbal?"

"I'm fine," said Frieda, sinking into the soft sofa. She disliked furniture that swaddled her. She liked to sit upright.

"So. Do you have anything you want to ask? Frank isn't here, of course."

"That's why I came. I assumed he'd be at work and your children would be at school."

"I don't understand."

"I wanted to talk about your affair with Robert Poole."

"How dare you?" She sprang to her feet and stood in front of Frieda, thin and straight, quivering with distressed rage. "How *dare* you?"

"Someone killed him, Aisling. It might be relevant."

"Get out of here."

"All right." Frieda stood and picked up her coat from the arm of the sofa, feeling in its pocket. "But if you want to tell me about it, here's my card." She hesitated, then added, "I'm not going to say anything to the police at the moment."

"There's nothing to say."

The two women stared at each other, then Frieda nodded at her and left. Through the window, she could see Aisling still standing where she'd left her, gazing down at the name card.

"Come in, come in, come in!" cried Olivia. She was in hostess mode, expansive and already slightly tipsy. Dressed in green velvet, her hair tied up, earrings dangling, she pulled Frieda into the house and kissed her on both cheeks, then rubbed off the lipstick marks with a licked finger. The hall was full of shoes. There was also a mouse-trap at the foot of the stairs, as yet mouse-less.

"Is she here?"

"Your solicitor woman —"

"Tessa Welles."

"Not yet. But she rang to say she was on

her way. She sounded *lovely.* She's bringing her brother."

"Why? Is he a solicitor too?"

"No, but she's going to the theater with him and they were coming from the same direction, so . . ." Olivia waved vaguely in the air. Her fingernails were chipped scarlet. "I said it would be fine."

"Of course. Have you got all the documents together?"

"Well. You see. That's a bit of a problem. I've done my best. You know how these things are. Stuff just disappears." And Olivia opened her eyes wide, as if she were a conjuror who'd done a magic trick.

"She must be used to it. Where's Chloë?"

"She's at some mobile club thing."

"What's that?"

"I don't really know," Olivia said vaguely. "It's all done on Facebook and, anyway, she's with Sammy and Sammy's brother and his friends and she *is* seventeen."

The bell rang, and she went to the door, throwing it open with such force that it banged back on itself, and Frieda caught a glimpse of two surprised faces before it shut once more.

"Sorry," said Olivia, reopening it. "Do come in."

They could only have been brother and

sister. It wasn't just that both were tall and rangy and had the same red-blond hair, although his was cut short and fading to a peppery gray. They had the same oval face and gray-blue eyes.

"Hello," said Tessa. She saw Frieda and gave her a smile of recognition. "This is my brother, Harry Welles."

Harry shook Olivia's hand and then Frieda's. "Don't mind me," he said. "I can sit in the car, if you like, or just perch somewhere while you talk. I've got plenty of work to be getting on with."

"Are you joining us?" Tessa asked Frieda.

"I asked her here for moral support," said Olivia. "I thought you might be some terrifying woman in a pin-striped suit. But I think I'll manage on my own. Come into the living room. It's a bit of a mess, I'm afraid. Though I tried to clear things up a bit."

"Where shall I put myself?" Harry asked Frieda.

"You could try the kitchen," said Frieda, dubiously. "It might not be in a suitable state. Shall we have a look at it?"

"Wow," said Harry, almost admiringly, as they entered. "I see what you mean."

"I could clear you a space at the table."

"Where are you going to be?"

"I thought I might clear up a bit. Although I'm not sure where to start."

"I tell you what, why don't I wash up?"

"That's out of the question."

"Why? I like washing up. Are there any gloves that would fit me?"

"No."

"Yes. Here they are." He snapped them on. "Perfect. Bring it on."

"This is inappropriate."

"Inappropriate?"

"Yes."

"You're uncomfortable."

"Yes."

He peeled off the gloves. "I don't see why. Perhaps you could make us some tea?"

"I don't want tea."

"A glass of wine? Tessa's driving. There are about four opened bottles that I can see."

"All right. I'll make you some tea and you can sit at the table."

She took the ashtray, the wine glasses, the mugs, and several smeared plates off the table, then collected the newspapers and magazines into a pile. There were several unopened letters, bills as far as she could tell, that she put on the side for Olivia to look at later. "Here. Take a seat."

"You're stubborn."

"Yes. I'll just wipe the surface."

"I'll put the kettle on, shall I?"

"Do you always make yourself at home like this?"

"Do I?" He looked surprised. "I don't know."

Frieda made a pot of tea and Harry Welles opened his briefcase and pulled out some papers that he put on the table in front of him, but he didn't seem inclined to work. Frieda could feel him watching her as she stacked plates in the dishwasher.

"What's your job?" she asked at last.

"I'm a financial adviser. There, that usually shuts people up."

"What kind of people do you advise?"

"All sorts. Some who are wealthy and want to know which offshore account to hide their money in, some who are struggling and can't make ends meet. I look after a few charities. You wouldn't believe what a mess people can get into with their money."

"I probably would."

"But you don't. I mean, get into trouble with your own money."

"No."

"Of course not. I hear you're a therapist."

"Yes."

Often people responded to her profession with a jokey, nervous comment about what she was reading in their behavior and manner, as if she had spooky X-ray vision. Harry Welles, propping his chin in his hands and looking at her, said, "Yes. I can see how someone would trust you." Then he added, with a casual ease, "Would you like to have dinner with me on Friday?"

Frieda handed him his tea. "All right," she said, surprising both of them.

"Good. Venue to be confirmed. What's your e-mail?"

She gave it to him and he jotted it down. Then he opened a folder, picked up a pencil, and started working. Frieda smiled to herself and attacked a particularly encrusted pan.

# 31

Frieda made normal tea for herself —
builder's, mahogany brown — and green
tea for Aisling Wyatt. When she handed the
mug across, Aisling put her hands round it.

"I feel I need to warm myself up," she
said. "It's so cold. I've felt it the whole
winter. It's been cold all the time. There
were days when I'd walk along the river and
I'd expect it to freeze. It used to freeze,
didn't it, hundreds of years ago? They'd
skate on the Thames."

"And have fairs on it," said Frieda. "Festi-
vals."

"It should have frozen this winter," said
Aisling. "It was so bitter."

She looked like a woman who got easily
cold — thin and highly strung.

"It's because of the old London Bridge,"
said Frieda.

"The old London Bridge? What did that
have to do with it?"

"It slowed the flow of the river," said Frieda.

Aisling looked around Frieda's living room as if she were gradually thawing out and becoming aware of her surroundings. "It's nice here."

"Thank you."

"You've got lovely things. Like this." She picked up a green porcelain bowl. "Where did it come from?"

"It was a present."

"Is this where you see your patients?"

"No," said Frieda. "Mostly I see patients at an office round the corner."

"Would you see me?" said Aisling.

"That wouldn't be right because of the way we met. But why would you want to see me?"

"Oh, just everything," said Aisling. "Because everything is a mess, because I haven't got the life I thought I'd have, because I hate myself. Is that enough to be getting on with?"

All the time she was talking, Aisling wasn't looking at Frieda. She looked into her tea, around the room, anything that would avoid eye contact.

"It sounds to me as if you should talk to your doctor first," said Frieda. "But of course I could refer you to someone."

Finally, Aisling looked directly at Frieda. "I suppose you don't want to," she said. "That's understandable. You're working with the police. That's your priority."

"I *am* working with the police."

Aisling gave a bitter smile. "And I read about you in the paper," she said. "It looks like you've got troubles of your own."

"If I've got troubles of my own, why did you want to talk to me?"

"When you asked me about Bertie, I thought you seemed sympathetic."

"And what do you think now?"

"That girl in the story said you used her. Is that true?"

"I was involved in rescuing her. But being rescued can be painful."

"Maybe what she meant," said Aisling, "is that you go into people's lives and shake things up, and then you leave and don't take responsibility for what you've done."

"Is that what you feel I've done to you?"

Aisling took a sip of her tea, then placed the mug very carefully on the little table in front of her. "When I met Frank, we were both working in the same firm. In the same department. If anything, I was probably doing slightly better than he was. Then we had Joe and Emily and, blah blah blah, suddenly I'm at home and he's been promoted and

I'm boring myself even saying the words, it's such a cliché. You know, I'm not supposed to be boring. When I was at college, I was the person who found other people boring. If when I was twenty-two I'd been able to see myself at thirty-two, I would have . . . well, done something drastic. Run away to South America." Now she gave Frieda a challenging look. "I know that you'll tell me to count my blessings. You'll say I've got two lovely children, a beautiful place to live, it was my own decision and I've got to take responsibility for it. You'll say that I must have subconsciously not enjoyed working in an accountancy firm and I'm just using the children as an excuse."

Frieda put her own mug of tea on the table, untasted. "Tell me about Robert Poole," she said.

"When Frank comes home and I show him things I've done in the garden or in the house, his eyes just glaze over. Bertie was different. He was interested, he had ideas. He also listened to my ideas." She paused, as if waiting for Frieda to speak, but Frieda stayed silent. She continued, almost as if she were talking to herself, "I never thought I'd feel like that again. I felt like I was being looked at. I know what you're thinking."

"You probably don't."

"You're thinking that I must be feeling guilty for being a bad wife and a bad mother. Well, it's not true. We made love when the children were out of the house. Emily's at nursery school four mornings a week and she goes to a child minder for three afternoons as well. And we'd make love in the children's bedroom. That was partly practical. I would probably have worried about some kind of smell on the sheets and I'd have had to wash them every time, and even Frank might have noticed something. But it was more than that. When we were lying naked in the children's room, with their things around, their toys, I felt like I was saying 'Fuck off' to all that, to the idea that that was who I was. I suppose that shocks you."

"No. Did you think about leaving your husband?"

"Not really," said Aisling. "No, not at all. Anyway, the sex stopped after a while, although the feeling of intimacy didn't. We talked about working together."

"Doing what?"

"He had plans as a designer, gardens but interiors as well." Aisling smiled. "We walked around Greenwich and looked at people's gardens. You could see that people have such a need for someone who can come into their homes and take responsibility and sort out their problems for them, so they can get on with other things. People have the money, but they don't know how to get what they really want. Anyone who comes up with a way to find these people can't fail. So we talked about creating a business like that."

"Did you do anything more than talk about it?"

Aisling dropped the eye contact and gave a shrug.

"What did you actually do?" asked Frieda.

"That's all you care about," said Aisling. "You're just being a policeman."

"I can't help you if you don't tell me the truth," said Frieda, "which means all of the truth. Even the uncomfortable bits."

Aisling put her hand over her mouth, then rubbed her face as if it were itching. "Some of this would look awkward if it came out, and now that he's dead, I don't know what will happen."

"If what came out?"

"I gave Bertie some support, that's all. Part of which was financial."

"How much?"

"A few thousand," said Aisling, almost in a mumble. "More than that. A bit more. Twenty-five. Maybe thirty, forty. Or something. It's my money as well as Frank's. We share everything. And I have my own account."

"Did you tell your husband?"

"I was going to tell him about the plans when they were more worked out. It would have been all right, but then suddenly Bertie was dead. It's a disaster in a way, I know, but we have quite a lot of savings. And he doesn't look at my bank statements. Why should he? I feel terrible about it, but it should be fine. It'll die down and go away, that's what I tell myself. I mean, this is nothing to do with Bertie's death, just about a mess in a marriage. Our mess — it's got nothing to do with anything else. You must see that."

Frieda held her gaze. "I'm sure you understand that I have to tell the police about this."

"No! Why? This has nothing to do with anything. I came to you because I trusted you."

"You came to me because I'd realized you had had an affair with Robert Poole."

"I thought you'd understand. I didn't think you'd judge me."

"I'm not judging you, Aisling. A man has been murdered."

"Not by me."

"I have to tell them."

"But Frank will find out. You won't tell him, will you? You can't anyway. You can't betray the secrets of a patient."

"You're not a patient," said Frieda. "But I won't tell him. You should think about doing so yourself, even if he doesn't discover it from the police."

"I can't. You don't understand what he's like. He'll never forgive me."

"Give him the chance. Anyway, I think he already knows."

Frieda had only been home a few minutes when the bell rang. She was on the way upstairs to have a shower, but now she turned round and went to the door.

"Hello? Are you Dr. Klein?"

A woman on her doorstep, young and fresh faced, with an expression that was both apologetic and eager. Frieda had the impression that she was ready to break into an enthusiastic smile, and that when she did there would be dimples in both her cheeks. She had curly chestnut hair cut quite short but still unruly, freckles on her cheeks and over the bridge of her nose, and soft brown eyes.

"I'm so sorry to turn up like this. My name's Liz. Liz Barron."

"How can I help you?"

She shivered. "It's horrible out here. Could I come in for a moment?"

"Not until you tell me who you are."

"Of course, sorry. I wanted to ask your advice on something. I was hoping you could help me."

"What's this about?"

"I'm a journalist for the *Daily Sketch.*"

"I see."

"I'm writing a feature, a kind of zeitgeist piece about the police force in the present climate of suspicion and cuts. Basically sympathetic, but trying to look at it from all points of view."

"I'm not a police officer."

"I know, I know," she said, blushing. "I'm probably not explaining myself very well. The thing is, my editor thought it would be a good idea to focus on a particular area or a particular story. I was wondering if I could talk to you about your involvement — with Dean Reeve, of course, and now with this man Robert Poole. I was so impressed by what you did and I know what Joanna Teale wrote about you. It was a really unfair piece. I thought it would be a great opportunity for you to put your side of the story, too. It must feel awful not to be able to set the record straight."

"Not really."

Liz Barron seemed undeterred. Her pleasant face glowed with sympathy. "You could tell me about what happened, then, and what you're doing now, and what it's like to be a consultant."

"No."

"And we could even talk about paying you expenses for your trouble."

"No."

Her expression didn't alter. "Do you feel responsible for Kathy Ripon's death?"

"I don't want to be rude, but I'm going to shut the door now."

"Why should the public pay for your help with the Poole case, when —"

Frieda closed the door. She went up the stairs and took her shower, standing for a long time under the needles of water, trying not to think.

"Well, well, well," said Karlsson. "So Mrs. Wyatt was cheating on her husband with our Robert Poole."

They were in a car on their way to Mary Orton's house. Frieda just stared out of the window.

"And he took Mrs. Orton and then got her to change her will."

"Tried to," said Frieda.

"He slept with Mrs. Wyatt, then took her money. Do you think he was blackmailing her?"

"I don't think he needed to. She said they were going to set up in business together."

"I've never heard it called that before," said Karlsson. "You reckon Mr. Wyatt knew?"

"There was something about the way they were together. They didn't look at each other, seemed almost scared to catch each other's eye. It felt to me then that they were both concealing something from each other. We know what she was concealing, but what about him?"

"So he knew?"

"Aisling Wyatt said he didn't. I'm not so sure."

Karlsson looked thoughtful. "He sleeps with your wife, steals your money. And then the body is found a mile away from your house. I'm looking forward to talking to Frank Wyatt."

"I told Aisling I was going to tell you and that she should speak to him before you did."

"What the hell did you do that for? Now he'll be prepared."

"Because it was the right thing to do."

"Right for who, Frieda? For her, or for

our investigation?"

"There's no difference. It's right, that's all."

"Whose side are you on?"

"I'm not on any side."

Karlsson breathed deeply, making an effort to stop himself saying something rude.

"What did you make of Mary Orton's sons?"

"I don't like them," said Karlsson.

"But there's no evidence against them?"

"They had a motive. They had a big bloody motive. The trouble is, I don't think they realized it until it was too late."

Mary Orton insisted on making a pot of tea and putting out biscuits. She was apologetic that she hadn't baked a cake. Frieda saw how her hands — liver spotted and with thick blue veins under the loose skin — shook as she set out the cups. She was wearing a dark green skirt and a white blouse, with a thin cardigan over the top. But the blouse buttons were done up wrong, showing the old-fashioned lacy vest underneath, and there was a ladder running up her tights. "We're so sorry to bother you again," she said to the old woman gently. "We just wanted to check a few things with you."

"Anything I can do to help." She picked

up her cup with clumsy fingers, setting the teaspoon ringing against its side.

"It's just routine," said Karlsson, soothingly. "We just want to confirm a few details. Such as when your sons last visited you, for example."

She looked at him, then down at her tea. "Why?" she asked.

"We just need to know who met Robert Poole," said Frieda. "It's nothing to worry about."

"I don't know when they came."

"Have they been this year?"

"They have very busy lives."

"I know. And they live a long way off so, of course, it's hard for them to get down," said Frieda.

"They're not bad sons."

"But you don't see them very much?"

"It's the grandchildren I mind about."

"They grow up so quickly," said Frieda. "A few months can make all the difference."

"I'd like to know them better," agreed Mary Orton. "No. Not this year."

"What about last year?"

"Couldn't they tell you themselves?"

"They both said they'd been down in the summer."

"Yes. That would be right."

"So, not for eight months or so." It felt

cruel to press her.

Mary Orton lifted her eyes. "Eight months," she said softly.

"Did you tell either of them about Robert Poole helping you with the house?"

"I didn't like to. I didn't want them to feel guilty."

"Because you'd already told them about the leak?"

"I don't like to make a fuss. They said it was probably nothing and, anyway, it would be all right when the spring came."

"I see."

"Your friend Josef," said Mary Orton, visibly brightening. "He's done a marvelous job with the roof and the boiler."

"I'm glad he could help you."

"Such a nice young man. He tells me stories about his country and I tell him about what London used to be like. He is very fond of my lemon drizzle cake. And he said he would make me a honey and poppy seed loaf that he used to eat as a boy, although he'll probably forget."

"I'm sure he won't," said Frieda.

"People are so busy nowadays. But when you're old and live alone, time goes so fast and yet at the same time very slowly. It's odd, isn't it?"

"It is odd."

"Nobody tells you, when you're young, what it will bc like."

"What is it like?"

"You become like a ghost in your own life." Just before they left, Karlsson stopped in front of the wooden urn that contained the ashes of Mary Orton's husband. He touched it very gently with his forefinger, following the whorls in the grain. "This is lovely and very unusual. Who made it for you?"

She came over to where he stood, looking tiny beside him. "It was made from an elm tree that fell over in our garden years ago. It felt right for Leonard's remains to be in something made from a tree he used to love."

"Mm." Karlsson nodded encouragingly. "Can you remember the name of the people who made it?"

She frowned, thinking, then said: "A company called Living Wood. I think. Though I could check. If I've kept the papers. Why?"

"It caught my eye. It's beautiful."

She beamed at him. Frieda saw the way he bent toward the old woman respectfully and turned away from them, feeling strangely moved.

"Why did you want to know who'd made that little urn?" Frieda asked, once they were back in the car.

"Mrs. Orton, Jasmine Shreeve, and Aisling Wyatt all have beautiful things made from wood in their house. It might be a connection."

"Oh! Yes, I see."

"Only might."

"That was perceptive."

"Why, thank you, Dr. Klein."

"Why have you taken up smoking?"

He glanced round sharply. "Who says I have?"

"Haven't you?"

"Can you smell it on me?"

"No. Just extra-strong mints."

"I don't want my children to know," he said, and was about to add something when he checked himself.

"You can say it, you know."

"No. I don't think I can." He turned on the windscreen wipers and the headlights. "God, don't you hate February?"

## 32

Living Wood was based in a small industrial unit in Dalston, occupying the bottom floor of a building that also housed an animal charity, a company making hats, and a manufacturer of signs. Inside, there was a different world. Wooden planks leaned against every inch of the walls. In the middle of the room there were large machines, saws, and planes, one of which was being run by a young man in a white vest, stooped over his work with sweat on his bare shoulders. The rich smell of resin hung in the air. Yvette had to shout to make herself heard. The man turned off the machine and stood up, wiping the back of his hand across his forehead.

She held up her badge. "Are you in charge of this company?"

"That's my dad. He's away. You can ask me."

The man looked at Munster, who was

examining a machine with a huge heavy blade.

"Careful," said the man. "That'll have your arm off if you press the wrong button."

"We have a list of names," said Yvette. "I want to ask you if they mean anything to you."

"All right."

She handed him the typed list. He glanced at it. "They're customers," he said. "A couple of them I don't recognize. I'd have to check on the computer, but they might be as well." He went over to a small space, partitioned off from the rest of the room, where there was a filing cabinet and a computer. He sat at it, tapped at the keys, opened a file of names, and scrolled down it.

"All except the last," he said. "Sally Lea. I don't know her, and she's not on our computer. We've made things for the others, some of them more than once. The Coles, for instance, we made them a bed out of an old ash tree that had blown down. Beautiful bit of wood. It took months."

"So you're saying they all bought things you made."

"We're not a shop, as you can see. People bring us wood from their garden and we turn it into objects. Usually bowls and chopping boards — but anything, actually. Mrs. Orton — we made her an urn for her husband's ashes."

"How do your customers find you?"

"We've got ads in a couple of magazines. Magazines for people who're doing up their homes."

"Was someone called Robert Poole a customer?" said Yvette.

"Robbie?" He looked at them curiously. "No. He wasn't a customer. He worked here."

"Did he? When?"

He thought for a moment. "Beginning of last year, just for a few months." Another man pushed open the door of the workroom with his shoulder and came in carrying two cardboard cups of coffee. "Darren, these two are detectives. They're asking about Robbie Poole."

"Why did he leave?" asked Yvette.

The two men exchanged looks.

"Is there a problem?" said Darren. "We don't want to cause any trouble."

"There's been a crime."

"It ended badly," said the young man. "Some money went missing. I felt really rotten about it."

"You thought it was him?"

"We thought it might have been. It seemed the only explanation. We confronted him and he was in a real state about it. It was bad. For everyone."

"But he left."

"I gave him a couple of weeks' wages to tide him over. Is he OK?"

"He's dead."

"What?"

"He was murdered."

"Fuck."

"Fuck," repeated Darren, with awe. "Fucking fuck."

"We found these names in his flat."

"Jesus. Why?"

"That's what we're trying to find out."

"Dead!"

"You've been very helpful. We might be back in touch." Yvette smiled at him. "But I don't think you should feel guilty about letting him go," she said.

# 33

When Harry picked Frieda up on Friday evening, he didn't tell her where they were going. She got into the back of the taxi beside him and he peered down at the screen of his phone. "I don't even know myself yet," he said.

"What do you mean?"

"Not knowing is part of the fun," he said. "It's in Shoreditch. That's all I can tell you."

"I don't understand. What happens when we get to Shoreditch?"

Harry tapped the phone. "Leave it to this," he said. "It'll tell us."

"All right," said Frieda. "I'll trust it."

"I need to warn you about something," said Harry. "I want to begin by being completely honest."

"That's always a bad sign," said Frieda.

"No, really. I just want to tell you in good time that you need to beware of my sister. Tessa Welles lives part of her life as a law-abiding solicitor, but she almost always has an ulterior motive."

"Why do I need to know that?"

"She phoned me straight after she'd met you, telling me all about you. She told me that she wouldn't rest until she'd brought us together."

Frieda glanced out of the window before answering. "I just said I'd come for a meal," she said at last.

"I know. I guess what I want you to tell me is if you're involved with anyone else."

"No."

"That's good. Why do I think there's a *but* coming?"

"I don't know. I wasn't going to add anything."

"Perhaps you've just broken up with someone."

Frieda met his gray-blue gaze. How long ago was "just"? She had parted with Sandy the December before last. She suspected that Harry would think fourteen months was a long time; most people would. How do you measure absence? There had been minutes that had become hours, and hours that had been like a desert with no horizon. There had been days dull and deadened as lead, and whole weeks when she'd had to force herself forward, inch by inch, across their expanse. How do you know when your heart is ready once more? Perhaps, for someone like her, the heart was never ready and had to be forced open.

"There was someone recently," she replied softly.

"Fortunate someone."

"No. I don't think so."

"But it's over?"

"He went away." Far away, she thought. America, another continent. "And I don't want to talk about it."

"I can't imagine how anyone —" Harry broke off. "Sorry. We've only just met, and I don't want to blunder in."

"It's OK."

"But I think you're beautiful."

"Thank you. Now, have you worked out where we're going or is it still a mystery to us both? We're nearly at Shoreditch."

"Right. Of course. Hang on." He looked at his phone again, then opened the glass partition and leaned forward to speak to the driver. "Perhaps you'd better let us off at this junction."

They got out in Shoreditch High Street.

"I used to work in an office near here," said Harry. "And at the time I thought — in fact, I didn't just think, I also said — that this was one part of London that would never come up. And about five years later I read an article in a U.S. magazine saying that Hoxton was the trendiest place on the planet." He tapped the screen of his phone. "Good. Just follow me."

They turned off the high street and Harry led Frieda through a maze of streets, occasionally referring to his phone. "Here we are," he said. "Allegedly."

They were standing in front of the steel door of what looked like a warehouse. Harry pressed a buzzer. A voice spoke through a hum of static.

"Harry Welles plus one," Harry said.

There was a click and he pushed open the door. They walked inside and up some metal stairs. At the top, another door opened and a woman met them. She was large, with glorious blond hair springing in curls and tendrils from her head, and was wrapped in a white apron with a single streak of dark red running down it. She led them inside to a small open-plan apartment, all bare boards and brick walls, exposed heating ducts and metal radiators. Large windows looked over the City of London. Of the five makeshift tables, four were already full. The woman led them to the empty one. They sat down.

"I am Inga," said the woman. "And I am

from Denmark. My husband, Paul, is from Morocco. We cook together. I will bring you wine and food and there is no choice. No allergies, no fads?"

Harry looked at Frieda. "Sorry, I forgot to ask."

Frieda shook her head and Inga left. She returned with a jug of white wine and a plate of pickled fish and sour cream. When they were alone again, Frieda looked across at Harry. "What the hell is this?"

Harry examined his plate. "It looks more Danish than Moroccan," he said.

"No, I mean this." She gestured around her. "The whole thing."

"Oh, this? It's a pop-up restaurant. You can find them if you know where to look."

"Pop-up?"

"They come and go, with strange people doing their own strange thing for little groups."

"Is it . . . well, is it legal?" asked Frieda.

"I hope so," said Harry. "Anyway, you should know. You're the policewoman."

"Not exactly."

He poured wine for both of them. "I'm fascinated," he said. "A psychotherapist who works for the police. How did that happen?"

"It's a long story."

"Good," said Harry. "I like long stories."

So, while the table filled with little plates of smoked meats, yogurts, savory pastries, Frieda told him about Alan Dekker, about the search for Matthew, about Alan's twin, Dean Reeve, and his wife, Terry, who had turned out to be a girl who had gone missing twenty years previously. She edited the story. She didn't tell him about Kathy Ripon's death or about her new certainty that Dean was still out there somewhere.

Harry was a good listener. He leaned forward across the table, but not too much, and he nodded, giving small murmurs of attention, but didn't interrupt. When she finished, he asked her about the case she was working on now with this character Robert Poole, and to her surprise, she found herself telling him. She described Michelle Doyce to him, and then, though she didn't talk about his victims, she talked about Poole as well.

"I can't quite make him out," she said.

"Well, you never met him, did you, and now he's dead."

"I still want to make sense of him. Perhaps that's the way to find out who killed him. On the one hand, he was obviously a con man. At the same time, he made people feel less lonely. He seemed to have had a knack for understanding their vulnerabilities and for comforting them."

"Isn't that what con men do? Worm their way in?"

"Yes. Maybe. It's just —" She stopped.

"Maybe?"

"Maybe I feel he was a bit like me."

Harry didn't seem surprised. He nodded, rolled some bread into a pellet, then said, "You mean he was like a therapist to the people he conned."

"Yes."

"That must be a pretty uncomfortable thought."

"Yes, it is."

"Yet I feel sure you're a terrific therapist."

Frieda snorted. "Now you're just trying to flatter me. You have no idea if I'm good at it or not."

"I'd trust you and I'd tell you things."

"Except you haven't. You've just been asking me questions and listening to me."

"Ask me something." He held his hands out, palms upward. "Anything."

"Anything?"

"Absolutely anything."

"Do you do your job because you like money?"

"Hmm. No, I do it because I understand money and how it changes people."

"Go on."

"A good accountant or financial adviser is a kind of artist. You can turn people's money into the most amazing creative possibilities, things they would never have dreamed of."

"So that they don't pay tax on it?" said Frieda.

Harry gave a humorous frown. "You're not from the Inland Revenue, are you?" he said. "It's just about seeing possibilities. For me, it's not really about the money at all. It's like counters in a children's game." He looked around the room. "It's like this. You asked if it was legal. Strictly speaking, it probably isn't. They've found a gray legal area somewhere between a restaurant and a private dinner party. And in that area they can develop their Moroccan-Danish creativity. What do you think?"

"It's London," said Frieda.

Harry looked puzzled. "What do you mean?"

"Gray areas," she said. "The things that happen in secret — good things, bad things, strange things."

"Which is this?" Harry asked.

"Good, I think," she said. "Until one day there'll be a fire here or somewhere similar and it won't seem such fun."

Harry's face fell. "There speaks the police-

388

woman."

"I'm not a policewoman."

"Sorry, of course you're not. Next question."

"Why are you still single?"

"I don't know."

Frieda raised her eyebrows and waited.

"I didn't think I'd be single at thirty-eight. I'll be forty soon — I always thought at forty I'd be settled down: wife, kids, house, you know. The life you're supposed to have. Of course, I've had relationships, some short and some long, and once upon a time I was engaged to a woman I thought I loved and who, I thought, loved me and then, well, it didn't work out. It petered away, and sometimes I can hardly remember what she looked like or felt like, as if it were a dream that happened to someone else. I think I've always felt" — he frowned and took a gulp of wine — "always felt that I was waiting."

"What for?"

"I don't know. For my real life to begin, the life I was supposed to have."

"Real life?" Frieda's words hung in the air between them.

"Real life, real love. I don't know."

Once, he had said to her, "I know you." He had looked into her eyes and he hadn't smiled and she could feel his gaze finding its way through the tunnels and secret doorways of her mind.

What had he seen? What had he found as he gazed into her? Had he found the real her, the one nobody else could reach?

The body doesn't matter. Not anymore. The splitting skin and the scabby mouth, the cropped and greasy hair, the protruding ribs and the strange bruises that have begun to flower on the pale, grubby flesh, unused to sun. What matters is the soul. "Don't listen to anything," the voices say to you. He said, "I know you. Put that in the scales. I know you." That counted for everything.

# 34

Their meeting was at seven, when it was still not fully light outside. There was yellow-brown tea that nobody drank and Garibaldi biscuits that none of them ate — Yvette took a large dusty bite of one, then looked surprised by her own action and embarrassed by the crunching sound she made, just when she was supposed to be talking, while Jake Newton looked at her pityingly.

She laid a chart on the table, and Karlsson, Frieda, and Chris Munster leaned forward to look at it. Jake tipped himself back in his chair, keeping himself balanced with his forefingers in a way that alarmed Yvette and irritated Karlsson.

"We thought we should try and account for what he did in his days," said Yvette, still swallowing biscuit, "where he was, who he saw, try and establish a pattern and any gaps."

"Go on."

"It's not exact, of course. We don't know enough, and a lot of it relies on memory. But look. These are the days he saw Mary Orton. She's in green. Jasmine Shreeve is red. The Wyatts are blue. The days he met up with Janet Ferris are dotted around, not surprisingly, and there are various days that are free. But it seems quite regular, doesn't it? I mean, more regular than you'd expect — as if he had a system and set aside times for each of the people he wanted something from."

"Mm," said Karlsson, musingly. "It does. Good work."

"But the odd thing is there are sets of days when he just disappears from the radar. Like, every ten days or two weeks, there are three or four days when there's no trace of him and, as far as we can tell, he wasn't in his flat either."

"So you think he was with someone else?"

"Possibly. Someone we haven't traced yet."

"Maybe another victim."

"It's a thought anyway."

"Has there been any response to the poster?"

"You know, dozens of people have come forward claiming knowledge, but they're all dead ends."

"He's a gardener, isn't he?" said Frieda.

They all looked at her.

"What do you mean 'he's a gardener'?" said Yvette. "What's that got to do with anything?"

"What you've done makes me think of gardening," said Frieda. "Gardening's all about different stages. You're planting seeds, watering plants, picking fruit, pruning dead wood. It looks to me as if he was in various stages of cultivating the people we know about. There are the ones he had only contacted by phone or presumably was going to contact at some point. Then there's our couple in Brixton, our first leads to him, whom he had visited once. There's Janet Ferris, to whom he seems to have been the perfect neighbor, kind and attentive. There's Jasmine Shreeve — he had something on her but hadn't used it yet, as far as we know. Then the Wyatts. He'd managed to extract money from Aisling, and it seems unlikely he wouldn't have put more pressure on her. Mary Orton, of course, he had deceived out of a large amount of money and also tried to persuade her to change her will."

"You're right," said Karlsson.

"If there's someone else we don't know about, someone he was seeing in those gaps,

I wonder where he or she fits into this. Was he done with them? Was he just getting started? Or was this person further along the line than any of them? Con men — they don't just cheat people of money. They like to have power. There are studies of people who have conned their victims for no financial gain at all."

Chris Munster spoke for the first time. "What I want to know," he said, "is, who is bloody Sally Lea?"

The booming in her head had gone. The sharp hunger had gone, and the fug of dizziness. Everything had a sharp outline. She could see clearly now, and her thoughts were like knives.

She was his inheritor. She would not let him down.

She stood up from the narrow bed, the ruck of sheets and itchy blanket. Her clothes hung off her and, with her fingers, she could feel how sharp her bones were: pelvis, collarbone, ribs, wrists, shoulder blades — her wings. To fly. At school she had been plump, with soft round hips. Curvaceous, her mother had said. Pudgy, her enemies had jeered. Now she was lean and hard. An instrument. His instrument.

She made her way to the long cupboard

under the bow of the boat, which stretched into darkness at its point. He had said that she mustn't, on any account. She had sworn: cross my heart and hope to die. But everything had changed. The rules were gone and the waiting was over.

She reached into the cupboard and pulled out the first packet, which was wrapped in several plastic bags against the wet, and put it on the table. Three more followed. Then she began.

Frieda only just got to the hospital in time. She was supposed to meet Jack in the lobby, by the rack of get-well cards, but he was late, and she saw him as he came hurtling through the revolving doors, his face flushed. He was wearing an odd jumble of garments — weekend clothes, she thought, or got-out-of-bed-in-a-hurry clothes: balding velvet jeans that used to be dark red, a shirt with brown and green geometric patterns under a cardigan with reindeers on it, probably a Christmas present from his parents, she decided. Only one of his sneakers had laces in it, so that he ran with an asymmetric hobble, sliding one foot along the ground to stop the shoe falling off.

"Sorry," he gasped. "Alarm clock. Public transport. Have you been waiting long?"

"Just a few minutes. It's fine. We don't have an appointment or anything. It's just a visit. I thought you'd be interested to meet her, and I know she likes visitors. We'll have coffee after and you can tell me about Carrie."

They walked up the stairs and along the corridor of gaudy murals, wheelchairs, and Zimmer frames, then through the double doors and into the ward. The woman in a Victorian nightie who did jigsaws was no longer there, but everything else looked unchanged. The bed that Michelle Doyce had occupied was now filled by a very large woman who stared at them blankly.

"She's through there," said the nurse, gesturing toward a door. "On her own. Orders." She raised her eyebrows at them, inviting a humorous response.

Frieda nodded. "Good."

Michelle Doyce's new room was small and poky, with peeling, light green walls. It would have been unremittingly grim but for a large window that let natural light into the room and led on to a fire escape. The metal stairs spiraled down to a courtyard that was filled, Frieda saw, with a nearly empty Dumpster and several overflowing refuse bins. She couldn't imagine any of the patients she had seen managing to maneuver their way down to safety. There was a cockroach under the miniature sink in the corner. She opened the window, picked the insect up with a tissue, and dropped it neatly into the Dumpster below. Jack pulled a face.

Michelle Doyce was sitting in the metal chair beside her bed. On the bedside table were several small scraps of paper, three plastic bottle tops in a row, an old dosette box, whose compartments now contained small curls of fluff and hair, five jigsaw pieces, and a few thin tabs of soap, presumably collected from the bathroom bins. This, Frieda reflected, was Michelle Doyce's way of making herself at home.

Michelle put a finger to her lips as they approached. "They're sleeping."

"We'll be quiet," said Frieda. "Can we sit at the end of the bed, or do you want us to stand?"

"You can sit if you're careful. He can stand."

Jack held out his hand. "I'm Jack," he said. "Frieda's friend. I'm glad to meet you."

Michelle Doyce looked at his outstretched hand as if she didn't know what it was, and after an awkward moment he dropped it to his side, but then she leaned forward and picked it up, examining it curiously, running her finger over his calluses, tutting over a broken blood vessel and torn nail, murmuring to herself.

"Look," she said, turning it over so the palm lay upward in her grasp. "Life lines."

"Will I live long?" Jack asked, smiling.

"Oh, no." She patted his hand softly, then let it go. "Not you."

Jack looked disconcerted, although he tried to smile.

"Do you remember me?" Frieda asked.

"You introduced us."

"My name's Frieda. We talked about the man who lived in your room."

"He never came back to me."

"Do you still miss him?"

"Where is he?"

"He's safe now."

Michelle Doyce nodded. She made one of her floating gestures, tracing a vague outline in the air with her blunt fingers.

"What do you remember about him?"

"His poor hand." She turned her face to Jack, her eyes milky. "Worse than yours."

"Just his hand? There's nothing else? Nothing you picked up?"

"I never steal. I look after things."

"I know that. Is there anything you need?"

"In the end."

"Where's your dog?"

"Everyone leaves. Ports and rivers."

"But your dog, has he left you?"

"They'll wake."

She pointed at the brown blanket pulled over the pillows.

"Is he in there?"

"Friends now. It took time."

"Can I see?"

"Promise."

"I promise."

With infinite gentleness, Michelle turned down the blanket. "There," she said proudly.

Under the blanket lay not just one soft toy, but two: the floppy-eared dog with button eyes that Frieda had given her, and a small pink teddy bear with a red heart stitched onto its chest.

"That's good," said Jack. "They can keep each other company."

"Here." Michelle lifted the dog into his arms, positioning it carefully.

"Where does the other one come from?" asked Frieda.

Michelle looked at her uncomprehendingly.

"Did someone bring him?"

"I look after her."

"I can see that. But how did she come here?"

"You never can tell."

■ ■ ■ ■

"So you have no idea how Michelle Doyce came by the teddy?"

"That's what I'm saying." The ward manager spoke loudly and deliberately, as if Frieda were hard of hearing or slow to understand.

"Or when she got it."

"That's right. No idea."

"Someone must have given it to her."

"It's just a cheap little bear," the woman said. "Maybe she took it from someone else's bed, or maybe someone threw it away and she picked it out of a bin. What's your problem? It makes her happy. She spends every minute of the day looking after them."

"I need to find out if someone else has been to visit her. How long do you keep your CCTV footage?"

"What footage?"

"I've seen several cameras round the hospital."

"Oh, them. They're just for show. Where do you think we'd get the money for the real thing? This isn't one of your hospital trusts, you know. It's hard enough to pay our nurses or get people to clean the floors, let alone have all the mod cons."

"So there wouldn't be anything on film?"

"I don't think so. Not from here, at any rate. There's a camera at the entrance, but they only keep footage for twenty-four hours."

"I see. Thank you."

Jack and Frieda sat in the downstairs café, which was really just two Formica tables in a corner of the lobby, next to the shop where Frieda had bought the button-eyed dog. A man in overalls trundled past them with a trolley full of magazines and newspapers that he threw in large bundles onto the floor. Frieda ordered a green tea from the bored-looking woman behind the counter, and Jack a cappuccino with chocolate on top and a dried-out blueberry muffin.

"Poor Michelle Doyce," he said. There was a line of froth above his upper lip.

"She seems much happier now."

"Because of those toys?"

"They're not toys to her. They're living creatures she can look after and love, and be loved by in return. It's what most of us want, after all."

"Yes," said Jack, gloomily.

"Tell me about Carrie. You've seen her twice, I think. How's it going?"

"Well." Jack brightened. He broke off a crumbling lump of muffin and posted it into his mouth. "I was so nervous. It was like going onstage. I took ages choosing what to wear, which isn't like me."

"It's natural," said Frieda. "So how did it go?"

"I was in my room at the Warehouse, waiting, an hour before she came. Paz was a bit startled. Carrie was ridiculously early, too. And she was nervous, Frieda. As soon as I saw her, I felt ashamed of my own anxiety. I'd just been thinking of myself, but she was going through the real thing. She came in and sat on the chair opposite me and took a long drink of water, and then I said that although I knew of some of the events in her life that had brought her to me, I wanted her to tell me in her own words. And she started to cry."

"What did you do?"

"I wanted to get up and hug her. But you would have been proud of me. I didn't do anything."

Frieda looked at him suspiciously. Was he being sarcastic? "What happened?"

"I gave her a tissue. She finished crying. She apologized. I said she didn't need to apologize. I said that when she was with me she could say anything, express any emotion. The thing is, she doesn't know what she feels — whether it's grief or anger, guilt or humiliation, or the simple sad fact that she doesn't have a child and all that she ever wanted was to be a mother."

"Probably all of those things."

"Yeah. Also, I think she was so used to being the strong one for Alan that now she doesn't know who she is or how to be. She has to learn again who she is in the world."

"It sounds as if it went well."

"I still don't know what that means. The second time, just before she left, she talked about how she'd thought she wanted to talk to someone like you, but that now she saw it was better to have a man."

"By which she meant better to have you."

"Does that sound rude?"

"No. It makes sense." She sipped her green tea. The woman in the shop was cutting open the plastic-wrapped papers and arranging them on racks. "I Want My Love Rat Back," read one headline.

"She said she used to hate you," continued Jack. "She blamed you for everything that happened, but — Frieda? What's up?"

Frieda pointed toward one of the tabloid newspapers. The *Daily Sketch.*

"Oh, my God," said Jack. "Is that you again? Just ignore it. It's not worth bothering about."

"I can't ignore it," said Frieda. She took the paper from the rack and brought it back to the table.

"It's not the main story," said Jack.

The main story was about a rock star in rehab. Along the bottom of the front page was a smaller story: dodgy doc in botched murder probe. Alongside there was a photograph of Frieda.

"Dodgy," said Jack. "Isn't that libelous?"

"I appeared before a medical tribunal. Maybe that's enough."

"Nice picture, though."

"Someone's taken it without me knowing," said Frieda. "In the street somewhere. They must have been following me."

"Is that legal?"

"I don't know."

"It's written by Liz Barron. Who is she?"

"I've met her," said Frieda. "She knocked at my door."

"What did she say?"

"Nothing. Now shut up. I need to read this."

Frieda took a sip of her tea. She took a few deep breaths, and then she forced herself to read the article word by word. She read the story on the front page, and when she turned it to continue reading, she gave a start. Accompanying the story was a photograph of Janet Ferris and the sketched portrait of Robert Poole that she herself had made, using the photo of his decomposing face. She finished the rest of the article slowly and deliberately, word by word. Then she sat back.

"What does it say?" said Jack.

"Read it for yourself."

"I don't really want to. Can't you just tell me?"

"All right," said Frieda. "I think the basic point is that at a time when the police force is facing severe funding cuts, it's inappropriate that they should be hiring a therapist. Especially a discredited one. Especially when they already have qualified experts, like Dr. Hal Bradshaw."

"Is he the one who appears on TV?"

"That's what they say. And somehow they've tracked down Poole's neighbor, Janet Ferris. She's not happy with the way things are going." Frieda picked up the paper and looked for the exact quotation. " 'The police aren't taking this seriously enough,' she says. 'Nobody seems to care. Bob Poole was a lovely man, and he was generous to a fault. He used to bring little gifts over, on the spur of the moment. We swapped books, even did a picture swap. He said it was like a change of scene for us both. I returned it, of course. I returned everything that belonged to him, there's nothing left. But I still can't believe I'll never hear his knock at my door or see his smiling face. He has been abandoned by everybody yet I will never forget him.' "

"How did the journalist find out about this woman?"

"I don't know."

"Did they talk to Karlsson?" said Jack, angrily. "Did he stand up for you and tell them all that you've done?"

Frieda ran her finger down to the end of the article. " 'A police spokeswoman said, "It is not our policy to comment on operational matters but Dr. Klein is not playing any significant part in the inquiry. We are always grateful for co-operation from any member of the public." She said that the investigation was continuing.' "

"That's not exactly a ringing endorsement," said Jack. "How does it make you feel, being written about like that? Don't you feel violated?"

Frieda smiled. "Violated? Are you being my therapist now?"

Jack looked embarrassed and didn't answer.

"So what would you say if you were my

therapist?"

"I'd ask you how the article makes you feel."

"And you wouldn't ask if I feel violated?"

"I wasn't saying that as a therapist," said Jack. "By the way, how does it make you feel?"

"It makes me feel like somebody else's property," said Frieda. "Which I don't like."

Jack picked up the newspaper and looked at it. " 'Abrasive brunette,' " he said. "That doesn't seem quite right."

"Which? Abrasive or brunette?"

"Both. And 'dodgy.' That's completely out of order." He put the paper down. "What I don't understand is why you put yourself through this."

"Now *that*'s a good question," said Frieda. "And if you were my therapist, we would spend a lot of time discussing it."

"Can't we spend time discussing it even if I'm not your therapist?"

Frieda rummaged in her bag until she found her phone.

"Do you ever switch it on?" he said.

"I'm switching it on now," she said. "I switch it on when I need to use it and then I switch it off again."

"I'm not sure that's really the point."

Frieda dialed Karlsson's number.

407

He picked up after a single ring. "I've been trying to reach you," he said.

"How did they find Janet Ferris?"

"You mean the journalist?"

"That's right."

There was silence on the line.

"Are you still there?" asked Frieda.

"Look," said Karlsson, "everybody knows that the press have contacts on the force."

"I didn't know that," said Frieda. "What does it mean?"

"It's a bloody disgrace," said Karlsson. "But regrettably, there are officers who leak material. For a fee."

"It didn't take long to become public."

"It's not exactly a state secret. We're funded from people's taxes. But I'm sorry. And I'm sorry that we didn't seem to be putting up much of a defense on your behalf."

"If Yvette Long objects to me being on the case, I'd rather she expressed it to me or to you than to a journalist." There was another silence on the line. "I suppose she already has expressed it to you. That's OK."

"It's not like that, Frieda."

She glanced at Jack, who was staring rather guiltily at the *Daily Sketch.* He looked up, and Frieda made a gesture at him, trying to convey that she would only be a minute. "What is it like?"

"That article was bollocks. Bollocks about you and bollocks about the case going nowhere."

"It makes you and your team look ridiculous. Whatever the phrase was . . ."

" 'Dodgy Doc.' "

"Yeah, thanks." Frieda was about to ring off when she remembered something. "I feel bad about Janet Ferris. I'd like to go and see her."

"She was talking rubbish to that journalist. Don't let it get to you."

"I don't mean that," said Frieda. "I think she needs someone to talk to."

"She's a lonely woman," said Karlsson. "I think she had a bit of a crush on Poole. But it's not our job to hold her hand. We just need to find who killed him."

"I'll see her on my own time," said Frieda. "Don't worry. I won't charge you." She switched the phone off and put it back into her bag.

"It was good to see you, Jack," she said. "Now I've got to go and pay someone a call."

"You're not going to hunt that journalist down and kill her, are you?" said Jack. "Don't bother. She's not worth it."

Frieda smiled. "She was interesting," she

409

said. "First she was like someone who wanted to be my friend. Then she wanted to tell my side of the story. Then she threatened me. As you can see, I've already forgotten about it. But she'd better not find herself drowning in a lake with me as the only person looking on."

"You'd dive in and save her anyway," said Jack. "I know you would."

"Only to make her feel guilty," said Frieda.

"She wouldn't. And then she'd write another piece about you, misrepresenting you."

Frieda thought for a moment. "Maybe I'd let her drown then."

# 35

They walked out together and Frieda hailed a taxi. She sat back and gazed out at the unfamiliar south London streets. They drove past parks, schools, a cemetery, and it might have been in another part of England, another part of the world. She thought of Janet Ferris and the reporter, Liz Barron. Frieda had just slammed the door on her, but Janet Ferris hadn't. She would have invited her in, made tea for her, talked to her, grateful to find someone who wanted to listen. Janet Ferris was a woman who had been ignored, who was somehow at the edge. And then, suddenly, she had found herself involved in a big story, the murder of someone she knew and cared for, and even then she had been ignored. Nobody had wanted to hear her story. At least Liz Barron had sat in her flat and let her talk.

Frieda rang Janet Ferris's bell, but there was no answer. She silently cursed herself for arriving without phoning ahead. She looked at the bells. Flat one was Janet Ferris. Flat two was Poole. She pressed the bell for flat three, then pressed it again. A voice came from a little speaker, so crackly that she couldn't make out the words. She said who she was and that she wanted to see Janet Ferris, but she didn't know if she was being heard. She waited and then heard steps. The door was opened by a tall young man with blond hair and wire-rimmed spectacles, wearing a sweater and jeans, and with bare feet.

"What is it?" he said. His accent was foreign.

Frieda remembered the file: a German student upstairs. "I want to see Janet Ferris," she said. "But she's not in. I wondered if you knew where she was."

He shrugged. "I'm upstairs," he said. "I don't see her come and go."

Frieda peered into the hallway for piled-up mail. She couldn't see any. "This is going to sound strange," she said. "I'm working with the police on the murder. I'm a bit worried about Janet's state of mind. Do you have a key to her flat?"

"You have identification?"

"No. I mean, not as police. I'm a therapist. I work with them." The man looked reluctant. "I'd only be a minute. Just to check she's all right. You can come in with me."

"I'll get it," he said. "One minute." He bounded lightly up the stairs.

Frieda wondered what she was doing. More of the dodgy doc. He came quickly back down.

"I am not sure of this." But he unlocked the door anyway and stood back, calling Janet's name.

Frieda stepped through the doorway and was immediately hit by the smell. Horrible and sweet at the same time: she recognized it as the smell of shit.

"Stay there," she said to the man, and walked through and into the living room with a lurching sense of what she was going to find. She almost bumped into Janet Ferris's body, the legs. She looked up. An extension cable had been looped round a wooden beam. The other end was tied round Janet Ferris's neck. Her body hung quite still, heavily and limply, as if it were a bag filled with sand. One leg was streaked with brown that ran down over her shoe and dripped on to the carpet. Frieda heard a sound behind her, a sort of gasp. She looked round at the pale, dismayed face.

"I said to stay out," she said, but not angrily. He backed away. She fumbled for

413

her phone. She felt calm, but her fingers were big, swollen, and clumsy.

Josef had never seen Frieda like this before: she, who was always so self-possessed, so strong and dependable, now sitting at her kitchen table, hunched over, her face half hidden by her hand. It made him anxious and protective, and it made him want to get her pot after pot of tea. He refilled the kettle as soon as he had poured the boiling water into the teapot. She hadn't wanted vodka, although he thought it would do her good and put a bit of color back in her face. He had baked her a honey cake the day before, spiced with cinnamon and ginger, whose rich smell when it was baking had reminded him of his mother, and also of his wife or, at least, the woman who used to be his wife, and had filled him with emotions both happy and sad. Now he tried to persuade Frieda to eat some, pushing the plate under her nose. She shook her head and pushed it away.

Reuben hadn't seen Frieda like this before either, although he had been her supervisor and her friend for years, and knew things about her that probably no one else in the world did. She wasn't crying — even Reuben had never seen her cry, although once, during a film, she had been suspiciously watery eyed — but she was visibly distressed.

"Tell us, Frieda," he said. It was early evening, and in an hour or so he was supposed to be going on a date with a woman he had met in the local gym. He couldn't remember if she was called Marie or Maria, and he was worried that he might not recognize her when she wasn't dressed in Lycra, a V of perspiration on her shapely back.

"Yes. Tell us start to end," Josef said. He poured them all another cup of tea, and then himself a shot of vodka to accompany it, from the bottle he'd slipped into his bag when the phone call from Frieda had come. He thought of laying his hand on the top of her bowed head, but changed his mind.

"I knew she was lonely." Frieda's voice was low; she spoke not to them but to herself. "When I read that story . . ."

"Dodgy Doc, you mean?"

She looked up with a grimace.

"Yes, Reuben, that one. It made me think about Janet Ferris all alone in her room, and how anyone knocking at her door would have felt like a friend. She is — was — a clever, attractive, and affectionate woman, and yet it seemed that she had somehow missed out on everything she most wanted in life. Robert Poole, coming in with his little gifts, confiding in her, must have meant a great deal to her. When I visited her, I could feel that she was distressed. But I put it out of my mind."

"You can't save everyone."

"I went there and I encouraged her to open up to me, say what she was feeling. That's a risky thing to do if you're not prepared to deal with the consequences."

"You were only kind," said Josef, soothingly.

"Band-Aid kind," Frieda said, and Josef looked confused. He took a mouthful of vodka, then chased it down with tea. "Kind to get her to give me her confidences and expose her feelings. Then I went away and filed my report for Karlsson and forgot about her. I'd ticked her off my to-do list."

"Ticked her off?"

"It means — oh, never mind." Reuben took Josef's vodka and absent-mindedly drank it, then filled the glass again, drank half, and handed it to Josef, who emptied it. "Are you saying you should have been more aware of her state of mind or that you helped to create it?"

"I don't know. Me, the police, that jour-

nalist — we all just used her. She was griev-
ing."

"He was just her neighbor."

"He made her feel hopeful."

"There is that."

"When I first came on to this case, the
police didn't really care about it. Karlsson
was different, but basically they wanted to
close the file. They thought the victim would
turn out to be some drug dealer or dropout,
and the murderer was a madwoman who
would be locked away in a hospital for the
rest of her life. Then when we discovered
who Robert Poole was, it still didn't matter
that much because he's some kind of creepy
con man. Who really minded that he was
dead? Janet minded. And now she's dead,
too."

"The problem," said Reuben, refilling the
glass with vodka and taking another gulp,
"is that you're losing sight of whether you're
a therapist or a detective." He stared into
the glass. "You don't know whether to catch
people or cure them."

Frieda took her hand away from her face
and sat up straighter. "That's one way of
putting it."

"The point is that a therapist is what you
are when someone comes to see you in a
room and takes on the role of the patient.

You're not a therapist to everyone you meet. You can't be."

"No," said Frieda, but not with certainty. "No, you're probably right."

"This is good for sad days," said Josef, filling three shot glasses to the brim. They each took one, raised it to the others, and swallowed it in one go. Even in her wretchedness, Frieda noticed how gradually Reuben was shedding his virtuous abstinence and returning to his old self.

"You need to sort this out," said Reuben. "In your own head."

"I'll think about it. I need to get this right. Now, you've got to go out soon, right?"

"Christ, Frieda! You should have been a spy."

"You've just shaved — there's still a fleck of foam on your neck, and you never shave in the evenings — and you've looked at your watch twice."

"Sorry."

"Who is she?"

"Just someone I met. Marie. Or Maria."

"You don't know?"

"I'll just have to avoid using her name."

"I'll be on my way soon. First, can one of you get me some milk from the fridge?"

"Milk?"

"Yes, please."

Josef fetched a carton of semi-skimmed milk from the fridge and handed it to her, with a glass, but Frieda took a saucer from the cupboard instead and went out into the hall where she had left a cardboard box by the door. Josef and Reuben followed her curiously. She prised open the box and put her hand inside.

"Out you come," she said, and lifted the cat Robert Poole and Janet Ferris had called Mog or Moggie on to the floor. It stood quite still for a few moments, its back arched and its tail high in the air.

"Where did you get that? Has it got fleas?"

"No," said Frieda. "Janet Ferris wouldn't have let it get fleas." She poured some milk into the saucer and put it under the cat's nose. It sniffed at it suspiciously, then lapped at it with a flicking pink tongue. Only when the saucer was empty did it move away and delicately start to wash itself, licking the side of its paw, then swiping it over one ear and down the side of its face.

"So, would you like a cat, Reuben?" Frieda asked.

"Ah, yes!" Josef squatted on the floor beside her and put out one stubby finger, making strange crooning noises and speaking in a language Frieda didn't understand.

The cat gave a piteous mew.

"I'm allergic," said Reuben, hastily.

"Is hungry," said Josef.

"How can you tell? Do you talk in cat language?"

Josef stood up and disappeared into the kitchen, the cat trotting behind him. They heard the fridge door open.

"That cold chicken is not for cats!" Frieda shouted after him, then turned to Reuben and asked, "Are you really allergic?"

"I wheeze and come out in hives."

"I guess I'll have to keep him."

"I don't believe it. Frieda Klein with a pet?"

"It's not a pet. It's a punishment," she said. "And now it's time for you to go."

She almost pushed them out, and when the door was closed she leaned back against it, as if to keep it shut. She took a deep breath and then another. Suddenly she heard a sound, something she couldn't make out. Was it from inside the house or outside? Far away or near? She opened the door and just a few yards away she saw a jumble of bodies — she couldn't make sense of it. It was a mixture of impressions: shouting, swearing, a fist, the sound of blows — men sprawling on the ground, entangled with

420

each other. As she stepped forward, she saw Reuben, Josef, and someone else she couldn't make out, gripping and hitting each other, rolling round. She shouted something incoherent at them and tried to grab one — it was Reuben's moleskin jacket — and an arm struck her and knocked her back. She sat down heavily. But her intervention had broken the spell. The men disentangled themselves, and Josef bent down to her:

"You hurt?"

Frieda looked beyond him at Reuben. He was panting heavily, and there was a glow in his eyes that alarmed her. Another man, young, dark haired, anoraked, a camera hanging from his neck, stood up and backed away. He raised his hand and touched his nose. "You fuckers," he said. "I'm fucking calling the police."

"Call the fucking police," said Reuben, still breathing heavily. "You're a fucking parasite. I'd like to see you in court in front of a fucking jury."

Frieda pushed herself up. "Stop this," she said. "Stop this, all of you." She looked at the photographer. "Are you all right?"

"You fuck off, too," he said, jabbing his finger at her. "I'm calling the police right now."

"Call the police," said Reuben. "I want you to. I fucking dare you to."

The photographer gave a strange, twisted nod and walked away, out of the mews and round the corner. The three of them watched him go. Reuben was touching the knuckles of his right hand, flinching slightly. Josef was shamefaced.

"Frieda . . ." he began.

"No," she said. "Just stop. Go. Go now."

"We're just looking out for you," said Reuben.

She couldn't bring herself to reply. She turned and left them, kicking the door behind her.

# 36

Frieda woke with the watery light of a late-February morning. The cat was sitting on the end of her bed, staring at her with yellow eyes, unblinking. She sat up. The brawl in the street had kept her awake and infected her dreams, in which, she knew, Dean Reeve's face had smiled at her out of shadows and corners. Why had it sickened her? Weren't they just protecting her? Didn't she herself know what it was like to behave impulsively? She forced herself to put it out of her mind.

"What do you know?" she asked. "What did he tell you, and what did you hear?"

Perhaps this cat had seen Robert Poole die and then poor Janet Ferris string herself up and kick away the chair. Or was that really what had happened? Frieda was uneasy with unformed thoughts and suspicions. She shivered and got out of bed. The sky was a pale streaked blue. Today it was possible to believe that spring might come, after such a long, cold winter. She showered and dressed in jeans, then went downstairs, the cat threading through her legs and meowing. She'd bought some cat food from the late-night shop down the road when she'd come home, and now she shook some dried pellets into a plastic bowl and watched while it ate. Now what should she do? Let it out? But then it might run away, heading for its old home, and get crushed by a car. Or leave it inside to pee all over her floor? She'd have to get a cat flap. Sighing, she laid down several layers of newspaper on the kitchen floor and shut the cat in there. She pulled on a thick jacket, picked up her manila folder and notebook, then left the house.

Number 9 was always busy on a Sunday morning, but two people were just leaving the table in the corner, and Frieda took her place there. Marcus was behind the counter, operating the espresso machine, steam hissing from its nozzles. Kerry was picking up plates from tables, delivering full English breakfasts or bowls of porridge. But she stopped when she saw Frieda. "Hello, stranger."

"I've been a bit busy. Where's Katya?"

Kerry pointed and Frieda saw the little

424

girl at a table near the door that led into their flats, bent over a pad of paper and writing furiously, her tongue on her upper lip. "I should be taking her swimming or to the park," said Kerry.

"She looks happy enough."

"She's writing a story. She's been at it since half past six this morning. It's about a girl called Katya whose parents run a café. Cinnamon bagel?"

"Porridge. And fresh orange juice. There's no hurry."

Kerry left and Frieda pulled open her folder. Inside was everything Karlsson had given her on the Robert Poole investigation and everything she had collected herself, including the *Daily Sketch* article from yesterday, which she turned facedown on the table so that the photograph would be out of sight. She read through it all: the discovery of Robert Poole's body by the woman from Social Services; the autopsy; the state of Michelle Doyce's room; Michelle Doyce's garbled account; the interviews with the people who lived in the house with her; the interviews with Mary Orton, Jasmine Shreeve, the Wyatts, and Janet Ferris. She noted the brief, clear statement by Tessa Welles, appended by a paper clip to the copy of Mary Orton's unexecuted will, and the statements made by Mary Orton's sons, in which Frieda felt she could hear their aggrieved self-righteousness. She read about the money trail, struggling to make sense of some of the vocabulary but understanding that Robert Poole's money had been removed by him from his bank account, transferred to another account that had been opened in Poole's name, and then emptied. She looked through the notes about the real Robert Poole, who had died years ago and whose photograph bore no resemblance to that of their victim. She stared at the sketch she had made and the visual produced by the police computers and read her own transcribed notes.

Her porridge arrived, and she sprinkled brown sugar over the top and ate it slowly, not interrupting her work. She made herself go through the *Daily Sketch* article once more, pausing, brow furrowed, when she came to Janet Ferris's appearance. Opening her notebook, she read what she had jotted down after seeing Janet: her loneliness, her affection for Poole, which was both romantic and motherly, her sense of duty. She'd put in brackets "cat" after this: the cat had been her inheritance from Robert Poole; caring for it, she was somehow still caring for him.

Frieda put down her spoon thoughtfully.

Depression is a grim and blinding curse: you can't see outside it. You can't see hope, or love, or how spring will follow winter. Frieda knew this, better than most, and yet she remained bothered by the cat. When Janet Ferris had decided to take her own life, she hadn't left food in the bowl for it or opened the window so that it could get out.

At last she got up, put her jacket on, left money on the table for her breakfast, and, calling good-bye, went out into the street. The wind was cool but not unkind. Usually on a Sunday morning, she would read the papers at Number 9, then go to the flower market on Columbia Road. But today she walked instead past Coram Fields and then up toward Islington and to Highbury Corner. She didn't know if Karlsson would be at home, but even if he wasn't, the journey gave her time to collect her thoughts. As always, walking was a way of thinking. The houses flowed past her, the pavements pressed against her feet, and the wind blew her hair back and filled her lungs.

At last she arrived at the Victorian semi-detached house where he lived in the lower-ground-floor flat. She had been there only once before, and then he had come to the door with his little daughter wrapped round him like a koala bear. Today he was alone, wearing running shorts and a sweat-drenched top, carrying a bottle of energy drink.

"Do you want to shower first?"

"Is something wrong?"

"You mean apart from everything else?"

"Yes."

"I don't know."

"Give me five minutes. You'd better come in." Frieda went down the steps and into the flat, stepping round a small tricycle and some red Wellingtons. "Put the kettle on," he said, and disappeared.

She heard the shower running, doors opening and closing. It felt too domestic and intimate, and she tried not to look at all the photographs of Karlsson-the-husband, Karlsson-the-father, Karlsson-the-friend. She filled the kettle and turned it on, opened cupboards until she found coffee and mugs, watched a blue tit on the bird table outside, pecking at some seed.

"Right." He stood beside her in jeans and a gray shirt, his face glowing and hair wet. "White, one sugar."

"You can put your own sugar in. You're not having the kids today."

"Later," he said brusquely.

"I'll make it quick, then."

"Why are you here?"

428

Frieda paused for a moment. "Before I say anything else, I'd better warn you about something."

" 'Warn,' " said Karlsson. "That means it's not something good."

"Reuben and Josef were at my place last night. They were trying to be consoling and they were drinking vodka and when they left there was a photographer outside and —"

"No," said Karlsson. "Let me guess. This is like you and the therapist in that restaurant. The incident that ended with you in a cell."

"Some punches were exchanged."

"What is it with you people? Was he hurt?"

"He was a bit knocked about."

"Well, it was two against one. Or was it three against one?"

"I came out and stopped it."

"That might get you a reduced sentence. Did he call the police?"

"I don't know," said Frieda. "I don't think so. I just wanted to warn you."

"We'll have to see what happens. What's the immigration status of your Polish friend?"

"He's Ukrainian. And I don't know."

"Try to keep him out of it. If he's charged, he'll probably be deported." Karlsson smiled thinly. "Any other crimes to report?"

"No, it's not that."

Karlsson's expression turned serious. "Yesterday must have been very distressing."

"I've spent this morning reading through the file."

"Instead of sleeping in, which is what you really need."

"I took the cat, you know."

"Yvette told me."

"When Janet Ferris killed herself, she didn't feed it or leave the window open. Before you say it, I know she was of unsound mind, but it doesn't feel right to me." Karlsson waited, and Frieda drew a deep breath. "I am not sure that she killed herself."

"You saw her, Frieda."

"I think she was killed."

"If I was your therapist —"

"Why do people keep saying that to me?"

"I would say that perhaps you need to believe she didn't take her own life because then you wouldn't feel so responsible for her death."

"I've thought of that, of course."

"You're upset, this has been a traumatic experience. But tell me, why on earth would anyone kill Janet Ferris?"

"She died after the article came out in the paper."

"Exactly," said Karlsson. "And you know what that does to you."

Frieda took the folder out of her bag, pulled out the *Daily Sketch,* and pointed to the paragraph. "She says here that Robert Poole told her things, confided in her. If whoever killed him read that, they'd be worried. Wouldn't they?"

Karlsson sighed heavily. "I don't know, Frieda. I don't know what they'd think. *I* think you're barking up the wrong tree."

"If someone killed Janet, I want to help find them."

Karlsson put his mug down. "Think about it, Frieda. Dean hanged himself, and you think he's still alive. Janet Ferris killed herself, and you think someone murdered her. Do you see a pattern?"

"Two events don't make a pattern."

"There's something about suicide that affects you very deeply."

Frieda glared at him and got up abruptly, the chair scraping the tiles.

"Where are you going now?" he asked. "You haven't touched your coffee."

"Now I've seen you, I'm going to Margate."

■ ■ ■ ■

Margate was where Dean and Terry had gone on holiday each summer, for ten days, taking his mother, June, until she'd needed too much care. Frieda had read that in Joanna's book, *An Innocent in Hell.* She had noted down the places they liked to visit: the beach, of course, and the old funfair with its wooden roller coaster. The shell grotto, the arcades. Joanna had written that Dean always bought humbugs from the old-fashioned sweetshop. Dean and his mother, June, had a sweet tooth: Frieda remembered the doughnuts he always used to bring to June Reeve, in their greasy brown-paper bag.

It was windy and wet when she arrived in the town. Not many people were on the streets, and the beach was practically empty, bits of paper and plastic blowing across it. She pulled her coat tighter around her and, putting her head down, walked swiftly to the B&B Joanna had mentioned, which was set back from the beach, with a sea view only from its top floor.

The man who came to the door had a livid birthmark covering one side of his face and was in a dressing gown over his clothes.

Frieda could hear the television in the next room, and smell meat frying.

"We're not open. It's out of season."

"I was hoping you could help me." Frieda had thought about what she was going to say and decided it was best to be straightforward. "I wanted to ask you about Dean Reeve."

A strange expression crossed both halves of the man's divided face, furtive and assessing.

"Who are you?"

"I'm Dr. Klein," said Frieda, hoping the medical tag would be enough. "Is it true that Dean Reeve stayed here?"

"I'm not sure I'm wanting that to get around. Might put people off. Then again, it might encourage them."

"How often did he come?"

"Ten years," he said promptly. "Every July. Him and his wife and his old mother."

"When did you last see him?"

"Must have been the July before . . . before he died."

"Not after?"

"How could it be after?"

"This might sound like a strange question, but you haven't met his brother, have you? They look — looked — identical."

The man peered at her. "Why would I

meet his brother?"

"I thought he might have come here. Out of interest. His name is Alan Dekker."

"Never heard of him."

"You've never even seen someone who reminded you of Dean?"

The man shook his head. "The thing is, he was always all right with me. Helped me mend the shower. I always thought there was something wrong with her, though."

"Her?"

"The old woman."

"But his brother never came?"

"I told you."

Frieda went through the town to the shell grotto that Joanna had written about so enthusiastically — an underground labyrinth whose every inch was lined with shells, in patterns and stripes and studded spirals. It made her feel slightly nauseated. But Dean had loved it here, said Joanna. He'd been obsessed with it. So she asked the woman at the desk, selling little boxes made of shells and postcards featuring shells, the same questions she had asked the man who ran the B&B.

"I don't know who you're talking about," answered the young woman. She had an Australian accent.

Frieda took a piece of paper from her pocket and unfolded it. "That's the man I'm talking about."

The girl smoothed it out and held it close to her face, then away from her, frowning. "No," she said.

"You're sure?"

"Course I'm not. Hundreds of people come through here. He could have done. I wouldn't remember."

Frieda walked back along the beach. The tide was coming in, little waves licking their way up the shore. An old man was the only other person she could see: he had a small, scruffy dog running round and round him, trying to get him to play, and every so often he stooped down very slowly, as if his back was creaking, and picked up a stick to throw for it. Frieda stared out across the gray, wrinkled sea and, for a moment, wished she was on a boat out there, alone and surrounded by water and sky.

# 37

Frieda had a meeting at the clinic. She arrived there early to go through her paperwork and catch up. Paz was on the phone, talking to someone; her job at the Warehouse seemed to consist of long and animated conversations with anyone who happened to call. Now she was waving her hands in the air, gesticulating to whomever was on the other end, her bangles clattering on her wrist, her long earrings swinging. She waved and made incomprehensible signs as Frieda passed. Reuben was in his room, but his patient hadn't arrived yet, and Frieda put her head round the door.

"How are your knuckles?" she said.

"We were just looking out for you," he said.

Frieda closed the door. "Defending my honor? What if he'd been carrying a knife? What if he'd fallen more heavily and hit his head?"

"We were doing what friends do."

"You were drunk. Or on the way to being drunk."

There was a pause.

"How's the cat?" he asked. He was sucking a mint. He was back on the cigarettes, she thought; he and Karlsson both.

"He woke me up at three by biting my toe. Also, he's eaten my jasmine plant and pissed in one of my shoes. Do you know anything about housetraining a cat?"

"No."

"I've asked Josef to put a cat flap in my door."

"Good idea. There's a woman in your office."

"I'm not expecting anyone."

"She looks a bit odd, like a toad."

Frieda walked down the corridor and opened her door. For a moment, she didn't recognize the woman who was sitting on the chair, her short legs curled under her, wearing a mustard yellow scarf wrapped round her gray hair.

"Hello, Dr. Klein."

"Hello."

"Or can I call you Frieda?"

"Whatever." She looked more closely and suddenly she knew. "You're Thelma Scott, aren't you?"

"Yes."

"Sorry I was slow to recognize you. When I last saw you, you were sitting in judgment over my treatment of Alan Dekker. You'll understand that I found the hearing rather intimidating."

"Of course."

Frieda suddenly felt so weary and dispirited she could hardly bring herself to speak. "What is it now?" she asked. "Is there a new complaint?"

Thelma took a tabloid from her bag and opened it. "Have you read today's paper?" she said.

"I don't read newspapers."

Thelma put reading glasses on and opened it. SHRINK IN STREET BRAWL, she read. "There's a picture of the photographer. It probably looks worse than it really is. 'Friends of controversial therapist Dr. Frieda Klein set on press photographer, Guy Durrant . . .' Well, I don't need to read the whole article out."

"I'd rather you didn't."

"I suppose the report is broadly accurate."

Frieda took the paper from Thelma's hands and looked at it. The story was written by Liz Barron again. She handed the paper back. "Broadly," she said.

"Who were the friends?" said Thelma.

"I've just come out of the office of one of them," said Frieda, pointing behind her.

"Reuben?" said Thelma. "Oh, for goodness' sake."

"I know."

"Are you all right?"

"What do you mean?"

"I don't pay much attention to gossip," said Thelma, "but I heard a story about you a year or two ago. It involved a colleague of mine and a fight in a restaurant in Kensington. It was probably exaggerated."

"I ended up in a police cell," said Frieda.

"I notice he didn't press charges. There was probably a reason for that."

"Yes, there was. Look, is this some disciplinary issue?"

Thelma looked puzzled. "If you mean, do I endorse public fighting by accredited psychotherapists — or even between accredited psychotherapists — then the answer is no." Thelma stood up. She was several inches shorter than Frieda. "I came because I was worried about the pressure on you."

"That's very kind of you, but this really isn't the best time, Dr. Scott."

"I just wanted to make sure you were clear about the BPC hearing. You weren't reprimanded. You weren't censured. I hope you understand that."

"You came all the way here to tell me so? Thank you. That's a kind gesture."

Thelma studied her closely. "I've looked you up," she said. "I've read some of your work. It's not entirely a battle, you against the rest of the world."

"I know. I've got a few people with me. I mean in my battle against the rest of the world."

Thelma pushed a hand into the pocket of her donkey jacket and pulled out Underground tickets with a business card. "Here," she said. "If you need someone to talk to sometime."

"Frieda thinks Janet Ferris was murdered," said Karlsson. "Might have been murdered."

Yvette took the coffees from a tray and passed them around the table. She looked at Jake Newton, who had spent the last couple of days assessing human resources management. "Did you want one?" she said.

He looked at the mugs as if they were a part of his evaluation. Chris Munster tore a sachet of sugar and tipped it into his.

"No," Newton said. "No. I think I'll pass on that."

Yvette took packets of sandwiches from a plastic bag. "Cheese and celery for you, boss. Tuna and cucumber for you, Chris."

440

She tossed the packets across the table. "Chicken for me." She looked at Newton. "Sorry. I didn't know you were coming."

"I'm just a fly on the wall," said Newton. "You don't need to feed me."

"Flies on the wall still have to eat," said Yvette. While Newton looked puzzled by that, as if he were trying to work out whether there was an insult behind it, she continued, "Is Frieda coming to the meeting to explain her theory?"

"She's seeing patients this afternoon," said Karlsson.

"How does the arrangement with her work?" said Newton.

"Good question," said Yvette.

"This isn't really the time or the place," said Karlsson, "but she receives a small retainer and she is entitled to expenses. None of which she has actually claimed. But I can provide you with details later, if you want."

"Thanks," said Newton. "I'd like that."

"She is also entitled to confidentiality," continued Karlsson, "which, unfortunately, she did not get when someone in this building leaked details of the investigation to the press."

"Whoops," said Newton, cheerfully.

"Nor did she receive proper support,"

added Karlsson, staring at Yvette, who turned pink and dropped her gaze.

"So," said Munster, "why does Frieda think Janet Ferris was murdered?"

"It's partly an instinct," said Karlsson. "She felt that Janet Ferris wasn't in a suicidal frame of mind. She should really be here to put her own case, but she said it was partly based on an assessment of her mood. Also, she had left her cat locked in. She didn't seem the sort of woman who would do that."

"I guess that the point about being suicidal," said Yvette, "is that you don't worry about things like that anymore. If you want to look after your cat, you don't kill yourself. Have they done the autopsy yet?"

"I just got off the phone with Singh."

"And?"

"He said that death was caused by asphyxia. That and the state of the body . . ."

"What do you mean 'state of the body'?" asked Newton.

"You don't want to know," said Yvette.

"She shat herself," said Munster.

"Really?" Newton's eyebrows went up.

"Loosening of the sphincter is a feature of hanging," said Karlsson. "As it is of other forms of death. It wasn't so much the evacuation of the bowels as the, er . . ." He made a gesture with his hands.

"The disposition," Yvette supplied.

"The splatter," added Munster.

"Please," said Karlsson. "Singh said there were no signs of any other injury, no bruising on her body. So, he said his view was that the death was a suicide. I asked him if he was sure Janet Ferris hadn't been strangled before she was hanged. He said one could never be sure. I asked him if it was possible that she was hanged forcibly. He said it wasn't *im*possible, but in that case he would have expected bruising, perhaps on the upper arms, and there wasn't any."

"So what was his final opinion?" asked Yvette.

"His *provisional* opinion is that it was suicide."

"Well, there we are."

"His job isn't to provide a theory," said Karlsson. "It's to report on the state of the body. Our job is to keep options open."

"We've got lots of options open," said Yvette. "They're all bloody open."

"That's why we're having this meeting." Karlsson took an angry bite from his sandwich, and the others waited for him to swallow. "At any moment, Crawford is going to ask where we've got to and, to be honest, I don't exactly know what we're going to say.

We don't know who Poole really was. We don't know within five days when he was killed, so we can't check alibis in any useful way. We don't know where he was killed, so we've got fuck-all forensics. We know roughly how he was killed, but we don't know why his finger was cut off." He paused for thought. "We know too bloody much about *why* he might have been killed. He was a con man and a thief. If someone fucked my wife, I'd want to kill them. If someone fucked my wife and got her to steal my money, I'd want to cut his finger off, feed it to him, and then strangle him with my bare hands. If someone cheated my mother, I'd want to kill him. If someone tried to get my mother to change her will so that she'd leave everything to a fucking con man, I'd want to kill him. If someone blackmailed me over my drinking problems, I'd also want to kill him. So . . ."

"But the Orton sons' alibis check out. Jeremy Orton was tied up day and night with some company takeover deal, and Robin Orton was in bed with flu."

"Alibis," said Karlsson, wearily. "I don't know. He could have got out of bed. And aren't there high-speed trains from Manchester?"

"Two hours and five minutes," said Yvette.

"What about Jasmine Shreeve?"

Karlsson gave a sour laugh. "From the sound of the TV programs she used to make, I'd give him a free pass for conning her."

"*House Doctor* wasn't that bad," said Munster.

"It bloody was," said Yvette. "Looking at people's psychology from their wallpaper."

"It was more of a guilty pleasure." Newton was in a good mood today, positively bouncy.

"Enough of the TV reviewing," said Karlsson. "However good or bad she was, she seems to have got off lightly. Maybe he really liked her, maybe he hadn't got around to conning her, or maybe he conned her in a way we haven't found out about yet. And then there's the possibility that he conned the wrong person, someone we don't even know about, perhaps someone in the past, and they caught up with him and taught him a lesson."

"That's a lot of maybes," said Yvette.

"And our main witness is insane and delusional. And our other main witness is dead." He took another bite of his sandwich. "None of this is good. But the question is: what do we do now?"

There was a long silence in which the only

445

sound heard was of sandwiches being chewed.

"Well?" said Karlsson.

"All right," said Yvette. "There are actually lots of things we know."

"Go on."

"We know that he earned his money by conning rich people. We know he slept with Aisling Wyatt and that he was probably going to blackmail Jasmine Shreeve. He fleeced Mary Orton and tried to make her change her will. As you say, there are lots of motives here — although the Jasmine Shreeve motive appears to be like the one for the Orton sons, a motive she didn't yet know about. We know he had a shed load of money that someone stole — or he put somewhere else, and we haven't managed to find out where." She paused. "Yet. We also now know how he found his victims."

"Do you?" Newton leaned forward. "I didn't know about this."

"Sorry," said Karlsson. "I wasn't aware we had to keep you up to date with all the details of our cases."

"They all used the same bank?" guessed Newton. "Or they all shopped at Harrods?"

"The second guess is warmer. They all bought very expensive items made of wood from a company where Poole briefly

446

worked. When he left, he took the list of clients with him, presuming — rightly, it seems — that they all had money to spare."

"That's clever," said Newton.

Karlsson thought he was enjoying himself far too much. "Unfortunately, it doesn't get us much further on." He turned to Yvette. "What do you think we should do next?"

"We lean on Aisling and Frank Wyatt. Separately."

"Lean on?" said Karlsson. "Meaning?"

"Give me some time alone with Frank Wyatt and put the following scenario to him: you confronted Robert Poole with what he'd done, you had a row, there was a struggle, you killed Poole by mistake, panicked, dumped the body. If he owns up to that, the CPS might well go for manslaughter, possibly even a suspended sentence if the judge is sympathetic."

Karlsson thought for a moment. "What about the missing finger?"

"Maybe there was a ring that would identify him."

"So he cut the finger off in a panic?"

"That's how we'll put it to him."

"And what about the money that was cleared out of Poole's account?"

"Poole could have done that himself to hide the trail."

"And it's now where?"

"Buried somewhere. Lost forever. Or in an account abroad." There was another silence. "Well, you never clear up everything."

"And Janet Ferris?"

"Suicide," said Yvette, promptly. "While the balance of her mind was disturbed."

Karlsson gave a grunt. "All right. We pull the Wyatts in for questioning. Before that, we dig up everything we can find about them." He looked at the desk diary. "Wednesday morning," he said. "First thing. Chris, you go and check out alibis for both of them before then."

"I think it's Jasmine Shreeve," said Newton.

There was a silence and a slow smile grew on Karlsson's face. "What?"

"Sorry," said Newton. "Ignore what I said."

"Well, we've already got a psychotherapist working on the inquiry. Why not a management consultant as well? Why do you think it's Jasmine Shreeve?"

"She's got more to lose than the others. I've seen interviews with her. She still has a hopeless fantasy that she's going to have a comeback. If she was humiliated by a con man, it would ruin any chance of that. And anyone who's seen her on TV knows how needy shc is. If she felt she had been betrayed, she could have done anything."

"Thank you for that," said Karlsson. "You'll forgive me if I don't send you off to interview Jasmine Shreeve for us. I'll talk to her myself. And if your theory turns out to be right, then Yvette and Chris will cook you a bang-up dinner."

"Why don't you do it yourself?" said Yvette.

"That wouldn't be much of a reward."

"And what's Dr. Klein going to be doing?"

"I think she was on the verge of dropping out."

"Why?" said Yvette. "Did she get fed up?"

"It looks like she took it out on that photographer." Munster grinned at Yvette, then caught Karlsson's eye and stopped grinning.

"She told me about it," said Karlsson. "It wasn't her, it was two of her friends."

"It's not very professional," said Munster. "She gets into the papers. Then there's a fight with a photographer and she's in the papers again. It's like having Britney Spears on the inquiry."

Karlsson shook his head. "I think she felt too involved. She felt she'd let Janet Ferris down." He screwed up the sandwich wrapping and tossed it at a bin. It bounced off the rim on to the floor. "It's not as if we're doing such a good job ourselves."

There was a knock on the door and a woman put her head round. "There's someone to see you, sir," she said apologetically.

Lorna Kersey was in her mid- to late forties, Karlsson guessed, with cropped brown hair and round glasses. She was wearing no makeup but had chunky earrings and several rings on her small hands. She was wrapped in a voluminous orange cardigan and was wearing snow boots, but she still looked cold. Her husband, Mervyn, was a small, plump man with silvering hair who looked older than she. He sat upright and still in his chair and pressed his hands together, as if he were praying. Every so often, Lorna would reach out and touch him gently — on his shoulder, his arm, his thigh — to reassure him, and he would glance toward her and smile.

"I don't want to waste your time," she said.

"I understand it's about Robert Poole. I'm in charge of the case and would be interested to hear anything you have to say."

"Well, that's the thing. The man we know

isn't called Robert Poole. He might be someone different."

"What is he called?"

"Edward Green."

"Go on."

"It was the poster. It was clearly him."

"And this man, Edward Green, you haven't seen him for a while?" She grimaced. "It's to do with our daughter."

"Hang on. Your daughter's not called Sally, is she?"

"Sally?" She looked bewildered. "No. She's Beth. I mean, she's Elizabeth, really, but she's called Beth. Beth Kersey."

"Sorry. Go on, then."

Lorna Kersey leaned toward him. Close-up, Karlsson could see the creases and lines on her face.

"We've got three daughters. Beth is the eldest. She's nearly twenty-two now. Her birthday is in March. Her sisters are younger. They're still at school, and I don't think that helped much." Karlsson saw her swallow, saw how her fingers pressed against the rim of the desk. "She's always been a troubled girl, from the moment she was born, you could say. A worry to us." She glanced at her husband, then back again. "She was unhappy, you see, and angry. She just seemed made that way."

"I'm sorry," said Karlsson. "Where is your daughter now?"

"That's it," she said. "We don't know. I'm trying to explain things, how we got here. What I'm trying to say is that she was always troubled. School was a problem for her, though she liked things like art and practical subjects, things she could do with her hands. And she was strong. She could run for miles and swim in the coldest water. She didn't make friends easily." She hesitated. "I'm sorry, you don't want to hear about all of that. What's relevant is that she had a wretched adolescence. She thought she was ugly and stupid, and she was lonely and very needy but hard to help. We did everything we could, but it just became worse as she got older. It was tearing us apart as a household. Then she started getting into trouble."

"What kind?"

"The trouble that teenagers get into. Drugs, probably, but there was always an anger, an unhappiness. She could be violent, to other people and to herself as well."

"Was she arrested?"

"No. There were police sometimes, but she was never actually arrested. We took her to see people. Doctors. Psychiatrists. She was referred to a counselor at the hospital, and then we went to someone private. I don't know if it was doing any good. Maybe we were just making her feel even more of an outsider and bad about herself. You don't know until it's too late if what you're doing is right or wrong, do you? There's no magic answer to things like this — you just hope that bit by bit something may change. It was all so — so mysterious. Baffling. We didn't know what we'd done to make her like this and — oh, it got so bad, we didn't know where to turn." She blinked, and Karlsson saw her eyes were full of tears. "I'm making this too emotional," she said, trying to smile. "It's probably not relevant. Sorry."

"Then she met this man." They were Mervyn Kersey's first words. He had a faint Welsh accent.

"The man you knew as Edward Green?"

"Yes."

"How did she meet him?"

"We're not sure. But she used to spend time just walking, sometimes all night. I think she met him then."

Karlsson nodded. This sounded like Robert Poole.

"We didn't know about him at first. She didn't tell us. She just changed. We both noticed it. At first we were glad: she was calmer, less volatile with us and her sisters. She went out more. We were just so relieved."

"But?"

"She was very secretive — furtive is the word, really. We started suspecting that she was stealing money from us. Not much, but there'd be cash missing from our wallets, stuff like that."

"And her sisters' savings," put in Mervyn Kersey. He spoke as if he could hardly bear to squeeze the words out. Karlsson thought he was ashamed.

"Did you meet him?" asked Karlsson.

"Yes. I couldn't believe it," said Lorna Kersey. "He was so — what's the word? — polite, personable. He was sweet to the girls and lovely with Beth. I should have liked him more than I did. This will sound awful. I didn't trust him because I thought he could have had anyone, so why would he choose Beth? I loved my daughter, but I couldn't see why a handsome, successful young man like him would go for a plump, unhappy, unglamorous, underachieving, and angry young woman. It didn't make sense. Does that sound callous?"

"No," said Karlsson, untruthfully. "So, what did you think?"

She looked at him unflinchingly. "I won't

say that we're rich . . ." she began.

"We are," said her husband. "By most people's standards."

"The point is," she continued, "that he would have known we were comfortably off."

"You thought he was after your money?"

"I worried."

"And now she's gone."

"She stole my bank card, emptied my current account, took a few clothes, and went."

"Where?"

"I don't know. She left a note saying we had controlled her for too long and tried to make her into someone she didn't want to be, and now she was free at last."

"Did she go with Robert . . . Edward Green?"

"We assume so. We never saw him again and we haven't seen her." She shut her eyes for a moment. "We haven't seen our daughter for thirteen months. Or heard from her, or heard anything about her. We don't know if she's alive or dead, happy away from us or wretched. We don't know if she wants us to find her, but we've tried and tried to. We just want to know if she's all right. She doesn't need to come home, she doesn't need to see us, if that's what she wants. We contacted the police, but they said there was nothing they could do about a twenty-year-old woman who had gone of her own free will. We even hired someone. Nothing."

"Did she have a mobile phone?"

"She did, but it doesn't seem to be operational."

"And this Edward Green looked very similar to this man?" Karlsson pointed at the poster of Robert Poole tacked to the board beside him.

"It looks just like him. But if he's dead, where's our daughter?"

She stared at Karlsson. He knew she wanted some kind of reassurance, but he couldn't give it. "I'm going to send two officers home with you. They'll need access to any documentation you have, the names of doctors. We'll be taking this seriously."

When they had gone, he sat in silence for several minutes. Did this make things better or worse?

Beth Kersey started with the photographs of her family. She had taken them with her when she'd left, on his instructions, but she hadn't looked at them. It was too painful and stirred up feelings in her that only confused and distressed her. He had looked at them, though, for a long time, when he'd thought she was asleep, and then he had wrapped them up in plastic bags and stowed them away with his other bags.

Now she laid them in front of her, one by one. She had a large box of matches that she had taken from the deck of the boat up the path one night, and she lit a match for each picture, letting it flare and then die down over a face, a group, a garden in spring. They were all lies, she thought bitterly. Everyone smiles for a photograph; everyone poses and puts on a public face. There was her mother with her camera expression, head a bit to one side, all tender and caring, butter wouldn't melt. And her dad, plump and sweet, when everyone knew he was a bully who'd made money by taking it from other people. Ed had explained it to her, why it was wrong, why the money didn't really belong to her father. She had forgotten the details, but they didn't matter. And her two sisters. There were days when she could barely remember their names, but she could remember how they'd been such goody-goodies, good at school and good at home, sucking up to their parents, coaxing money and favors out of them with their winning smiles. She knew that now. Once she had simply thought them better than her at belonging in the world, easier in their skins than her, blessed where she was cursed. Now she stared in the leap of flame at Lily's narrow face grinning between two tight plaits, Bea's solemn gaze. Then she was looking at herself. Elizabeth. Betty. Beth. She wasn't that person anymore, sloppy and angry, anxious to please and knowing she wouldn't. She was thin now, muscle and bone. Her lip sneered under its gash. Her hair was short. She had passed through fire and come out purified.

## 38

Josef was painting Mary Orton's baseboards white. As he drew the brush along the wood, he tried not to think about his children. His chest burned when he pictured them at home without him, or when he remembered the last time he had seen them. He had tried to hold them too tightly and they had shrunk away from him, from the smell on his breath and the wildness in his eyes. So he concentrated on the smoothness of the paint. He looked up from his work to find Mary Orton standing behind him, her hands clutching a dishcloth and her face anxious.

"I can help?"

"I want to show you something."

Josef laid the brush on the lid of the tin and scrambled to his feet. "Of course, show me," he said reassuringly.

"This way."

She led him upstairs to her bedroom, the

one room of the house he hadn't been into. It had high ceilings, patterned wallpaper, and its large window looked out on to the garden, where spring bulbs were at last pushing their way through the cold soil. She went to a small bureau, opened it, and fumbled in the small drawer for something. He could see she was agitated. Her fingers were clumsy and her breath labored.

"Here."

She turned and put a folded piece of paper into his hands, and he stared down at the lines of blue ink, the frail, old-fashioned handwriting, all the letters looped and crossed.

"This is what?" he asked. "Really, my English not good, Mrs. Orton."

"I did make a will," she whispered. There were tears in her eyes as she stared at him. "I was going to give a third of it to him. We drew it up together, and we got a neighbor down the road to witness it. Look. Here is their signature and mine."

"I am sorry," he said. "I am wrong person here."

"Because they never come to see me. They don't care — and he cared."

"He?"

"Robert. He spent time with me, like you have. To them I'm just a burden. I suppose

I should just burn this. Or is that wrong?"

Josef stood and held the piece of paper in his paint-smeared hand. He shook his head.

"What shall I do?"

"I don't know. I give it to Frieda."

Frieda walked home across Waterloo Bridge. They'd seen a film and then gone for a late meal at a Moroccan restaurant, where the air had smelled of cinnamon and roasting meat. Afterward, she had felt a sudden need to be alone. He was obviously disappointed, but something was holding her back. He had kissed her on the cheek and gone.

She walked slowly, and when she was halfway across the bridge, she stopped as she always did. Usually it was to look up-river at Parliament and the Eye and down-river at St. Paul's, but this time she just leaned on the railing and stared down into the water. The Thames never seemed to flow as a river should. It moved more like a vast tide, and with the tide there were eddies and whirlpools and clashing currents. After a few minutes, she didn't even see the water. She thought of the film she had just watched and of Robert Poole, whoever he really was. She thought of the traditional child's fantasy that you are the only real person in the world and everybody else is an actor. Poole had been a sort of actor, taking on a different character for everyone he met, giving them the person they needed, the person who would seduce them. Then she allowed herself to think about Harry, in his light gray suit with his gray-blue eyes and his crisp white shirt, the way he bent toward her when she spoke and took the crook of her elbow when they crossed the road. The way he watched her and seemed to be trying to hear the things she would not say. It had been such a long time since she had let anyone come near her.

Gradually her thoughts stopped being specific, stopped being about anything at all but swirling and dark, like the river beneath her. Out of that darkness came a face and a name: Janet Ferris.

Frieda shivered. It was cold and exposed on the bridge. As she turned toward home, she looked at her watch. It was a quarter to midnight. Too late to phone Karlsson. She walked home quickly, got into bed, and lay in the dark, agitated, her eyes burning. She wanted it to be day again, but day took a long time to come.

# 39

Frieda had seen three patients, one after another. She was aware that her mind was partly elsewhere, and she made a steely effort to concentrate, to be professional, precise. Or was she just playing the part of the attentive, sympathetic therapist? Maybe it was all a performance, once you got down to it. After the final session she wrote her brief notes, walked outside, flagged down a taxi, and twenty minutes later she was outside the house in Balham.

Karlsson and Jake Newton were standing on the doorstep. Karlsson was talking on his mobile. He nodded at her but continued talking. Newton smiled. "Hi," he said. "How are you doing?"

Frieda found the greeting strangely difficult to respond to. "I don't know," she said. "OK."

"Cheers." Karlsson put his phone into his pocket. He looked at Frieda. "Afternoon."

"You didn't have to come yourself," said Frieda. "I just wanted someone to let me in."

"I was curious. I wanted to know what you were up to."

"And I want to see what a consultant does," said Newton.

"I thought *you* were a consultant," said Frieda.

"Pretend I'm not here."

"By the way," said Karlsson, "there's something else." And there, outside Janet Ferris's home, he told Frieda about Beth Kersey and her involvement with Robert Poole. Frieda frowned as he spoke.

"That must account for Poole's missing days," she said.

"It may," said Karlsson.

"You've got to find this woman."

"Well, yes. That was our plan."

"And you need to find out about her medical history."

"We'd thought of that as well."

"If you get the name of the psychiatrist who treated her, I might be able to talk to him unofficially."

"We'll see about that."

"I thought criminal investigations were about eliminating suspects," said Frieda. "In this case, new ones keep popping up."

"In this case," said Karlsson, "it's difficult to tell the suspects from the victims. But at least it stops you thinking about Dean Reeve."

Frieda turned on him an expression that was almost fierce. "I think about Dean Reeve every day. And when I go to sleep, I dream about him."

"What can I say?" said Karlsson. "I'm sorry. But now, why are we here? What's this about?"

"I wanted to see Poole's flat, as well," said Frieda.

"Let's see it then." Karlsson took out a bunch of keys and examined the paper labels attached to them. Nobody spoke as they made their way into the house and then up to the flat. As they stepped inside, Frieda recognized the musty smell of a house nobody lives in, of a place where nothing is moved, no window opened, no air breathed. They stood in the main room. Frieda felt constrained: she'd wanted to be alone for this. "Did you bring the photographs?" she asked.

Karlsson took out a file from his bag. "These were taken when Janet Ferris's body was found."

"That's no good," said Frieda. "What about before, when you first came here?"

"We don't have photographs of that."

"Why? Wasn't it a crime scene?"

"No. It wasn't. Not that we knew of. And we had the room. We didn't need to photograph it."

"Fine," said Frieda.

She stood in the middle of the room and looked around, slowly, trying to examine everything.

"What are you looking for?" said Newton.

"Shut up," said Frieda. "Sorry. I didn't mean that. Please, just give me a moment."

There was a long silence. The two men looked at each other awkwardly, like people who had arrived too early at a party and were stuck with each other. Finally, she turned to Karlsson. "If you closed your eyes, would you be able to describe everything in this room?"

"I don't know. Most of it."

Frieda shook her head. "Years ago, I didn't take many notes after my sessions. I thought that if it was important I'd remember it. My remembering it would be a sign it was important. But I changed my mind. Now, if it's important, I write it down." She pulled a face, signaling frustration. "I don't know. There's something, but I can't quite grasp it."

"What is it?" said Karlsson.

"If I knew . . ." she began. Then she frowned. "Can we go downstairs? Do you have the key to her flat?"

Karlsson pulled out the bunch of keys. "Somewhere here," he said. "I feel like a jailer in an old movie."

"How do you decide when to give up?" said Newton, as they were walking downstairs.

"Is this for your report?" said Karlsson.

"I'm just curious."

"There's never a moment. But the urgency goes, people are reassigned."

Karlsson unlocked the door, and they walked into Janet Ferris's flat. Frieda found this abandoned space sadder. There was a mug on the table, a book next to it. She could imagine Janet Ferris walking in, picking it up, and carrying on. She tried not to think of that. It was a distraction. She looked around the room. She felt she was searching for something — and suddenly she found it. She turned to Karlsson. "Do you see that picture? Of the fish."

"Yes."

"Do you like it?"

He smiled. "I think it's lovely. But you'll have to leave it here. Nowadays we're not really allowed to help ourselves."

"When I first saw Poole's flat, this paint-

467

ing was there. Not here."

"Really?"

"You read the newspaper article. Janet Ferris said that Poole used to lend her things. Among other things, he gave — or lent — her a painting, and she lent him one of hers. She said she returned it and took hers back."

Karlsson's brow furrowed. "Interfering with a crime scene," he said, then caught Frieda's eye. "Or a semi-crime scene. Well, no harm done."

"We should go upstairs again," said Frieda.

Back in Poole's flat, Frieda stood once more in the center of the room. She looked at the pictures on Poole's wall. There were five: the Eiffel Tower, a Madonna and Child, a sun in a seascape, a poppy field, and a pine tree with the moon behind it. Frieda took a pair of transparent plastic gloves from her pocket and put them on. "I bought these from the chemist," she said. She glanced at Newton. "Don't worry. I'm not going to charge them to the taxpayer."

She walked to the picture of the Madonna, lifted it from the wall, and stepped back. She placed the picture on the desk. She turned to Karlsson. "What do you see?"

"A rather crappy picture," said Karlsson.

"I don't think that's worth stealing. I prefer the one of the fish."

"No," said Frieda. "Look at the wall where the picture was." Frieda picked up the picture and held it next to the mark. "It's not the same size."

"But . . ." Karlsson began, and stopped.

"Maybe it's the same size as the fish painting that was hanging here until the woman took it back," said Newton.

"But that was here for only a few weeks," said Frieda. "Those marks take years."

"I don't know what this is about," said Karlsson. "Poole might just have got tired of his pictures and moved them around."

"You're right. That's possible. Let's see." Frieda lifted the pine tree painting off the wall.

"Different shape," said Karlsson. "See?"

Then in turn Frieda took down the other three paintings. In each case the mark was smaller than the painting.

"There we are," said Karlsson. "Poole did some rehanging before he disappeared. I'm not sure this was worth coming all the way down to Balham to see."

Frieda didn't reply. She just looked at Karlsson, then at Newton. A smile slowly appeared on his face.

"They shouldn't all be smaller."

"What do you mean?" said Karlsson.

"Shall we rearrange them?" said Frieda.

"What do you mean?"

She picked up the Madonna and Child and held it against one of the patches on the wall. "What do you think?"

Newton shook his head. "The picture's too big." She moved it along the wall. "That's right," he said.

She did the same with the other pictures, holding them one by one against the shapes on the wall, while Karlsson and Newton nodded or shook their heads. They were left with two pictures and two spaces. The pine tree was slightly smaller than one space and much larger than the smallest. The seascape was larger than both spaces.

"They don't fit," said Karlsson.

"That's right."

"Now there are two pictures," continued Karlsson, "and two spaces, which neither of them fits. It's doing my head in, and I don't even know why I should be caring about it."

"But it's interesting, isn't it?" said Frieda.

"He could have got rid of a painting," said Newton, "and bought two new ones."

"They came with the flat. He wouldn't have got rid of them. Except this one." Frieda touched the picture of the pine tree.

"It's cheap and nasty but it's new, don't you think?"

Karlsson examined the shiny frame. "It does look new."

"It must be around here somewhere," said Frieda.

"What?" said Karlsson.

"One of the pictures."

"Where?"

"It'll be somewhere. Down the side of something, somewhere out of the way."

Newton found it under Poole's bed, where it was stowed with an old mattress. He carried it through with an air of pride. It was a picture of a windmill and a horse. There was something synthetic about the colors so it seemed to shimmer.

"No wonder he kept it under the bed," said Karlsson.

He took the painting and held it in front of the larger patch. It was the right size. "All right. Now we've still got a painting too many."

"No," said Frieda. "We've got *two* paintings too many."

She walked across to the pine dresser that stood by the wall farthest from the window and knelt down beside it. "Look," she said.

Karlsson and Newton peered down. Frieda pointed at two small depressions in the carpet.

"It's been moved," she said. "Just a couple of feet. But . . ." She paused for a moment. "Let's move it back."

The three of them took hold of the dresser and moved it back.

"Bloody hell," said Newton.

Where the dresser had been, there was another patch on the wall. They could see at a glance that it was the same size as the seascape, but Karlsson held it up to confirm it.

Karlsson turned to Frieda. "So, what the fuck does it mean?"

"It means that someone's been here," said Frieda. "With all the risks it entailed, someone had to come here."

Back outside the house, Karlsson asked Jake Newton if he could give them a moment. He and Frieda walked a few paces along the road. When Karlsson spoke, it was without looking at her. "I talked to your friend Reuben," he said.

"What about?"

"About the encounter they had with the photographer outside your house. I wanted to be clear about what had happened. Obviously, if the two of them had made an unprovoked attack on the man, it could

472

potentially be treated as a serious case of assault." Now Karlsson stopped. His hands were in his pockets against the cold. "Reuben — Dr. McGill — told me that the photographer had obstructed your other friend, Josef, and then struck him. While Reuben was trying to separate them, he inadvertently struck the photographer in the face."

"Inadvertently?"

"Yes. Since there were no other witnesses . . ."

"I was a witness," said Frieda.

"Apparently you arrived only when the incident was almost over. Even if the photographer disputes their version, I'm clear that no action will be taken."

"Are you sure you didn't coach Reuben about the best way of getting out of this?"

"For God's sake, Frieda, just let it go."

"What do you think of people who just let things go because it's convenient?"

Karlsson took time to speak, breathing deeply. "What I think, first, is that if there had been a conspiracy to pervert a police inquiry between me and Reuben, then I would be dismissed and he would be struck off. And what I think, second, is, don't be so fucking pompous."

This is how it begins, Frieda thought.

Then she looked harder at Karlsson. "Are you all right?" she said.

"Yes."

"Really?"

"I'm fine," he said. "Of course, things are a bit, you know . . ."

"Like, what things?"

"Well, for example, my children are going to live in Spain with their mother."

It took Frieda a few seconds to register what he had just said. "That's tough for you."

"Yes."

"How long for?"

"Two years."

"Two years is a long time when they're so young."

"Tell me about it."

"Why is she taking them away?"

"Her new partner has been offered a promotion there."

"Did you try to make her change her mind?"

"I'm not going to stop her, but she knows how I feel."

"How do you feel?"

Now he turned away, as if he was embarrassed. "I work. I come back to an empty flat. I live for the days my kids come — and now they won't. Oh, I'll go and see them, of course, and they'll come for holidays, but he'll be the real father."

Fathers and their children, thought Frieda, remembering Josef's brown eyes but seeing Karlsson's drawn face.

Jake Newton was talking on his mobile.

"That arsehole Newton," Karlsson said now, "wants to be taken on a tour of the custody suites."

"I can walk from here," she said.

She touched him on the cheek with two fingers, very lightly.

"I haven't told anyone."

"I'm glad you told me."

"I didn't mean to."

"Well, thank you. And I'm sorry to add to your troubles." And she was gone.

# 40

"I'm glad you called!"

Frieda was in her room, gazing down at the wasteland outside the mansion block. Patches of grass and small scrubby plants were springing up where the bulldozers had been. Children pelted across the open spaces. A woman with a tiny ball of fluff on a leash pushed her way through a break in the fence and stepped into the wasteland quite casually, as if it were a park.

"Good. Although I was actually ringing you on business."

"Oh. Well, that's better than nothing," Harry said ruefully.

"I was hoping you could meet me at Olivia's house in the next few days and sort out her finances a bit. I don't think she's filed her tax returns for years, or kept any records. It's all a bit of a mess. I thought while your sister sorted out her legal affairs, maybe you could have a go at her financial ones."

"Tonight?"

"What?"

"I could come straight after a meeting near Old Street. About six?"

"Really?" Frieda asked doubtfully. She had been thinking of going straight home after her last patient and spending a longed-for evening alone.

"If your sister-in-law is available, of course."

"I'll call her now."

"And after, if you felt like it, you could invite me to have a glass of wine with you."

"All right, I give in." She smiled and put the phone down. That morning, she'd had an e-mail from Sandy. He was coming back to the UK for two weeks, he said; his sister was getting married. There was a party at Lauderdale House in Highgate, which he and Frieda had once visited together. He wanted to see her. Please. She had read the e-mail and deleted it. But, of course, she could still reply. She could still say yes. Or she could say no. No: that bit of my life is over. I can imagine going on without you.

Now here she was, just before six, in Olivia's house again. Kieran, the funeral director's accountant, was there as well. He was sitting at the kitchen table with a large pile of broken china laid out in front of him on a sheet of newspaper, a tube of superglue, and a piece of pink sandpaper. Frieda watched as he patiently matched fragments, his glasses perched on the end of his nose and a look of concentration on his face. He was happy, she thought, lost in his task.

"He's mending all my favorite broken china," said Olivia, exuberantly. "Tessa's sorting out my alimony, your new friend Harry's dealing with the taxes, and Kieran's putting my life back together."

"And what are you doing?" asked Frieda, feeling irritated by Olivia's radiant assumption that someone would always sort out the havoc she created.

"Me? Pouring wine? No? Tea, then?"

"Tea would be good."

"Tessa's coming as well. Did I tell you?"

"No."

"Just to drop off some forms I need to sign or something. You know that woman has *literally* saved my life."

"That might be putting it too strongly. Where's Chloë?"

"Out with friends, I imagine. I haven't seen her."

"It's Wednesday."

"Yes?"

"Does she often go out on a school evening?"

"Frieda, she's seventeen. What were *you* doing when you were seventeen?"

There was a knock on the door and Frieda went to answer it. Harry and Tessa stood on the doorstep, and once again she was struck by how similar they were. Harry, looking serious, was wearing a dark suit and a pale green shirt. He smiled at Frieda and his face softened, but he didn't greet her with his usual effusiveness. Tessa nodded at Frieda and held up a thick brown envelope.

"I'll get Olivia to sign these and be on my way," she said.

"It's good of you to bring them round in person."

"I was more or less passing," said Tessa. "It seemed simpler, and I'm trying to speed things up a bit."

Olivia called from the kitchen, offering coffee or something stronger. Everything had to be personal for her, thought Frieda. She couldn't just have a solicitor or a financial adviser; she needed to make them into her friends, spectators of her personal dramas. She kissed Tessa, then took Harry's hand in both of hers and held it for longer than necessary. She introduced them both to Kieran, who nodded, blushed, and returned to his painstaking work. She put her large signature on the papers Tessa laid in front of her, then kissed her again, in farewell.

She turned to Harry. "How are we going to do this? I've tried to collect any of the old statements and receipts I've got, but I warn you, I've let everything slide dreadfully."

"We should go into your living room, away from these two, and start trying to put some order into your affairs," said Harry, gravely. "It will take some time. This is just the start, when I'll assess your needs, but we're going to try and build up some kind of record for you and see what we've got. Anything you've kept will be useful, and I can try to fill in the gaps. I'm going to create a system for you that you should be able to keep to in the future. All right?"

"I already feel in safe hands," said Olivia, beaming up at him. Frieda wondered if she was on some new kind of medication.

"Good," said Harry.

Frieda scrutinized him for any hint of mockery or contempt, but could find none. He seemed more like a doctor with a patient than a financial adviser with a client.

"Right!" said Olivia. She swept the bottle

of wine from the table and grabbed a glass.

"Just tea for me," said Harry. He glanced briefly at Frieda. "Will you still be here when we're done?"

"It depends on how long you take."

"I'd say about an hour."

"In that case, I'll be here."

"Good. There's something I'd like to say to you."

Frieda helped Kieran mend pottery. Some of the pieces she recognized: the old Indian tree platter that had belonged to a set her grandmother used to own. It must have passed to David, and from him into the unsafe hands of Olivia. The white bone china teapot, whose handle Kieran now stuck expertly back into place, delicately sanding away the tiny ridge of glue that was left when it dried. She remembered — she thought she remembered — her mother pouring tea from it. It gave her a strange feeling to see these pieces lying in broken bits on Olivia's cluttered table, yet there was something consoling in the way Kieran was putting them back together. He felt her gaze and glanced up. "It's satisfying," he said. "And restful."

It occurred to Frieda that, for a man who liked rest, he had chosen a very restless partner in Olivia, and he must have sensed something of this because he suddenly said, "Olivia has been good for me."

"I'm glad," said Frieda. She excused herself for a moment and went into the hall to make a call to Chloë. The phone rang and rang and then switched to voice mail. She ended the call and was about to turn her mobile off again, when it vibrated in her hand.

"Frieda?"

"Yes. Where are you, Chloë?"

"What do you mean, where am I?"

"I mean, where are you?"

"I'm at home. Why?"

"At home?"

"Is something wrong?"

"I thought you were out."

"What are you talking about?"

"This is ridiculous. Hang on."

She ran up the stairs and knocked on Chloë's door, which opened a crack to reveal Chloë's bewildered face.

"What? Frieda? I don't get it."

"I was downstairs. I've been here since six. Olivia thought you were out."

"Yeah, well."

"You've been here all the time?"

"Yeah."

"Why didn't you let Olivia know you were in?"

"She didn't ask. I didn't think she'd be interested."

"When did you get back from school?" Frieda looked at her niece's sullen expression. "Did you go to school?"

"I had a headache."

"Does your mother know?"

A shrug. The door opened a bit wider. Frieda could see the litter of the room. "Did you go yesterday?"

"What is this? Interrogation time?"

"Did you?"

"Maybe not."

"Why?"

"I didn't feel like it."

"When did you last go?"

"Monday. For a bit."

"And Olivia doesn't know about this?"

"Not until you tell her."

Frieda paused. She looked at Chloë's face and the dim, jumbled interior of her room. "You're going to school tomorrow," she said. "In the evening, I'll collect you from here at seven o'clock and take you for a meal somewhere and we can talk. All right?"

Another shrug.

"Chloë?"

"K."

"And you'll promise to go to school?"

"Yeah."

"Have a shower now. Put on some clean clothes, do a bit of work, and then come downstairs and have a meal with your mother. All right?"

"Maybe."

"Chloë, I'm serious."

"OK. Is he here?"

"Kieran?"

"Yeah."

"He's in the kitchen, mending Olivia's broken china. Why? Don't you like him being here?"

"She forgets about me even more." She added grudgingly, "He's all right, though. He pays attention."

"Right. Shower. Meal. Work. Up in the morning at a proper time — I'll call you to make sure you are — and then off to school. Be waiting for me at seven."

As she went downstairs, she heard Olivia's thin, violent screech of laughter from the living room and Harry's steadying voice in response. The door opened as she came into the hall.

"All done for now," said Harry, cheerfully. "I think we've made some headway."

"Good." She turned to Olivia. "Chloë's

upstairs in her room."

"Is she? Mysterious child!"

"She needs a proper supper."

"Kieran's cooking."

"Cooking for three, then. And pay her proper regard."

Olivia made a face at Harry. "See how scary she is!"

Harry put on his coat. "Are you leaving now?" he asked Frieda.

"Yes. We can go together. 'Bye, Olivia," she added, cutting Olivia off mid-exclamation.

They walked in silence down the street, and when they came to the main road, Frieda said, "There's a bar just along the road that's OK."

Harry ordered a glass of red wine for himself, a ginger beer for Frieda, and they sat at a table in the corner. "Are you all right?" he asked.

"Family stuff," she said.

"I gathered."

"Are her finances in a dreadful state?"

"I've seen worse. That's not what I wanted to say."

"Go on."

"I've been thinking about you." He held up a hand before she could speak. "Not just about what I feel — that's not what I want to talk to you about. I don't want to be oppressive in any way. I've been thinking about what you've been going through recently. I get the impression you're not good at confiding in people, but I know you've been having a rough time with everything that's been going on, and I think you're being extraordinarily strong and impressive about it, and I would very much like to help if I can. If only by being someone you can turn to, talk to." He sat back and ran his hand over his brow in self-mockery. "There. It's not often I speak without irony for more than one sentence."

"Thank you," said Frieda, simply.

"You're welcome."

"What do you know about my rough time?"

"The complaint against you, and that book, then all the awful stuff in the papers."

"It's been worse for other people."

He took a small sip of his red wine. "And you finding that poor woman's body."

"How did you know that?" Frieda asked.

"Sorry. Olivia told Tessa and Tessa told me."

"How did Olivia know?"

"I think her daughter told her. But before you ask, I've no idea how she knew."

"I see."

"I haven't been spying on you. It was hard to avoid."

"I understand that." She looked at him, and he didn't drop his eyes.

"How do you deal with it all?"

"I'm not sure that I really do." She twisted her glass round. "It's like winter. I just trudge through, head down, and hope that spring won't be delayed."

That was it, she thought, the Frieda Klein method of survival, but not one she would recommend to her patients or her friends.

"You just endure."

"I just try to endure."

"And if you can't?"

"I don't have a choice."

Was that true? There had been times in her life when she had been so engulfed by darkness that she had had to grope her way through it, blindly, without hope and without expectation. "You just keep going because you keep going." Who had said that to her? Her father, and look at him, after all.

"If you feel you can't, remember there are people who would like to be there for you."

"You hardly know me."

"I know enough."

She lifted her glass and took a fiery sip. "I'm fine, really. Just a bit tired."

"Is it this case?"

"Partly." She frowned to herself, then continued, "When I first got involved with the police, it was because of the disappearance of a child. Two children, in fact."

"I know," said Harry. "I read about it."

"That was a crime everybody wanted to solve. It's different with this man, Robert Poole. All we know about him is that he cheated people and exploited them. As your sister noticed, though she seemed to be the only one who did. I think what they mainly feel is that he's not worth the trouble. Mainly they wish the case would just go away."

"What does that mean?"

"I suppose I'm discovering that the police are like everybody else. There are some parts of their work that interest them more than others."

"That reminds me of my cleaner," said Harry. "She's from Venezuela. She loves dusting and she loves putting things into piles. What she doesn't like is washing the really nasty bits behind and under things."

Frieda smiled. "In that analogy, Robert Poole is the bit behind the fridge that you can't be bothered to wash because it means you have to move it."

"I don't think I've ever even thought of

cleaning behind my fridge."

"But when you *do* move the fridge," said Frieda, "you'll find something strange or something really important that you lost years ago."

Harry looked puzzled. "Are we talking about cleaning now or is this something more profound?"

"That's probably enough of the fridge comparison."

He touched her hand. "That stuff in the paper about Janet Ferris and Bob Poole: I'm sorry about it. You don't deserve it."

"I wonder," said Frieda. "But thank you. I must go now. It's been a long day. I'm grateful to you, Harry."

"My pleasure," he said softly. "Will you be in touch?"

"Yes."

"I'll be waiting."

He watched her as she rose from her chair, gathered up her coat and bag, and walked with her swift, decisive steps from the bar. Outside, she passed by the window but didn't turn her head toward him. He sat for a while after she had left, taking time over the last of his wine, thinking about Frieda's face.

# 41

The Kerseys' house was in Highgate, near
the top of the hill. It was large and old, with
gabled windows, uneven stone floors, and
low ceilings. From the kitchen where she
sat, Frieda could see London spread out
beneath her. An ancient spaniel lay curled
near the fire. It twitched in its sleep and occasionally gave piteous murmurs. Frieda
wondered what dogs had nightmares about.

"Mervyn was going to be here as well, but
at the last moment something came up.
Well, actually, he just couldn't face it." She
grimaced at Frieda. "He's taken this so
hard. He feels it was his fault."

"What, exactly?"

"Everything that happened with Beth.
That's being a parent for you, of course. Do
you have children?"

"No."

"You blame yourselves, of course you do.
Anyway, it's just me."

"Just you is fine. Thank you for seeing me. I work with Detective Chief Inspector Karlsson. I'm a doctor, not a detective."

"What kind of doctor?"

"I'm trained as a psychiatrist, but I work as a therapist."

Frieda was used to the expressions that crossed people's faces when she said this, but Lorna Kersey's suggested something different — a flicker of anticipation, watchfulness.

"Did your detective want you to talk to me because Beth was disturbed?"

"Would you say your daughter was disturbed?" Frieda asked. "Rather than simply unhappy and confused?"

"I don't know. I've never known. I ask myself all the time. Was it because of her childhood? Were we bad parents? Did she need medical help or did she need understanding and kindness? I don't know. I don't know what the word means to people like you."

"Your daughter received treatment. Is that right?"

Lorna Kersey waved a hand in the air. "We were desperate. Counseling, therapy, drugs, you name it." She pinched the top of her nose between her thumb and forefinger, sharply, and closed her eyes for a moment.

"I hate to think of her out there, alone," she said. "I can't begin to tell you how much I hate it. The thought of what she'll do."

"Do you mean, to herself?"

"Well, yes. That too."

"To other people?"

"I don't know! I haven't seen her for so long. I never thought she could manage on her own. I can't imagine what she's doing or how she is."

"What kind of drugs was she on?"

"Why does that matter?"

"What were they for? Were they anti-depressants?"

"I can't remember their name."

"But were they because she was depressed, or were they for something else?"

Lorna Kersey laid her hands flat on the table in front of her and stared at them. Then she looked up at Frieda. Her eyes seemed sore behind her round glasses. "She had these episodes," she said. "I'm an expert now. I've read the books, I've talked to experts. You're not meant to say, 'She's a schizophrenic.' You say, 'She had schizo-phrenic episodes.' That's meant to make us feel better. Either way, they were terrifying."

"I know," said Frieda.

"No," said Lorna Kersey. "If you don't have a child, you can't know."

"We'd like to try and help you find her."

"You think she may have killed him?" whispered Beth's mother. "You think my Beth may have murdered him?"

"I'm not a detective."

"So what happens next?"

"We need to find her for you."

# 42

"Are you ready for this?" said Karlsson.

"How do you mean?" said Frieda.

"I'm just trying to be encouraging. Wyatt's got his lawyer with him. Don't let him put you off."

"Put me off what?"

"Nothing," said Karlsson. "I didn't mean anything. Just be yourself. Remember, this is what you do, what you're good at."

"What you want," said Frieda, "is for me to get Frank Wyatt to confess to killing Robert Poole."

Karlsson held up his thumb and first finger, almost touching. "We're this close to having the evidence to charge him. This close. But, yes, it would be helpful. I should warn you. I've just spent an hour with him. I dangled the idea of a manslaughter charge in front of him. I said he might even get a suspended sentence. But he's not biting. So, it would be nice if you could work your magic on him."

"I'm interested in talking to him," said Frieda. "But I don't want you to get your hopes up."

"No pressure," said Karlsson, as he opened the door and led her into the interview room. Frank Wyatt was sitting at a table. The jacket of his gray suit was draped over the back of his chair. He was wearing an open-necked white shirt. Beside him was a man dressed in a suit and tie. He was middle-aged, and his hair was not so much balding as thinning. His pale scalp showed through short dark wisps. As the door opened, the two men drew apart from each other as if they had been caught saying something embarrassing.

"Mr. Joll," said Karlsson, "this is my colleague, Dr. Klein." He waved Frieda toward the chair opposite the two men, then went and stood to one side, slightly in the background, so that Frieda felt he was looking over her shoulder, checking on her. As Frieda arranged herself on the chair, Karlsson stepped forward and pressed a button on the sound recorder on the table. She saw a digital counter, but she couldn't read the figures.

"This is a resumption of the interview," said Karlsson, sounding slightly self-conscious. "We've now been joined by Dr. Frieda Klein. Mr. Wyatt, I'd like to remind you that you're still under oath."

He nodded at Frieda, then stepped back behind her, out of her sight. Frieda hadn't really thought about what she was going to say. She looked across at Wyatt. His eyes flickered. He was angry and defensive. Both his hands were resting on the table, but Frieda could see that they were trembling.

"What did you think of Robert Poole?" she said.

He gave a sort of laugh. "Is that the best you can come up with? What do *you* think?"

"Do you want me to answer that?" asked Frieda. "Do you want me to tell you what I think?"

The lawyer leaned across. "I'm sorry. Mr. Wyatt is here as a courtesy. He has made it clear that he is eager to cooperate but, please, if you have relevant questions, then ask them."

"I've just asked a question," said Frieda. "And then Mr. Wyatt asked me one. Now, he can answer mine or I can answer his."

Joll looked at Karlsson as if appealing to his authority to put a stop to all this. Frieda didn't turn round.

"What I'm meant to say," said Frieda, "is that you found out that Robert Poole had slept with your wife and that he'd stolen your money. He'd cheated you and made a fool of you. You had to get back at him."

There was a pause.

"Yes?" said Joll. "Is there some question at the end of this?"

Frieda continued to gaze at Wyatt. He leaned back in his chair and ran his hands through his hair. "Is that what you wanted me to say?" she asked.

"I don't know," he said. "And I don't care, really."

"What I want to know is why, when you started to see what was going on, you didn't confront your wife. Why didn't you talk to her instead of hiding your feelings away and brooding over them?"

Now Wyatt leaned forward, his head in his hands. He mumbled something.

"I'm sorry," said Frieda. "I couldn't make that out."

He looked up at her. "I said, it was complicated."

"You found out, but you couldn't talk to your wife about it. So what did you do?"

Wyatt looked uneasily around, over Frieda's shoulder at Karlsson, at Joll. She felt he was avoiding her gaze.

Suddenly Karlsson spoke. "You confronted him, didn't you?"

Wyatt didn't reply.

"Well?" Karlsson's tone hardened.

Wyatt looked at the floor. "I talked to him," he said, in a low voice.

"Stop this," Joll said. "I need a moment alone with my client."

Karlsson gave a thin smile. "Of course."

Outside, Karlsson broke into a grin. "Excellent," he said. "If his lawyer's got any sense, he's telling him to confess." He glanced at Frieda and frowned. "You should be enjoying this. You know, the thrill of the chase."

"It doesn't feel like a chase to me," she said.

After a few minutes, they had resumed their positions. For Frieda it felt artificial now, as if they were all actors, resuming a rehearsal after a break for tea.

"Mr. Wyatt would like to explain," said Joll.

Wyatt coughed nervously. "I talked to Poole about the money."

"I bet you did," said Karlsson.

"When I asked him about it, it was more complicated than I expected." Wyatt was speaking in a low, miserable tone. "You've heard about him. When he talked about the money, it sounded convincing, or sort of convincing. He talked about his business plans. We ended up having a drink. It almost felt like I was the one in the wrong."

"Where was this?" asked Karlsson.

"At our house. My wife was out. She didn't know — didn't know I knew."

"Why didn't you tell us about the meeting before?"

"I don't know," said Wyatt. "It was difficult to explain."

"That's true," said Karlsson. "And you haven't managed to explain it. Frieda? Is there anything you want to say?"

"I want to go back to my original question," she said. "What do you think of Robert Poole now?"

"I don't know that I can answer that," he said. "And, anyway, what does it matter what I think?"

"It does matter," said Frieda. "Some people would say that you couldn't do anything worse to a man than what he did to you."

"Thank you for that," said Wyatt. "Is that what they pay you for?"

"What interests me," said Frieda, "is that you really don't seem all that angry with him."

Now Wyatt became wary, uneasy, as if Frieda were laying a trap for him to walk into. "I don't know what you're getting at."

"What did you mean when you said that talking to Poole was complicated?"

"I meant just what I said."

Frieda left a silence before speaking and looked at Wyatt closely. "I never met Poole," she said. "I've only heard about him. But it sounds to me as if when people met him they thought he recognized them, that he knew them. And that can be uncomfortable."

"I don't know what you're talking about."

"I wonder," said Frieda, "whether you really feel that in some strange way you almost deserve what he did to your wife. I was going to say did to you, but that's not what you feel, is it?" She left another silence. "What I'm wondering is whether you feel that Robert Poole was looking after your wife in a way that you hadn't been doing for a while."

Wyatt swallowed nervously. He flushed. "That sounds a bit pathetic."

"I don't think it's pathetic at all," said Frieda. "Do you think it's possible that when you learned about what Robert Poole had done, even when you learned he'd been sleeping with your wife, you didn't feel all that angry? A man is supposed to feel angry with the man who has slept with his wife, but it wasn't quite like that, was it? Or not only like that." Now Wyatt was staring at her blankly. "I believe that you were confused. You were humiliated, of course. Maybe you had some fantasy of revenge. But I believe you're a thoughtful man, and mainly you thought about your marriage, about your children. Perhaps you wondered how you could have let things get that bad."

When Wyatt spoke, it was in little more than a whisper. "What's your point?"

"You'd gone to sleep in your marriage," said Frieda. "Robert Poole showed you something. Maybe he even woke you up."

"I couldn't believe it," said Wyatt, slowly. "Everything was a lie, everything I'd believed in."

"Have you talked to your wife about that feeling?"

Wyatt shrugged. "A bit. It doesn't make much sense to me, so it's hard to talk about it to someone else."

"You should try."

Joll coughed. "Excuse me," he said. "I'm not clear about the relevance of this."

"No," said Karlsson. "I agree. I think we can stop for the day."

As they left the interview room, he gestured at Frieda to follow him.

"What was that?" he said. "We had him. We were on the verge of getting him to

501

plead. What was all that? Where was the old Frieda?"

Frieda looked at him with a curious expression. "Wouldn't you like to have met him?"

"Who?"

"Robert Poole."

Karlsson seemed to be having trouble speaking. "No," he said. "No. And nor should you, Frieda — because he's dead and beyond your attempts to understand him or rescue him or change what happened."

Chloë was waiting. Frieda noticed that she had washed her hair and put on a clean white shirt over her miniature stretchy black skirt. She wasn't wearing any makeup and looked vulnerable and childlike. There wasn't any sign of Olivia.

"Tapas OK?" asked Frieda.

"I don't eat meat anymore."

"That's OK."

"And only sustainable fish."

"Fine."

"There aren't many of them."

The restaurant was only a few minutes away, in Islington, and they walked there in silence. It had been raining earlier, and the car headlights wavered in the long shallow puddles. Only after they'd taken their seats at a rickety wooden table by the window did Frieda speak.

"Did you get to school today?"

"Yeah. I said I would."

"Good. Was it all right?"

Chloë shrugged. Her face was slightly puffy, thought Frieda, as though she had cried a great deal. Her arms were covered by her shirt, so she couldn't see if she'd been cutting herself again.

They ordered squid, roasted bell peppers, a Spanish omelette, and a plate of spring greens. Chloë cut a tiny squid ring in half and then in half again, put it into her mouth, and chewed very slowly.

"Let's take one thing at a time," said Frieda. "School."

"What about it?"

"You did really well in your GCSEs. You're bright. You say you want to be a doctor . . ."

"No. *You* say that."

"Do I? I don't think so."

"Anyway, people do. Adults. My dad. Teachers. There's this road you're expected to be on. You're supposed to do your GCSEs and then your A levels and then you go to uni and then you get a proper job. I can see my whole life in front of me like a great slab of tarmac. What if I don't want it?"

"Don't you want it?"

"I don't know." She stabbed her fork into the bright green pepper and juice spurted out. "I don't know what the point of any of it is."

"You've had a hard time, Chloë. Your father left —"

"You can use his name, you know. He's called David, and he's your brother."

"OK. David." Even saying the name left a nasty taste in her mouth. "And Olivia has a new boyfriend."

"Guess where she is now," said Chloë.

"I suppose she's with Kieran."

"Wrong. Guess again."

"I can't," said Frieda, uneasy under Chloë's interrogation.

"It's that accountant or whatever he is. The one you brought round."

"I didn't bring him round."

"I know what's going on," said Chloë.

"What do you mean?"

"I know I'm just a teenager, but even I can see that it's really about you."

"I don't even know where to start with that," said Frieda.

"I can see the way he looks at you. He's using my mother as a way to impress you. What do you think of him?"

"What do you think of him?"

"Auntie Frieda, you've got a really bad habit of always answering a question with another question."

Frieda smiled. "It's lesson number one in therapist school," she said. "It's the way of avoiding being put on the spot. So that whatever your patient says to you, you just say, 'What do you mean by that?' And then you're off the hook."

"But I'm not your patient. And you're not off the hook."

"We were talking about your mother."

"All right then, let's talk about my mother," said Chloë. "I think she doesn't care about me."

"I think she cares a lot, Chloë. But, you know, she's not just your mother; she's a woman who feels she's been humiliated, who's worried about the direction of her own road, if you like, and who's just met a new man."

"So? She's still meant to be my mum. She can't just behave like a teenager herself. That's supposed to be me. It feels scary sometimes. Like there's no solid ground under me."

This was so exactly what Frieda felt about Olivia that she took a moment to answer. "You're right. And maybe you and I could talk to her about it, try to explain what you're feeling, and draw up some ground rules. But give her a chance to change as well. Leave doors open. She can be good at acknowledging when she's wrong."

"Why should I give her a chance when she doesn't even notice me?"

"Is that what you think?"

"I don't think it, I know it. She's so wrapped up in her own mess, she can't see mine. I get home and I don't know what I'll find. Sometimes she's drunk. Sometimes she's crying. Sometimes she's hyper and wants to rush out to the shops with me to buy me ludicrously expensive clothes or something. Sometimes she's shouting at me about Dad and what a wanker he is. Sometimes she's in the bath and she doesn't even wash it out after she's used it — she leaves hair and tide marks all over it. It's disgusting. I have to clean up after her. Sometimes she cooks and sometimes she forgets. Sometimes she wakes me up in the morning for school and other times she doesn't. Sometimes she's all over me, hugging me and telling me I'm her precious darling or something, and sometimes she snaps at me for no reason. Sometimes Kieran's there — actually, it's best when he is. He's calm and kind and he talks to me. She doesn't ask about my work, she doesn't open letters from school, she forgot to go to my last parents' evening. She couldn't care less."

Frieda listened while Chloë talked and talked as though the floodgates had at last been opened to a gush of fear and wretchedness. She didn't say much, but anger swelled inside her until she could barely contain it. Privately, she made plans. She would talk to Olivia and make her see the consequences of her disordered life on her daughter; she would go with Chloë to talk to her teachers and make a schedule of work; she would — this last resolution made her feel slightly dizzy, as if she were peering over a cliff edge — talk to her brother, David.

Half a mile along Upper Street, in a new wine bar that had been extensively refurbished so that it looked as if it had been there unchanged since the nineteenth century, Harry was topping up Olivia's wine glass. She took a sip.

"It seems a bit cold," she said. "For a red wine."

"I think it's meant to be cool," Harry said. "But I can get them to warm it up for you."

Olivia took another sip, more of a gulp. "It's fine. I'm sure you're right."

"You know what they say, white wine is

always served too cold and red wine too warm."

"No," said Olivia. "I didn't know they said that. I just drink it, I'm afraid."

"Which is the right attitude," said Harry. "But what I'm really here to talk about is this." He put a folder on the table and pushed it across to her. "I've gone through everything. I've looked at your accounts and credit card bills. I've written out a plan for you, made some suggestions. The situation isn't as bad as you told me. And I've found some standing orders you've been paying for services you no longer get. I've written some letters for you to reclaim the overpayments, so you should get a bit of a windfall."

"Really?" said Olivia. "That's amazing. But I must say, I feel a bit embarrassed by all of this. I've dealt with my affairs for years by not opening letters or throwing documents away without looking at them and hoping for the best. And now you know all my most shameful secrets."

"That's my job," said Harry. "Sometimes I feel a financial adviser ought to be like an old-fashioned priest. Your client, or parishioner, or whatever, has to confess everything, all the sins and omissions and evasions and then —"

"And then you can give me absolution?"

said Olivia.

Harry smiled. "I can show that once you get everything into the open, look at all the figures, it's not so bad. What causes problems is when you have secrets, when you don't face up to things."

"It's awful, though," said Olivia. "You've done so much for me, and I didn't . . . I can't . . ." She started to blush and covered her confusion by taking an even deeper gulp of wine.

"That's all right," said Harry. "I've been clear from the start. Frieda is paying for this and, between you and me, I'm doing it at a reduced rate."

"I don't see how you can make a living, if you keep doing favors like this."

"It's for my sister. She was helping Frieda, and I'm helping Tessa."

"I didn't know Tessa was such a friend of Frieda's."

"They only just met," said Harry. "But Frieda's the sort of person you hit it off with."

Olivia gave a knowing smile. "Yes, isn't she?" she said.

Harry laughed. "I've got no ulterior motives," he protested. "I promise."

"Yes, yes," said Olivia. "I believe it. So what do you make of my sister-in-law?

You're intrigued, aren't you? Admit it."

Harry held up his hands. "Of course I admit it. I've gotten to know Frieda and spent time with her, but I still don't really know what makes her tick."

"And you think I do?"

"I can't help noticing that you were married to Frieda's brother, and you had what I take to be a troubled breakup."

"You can say that again."

"Yet Frieda has stuck by you instead of her brother."

Olivia picked up her glass but put it down again without drinking from it. "Maybe she feels she needs to keep an eye on her niece. Sometimes I've not been the most stable parent in the world."

"What about her brother?"

Olivia ran a finger round the rim of her glass. "I've never been able to get it to make that sound," she said, then looked drunkenly thoughtful. "Frieda has a very complicated relationship with her family."

"How do you mean?"

"Why don't you ask her?"

"I get the impression she doesn't like being quizzed about her private life."

"She scared me when I first met her," said Olivia. "Sometimes she'd look at me or listen to me and I'd get the feeling she was looking right into me, knowing everything about me, all the things I didn't want anyone to know. Like you, when you saw all my papers and checkbooks that I'd kept hidden. When David left, I stopped hearing from quite a few people that I'd thought of as friends, but Frieda was there, admittedly sometimes being sarcastic or silent the way she can be, but she did things that were necessary. Or mostly necessary."

"Why does she do all this stuff with the police?" asked Harry. "She's been attacked, she's been written about in the papers. Why does she put herself through it?"

Now Olivia took another gulp of wine, and Harry topped up her glass once more. "Thanks. Is this how you normally meet with your clients? I hope not. Anyway, the thing is, when I decide to do something, it's because I know I can do it, and it won't be too demanding and it won't give me any grief. The basic way to understand Frieda is to look at me and then think the opposite. I don't know why Frieda does these things, and when I hear that she's done something, I never understand why. I don't know why she helps me. I certainly don't know why she puts herself through the purgatory of trying to keep Chloë on the straight and narrow." Another gulp of wine. Her voice was thickening now, as if her tongue was just slightly too large for her mouth. "For example. What was I saying?" She paused for a moment. "Oh, yes. The newspaper article. I saw that, and if it had been about me I would have crawled into a hole and pulled the hole in after me. Whereas, Frieda, Frieda, she's like one of those animals, a badger or a stoat. If you mess with their den, they become dangerous and . . . Well, I'm exaggerating. I'm making her sound feral. But she's stubborn and bloody-minded. In a good way. Ninety-nine percent of the time. Or ninety-five."

Harry waited a moment. "I think Frieda has secrets," he said. "I mean, she's someone with a hidden grief. Do you know what I mean?"

Now there was a long pause. Harry felt that Olivia was suddenly reluctant to meet his eyes. "It looks like you do know what I mean," he said. "And, as you can tell, I'm falling for her. I'd like to know."

Finally she looked round. "Well, you know what happened with her father?"

"No," he said. "No, I don't."

After Beth had finished with the photographs, there were his notes. There were pages and pages of them, and at first it was

hard to make sense of what she was reading. Sometimes they seemed like short
stories, and then they became lists — lists
of odd things. Exercises to do to lose weight;
plants and where to get them from. Some
things had a neat tick by them, or were
crossed off. There were figures, but she
couldn't make any sense of those, so after a
while she stopped trying, although she knew
that some of the numbers were quite long
and had pound signs in front of them. Bit
by bit she realized that she was reading
about different people. They had names,
addresses, dates of birth, relatives, jobs.

He had written about her parents, and he
had put down all the things they liked and
didn't like, all their hobbies, the charities
they subscribed to, and the events they attended. He had even done the same for her
sisters. He had drawn a map of the house
and garden, putting in the studio shed at
the end, where her mother played her cello
sometimes and where her father kept his
paints. She hadn't grasped how closely he
had listened to her, and it made her eyes
prick with tears to know that even when
he'd seemed aloof, he was thinking of her
and looking out for her. He had left this for
her, Beth thought, as a gift, and he had gone
to such a lot of trouble — but why? She

stared and stared at the words, until the lights in her eyes flickered and made her dizzy. She knew she had to find some food, make herself stronger.

She crawled out of the hatchway, her cheeks scraping against the metal rim of the opening. She hadn't been out for a while and her body felt stiff, as though it had hardened into crookedness. She made herself jog up and down on the spot for a while, feeling how pain knifed in her chest and bounced up and down in her skull. Like those tennis balls she used to bounce on her tennis racket, counting up, trying to beat her record. When was that? She could almost see her fat child's knees and the yellow sun, like a yolk, in the sky, but now everything was dim and dark and ragged and the water was oily, and when she walked, her body slid about on the muddy path.

She reached a boat she knew was inhabited. She wasn't being careful enough, but perhaps it didn't matter so much anymore, because he was gone and everything was over, except the thing she had to do in his name. In his name. Like a disciple.

The lights were off and the boat felt deserted. There were bikes chained to the top, and when she scrambled onto the deck, the chains rattled and she lay quite still for a moment, flat against the icy wet wood, but nobody came. She pulled at the hatch and it creaked open, and she lowered her body into the snug interior. It was much, much nicer than hers. It was warm, neat, there was a good smell to it, of clean bodies and fresh food. You could call it a home. You couldn't call hers a home. It was a hole. A dank ghastly pit. There was still enough light outside to see the shapes of things, and she found the small fridge and pulled it open. Milk. She took that out. Spreadable butter. Two wholemeal rolls. And there was half a chicken under shrink wrapping. Half a chicken. Golden skin. Plump thighs. Her mouth filled with saliva and she lifted the wrapping, tore off a piece of meat, stuffed it into her mouth, and swallowed it almost without chewing. Blood roared in her head, and she thought she might be sick. She tore another piece and pushed that in too. Her gashed lip hurt and her throat hurt and her stomach shrieked.

There was a sudden sound from the front of the boat, through the little closed door, and she froze, though fear coursed and thundered through her body. Someone was humming. Someone was there. A few feet away. Probably sitting on the toilet or something. They'd come out, find her with her mouth full of chicken. Call the police. Everything would be over. Finished. Wrecked.

She grabbed the chicken and the milk, pushed the tub of butter into her pocket, held the plastic bag with the rolls in her teeth, and tried to clamber one-handed through the hatch. Her shoelace got caught in the corner and she yanked her foot hard. The humming stopped. She hauled herself into the air and stumbled across the wooden roof, then leaped onto the path, dropping the chicken into the mud. She picked it up and ran, her breath in sobs, the plastic bag still clenched between her teeth. *Please please please please.* She pushed her way through a thick, overgrown hedge beside the path, feeling the nettles brush her hands and, when she crouched down, her neck and face. A shape was standing on the deck of the boat, staring out. It lifted a torch and swung the beam around. She could see it bob across the water, the shattered buildings on the other side, the path, the hedge. She felt it in her eyes so she shut them and didn't breathe.

The light went off. The shape disappeared. She waited. Her ankle throbbed. She took the bag of rolls out of her mouth and laid it in front of her. She could smell the chicken, which made her feel both sick and excited. She didn't know how long she waited, but at last she crept back onto the path and hobbled toward her boat, clutching her booty.

She'd done it. Now she had food and she could make herself strong again, enough to see her through. After that, it didn't matter. She would have kept her promise to him. She chewed another piece of muddy chicken, grit in her mouth. His trusty soldier, his servant, his beloved.

# 43

Frieda caught the fast train from King's Cross. It took less than fifty minutes, speeding her out of London and into Cambridge before she had time to change her mind. She stared out of the window, watching London as it blurred into meadows and waterways and the back gardens of houses facing a road she couldn't see. There were newborn lambs in some of the fields, and banks of daffodils. She tried to concentrate on the landscape rushing past and not think about what lay ahead. Her mouth was dry and her heart beat faster than usual, and when she arrived in Cambridge, she went first to the Ladies to check how she looked. The face that stared back at her from the tarnished mirror above the chipped basin was quite composed. She was wearing a dark gray suit and had tied her hair back severely; she appeared professional, competent, unyielding.

She had wanted to meet somewhere public, preferably his office among the computers and strangers, but he'd told her he would be working from home that day; if she wanted to see him, that was where she had to come. His territory and his terms. She had never been there, and he had had to give her the address. She had no idea what to expect — whether his house would be in town or out of it, large or small, old or new. It was out, about ten minutes by cab, into leafy semi-countryside or tastefully rural suburbia; large, though not as large as some of the houses in the village; and moderately old, with a red-tiled roof, gabled windows, a porch over the front door, a willow tree in the drive whose branches fell almost to the gravel. It was nice, Frieda admitted to herself. Of course it was. He'd always had good taste, or, at least, the same kind of taste as she. However far you run from your family and try to expunge them from your life, they follow you.

The man who opened the door when Frieda rang was noticeably her brother. He was slim, dark haired, although his hair was turning silver at the temples, dark eyed, with high cheekbones and a way of holding his shoulders back that was her way, too. But, of course, he was older than he had been at their last meeting, and his face had tightened into an expression that was both angry and ironically amused. She hoped she didn't look like that. He had dressed in a gray shirt and dark trousers, and she had the horrible feeling that he, too, had carefully chosen his clothes for this visit, and had chosen almost identically to her. They were almost like twins, she thought, and shuddered, remembering Alan and Dean.

"David," she said. She didn't smile or step forward to hug him or even shake his hand. She simply watched him.

"Well, well." He didn't move either. They stared at each other. She saw a tiny pulse jumping in his cheek. So he was nervous. "I'm honored, Dr. Klein." He emphasized the "Dr." as if mocking it.

"May I come in?"

He stood back, and she entered a spacious hallway, with a rug over the wooden floor, a chest to one side with a bowl of spring flowers on it, a portrait hanging on the wall. She wouldn't look at that, she mustn't — and she steadfastly averted her eyes from it as she followed David into the living room.

"I've just made a pot of coffee," he said. "You told me you'd be here at half past three and I knew I could reliably set my

520

watch by you. Ever prompt. Some things never change."

Frieda squashed her impulse to refuse coffee, and took a seat while he went into the kitchen, returning moments later with two mugs.

"Black, as usual?"

"Yes."

She was pleased to see how steady her hands were as she took a small sip. There was bitterness in her mouth, and the coffee tasted hard and full of minerals.

"Still treating the diseases of the rich?"

"I'm still working as an analyst, if that's what you mean."

"I've been reading about you in the paper." David slid his eyes across her face to gauge her reaction. Frieda felt as if someone jabbed her with something sharp. "Very interesting."

"I'm here to talk about Chloë."

David's smile thinned into a straight line. "Is this about Olivia's maintenance money?"

"No."

"I've had enough of her complaints, and of her solicitor's letters. Who is this Tessa Welles, anyway? She suddenly appeared out of the blue. I suppose that was your doing."

"Olivia needs help. But that's not —"

"What Olivia clearly needs is to pull

herself together. I'm not going to continue supporting her in her life of leisure. That's final."

Frieda said nothing, just looked at him.

"I know what you're thinking." He leaned forward. She could see the fine lines round his eyes, the flecks in his irises, the slightly cruel curve of his lips, the continuing pulse in his cheek. She could smell him, too — shaving lotion and coffee and something else, some smell he had had since he was a small boy who used to slap the back of her leg with a plastic ruler.

"You live in a lovely house just outside Cambridge," she said. "This is a new carpet. You're wearing a watch that would pay for Chloë's first year at university. There's a gardener out there, weeding your flower-bed. Nobody's asking you to be generous. Just fair."

"Olivia was a mistake. She's a rude, messy, selfish woman. Actually, I think she's unhinged. I'm well shot of her."

"You have a daughter with her."

"She's her mother's daughter," said David. "She talks as if she has contempt for me."

"Perhaps she does."

"Did you come all this way to insult me?" he asked, then added, softly, "Freddy?"

The old nickname might once have been used affectionately, but not now, not for a very long time.

"She's a teenager," she said, keeping her voice steady and her face neutral. "Life is hard for a teenager at the best of times. Think: you left her mother for a younger woman, and you left her as well. You're holding back money, and she's watching her mother go to pieces. You rarely see her, and sometimes you make arrangements that you then default on. You go on grand holidays with your new wife and don't take her. You forget her birthday. You don't go to her parents' evenings. Why shouldn't she have contempt for you?" She held up her hand to stop him from interrupting. "For someone like Chloë, feeling anger and contempt is far easier to deal with than feeling wretchedness and fear, which is what she's really feeling. Your daughter needs a father."

"Finished?"

"No. But I want to hear what you have to say."

David stood up and went to the window. Even his back looked angry — yet Frieda had a sudden clear flashback of sitting on those shoulders, holding on to his head with one hand and with the other reaching down some fruit from the tree at the bottom of their garden. She could almost feel the cool heaviness of the plum in her hand, its bloom against her fingers. She blinked away the memory and waited. David turned round.

"I don't know how you can sit here, in this room, and talk to me about what teenagers are like and what parents feel."

He wanted to hurt her.

"You weren't a parent last time I looked. How old are you? It won't be so very long before you're forty, will it?"

"This is about Chloë."

"It's about you thinking, after everything, you have the right to come here and tell me what to do with my life."

"Just with your daughter. And if I don't tell you, who will, until it's too late?"

"What do you think she's going to do? Slit her wrists?"

She gave him a look so fierce that she could see he was shaken. "I don't know what she could do. I don't want to find out. I want you to help her." She took a deep breath and added, "Please."

"This is what I will do," he said. "Because I had already decided to, not because you've asked me to. I will see her every other weekend, from Saturday afternoon, until Sunday afternoon. Twenty-four hours. All right?" He picked up his electronic organizer and started pressing buttons, very business-like. "Not next weekend, or the one after, though. We can start at the beginning of April. You'll see to it that she knows?"

"No. You have to ask her if that's what she wants. She's seventeen. Talk to her. And then listen."

He slammed the organizer on the table, so hard that his mug jumped.

"And please don't tell her I came to see you. She'd feel humiliated. She needs you to want to see her."

A door slammed and someone called his name. Then a pretty young woman entered. She had blond hair and long legs. She must have been in her late twenties, though her style was of someone younger — someone of Chloë's generation, thought Frieda.

"Oh," she said, in obvious surprise, laying one hand against her stomach. "Sorry." She looked inquiringly at David.

"This is Frieda," he said.

"You mean — *Frieda* Frieda?"

"Yes. This is my wife, Trudy."

"I'm just going," said Frieda.

"Don't mind me." She picked up the two coffee mugs, making an odd little grimace of distaste as she did so, and went out of the room.

"Does Chloë know?" asked Frieda.

"What?"

"That she's going to have a sibling."

"How the fuck?"

"You have to tell her."

"I don't have to do anything."

"You do."

She walked back to the station. She had plenty of time before Sasha's birthday party, and although the day was gray and foggy, threatening rain, she needed to be outside in the cleansing wind. She felt polluted, defiled. At first, as she made her way rapidly up the lane lined with bare trees and muddy fields, she thought she would actually be sick, but gradually her feelings began to settle, like something sinking back into darkness.

Sasha opened her front door to find a couple she didn't know outside. She felt a brief moment of panic. Were these some old friends she'd forgotten about? The two of them had easy, cheerful expressions, as if they were both in on a joke. The man put his hand out.

"I'm Harry Welles, a friend of Frieda's."

A relieved smile broke over Sasha's face.

"Frieda said you were coming. She's told me all about you."

"I'm a bit worried about what Frieda might mean by all about me," said Harry. "I've brought my sister, Tessa, as well. Is that OK?"

"Great." Sasha stepped back. "Come in out of the cold. Dump your coats and then join us."

They went up the stairs together to a small bedroom, where the bed was already piled with coats and jackets. Harry picked up a photograph that was on the little table: Sasha and another young woman standing arm in arm in front of a tent, wearing shorts and hiking boots. "Do you think she's gay?" he asked.

Tessa snatched the picture out of his hands and put it back on the table. "Do you fancy her as well?" she said.

"I was thinking of you," he said, and she responded with a playful slap. They headed back down to the music and hubbub of the party. Tessa watched Harry as he entered the main room. He looked at ease, handsome, and full of an amiable curiosity. Of course Frieda liked him.

And there was Frieda, in a corner of the room holding a glass of what looked like mineral water, wearing a dress the color of moss that shimmered slightly when she moved. Tessa noticed how shapely her legs were, how slim her figure, and how upright she stood. She was talking to an older man with gray hair and a thin, unshaven face. He was wearing a tatty pair of jeans, a gorgeous patterned shirt, and a bright cotton scarf wrapped round his neck. A pretentious abstract artist or another psychotherapist, she thought, as she and Harry approached. It looked as if they were having a serious conversation, almost an argument.

"Am I interrupting something?" Harry said.

"Frieda has problems with her friends helping her," said the man.

"What Frieda has problems with," said Frieda, "is that her friends might get arrested while trying to help her."

"Arrested?" said Harry.

"Don't ask," said Frieda.

Harry kissed her, first on one cheek, then, lingeringly, on the other. She didn't draw back, but put a hand on his arm, holding him by her side. She smiled at Tessa, apparently unsurprised to see her, then introduced them.

"Reuben McGill, this is Harry and Tessa Welles."

"Brother and sister," said Harry.

"Well, any fool can see that," said Reuben.

"Really?"

"Cheekbones," said Reuben. "And the ears as well. Dead giveaway."

"Reuben's a colleague of mine," said Frieda. She lifted a hand in greeting, and an olive-skinned woman, with dark hair tied in a dramatic bandanna and wearing turquoise eye shadow, came toward them, swaying slightly. "And here's another colleague. Paz, Harry and Tessa."

"I am already drunk," said Paz, solemnly, forming her words with care. "I should have paced myself. But I am a very bad pacer. My mother used to make me drink a glass of milk to line my stomach before going out. I hate milk. Sasha says I have to dance." She tucked her hand through Reuben's arm. "Will you dance with me, Reuben? Two people with broken hearts?"

"Do I have a broken heart?"

"Of course."

"You're probably right. Just a bit broken in many places. Multiple hairline fractures. Is your heart broken as well?"

"Mine?" said Tessa, startled.

"You don't look like someone with a broken heart. I can usually tell."

"How?"

"Something in the eyes."

"Ignore him," said Frieda. "It's his chat-up line."

"You look beautiful, Frieda," said Harry, softly, as though there were no one else in the room but them. Reuben's eyebrows went up and Paz giggled. Frieda ignored them. "Can I get you a drink?"

"I have a drink." She raised her glass of water.

"A proper drink."

"I'm fine."

"I'll get myself one, then. Tessa?"

"A glass of wine, please."

"I'll be right back."

They both watched him as he edged his way through the crowd. Sasha came up behind them and put her arms round Frieda, kissing her on the crown of her head. "Thank you," she said.

"What for?"

"I don't know. It's my birthday and I wanted to say thank you."

Tessa saw the two women exchange an elusive smile and felt a shiver of — what was it? Was it envy of their intimacy? Sasha drifted away, pulled into another group of people. Frieda turned as a young man in an orange shirt that clashed with his hair claimed her attention. He seemed a bit stoned and his hair stood up in peaks. He waved his hands around and leaned toward her with burning eyes, but she stood quite still as she listened. There was a quality of deep reserve about her, thought Tessa. She was in the room and yet somehow standing back from it. She gave you her full attention, and yet at the same time you felt she had a core of isolation, of separateness. It made her a kind of magnet.

The party continued. A small, scruffy band arrived and set up in a corner. The rain stopped and a half-moon sailed between the clouds that were breaking up. In the little garden at the back of the house, smokers gathered in small clusters. At one point, Tessa saw Harry standing there with Frieda, talking to her. He was much taller than she was, and was gazing down at her with an expression that Tessa — who knew her brother very well — found hard to read.

"You watch your brother?"

She turned to face a large man with big brown eyes and a scar on his cheek. He smelled of tobacco and something else that she found hard to place, wood or resin. "Not exactly."

"Some vodka." He held up the bottle in his hand. His lips and eyes gleamed. "And then we will dance."

"I'm not a great one for dancing."

"That's why the vodka first."

"You are Frieda's friend."

"Of course." He reached for a small tumbler, poured a couple of fat fingers of vodka, and gave it to her. She sipped it warily while he gazed at her.

And he pulled her into the center of the room. The band was playing some plaintive kind of music, not suitable for dancing at all, but he didn't seem to mind. He danced entirely without self-consciousness. Even with her chest stinging from the vodka, Tessa felt awkward. The music speeded up and so did the man. He was like an acrobat, agile on a tiny spot of carpet. Music seemed to ripple through him and people were cheering him on. Soon Tessa stopped and watched him too.

"Who is he?" Harry was beside her.

"A friend of Frieda's."

"For a recluse, she seems to know a lot of people."

A young girl had joined the man now, her bright yellow plaits swinging wildly.

"Where's she got to?"

"She was talking to Sasha and a man wearing high-heeled boots and a tiara, so I came to see how you were doing. She'll be back."

"Everything all right?"

"Very all right."

"Harry," she said, with a note of warning.

"I'm just having some fun."

Frieda tried to escape from the party without anyone noticing her, as she always did. She hated the ritual of farewells, hovering at the door. After she had collected her coat, Josef accosted her clumsily on the stairs.

"Frieda," he began, then stopped. "I forget . . . no, yes, I finish with Mary Orton and she give me something . . ."

"I'm going to have a talk with you," said Frieda, "when you're sober. What if you'd been arrested for punching that photographer?"

"But I think it might be important."

"What if he'd had a journalist with him? Then Karlsson wouldn't have been able to pull strings and you'd have been back in Ukraine."

Josef looked crestfallen. "Frieda . . ."

"No," she said. "I've got to rush."

It was only half past nine. She took the Underground from Clapham North all the way to Archway. She walked up Highgate Hill, past the stone cat, safe behind its grille. She was glad she had drunk only water. She wanted a clear head. As she reached Waterlow Park, she stood and looked through the locked gates. The clouds had gone and the moon was bright on the grass, which glistened slightly, still wet from the earlier rain. Suddenly she looked round. Had she heard something? A step? A cough? Or did she feel someone looking at her? There was a group of teenagers on the other side of the road. A couple, arm in arm, walked past her.

It took her barely a minute to reach the wedding party. In the main room, the dinner was over, the guests clustered. The air hummed with their talk, and music was playing. Some people were on the wooden dance floor — including a gaggle of children, who were holding hands and giggling, kicking up their legs and knocking into each other. There was a table at the far end on which stood the tall vases of flowers and the remains of the feast. Frieda saw a tall, dark-haired woman in a long ivory dress with red flowers in her hair, moving slowly in the arms of a man with ginger hair. That would be her, she thought.

She stood, unnoticed, and watched. It was like an old film, grainy and slightly blurred. A man came past, holding a tray of champagne glasses; seeing her, he offered her one, but she shook her head. She could still go away, and for a moment it was as if her life hung suspended in front of her. One move and everything would change.

Now she saw him. He was standing at the far end of the room, his head bent toward an older woman who was talking animatedly. He wore a dark suit and a white shirt that was open at the neck. He looked thinner, she thought, and perhaps older as well, but she couldn't tell because he was too far away from her, and the room lay like a year between them.

Frieda took off her coat and her red scarf and put them on a nearby chair. She did what she always did when she was scared: pulled back her shoulders, lifted her chin, and took a deep, steadying breath. She started across the space, and it seemed to her that everything around her slowed: the dancers, the music, her own footfall. Someone brushed against her and apologized. The woman in the ivory dress, Sandy's younger sister, spun gently by, with his cheekbones and his eyes and the seriousness of his happiness.

Then she was there, and she waited until something made him turn his head and there he was, looking at her. He didn't move, just looked into her eyes, and she felt that a hole was opening up inside her, undoing her. He didn't touch her or smile.

"You came."

Frieda made a small gesture with her hands, palms upward. "I found that I had to."

"What do we do now?"

"Can we go outside?"

"Shall we go into the park?"

"It closes at dusk," Frieda said.

He smiled. "That's the sort of thing you know, isn't it? Which parks close at night and which don't."

"But there's a terrace at the back."

They made their way out. His sister saw them and started to say something, then stopped. Frieda didn't pick up her coat, and the cold air hit her, but she welcomed it. She felt alive again, and it didn't matter if it was pain or gladness that coursed through her.

Even from there, they could look down on the City, and behind them they could still hear the music and see the lights of the house.

"Not a day has gone by," said Sandy, "when I haven't thought of you."

Frieda put out a hand and ran a finger over his lips. He shut his eyes and let out a small sigh. "Is it really you?" he whispered. "After all this time."

"It's really me."

When at last they kissed, she felt the warmth of his hand on her back through the thin fabric of her dress. He tasted of champagne. Her cheeks were wet, and at first she thought she was crying but then realized that the tears were his, and she wiped them. "Where are you staying?" she said.

"At my flat. I was going to sell it. But it fell through."

"Can we go there?"

"Yes."

In the taxi they didn't speak all the way to the Barbican. They didn't speak in the lift. When he opened the door of his flat, it was both familiar and a little sad. A bit musty, a bit abandoned.

"Turn round for me," he said.

She turned and he undid the zipper of her shimmering dress, and it fell to the floor. She stood among its green folds like a mermaid. It had been fourteen months, she thought. Fourteen months since he had left. The moon shone through the curtains and in its light she looked at his intent face and his strong body. Then she closed her eyes and lost herself, let herself go.

# 44

When Frieda woke, it was four in the morning. His body was warm and smooth against her. She slipped out from under the covers. In the dark, she was able to find her clothes and pull them on. She held her shoes in her hand, so they wouldn't clatter on the wooden floor. She heard a murmur from the bed. She leaned down and softly kissed the back of his head, the nape of his neck.

As she began to walk, she felt as if she were still asleep. It was dark and still and cool. She walked up Golden Lane, which turned into Clerken-well Road, and she realized she was making her way along what had been London's city walls. Once, this would have been a walk through gardens and orchards and across streams. That would be what the tourist guides would tell you. But Frieda thought of what must have come after that: the sheds, the rubbish heaps, the jerry-built houses, the squatters, the chancers, as the countryside slowly gave up and died.

She turned to make a circle back toward home. Now it was offices and council estates and small galleries, and the traffic that never stopped and a few stragglers, ending the day or beginning it, on the pavements. Someone approached her and asked if she wanted a cab. She pretended not to hear.

This night, or this morning, the city felt slightly different. Was it the clarity that comes from the cold darkness and the stillness? That she had opened herself to someone again? She thought about the night and felt a shiver. She looked around. She had been walking almost unconsciously and needed to orient herself. At this time of day, three, four hundred years ago, it would have been busy, full of carts loaded with food, livestock being driven into the city. She looked up and saw the street name, Lamb's Conduit Street, and smiled at it, as if it were echoing her thoughts. It sounded sweet, but by this part of their journey the lambs would have started to stir and become agitated, smelling the stink of the Smithfield slaughterhouses blown up from the river.

She looked around. Again that feeling.

Always she walked in London at night, because it was then that she felt alone and untouched. Now it was different, and it wasn't just the thought of Sandy, asleep in his flat. It was something else. She thought of playing Grandmother's Footsteps as a little girl. You looked round to see if you could catch anyone moving. Every time you looked, the players would be still but closer. Until they got you.

When she arrived home, it was half past five. She took off her clothes. She could smell him on her. She stood in the shower for twenty minutes in the spray of water, trying to lose herself, trying not to think, but she couldn't stop herself. She realized she had to phone Karlsson. It was still much too early. After she was dry, she sat in her armchair downstairs, tired but fiercely awake, her eyes stinging. She heard birds singing outside. Against all the evidence, spring was coming. Just after seven she got up and made herself coffee and toast. At one minute past eight she phoned Karlsson.

"Oh, it's you," he said.

"How did you know?"

There was a pause. "You do know about mobile phones?" he said. "That your name shows up when you ring me?"

"You probably don't want to hear from me."

"I always want to hear from you."

"I know you were disappointed in my interview with Frank Wyatt."

"We all have our off days."

"It wasn't an off day," she said.

"You didn't get him to confess."

"That's true," said Frieda. "Are you charging him?"

"As I said, we're putting the file together. I'm just trying to tie up some loose ends. I'm going over to the Michelle Doyce flat today. We're going to have some of the contents boxed up."

"When are you doing it?"

"I've got some meetings this morning. Sometime in the afternoon."

"Can I come? I'd like to see it."

"You've seen it already, haven't you?"

"I saw it from the outside, when we looked at the alley, but I never went in."

"All right," said Karlsson. "You can join us."

"Could I see it before they start packing things up?"

"I'll meet you there at half past ten."

The phone rang again.

"You ran away."

"I didn't run away. I needed to get away. I

needed to think."

"About how you'd made a mistake."

"No, not about that."

"So I'll see you."

"Yes, you'll see me."

Frieda didn't go straight to the house. She took the Underground and then the light railway across the Isle of Dogs and under the river to the *Cutty Sark*. She got out and walked west until she was standing outside the Wyatts' house. There was a light on inside. She turned toward the river. The tide was high, the water pitching against the Embankment. A tourist boat chugged past. Two children waved at her. She continued walking along the bank, first past the other apartments, then a yacht club, fenced off, then the entrance to a wharf with a uniformed man sitting in a booth. Guarding what? Frieda thought. He looked at her suspiciously. He stepped outside and walked toward her. "Can I help you?" he said.

"Are you always here?" she asked.

"Why do you want to know?"

"I just wondered."

"I'm not always here," he said. "But someone is. If you want to know."

"Thank you," said Frieda, and continued westward, past the railings of a primary school and the site of a warehouse being demolished that was entirely boarded up and inaccessible. And then she reached Howard Street and found herself standing outside the house where it had all started.

"Yes," she said to herself. "Yes."

Frieda stared at Michelle Doyce's living room, then noticed that Karlsson was looking at her and smiling.

"What?" she said.

"It's like the sea," he said. "People can describe it to you, but you have to go and look at it yourself. Quite a collection, isn't it?"

Frieda was almost dazed by the room, which was somehow both obsessively neat and horribly chaotic. She saw shoes, stones, feathers and bones of birds, newspapers, bottles, silver wrappers folded into squares, glass jars, cigarette butts, dried leaves, dried flowers, little pieces of metal that looked as if they had been salvaged from machines. There were beads and clothes and assorted cups and glasses. Where even to begin?

"I'd like to see Jasmine Shreeve do one of her programs here," said Karlsson.

"What do you mean?"

"That program where a psychiatrist judges you by looking at your home? This one would give them a bit of a fright." His tone changed. "Sorry. I know it's not funny."

"Actually, I sometimes think I might learn more about my patients by looking at where they live than listening to what they say." She shook her head and said, almost to herself, "I should have come here before. This is like looking inside Michelle Doyce's head."

"Which is not a pretty sight," said Karlsson.

"Poor woman."

"Have you seen things like this before?"

"I don't really deal with acute psychiatric disorders," said Frieda, "but obsessive hoarding is quite a common symptom. You must have heard about people who can't throw anything away, newspapers, their own shit."

"All right, all right," said Karlsson. "That's too much information. Being *here* is bad enough without hearing about things that are even worse."

Frieda felt herself flush, as if she were going to faint. But the feeling seemed to be in her brain. When she spoke, it was in a whisper: "I don't like this case."

Karlsson looked at her curiously. "You're not supposed to like it. It's not a night at the theater."

"No," Frieda said slowly. "I don't mean that. It's just that nothing seems to fit. We're standing in a crime scene that isn't really a crime scene. The victim seems to be the main perpetrator. And the motives are obvious, but they don't seem enough. And then there's Janet Ferris. She must have been killed because she saw something. Let's say, for the sake of argument, that it was Frank Wyatt. Why would he have gone there? We'd already connected him to Poole."

She shook her head.

"I don't feel we're seeing the whole story. I keep thinking about Beth Kersey. Poole used people. He tried to change Mary Orton's will but failed. He took some money from the Wyatts. Probably he was going to steal from Jasmine Shreeve. What was he going to do with Beth Kersey? Have you had any luck getting her medical details?"

"That's a dead end," said Karlsson.

"It's not. It's crucial."

"We can access her medical records if she's a suspect or a victim of a crime. At the moment, she is an adult who hasn't even been reported missing, and we're here because you said you wanted to be here."

"All right, all right," said Frieda, trying to clear her mind. "So, the idea is that Michelle Doyce found Robert Poole's body outside in the alley by the house. She brought him in and stripped him and washed his clothes and folded them up, in the process probably removing any hair or fibers."

"That's right."

"She tried to help," said Frieda. "She saw Robert Poole as someone in trouble, and she tried to be a Good Samaritan, but in the process she ruined things."

"Exactly. She couldn't have done a better job of getting rid of the evidence if she'd done it deliberately."

Frieda looked around, trying to take it all in. The sheer mass of it made her head ache. "This really is like her mind," she said. "When most of us go out, we bring back things in our memory or maybe we take a photo. But she just brought the things back."

"She was a real magpie," said Karlsson.

"Yes." Frieda frowned. "Yes, she was."

"You make that sound interesting. It's just what you say about people who collect things."

Frieda looked at the window. The day had gone gray. "Are there lights?"

Karlsson went to the doorway to switch on the ceiling light, and then, with his foot, an old standard lamp in the corner. Frieda stepped forward and looked at it more closcly. Suspended from short pieces of thread around the frame that held the lampshade were what looked like beads and pieces of glass. Frieda peered at them one by one. "Magpies don't collect just anything," she said. "They collect sparkly things."

"I don't know much about them," said Karlsson. "When I see them, they're mainly pecking at dead pigeons."

Frieda took a new pair of surgical gloves from her pocket and put them on.

"Are you still buying those yourself?" said Karlsson. "We can get them for you."

"Remember what Yvette said about Michelle Doyce? That she was the saddest woman she'd ever met? This room is like that. Those dead bits of bird, the newspaper, the old cigarette butts smoked by other people. They contain a sadness that I don't even want to think about. But the sparkly things are different. They're pretty."

"If you like that kind of thing."

"Come and look at these."

"Really?"

"Yes."

Karlsson stepped forward.

"What do you see?" she asked.

"Bits of glass."

She cradled one of the other little dangling objects in her gloved hand. "What about this one?"

"It's a bead."

"Describe it to me."

"Well, it's not exactly a bead. It's a sort of shiny metal cube, with a bit of blue at the center."

"I think the blue might be lapis lazuli," said Frieda. "And the shiny metal could be silver."

"Nice."

"What else?"

"Are you serious?" asked Karlsson.

"Yes."

He strained his eyes. "There's a little metal thing on two of the sides."

"Which is?"

"I don't know."

"Do you think it might be for attaching it to something?"

"Maybe. Or maybe not."

"And look," said Frieda. "There are two more here and one on the other side. Just the same."

She stood back. Her eyes had been dazzled by the proximity of the bulb. "There should be others."

"You mean beads like that?"

"Yes. Beads like that."

She began pacing around the room.

"Frieda . . ."

"Shut up," said Frieda. "Find the others."

She found three, ranged along the windowsill. Karlsson found four in a glass, arranged around the stub of a candle, standing in its own dried wax. Another four were placed along the frame of the door.

"This is like a children's party," said Karlsson.

Frieda had stopped. She was standing in the middle of the room with her eyes closed. Suddenly they opened. "What?" she said.

"I said, it's like a children's party. You know, like an Easter egg hunt, or something like that."

Frieda ignored him. She took the three beads from the windowsill, placed them in the palm of her hand, and stared at them closely. She turned to Karlsson. "Have you got a flashlight?"

"No."

"I thought policemen carried flashlights."

"In films made in the 1950s. I'm afraid I don't have a truncheon either."

She walked over to the standard lamp, lifted the shade off, and held her hand close to the bulb. She looked at them so intently that her eyes hurt.

"Yes?" said Karlsson.

"Look at this one." Frieda pointed at one of the beads.

"It's a bit grubby," said Karlsson.

"Do you have something we can put these in?"

Karlsson took a transparent evidence bag from his pocket and Frieda dropped them in, one by one.

"What do you think they are?" asked Frieda.

"Beads."

"And what do you get if you join beads together?"

"A bangle of some kind?"

"Or if you have more beads?"

"A necklace, maybe. But aren't these just something that Michelle Doyce found somewhere?"

"That's exactly what they are," said Frieda. "She found them joined together and took them apart and used them to decorate her room. These are nice. And they look handmade to me. And valuable. She didn't just find them on the pavement."

"So . . ."

"So you've got to stop your guys packing this stuff away. Instead, they've got to find as many as they can. There'll probably be fifteen or twenty more, at least. Then show a photograph of them to Aisling Wyatt. And you said that one of them was dirty. Find out what the dirt is."

"Of course, it could be that they're just beads," said Karlsson.

When the phone rang, Frieda knew it was going to be Karlsson. It almost rang with Karlsson's accent.

"Do you want the good news or the good news?" he said.

"What happened?"

"You're forgiven," said Karlsson. "Completely forgiven. Aisling Wyatt has identified the necklace. She said it 'went missing' a few weeks ago. What an amazing coincidence. Our trophy collector at work again. Robert Poole clearly took things from whomever he conned and redistributed them — some kind of power game. And that's not even the best bit. You knew, didn't you? Though fuck knows how. The dirt on the necklace was blood. Robert Poole's blood." There was a pause. "You know what this means, don't you? It means we can charge Frank Wyatt."

"No," said Frieda. "What it means is you can't charge Frank Wyatt."

"Joanna," said Frieda, "where else did Dean like to go? Apart from Margate."

551

"It's in the book. Can I have another beer?"

"Of course. I'll get one in a minute. I've read the book."

"Did you like it?"

"I thought it was extremely interesting."

"Fishing. He liked to go fishing. Anywhere — canals and flooded gravel pits and rivers. He could sit there all day with his tin of maggots. Drove me mad."

"What happened to his fishing rods?"

"I sold them on eBay. I didn't say who they'd belonged to."

"Anywhere else, any particular town?"

"We didn't travel much. When he was a kid, he said he and his ma used to go to Canvey Island."

"OK."

"Why? Why d'you need to know?"

"I'm tying up loose ends," said Frieda, vaguely.

Joanna nodded, as if satisfied. Frieda got her another beer and watched her as she drank it, froth on her upper lip.

"I'm surprised you've got the nerve," she said, when she'd finished it. "After everything."

"You didn't think we'd meet again?"

"No. I'm in the new chapter of my life.

That's what my editor said to me. You belong to the old one."

# 45

It was in the middle of the night when the voices came back. They started as a murmur that Beth could barely distinguish from the lapping of the water against the hull and the rustle of the trees by the bank and the spatter of rain on the roof. She knew the voices were coming for her, and she tried to hide from their anger, shut them out by wrapping a pillow around her head, blocking her ears, but gradually the voices became clearer, then settled into one voice, harsh, heavy, deep, coming out of the darkness close by and surrounding her.

It was angry with her. It asked questions she couldn't answer. It made accusations. It knew her secrets and her fears.

"You let him down."

"No, I didn't let him down."

"He went away and you forgot him."

"No, I didn't forget him."

The voice said terrible things to her, told

her that she had done nothing, that she was nothing, that she was useless. She told him about the photographs and the documents, but the voice just continued with its harsh accusations.

"It's the same. It's always the same. I speak and you don't listen."

"I do listen. I do listen."

"You're nothing. You do nothing."

Beth started crying and waving her head from side to side, banging it against the wooden wall above her bunk, anything to shut the voice out. Slowly, as the room grew lighter, the voice faded and left her aching, rubbing her tear-blotched face.

She got up and searched through Edward's papers until she found the pages she wanted. She wasn't nothing. She wasn't useless. She stared at the words and stared at them, committing them to memory, saying them to herself over and over again in a sing-song voice. Then she fumbled through the cutlery drawer until she found what she wanted. The knife and the stone for sharpening it. She remembered, from when she was a child, her father in the kitchen telling her mother, "Women don't understand." And then she'd hear the noise, the knife edge scraping against the gray stone with the hint of a spark. "This is how you sharpen a knife. This is how you sharpen a knife."

Frieda took a deep breath before she made the call.

"Frieda," Harry said.

"You sound cross."

"You can tell that from just one word?"

"But you are."

"Why would that be, Frieda?"

"Where are you now?"

"Where am I? I'm near Regent's Park, with a client."

"Are you free?"

"When?"

"Now. For a quick lunch. I've got an hour."

"Nice of you to fit me in."

"I'd like to see you for lunch, if you have the time."

"I don't know," he said. "All right, then. Where?"

"There's a little place that's quite near you — Number 9, Beech Street. Quite near my house. I can be there in ten minutes."

"I'll get a taxi. One thing, though: I don't really like being made a fool of."

"I understand that."

"Back to wearing dark clothes, I see."

Frieda glanced down at what she was

wearing — all blacks and somber blues —
and smiled. "I guess so."

"I liked what you were wearing last night."

"Thank you."

"You looked beautiful."

She didn't reply, but studied the offers
chalked up on the board. Marcus came over
to take their order. His eyes were bright with
curiosity.

"Goat's cheese salad, please," she said
briskly.

"Same," said Harry.

"And tap water."

"Same." He put his chin in his hands and
studied her, thinking she looked tired. "So
what happened?" he asked.

"You mean last night?"

"Yes."

"I don't know."

"Come on, Frieda."

"I'm not being coy. I want to be honest
about it. I didn't know in advance that I
was going to leave like that. I just had to. I
can't really explain."

"You could have told me, though. I was
waiting for you to come back and feeling
idiotically happy. Then bit by bit I realized
you'd deserted me and I was this stranger
at a party who'd been dumped."

"I just couldn't stay there."

"I thought . . ." He stopped and gave an awkward smile. "I thought you liked me. Were coming to like me, at least."

"I do. I'm sorry I left you like that last night. It was wrong of me."

Their salads arrived. Marcus winked at Frieda, who raised her eyebrows at him sternly.

"Is it because of all the things that are going on?" asked Harry, prodding his goat's cheese with a fork. He didn't really like salads. Or goat's cheese. "With this investigation and all that you've had to go through, I mean. That woman who killed herself, I forget her name, and the newspaper articles, and the general ugliness of it all. It must be tough."

Frieda considered. "I sometimes think I made a mistake in getting involved at all," she said at last. "I'm not entirely sure what my motives were. I've always said, always believed, that you can't solve the mess of the world, only the mess inside your own head. Now I'm interviewing suspects and wandering around crime scenes. Why?"

"Because you know you're good at it?" suggested Harry.

"I probably shouldn't be talking about this to you. But I don't know the rules for a police investigation. I don't know where the boundaries are."

"Can I say something?"

"Of course."

"You're someone that people tell their troubles to. Maybe you find it hard when it's the other way round. You can say what you like to me. I'm not going to run to the newspapers."

"That's kind of you."

"What's troubling you about this investigation?"

"The police think they know who it is."

"That's good, no?"

"They've found new evidence."

"What was that?"

"Something in the room where Robert Poole's body was discovered, something that was in his pocket when the body was found. I think they're going to charge someone soon."

"Who?" asked Harry. He took a small sip of water.

"Now that really *would* be breaking a rule," said Frieda.

"But you're not happy?"

Frieda looked steadily at him. Her expression of concentration almost scared him.

"It's not just the investigation," she said. "The fact is, I've had it with all this. At first I enjoyed being involved in a police investigation. It was like an escape from my real life. But now, when I've been attacked by people saying, 'What the hell is this analyst doing here?' — well, I mainly agree with them. So, I'm going to do this last thing and then I'm out of here."

Harry smiled at her. "What's this last thing?"

"Oh, you don't want to hear all the boring details," said Frieda.

"I do," said Harry. "I'm interested in what you're doing, in the things that make your life so complicated."

"All right," said Frieda. "It's about Michelle Doyce, the woman who found the body. She's in a psychiatric hospital down in Lewisham, and she'll probably never leave. The police have hardly bothered with her, she's so obviously delusional. But I've stayed in touch with her. I've seen her from time to time, and just recently she's been getting more lucid. She was terrified by the noises in the ward, all the other people, and it made her worse. But they moved her to a room on her own, and she calmed down and she's starting to talk about things."

"What does that mean?"

"Michelle found the body and brought it back to her room. But from what she's started saying, I think she did more than that. I think she saw who dumped the body."

There was a pause. With great care Harry took a piece of goat's cheese, put it on a piece of toast, chewed it, and swallowed. "What do the police say?" he asked.

"They're not interested," said Frieda. "They've got their own case and they're happy with it."

"So is that it?"

"No. I've come to know a neurologist who's an expert on these extreme syndromes. I'm going in with him on Monday. He's going to give her a cocktail of medication, and I'm convinced she'll be able to tell us exactly what she saw. Then I'll give her statement to the police, and they can do the inquiry the way they should have done it in the first place, which is properly. But they'll have to do it without me. I'm done."

"Why do you do this?" said Harry. "You can't do everybody's job for them. Aren't you just tempted to walk away now? To get your life back?"

"And watch an innocent man go to jail?" she said. "How could I possibly?"

"The police might just manage to get the right person themselves," he said. "Otherwise they wouldn't be called police."

Frieda shook her head. "Without this, they'll go with the case they've got already and move on to something else." She looked suspiciously at him. "Don't you like goat's cheese salad?"

"Not much."

"Why did you order it?"

"It doesn't matter. I'm not hungry, anyway. You know I'm mad about you, don't you?"

"Harry . . ."

"Don't say anything. Please don't say anything. You know, anyway. That's why I'm here, ordering goat's cheese and babbling." He put his hand out and touched her face. She sat quite still, her eyes fixed on his. Marcus, washing espresso cups at the counter, watched them.

"Do I stand a chance?"

"Not yet," said Frieda. She shifted away from him very slightly, and he sighed.

"Why?"

"Bad timing."

"But one day?"

"I need to go now. I have a patient."

"Don't go yet. Please. What do I need to do?"

"It's not like that."

"No. Tell me. Give me an order."

"All right." Her voice was almost a whisper. "Leave me alone."

∎ ∎ ∎ ∎

Frieda finished work just before six. It was twilight, and a damp wind was blowing through the streets. She turned up the collar of her coat, pushed her hands deep into its pockets, and began to walk toward her flat, which felt far off and infinitely desirable. Then someone touched her softly on the shoulder and she turned and saw Harry. "Were you waiting for me?" She sounded angry.

"I've been here for over an hour. I wanted to talk to you."

"I'm going home."

"Can I come along?"

"Not this evening."

"All right. Can I say something to you?"

"What is it?"

"Not just on the street. Here — can we talk in here?" Harry gestured toward the wasteland that Frieda looked at from her room every day. In the darkness, it seemed larger and wilder than it did when she stared down at it during the day. Weeds had sprung up. Kids had made strange structures from the boards and metal sheets that the workmen had left when they'd abandoned the site. The remains of a bonfire lay near the gap in the fence where Harry stood, its embers still giving out a glowing pulse. He held back a loose part of the fence.

"I don't think so," said Frieda.

"There's a bench near here," said Harry, coaxingly. "I saw it when I walked past earlier. Just a minute, Frieda. Hear me out."

Frieda hesitated, then stepped nimbly through the gap in the fence. Harry followed her and pulled it close.

"Tell me."

"Let's find this bench of mine."

"I don't need to sit down."

"This way."

They walked further into the enclosed space. There were craters in the earth; a small crane stood motionless in front of them.

"Frieda," said Harry, in a murmur.

"Yes?"

"I'm sorry."

"Why?"

"Because you see, my darling . . ."

He didn't finish his sentence because a figure suddenly rose from the ground in front of them — an ancient man wrapped in a blanket, with a bottle in his hand and a strange rusty moan coming from his mouth.

"He was asleep," said Frieda. Then, to the

man: "I'm so sorry to have frightened you."

He lifted the bottle to his mouth and tipped it so it was nearly vertical, and drank.

"We're going," said Frieda. "It's all right. We'll leave you in peace."

"Lady," he said, and followed them as they made their way back to the fence, through the gap.

"What was it you wanted to say sorry for?" asked Frieda.

Harry stared at her. It seemed hard for him to speak. He looked around at the people bustling past, on the way from work, heading home or to the pub for a drink.

"I wanted a word in private. I couldn't come to your place, could I? Just for a moment."

"Not now."

"All right," he said at last. "It can wait."

## 46

Michelle Doyce liked the hospital food. It was soft and grayish. It didn't look like anything. There was something that tasted a bit like fish, with a thick gray sauce. But there were no bones, no shape. There was something that tasted a bit like chicken, also with a thick gray sauce, also with no bones and no shape. It never looked like it would move, like it would speak to her. She didn't like the days. There were too many things all around her that felt like they were trying to batter at her head, colors and sounds and prickings on her skin, intertwining and tangling so that she couldn't tell what was the color and what was the sound. It was all just there, like a storm she was wandering around in, lost.

People came and went. Sometimes they moved so quickly and spoke so quickly that it was all a blur, and she couldn't make them out. It was as if she were standing on a station platform and they were on a train that wasn't stopping, that was racing past at a hundred miles an hour. Sometimes they would try to say something, but she couldn't catch it. It had been the same with the other patients in the ward. She had seen them and heard them, as in the flashes of a strobe light, and they always seemed to be screaming, shouting in pain or anger or despair, and she felt their pain and anger and despair herself. It was like spending day after day surrounded by road drills and sirens and electric buzzers and flashing light, with jagged stabbing knives in her eyes and her ears and her mouth. Every day she found things and hid them, then ordered them carefully. There were pieces of leftover soap from the bathroom, a little piece of silver wrapper from a pill container, a piece of Band-Aid, a screw. She arranged them in a pill box that had been left on the shelf by her bed. She would look at them and suddenly realize they were in the wrong order, take them out again, and put them in the right order.

Mainly it was bad. She felt she had been put out on a rock in the middle of the sea where she was completely alone, too hot or too cold, too dry or too wet, and she could never sleep because if she slept she would be washed off and battered and swept away and lost.

But it had gotten better when she was moved into a room of her own, as if she had escaped into a quiet little hole, away from the drills and the flashing lights. There was a TV. She would sit there, and at first the speckly light and the jagged sound would be a torment, but it was also soothing, like something warm washing over her, and she would watch the moving shapes for hour after hour. There were magazines as well, bright, smiling faces looking at her, asking for her friendship and her approval. She could hear them talking to her and she would smile back and sometimes she would catch them talking about her and she would shut the magazine, trap them, teach them a lesson. And there was the nurse. Sometimes she was white but with an accent; sometimes she was Asian; sometimes she was African. But she would lead her through a bright corridor, so bright that it dazzled her eyes, and sit her in a chair and lean her back and wash her hair. She could feel the fingers warm on her head. The feeling reminded Michelle Doyce of something long, long ago, deep down, where she was being held and kept safe. Then there were the two animals: the teddy bear and the dog. They sat on her bed; they slept with her. The dog had buttons for eyes. She knew they were only toys. But she had a feeling. She couldn't stop the feeling. Like a child lying in bed with a heavy, sleeping parent beside them. Not moving but warm and alive. They knew things; they were watching. When the noises and the lights got too much, she could look at them, feel them against her.

Best of all was when the lights went away and the noises sank like a storm blowing itself out. There would be a shout and a murmuring and a flickering and the lights would go out. It didn't get dark straight away. The light stayed in Michelle Doyce's eyes, like a dull ache, an afterglow of sour green turning to dirty yellow, then back to green, gradually fading to brown and to black. The darkness felt warm. Now even the lights felt more friendly. They blinked outside, in through the window, from far away in the night. They blinked inside, lights on machines, red and green and yellow. Even the noises were friendly, beeps and meeps. Sometimes, far away outside her room, there were groans and moans and cries that reminded Michelle Doyce of all the pain, but the dark was like a big furry cloth that mopped up the messy noises and squeezed them out somewhere into a river that would carry them away. The day wasn't for waking and the night for sleeping. It was all a sort of long doze, and she wasn't sure whether the pictures in her head and the voices were on TV or whether they were the people coming and going in the ward or whether they were stories she was telling herself, and what did it matter anyway?

But the nights were good. The lights became soft and the sounds softened, too, and the sharp edges of things became rounded. Michelle Doyce would have been happy for life to be like this always, and to go on forever and ever, sleeping and waking, warm and safe.

Voices came out of the darkness. They were part of her dream. She had been walking in a street and then she had been back somewhere inside, somewhere that seemed familiar. She was making tea. She filled the kettle and prepared cups and saucers. A bear and a dog with button eyes were sitting at the table.

"Michelle," said the quiet voice in the darkness. "Michelle Doyce."

There were two shapes in the black night. Two dark shapes, dark against the darkness, moving around her bed.

"Michelle," said another voice, right by her ear. A hiss, a whisper, but lighter. That had been a man. This was a woman.

"Is it her?"

Michelle Doyce didn't know if her eyes were open or closed, but she saw a tiny light, a firefly, floating in the dark, at the foot of the bed. It showed up the ghost of a face, a man's face. She felt something out there in the darkness, pain or anger or fear.

"Yes, it is," said a voice. The woman's again.

Michelle Doyce opened her mouth. She wanted to say something, but it came out as a groan and then the groan stopped. Something was stopping it. The blackness had become blacker. She wasn't making a sound. She couldn't make a sound. There was a weight on her, heavy and black, and she felt she was sinking down under it, down into a dream that was itself becoming dark, so that she was sinking out of the dream and fading and sinking.

Everything changed. There were lights, lights so harsh that they were like jangling sounds so that she couldn't see anything and couldn't hear anything. There were lights and there was shouting and she could cry out and breathe. She had been deep, deep underwater, and now she had been pulled out and was lying on the shore. Michelle Doyce breathed and breathed. She couldn't. It was like she couldn't pull the air inside her. Her breathing didn't work. She couldn't get the air in. She started to panic and flap and cry and shout. She flapped like a fish on the land, drowning in the air.

Then she felt a hand, cool on the side of her face, and a voice speaking to her out of the blinding light. She felt a breath on her face, a sweet and cool breath.

"Michelle," said the voice, soft and close. "Michelle. It's all right. It's all right. You're all right."

The voice spoke like it was telling her a story, soothing her to sleep. She felt the cool breath on her face. She felt she could breathe again, as if she were breathing in that cool breath, as if it were going straight inside her.

"Michelle, Michelle," said the voice.

Michelle Doyce opened her eyes. The light dazzled her so much that she could see nothing except blue and yellow dots popping before her eyes. Slowly a face took shape. She heard the words and felt the voice's fingers, cool and slow on the side of her face. She knew the face. The woman with the dark eyes and clear voice.

"You," said Michelle Doyce.

"Yes," said the woman, close, so she could feel her clean breath. "It's me."

# 47

Karlsson took Frieda by the crook of her arm, in an unfamiliarly protective gesture.

"They've had their rights read to them and they both have legal representation with them now. As you can imagine, Tessa Welles is aware of her legal situation."

"Have you been in with them already?"

"I was waiting for you."

"I came as soon as I could. I didn't want to leave Michelle alone."

"Is she all right?"

"For a woman in Hell, she's all right. I called Jack. She knows and likes him. He's not threatening. She finds the reddish color of his hair soothing. I said I'd go back later. And I'm going to call Andrew Berryman, a doctor who knows about Michelle. We've got to help her. She's a suffering human being, not a medical curiosity. We owe her that much at least."

Karlsson looked at her with concern. "Are

you all right?"

"I used her as bait," said Frieda. "That seems to be what I do with people I'm supposed to be caring for. She was like a worm with a hook pushed through her, and I did it to her."

"You got the fish, didn't you?"

"First, do no harm," said Frieda.

"What?"

"It's the oath that doctors are meant to swear."

Tessa was sitting in the interview room, her hands folded on the table in front of her, looking composed, although Frieda noticed that there were shadows under her eyes and every so often she licked her lips. The man who sat beside her was in his late fifties; he had a thin, clever face; his eyes were bright and watchful.

Yvette and Karlsson sat opposite Tessa; Frieda took a seat to one side. Tessa swung her head round and stared at her; there was a very faint smile on her lips, as if she knew something that Frieda didn't.

"Miss Welles," said Karlsson, courteously. "You understand your rights and that everything you say is being recorded."

"Yes."

"You've been arrested on suspicion of the

attempted murder of Michelle Doyce last night. We shall also be questioning you in regard to the murders of Robert Poole and Janet Ferris. Is that clear?"

"Yes," said Tessa, in a detached tone.

"Your brother is next door. We'll be talking to him as well. We just wanted to hear your side of the story first."

Tessa looked at him and said nothing.

"All right. Perhaps you should hear our version of your story." Karlsson picked up a folder and leafed through it, allowing the silence to settle around them. The muscle in Tessa's jaw tightened, but she didn't move.

"Robert Poole," said Karlsson at last. "You met him when he came to your office with Mary Orton, who wanted you to make a new will in his favor. You chose not to proceed. You mistrusted his motives."

Tessa stared straight ahead, not meeting Karlsson's gaze.

"You were quick to recognize that," said Frieda. "It was impressive."

"But then you saw him again," continued Karlsson. "What happened?"

"I've nothing to say," said Tessa.

"It won't matter." Karlsson turned to Frieda. "What do you think happened?"

"We're not here to listen to speculation,"

said the solicitor. "If you have questions to put to Miss Welles, then go ahead."

"I'm inviting Dr. Klein to put a scenario to your client. That's a kind of question. She can then confirm or deny it." He looked at Frieda, who had been thinking hard.

She pulled a chair over from the wall and sat beside Karlsson, facing Tessa. Now Tessa stared at Frieda. For a moment she thought of the children's game in which you had to stare at each other and try not to laugh.

"I never met Robert Poole," Frieda said. "I've never even seen a photograph of him. At least, not when he was alive. But I've met so many people he got involved with that I almost feel I knew him. When you refused to execute the will, most people would have felt humiliated or exposed, but he would have been intrigued by you. He was used to having power over people, but you'd escaped him. You were a challenge. So he got back in touch. What did he say? Perhaps he wanted to explain the situation to you, show you it wasn't the way you thought.

"You were intrigued as well, and a bit amused. There was something charming about the way he just wouldn't give up. So you began an affair with him out of a certain curiosity, just to see how he worked."

A contemptuous smile formed on Tessa's face. "That pornographic fantasy says more about you than it does about me," she said.

"And then he fell for you. He saw you as a kindred spirit. You encouraged him, and he told you about Mary Orton, Jasmine Shreeve, Aisling and Frank Wyatt."

"And Janet Ferris," said Yvette harshly.

"Leave that for a moment," said Frieda. When she resumed, it was almost as if she were talking to herself, puzzling something out. "There was something I couldn't quite put my finger on. Jasmine Shreeve, Mary Orton, the Wyatts, his victims. They were obviously hiding things, in their different ways, and they felt guilty and ashamed and upset. They contradicted themselves. That's what people do. They're not coherent. Things don't add up. But you weren't like that. Your relationship with Poole was completely uncomplicated. You were the only person he never got to. It was just about the money."

She glanced at Karlsson, who nodded.

"Once you discovered how much money he had," Karlsson said, "and how he'd got it, the idea was simple. The best person to steal money from is someone who's stolen the money himself, because he can't go to the police. Did he tell you about the money to try and impress you? So you and your brother decided to help yourselves. Harry knew about bank transfers and setting up fake accounts. Con the con man."

"No," said Frieda.

"What do you mean?"

"It wasn't just stealing stolen money," she said. "It was even better than that. When did you discover that he was using a stolen identity? Did he boast about it to you? Or did Harry discover it when he checked up on him?" Tessa just stared at her but didn't speak. "Because that's even better," Frieda continued. "Not just stolen money that won't be reported to the police, but stolen from a nonexistent person, someone with no history."

"It wasn't me . . ." Tessa began, but stopped.

"Was it Harry's idea?" said Frieda. "It doesn't matter. You know, I've tried not to think about the last few minutes of Robert Poole's life. You probably imagined that a threat would be enough, like in the old days when you could get a confession just by showing the instruments of torture." Suddenly she felt as if she were alone with Tessa and her voice became quiet. "What was it? A bolt cutter? A pair of secateurs? But he didn't believe you, did he? He didn't think you, Tessa Welles, would really go through with it. So you crammed a rag of some kind into his mouth and then you did it. It's hard to cut off a finger, the bone and the tendon and the gristle, but you, or Harry, did it, and he told you what you wanted to know to get at the money. Then you strangled him. But that was easy after the finger.

"But this wasn't an improvisation. It wasn't a Plan B. You knew about the Wyatts. You knew Poole had helped himself to her necklace. You knew where you were going to dump the body in order to frame Frank Wyatt."

"I'm sorry," said the solicitor. "Is there a question somewhere in this?"

"It's all a question," said Karlsson. "Will Tessa Welles admit to it?"

The solicitor looked at Tessa, who shook her head.

"Robert Poole's flat was interesting," continued Frieda. "I don't mean your painting, which was hanging in Janet Ferris's kitchen. We know about that. I mean that you weren't clever enough about the evidence in his flat."

"What do you mean?" said Karlsson, twisting his head to look at her. "There wasn't any."

"That's right," said Frieda. "They left

everything relating to his victims, but there was no reference to Tessa at all. Pages had been torn out of Poole's notebooks, but the names of the victims were left there. Which suggested that the pages had been torn out by someone else."

"What it suggested to you is not evidence," said Tessa's solicitor.

"You killed Robert Poole," said Karlsson. "You killed Janet Ferris."

"The coroner's verdict was suicide."

"You killed Janet Ferris," repeated Karlsson. "And you tried to kill Michelle Doyce because you thought she knew something."

There was a faint flicker in Tessa's face.

"She didn't." Frieda leaned forward once more. "Michelle Doyce was no threat to you. She had nothing to tell me; I just let you and Harry believe that, God forgive me."

"That's enough for now," said the solicitor, standing up.

"You would have killed her, just in case," Frieda continued quietly. "You and your brother. How does it feel?"

"I don't know what you're talking about."

"How does it feel to find out what you're capable of?"

"Enough. My client has nothing further to say."

"You're going to have to think about that, Tessa. Over the years."

Harry Welles was wearing a thick gray pullover and black jeans. It was the first time that Frieda had seen him casually dressed; he had always been in a suit or a smart jacket, carefully groomed and impeccable. She considered him: many people would think him an attractive man. He had the self-conscious charm of one who is confident of getting his own way. Olivia positively cooed when she talked of him.

She took her seat in the corner and met his eyes. His solicitor was a woman, young, trim, and pretty, who gestured with her hands whenever she spoke and sometimes tapped her pink-tipped fingers on the table.

He had no comment about the torture of Robert Poole, no comment about his murder, nothing to say about the planted evidence and the dumping of the body, silence over Janet Ferris's death.

"I don't get it," said Karlsson. "You were caught in the act of attempting to murder Michelle Doyce. It's cut and dried. You're going down, you and your sister. You've got nothing to lose. Why not tell us? It's your last option."

"As you say," replied Harry pleasantly,

"you don't get it."

"You think nobody is quite as clever as you," said Frieda. "Isn't that right?"

"I was wondering when you'd speak."

"You and Tessa think that you're superior to everyone else, and it makes you feel impregnable."

"It takes one to know one."

"And contemptuous."

"I wasn't contemptuous of you, was I? On our little dates?" He raised his eyebrows at her.

"Our dates?" Frieda gazed at him speculatively. "Do you want to know what I thought about them? I've been on dates with other men, and sometimes they were interesting, and sometimes they were embarrassing, and sometimes they were charged with possibility. With our dates, there wasn't anything. It was like a performance. There was nothing behind the words."

"Fuck you. You won't be so calm when everything comes out. You like your privacy, but I *know* things, Frieda. You'll be surprised by the things I know." He leaned toward her. "I know about your family, your father, your past."

Karlsson stood up, with a violence that sent his chair skidding across the floor. "As your solicitor should have said, this interview is over."

He turned off the tape recorder, then went to the door and held it open for Frieda. "Thank you," she said, then looked at Harry for the last time.

"You called him Bob," she said.

"What?"

"You asked about Bob Poole when we were in the pub. That was stupid of you, don't you think? After that I knew for certain. One word, Harry. One syllable."

Then she left the room, her chin raised.

"Are you OK?" asked Karlsson.

"I'm fine."

"That stuff he said about —"

"I said, I'm fine. It's all right. It's over."

"You're sure."

"But there's something else."

"Go on."

"Dean Reeve. Hear me out. I know he's alive. I think I sense him sometimes. I can't get rid of the feeling that I'm in danger."

She didn't go straight back to the hospital but took the bus to Belsize Park and walked toward the Heath. After a long winter's corridor of darkness and unyielding cold, spring was arriving — in the new warmth of the air, in the daffodils that were everywhere. The sticky buds were just beginning to unfurl on the horse chestnut trees. After the ice and the darkness, balmy days would arrive, long evenings and soft mornings.

She rang the bell, waited, rang again.

"What?" said the voice on the intercom, sounding cross.

"Dr. Berryman? It's Frieda Klein."

"It's Sunday. Don't you ever bother to ring ahead?"

"Can I talk to you for a moment?"

"You are talking to me."

"Not like this. Face-to-face."

There was an exaggerated sigh, and then he buzzed her up. She followed the stairs to the top flat, where he was waiting by the open door. "I was playing the piano," he said.

"How's it going?"

"Not much progress."

"I've come about Michelle Doyce."

"Is she still alive?"

"Yes."

"Any developments?"

"Yes. You and I are going to make sure she is put in a more appropriate institution, where she is properly cared for and can be surrounded by the things she loves."

"We are?"

"Yes."

"Why?"

"Not because she is a medical curiosity but because she's in distress and she is our responsibility."

"Really?"

"Yes, really." Frieda nodded at him. "It was you who gave her the teddy, wasn't it?"

"I don't know what you're talking about."

"Pink, with a heart stitched on to its chest."

"The shop had a lousy selection."

"Don't worry — I won't tell anyone. You don't know how much trouble it caused," said Frieda. "But it was a nice thing to do. And it helped, in a way."

As she walked down the stairs, she heard the sound of badly played Chopin behind her.

# 48

"Did you see the news today?" Yvette asked Munster. "Money for the police is being cut by twenty-five percent. How the hell are we going to manage that? I'll probably be working at McDonald's in six months. If I'm lucky."

"It's about efficiency," said Munster. "Cutting bureaucracy. Frontline services won't be affected."

"Crap," said Yvette. "The bureaucracy is me, sitting here trying to prepare a file for the CPS. How's that going to be cut? That's what that idiot Jake Newton was here for, wasn't it? Looking for who to cut. Where is he, by the way?"

"I suppose he's writing his report, just as we're writing ours. Speaking of which, we've got to explain these pictures for our report."

"Oh, shit," said Yvette. "I was hoping someone else would deal with them. It's like, I don't know, like an old sweater. A bit of wool comes loose and you think you've sorted it, but then something's gone wrong with the sleeve. What I can't understand is that you've killed someone, you've got the body dangling in front of you, and you start rearranging the pictures. And moving furniture around. Is this just some crazy theory of Frieda Klein's? Couldn't they have just moved two of the pictures? Take the big one to cover the patch, move the furniture. Replace the smallest picture with the one they'd brought. Wouldn't that be simpler?"

"There's a reason why not. I just can't think of it."

Karlsson came into the room, followed by Frieda.

"Everything all right?" asked Karlsson.

"We were talking about the pictures," said Yvette. "For the report. We can't get it straight in our heads."

"Frieda?" Karlsson turned to her and waited.

Frieda considered for a moment. Yvette thought she seemed tired, dark around her eyes.

"OK," she began. "Six pictures of different sizes. Poole took the third smallest, stowed it under his bed, and replaced it with the picture he'd taken from Tessa Welles, the one he gave to Janet Ferris and that she then put back." She gave a small sigh. "Poor thing. Sometimes I think it's people's attempt to do the right thing that destroys them. Anyway, imagine the scene. Tessa and Harry Welles have killed her. The picture they have brought is too small for the space, but it will fit where the second smallest picture hung. The second picture will fit where the smallest picture hung. There is still a gap, which they cover with the next biggest picture, so they move each picture to cover the smaller patch. This leaves them with one large blank patch, which they cover by moving the dresser, and one little painting, which they take away with Tessa's."

"Wasn't there an easier way?"

"It depends how you look at it," said Frieda. "You've got to remember that they were in a state of extreme stress. There was a body hanging in front of them. They were having to improvise. They solved one problem at a time, and I think they managed it pretty well. There was another reason as well. By moving all the pictures, they disguised which was the important one."

"I think I'll have to see it written down," said Munster.

"There is the alternative theory," said Yvette. "Which is that Poole just wanted to rearrange his pictures."

589

"That was what I thought," said Karlsson. "So this morning we went to Tessa Welles's flat. We found the painting, the real one with the bloody pine tree and the moon, and they've got it downstairs where they're going over it. Unofficially, there are several sets of prints on the frame."

"So they would have got away with it if they hadn't made a mistake with the bloody pictures?" asked Munster.

"No. Lots of small things didn't add up. But it was all vague at first," said Frieda. "With everyone else Poole met, he found their weakness, got under their skin. But Tessa got under Poole's skin. That was interesting. Their eagerness to get involved with me seemed a bit strange. It may sound crazy, but it was as if they wanted to become part of the inquiry."

"It doesn't sound crazy at all," said Karlsson. "It's part of our training. It's not at all uncommon for perpetrators to hang around the fringes of the investigation, even to try and get involved. It's to do with control. At least, that's what the textbooks say."

"The Welleses were big on control," Frieda said. "It all smelled funny to me, but finding Aisling Wyatt's necklace was the key thing."

"Which implicated the Wyatts," said Munster.

"The people it definitely didn't implicate were the Wyatts. I know that people leave things at murder scenes, but not an expensive necklace. It's just the sort of thing that Poole would have helped himself to, though, and shown off to Tessa. Even given to her."

"So why did it end up in Michelle's flat?" said Munster.

"I walked the route from the Wyatts' flat along the river to where Michelle Doyce lived. Tessa and Harry Welles must have checked the same route in their car. They wanted to dump the body as close to the Wyatts' place as possible, and Howard Street is closest to where you could pull a car up to an alley and leave a body without being seen. And they put Aisling's necklace in his pocket. It was as if they thought the police were really thick and needed to be led by the nose."

"How did you know that Tessa had had an affair with Poole?"

Frieda shrugged. "It was more or less a guess," she said. "Poole stopped sleeping with Aisling Wyatt at about the time he met Tessa. It seemed likely. When Tessa described the idea as pornographic, I knew I'd been right. But even when I'd started to

591

feel queasy about Tessa and Harry Welles, I knew that probably none of it counted as real evidence. Even Harry calling him 'Bob' to me, that one time. And whatever you think of me, I do understand you can't simply follow your intuition. That's what lynch mobs do. I felt certain the Wyatts were innocent but that someone else could be guilty aside from Harry and Tessa. What about Beth Kersey, for instance?" She rubbed her face. "So I used Michelle Doyce as bait. For my sins."

"You were sure they'd kill her to protect themselves?" said Munster.

"I felt they had a taste for it," said Frieda. "And that this was something they could do. I'd imagine that murder gets easier after the first one or two."

"So," said Karlsson, "it's the end of the case. We've found Robert Poole's killers, and Janet Ferris's. The one person we haven't found and never will is Robert Poole himself. That's not even his name. He's not Edward Green either. He's a mystery, a blank."

"Perhaps that's why he was so successful at what he did," added Frieda. "He became whoever people wanted him to be. He was everyone and no one, the perfect con man. I wonder who he was to himself."

"This is the time when we're supposed to go to the pub and celebrate."

"And," continued Frieda, "what was he to Beth Kersey? That's what I keep wondering. Where is she? Is she still alive? Poole preyed on people's weaknesses, their sadness, their little failures. But Beth Kersey's vulnerability is on a different level."

"I don't know what to say, Frieda," said Karlsson. "Except what about that drink?"

"No," said Frieda. "I'm going to see Lorna Kersey."

As she left the office, she saw Commissioner Crawford and Jake Newton at the end of the corridor. Newton glanced at her, then away.

# 49

A woman brought them coffee in the garden room. Outside, a man was working in the rose garden, pruning, tying up branches. Frieda found it difficult to believe they were in the middle of London.

"I thought you were coming to bring me news," said Lorna.

"I came because I want your help," said Frieda.

"It's meant to be so easy to find people nowadays, with mobile phones and the Internet and everything."

"But that's not the issue. As far as the police are concerned, your daughter is an adult and she's free to leave home and disappear, if that's what she wants."

"But she's not an adult," said Lorna. "Or, at least, she's not well."

"That's why I'm here," said Frieda. "I need to find out more about her mental state. You said that she had experienced schizophrenic episodes, but that can be anything from mild delusions to a complete loss of autonomy. I mean, you can be a danger to yourself and to other people. For example, did *you* ever feel threatened by your daughter?"

"Oh, no," said Lorna. "She wasn't overtly hostile, or not usually. She was always trying to help. That was her problem. When she was a teenager, she tried to paint her own room."

"That doesn't sound so bad," said Frieda.

"It was the way she did it. It was disastrously messy, but there was always something more than that, something frightening." Lorna picked up her coffee cup, then put it down without drinking from it. "I've had my own difficulties in my life from time to time. You may look at this house and think everything's fine with me."

No, Frieda thought. She didn't think that for a single moment.

"I know what it's like for things to feel a bit meaningless sometimes," Lorna continued. "But you have your family and your friends and your work to help you keep stable. But with Beth, in her bad patches, it was seeing what life could be like if all of that was gone."

"I know she could be a victim. I'm asking

if she could also be violent," said Frieda.

"I don't want to talk about things like that," said Lorna. "I just want her to be safe."

Frieda glanced out of the window. The gardener was cutting a rose bush back so hard that it was little more than a collection of stumps. Could it survive that? "Was your daughter ever forcibly committed for psychiatric treatment?"

Lorna shook her head in disapproval. "We didn't want anything like that," she said. "She received help when she needed it."

"Was she seeing a psychiatrist at the time she disappeared?"

"She was receiving some treatment, yes."

"Do you know the details of the treatment?"

"No," said Lorna. "But I don't think it was much help."

"Do you remember the doctor's name?"

"I don't think she was right for Beth. She got worse, if anything."

"But what was her name?"

"Oh, I don't know," Lorna said impatiently. "Dr. Higgins, I think."

"Do you remember her first name?"

Lorna was growing visibly more irritated. "E-something. Emma, maybe. Or Eleanor.

They weren't any help, though. None of them."

It had been a bad night. They'd been angry with her, a chorus of angry voices, shrill and harsh and high and low and jangling, and she didn't know how to make them stop. They were Edward's words, things he'd said to her, but they had come alive inside her skull and they wouldn't stop — he wouldn't stop. Beth knew she had to leave. Was it the sort of thing you could run away from? She felt like she had the worst kind of headache, the one where insects are inside your head, chewing and crawling and scratching, and she wanted to escape so that the ache would stay behind. She thought of setting fire to herself, burning the insects to death, like when people set anthills on fire and the ants run round and round in circles, as if that would do any good. Or she could get into a freezer, like the chest freezer her parents had in their scullery. It would be such a relief to get inside, into the fierce cold, sharp as a knife, pull down the top, lie in the dark, and feel the insects go to sleep.

But no. That wasn't allowed. That was what Edward said, what the voices had been saying. Everything went wrong when she thought about what Beth wanted. Everything had always gone wrong. Beth was bad. Beth was the bad person inside her head. What was important was to think of other people. Edward. Everyone else was the enemy. Especially Beth. She would deal with Beth later. But first, dimly, distantly, she felt she should eat, like putting fuel in a car. She just needed to get there, do what Edward wanted, and that would be enough. She found some pieces of the chicken, dry and hard. She chewed at them. She took the last of the bread, rock hard now, smeared it thickly with butter, and pushed it into her mouth, chewing it into a thick paste that was difficult to swallow. She needed to wash the paste down with water. Glass after glass of water. The milk smelled of cheese, but she drank it anyway. The heavy, full feeling was a comfort, weighing her down, stopping her floating away.

She came out on deck and stepped on to the towpath. It was sunny and cold. The sunlight hurt her. She could even hear it. The voices wouldn't stop, even in the daytime. Just nagging and nagging at her.

"Leave me alone, leave me alone," she said. "I can hear you. I'm doing it. Just leave me alone. They said it to me already, all right?"

Now she heard another voice and this one

was just stupid and it was even worse than the others. This voice came out of a real person, and he was standing on the towpath next to her. He had long hair and a sort of patchy horrible beard, as if he were ill or something. The man was reaching out and touching her and she could even smell him, he was so close, but she couldn't see him properly because of the brightness of the sun, which dazzled her. He was a dark shape, with sparks around his edges, like when the sun shone on the ripples on the canal. Then she remembered. She had it with her. She'd been sharpening it the whole night long, like her dad used to. She pulled it out and held it in front of her and the funny thing was that she suddenly saw the man clearly and he looked so surprised.

But it didn't matter, really, because the main thing was that she had somewhere to go. She turned away from him, where he'd sat down like a fool, and ran away along the towpath, away from the sun.

Like many doctors' addresses and phone numbers, Emma Higgins's were unlisted, which meant that it took Frieda three phone calls, two quite long conversations, a promise to meet up for a drink, an Underground journey, and a short walk before she found herself outside a smart terraced house in Islington, just off Upper Street. She hadn't dared to phone. She had only one chance, and it would be better face-to-face.

The woman who opened the door was wearing a purple knee-length dress and large earrings. She had on her party makeup, heavily lined eyes and red lips, blusher on her cheeks. Frieda could hear a hum from behind her and there was a glow from what must be the kitchen at the back of the house. It looked as if she had interrupted a dinner party.

"Are you Dr. Higgins?"

"Yes," she said, puzzled and irritated.

"I work as a consultant with the police, and I'd like to talk to you for just a couple of minutes."

"What?" said Dr. Higgins. "At this time of night? We've got people here."

"Just one moment, that's all. A patient of yours, Beth — or Elizabeth — Kersey, went missing a year ago. She's still missing, but she was involved with someone who was later murdered."

"Beth Kersey? Missing?"

"That's right. I wondered if you could tell me anything about her."

There was a pause. Dr. Higgins seemed to be remembering something. "Of course I can't," she said, with an almost disgusted expression. "She was a patient of mine. You know that. What the hell do you think you're doing, coming to my house at night, asking me about something private?"

"I don't need to know any clinical details," Frieda said. "I want to find her, and I'd like to know, even in general terms, about the kind of risks involved with her condition."

"No," said Dr. Higgins. "Absolutely not. And, in fact, I want your name, so I can make a complaint about your behavior."

"You'll need to get to the back of the queue," said Frieda.

"What are you talking about? And if you're working with the police, where are they? How did you get my address?"

A man appeared beside her, in a blue cotton shirt, loose outside his blue jeans. "What's going on, Emma?"

"This is someone who says she's a doctor . . ."

"A psychotherapist," said Frieda.

"Even worse, she says she's a psychotherapist and she wants to know about Beth Kersey."

The man looked startled, then angry. "Beth Kersey? Do you know her?" he said.

"No."

The man took Emma Higgins's left hand

and held it up. "Do you see that? What do you think it is?"

There was a pale line, three or four inches long, on Dr. Higgins's forearm.

"It looks like a scar," said Frieda.

"It's called a defense wound," said the man. "Do you know what that is?"

"Yes, I do," said Frieda. She looked at Dr. Higgins. "Did Beth Kersey do that to you?"

"What do you think?" said the man.

"I need your opinion," said Frieda. "She'll have been without her medication for a long time. What are the risks?"

"The answer is 'No comment,' " said Dr. Higgins. "As you well know, if you want access to her medical records you need a court order. And I'm also going to make that complaint."

She shut the door without another word. Frieda stood by the railings. As she dialed Karlsson's number, she heard raised voices from inside, the man saying something and Dr. Higgins answering angrily.

Karlsson sounded tired. When she told him about Dr. Higgins, she expected that he would be irritated by her acting without telling him but interested in what she had found out. But he didn't react at all.

"Don't you see?" she said. "She's violent."

"It's all in hand," said Karlsson.

"What do you mean? You need to step up the search for her and you need to establish who may be at risk."

"I said, it's all in hand. And we need to talk."

"Shall I come into the station?" said Frieda. "I'm seeing patients all morning but I could come afterward."

"I'll come to you. When's your first patient?"

"Eight o'clock."

"I'll be outside your house at seven fifteen."

"Karlsson, is something up?"

"I'll see you tomorrow."

## 50

"Would you like to come in for coffee?" said Frieda.

"No, thanks," said Karlsson. "You like walking, don't you? Let's go for a walk."

He headed north, his hands plunged into the pockets of his dark coat. His face looked swollen in the fiercely cold wind. When they reached Euston Road, it was already jammed in both directions with the largely stationary commuter traffic.

"You've got to love it, haven't you?" he said, and turned left, walking so briskly that Frieda had almost to run to keep up with him.

She grabbed him by the arm, forcing him to stop. "Karlsson," she said. "I know what this is about."

"What?"

"When I was in the station, I saw Jake Newton. He wouldn't meet my eye. He's delivered his report, hasn't he?"

Karlsson was silent, breathing out clouds of vapor. "That sharp-suited little cunt," he said. "I cannot believe we took that grinning little fucking oaf along with us and let him fart around with his fucking fly-on-the-wall act."

"So he's not too keen on freelance contracts," said Frieda.

"Oh, he's keen on contracts. For the office work, bureaucracy, management, there'll be freelance contracts out of our fucking arse."

"Karlsson," said Frieda. "You don't have to do the big sweary policeman thing for my benefit. It's fine. So, I'm out."

"Yes, Frieda. You're out."

"Not that I was ever really in. After all that, you never got a contract for me to sign."

"Well, that's the whole point about money-saving measures," said Karlsson. "You don't expect them to save money, do you? 'Dysfunctional operational procedures.' Those were his words. 'Management organization unfit for purpose.' Those were more of them. Do you know what makes it worse? I tried to impress him. I feel like some teenage boy who's tried to impress a girl he didn't really like in the first place and she's laughed at him. It's not just you. There are going to be cuts everywhere."

Frieda put her hand on his arm again, gently this time. "It's all right," she said.

"And after all you did in this case, getting the Welleses, I can't believe it."

"It's all right."

He pushed his hands more deeply into his pockets and looked embarrassed. "And despite me being sarcastic with you and shouting, it was, you know . . . having you around . . . I mean, anything's better than someone like Munster."

"Yes," said Frieda. "Me too."

"How do you get out of this place?"

"This way," said Frieda, and turned east. "But what about Beth Kersey?"

"I told you," said Karlsson. "It's in hand." He gave a faint smile. "You remember Sally Lea, the name in Poole's notebook?"

"The one we never found."

"It's not a woman," said Karlsson. "It's a barge on the Lea River up near Enfield."

"How do you know?"

"There was an incident yesterday. A resident of the adjacent barge called the emergency services. He'd been stabbed by a young woman. She had stolen food from him. She was acting strangely, talking to herself, and when accosted, she pulled a knife."

"Beth Kersey," said Frieda. "Did they find her?"

"No," said Karlsson. "But they found where she'd been living and a whole pile of Poole's stuff, papers, photos, the lot. Some officers are going to spend the day going through it, for what it's worth."

"What was this barge like?" said Frieda.

"What can I say? A barge is a barge."

"I mean inside, where she'd been living."

"I didn't see it myself. But from what I heard, it was pretty gross. It sounds like she'd been stuck there on her own, foraging for herself, ever since Poole died."

"Is that it?" said Frieda. "Pretty gross?"

"I know what you're saying," said Karlsson. "You want to go and look at it for yourself. I'm sorry, Frieda. Look, I know it seems messy. We'll probably never know who Poole really was. We don't know where he was killed. It looks like the money that the Welleses took from him has been safely stashed somewhere beyond our reach. Clearly that's one of the things Harry Welles is good at." He stopped and looked around. "But we got them. And the rest is in hand. We've put a protective unit on the Kerseys until we find their daughter, which won't take long. From what I heard about the state of that barge, she won't be able to look

after herself for long out in the big world
—" He stopped suddenly. "And now I've
got to get to work. Where the hell are we?"

Frieda pointed upward at the BT Tower.
They were standing almost directly beneath
it.

"That looks familiar," said Karlsson.
"Didn't there used to be a restaurant up
there? A rotating restaurant?"

"Until someone set off a bomb," said
Frieda. "A pity. I'd quite like to go up there.
It's the only place in London where you
can't see the BT Tower."

Karlsson held out his hand and Frieda
shook it. "I should probably move to Spain,"
he said.

"You're needed here," she said.

As they parted, Karlsson said, "At least
you can return to your real life now, Frieda.
You can put all this mess behind you. And
Dean Reeve. Let him go, will you?"

Frieda didn't reply. When he had turned
the corner, heading down toward Oxford
Street, she stopped and leaned against a
lamppost. She felt the metal cold against
her forehead as she took deliberate deep
breaths. "It's all right," she said. "It's all
right."

She took her phone from her pocket and
switched it on. There was a message and

she called straight back. "Sorry," she said. "Things have been a bit funny, but it's over now . . . Yes, that would be good . . . No. Just come to my house."

Frieda woke in darkness and felt the unfamiliar presence. A sag in the bed, breathing, a touch against her thigh. She moved as if to sit up, get out of the bed, get dressed, leave.

"Easy," said a voice, and Frieda lay down. She felt the sheet pulled back and a hand touching her body and his face against hers, the touch of lips on her cheek, her neck, her shoulders.

"A friend of mine was at a dinner," said Sandy. "He was a feisty guy, always up for a disagreement. He got into a row with a woman there, shouted at her, told her to fuck off, stormed out of the place, slammed the front door, found himself in the street, and realized he'd walked out of his own house."

"All right," said Frieda. "I get it."

"It feels like you're always about to leave. Just get up and walk away somewhere."

"That's what I do, when I'm afraid. When I can't sleep, which is most of the time, when my head is buzzing, when I'm confused, when I feel I just can't stay still, I go out and walk. And walk."

"And lose yourself?"

"No. I don't lose myself. I know my way around."

She felt both his hands on her now, his face on her.

"You smell nice," he said.

Frieda didn't know what she was feeling. Suddenly she thought of herself as very little, her father throwing her in the air and catching her; she was screaming and not knowing whether she was screaming with pleasure or with fear. She ran her fingers through Sandy's damp hair. She was damp too. "I probably smell of you," she said.

They lay for a moment in silence, tangled in each other.

"Is that what you feel?" said Sandy. "That you'd like to get up and walk somewhere?"

"That's what I feel most of the time."

"Do you always walk alone?"

"Not always."

"So if you were going to take me for a walk, where would we go?"

"Rivers," she said. "Sometimes I walk along the old rivers."

"You mean like the Thames?"

"No," said Frieda. "Obviously the Thames is a river. But I don't mean that. I mean the old rivers that flow into the Thames. They're buried now."

"Buried? Why would anyone bury a river?"

"I wonder that," said Frieda. "Sometimes I think people invent different kinds of reasons. They're a health hazard or they get in the way or they're dangerous. Sometimes I think rivers and streams make people uncomfortable. They're wet, they move, they bubble up out of the ground, they flood, they dry up. Better just to put them out of sight."

"So which vanished river shall we walk down?"

"The Tyburn," said Frieda. "Would you like to do that at the weekend?"

"I want you to tell me about it now," he said. "Where's it start?"

"It should start in Hampstead," said Frieda. "The source of the river is on Haverstock Hill. There's a plaque there. Except that the plaque is only in the approximate place. The actual source is lost. It's the only plaque I've ever seen that actually makes me angry. Can you imagine losing the source of a river? You have this spot where a spring bubbles clear water out of the ground and it flows down to the Thames. Then not only does someone decide to build on top of it but they actually forget where the spring was."

"It sounds like a bit of a bad start."

"I'm not some kind of tourist guide. I don't want you to get the idea that I just love London. In fact, I hate it a lot of the time. There are bits of it I hate all the time. So, anyway, you'd walk through Belsize Park toward Swiss Cottage. You can feel the slope that the river ran down. Then to Regent's Park and along the side of the boating lake."

"As we walk, you can talk to me about how you're feeling," said Sandy. "I suppose you should be feeling a bit bruised, especially with all the press."

Frieda found it strangely easy to talk to the voice in the darkness, not seeing the response, just feeling him. "From when I was little," she said, "I used to have a fantasy that I was invisible. I don't mean sometimes, I mean all the time, and I mean that I believed I really was invisible. But it turns out not to be true, so basically I feel like I've been taken out into the town square, flayed, and then had salt and sulfuric acid rubbed into my flesh."

"But you'll get over it."

"I'm already over it."

"So where are we now?"

"The river probably flows through the boating pond."

"Probably?"

"It's hard to find out. And then we walk out of the park and down Baker Street."

"Past Madame Tussaud's."

"That's right."

"Is it worth going to?"

"I've never been."

"Really? Have you been to the Tower of London?"

"No," said Frieda.

"I went when I was a kid."

"Was it good?"

"I don't really remember it," he said. "So where are we now?"

"This is the nice bit of the walk. You go through Paddington Street Gardens, which is a minute's walk from Madame Tussaud's and nobody knows about it, and across Marylebone High Street and down Marylebone Lane. Just for a bit you feel that you're walking along the bank of a stream as it flows through a little village just outside London. Except there's no stream. At least, not one you can see. It's there somewhere."

"You caught them," said Sandy.

"*They* caught them."

"Admittedly you didn't get full acknowledgment."

"Maybe I like doing without acknowledgment."

"Your invisible thing again. So those two,

that brother and sister, they just did all that for the money? Tortured that guy and killed him?"

"This is the bit of the walk I hate," said Frieda. "Suddenly you leave the village and you're right in the West End. The river became the boundary between two grand estates, and all that's left of it is awful big buildings, hotels, offices, garages. Robert Poole understood everybody, but he didn't understand Tessa and Harry Welles. He couldn't talk his way out of that one. They just wanted his money. It took only one finger for him to give them the details."

"Nice."

"But they got a taste for it. It's funny . . ." Frieda paused. "You're sure you don't want to sleep?"

Again she felt his touch.

"I wouldn't want to sleep tonight, even if I could."

"Well," she continued, "there's a difference between doing something and being something, but they merge into each other. I mean, you play the piano a bit, and then more and more, and at some point you become a pianist. That's who you are. That's your identity. They killed Robert Poole just for the money. They got trapped into killing that poor woman, Janet Ferris, and at that point they thought, We can do this. It stopped being just about the money and became about power. They got off on it. That's why they got involved with the investigation. It was about control, about showing they were better than us. Harry took it even further. If he could get to me, if he could fuck me, that would be the real demonstration of his control."

There was a silence for a time.

"You were on to him?" said Sandy. "It wasn't going to happen, was it?"

"He was never my type. The one who really interested me was Robert Poole."

"Is he your type?"

"No, no," said Frieda. "What haunts me is that he was a bit like me. Or I'm a bit like him. But he was better than me. At least, he was too good for himself. He was just a con man. He only needed to steal their money, but he had too much empathy. He was too interesting. It caught up with him."

"You couldn't save him," said Sandy. "His death was like, I don't know, the stipulation, the basis for it all. Anyway, where are we now?"

"It gets better," said Frieda. "We cross Piccadilly and we're at Green Park. You look across it and you can almost see the riverbed, where it ought to be. We walk through

615

the park, except that it's probably blocked by the preparations for the wedding."

"What wedding?"

"You know, the wedding. The royal wedding."

"Oh, that."

"But we make our way across, then round the edge of Buckingham Palace. The actual river flows under the palace. When I'm dictator and all the hidden rivers of London are exposed again, the palace will have to be demolished . . ."

"A small price to pay."

"And then we get to Victoria, which is even worse than the bit around Grosvenor Square. It's like a Fascist traffic island in the middle of a motorway and then a horrible street that's like the back of a hotel, where the deliveries are made and the rubbish taken out. But then you walk down Aylesford Street to the river and that's nice."

"Do you finally get to see the Tyburn?"

"You're not meant to," said Frieda. "It flows in a pipe under a house on the Embankment. But I once went round the side, climbed over the railing and down some metal steps on to the mud by the river at low tide. I sat by the outlet. After all that it was just a dribble. Hardly worth the trouble."

"I can't believe it," said Sandy. "You remember all that."

"I do the walks in my head sometimes. To try to get to sleep. It doesn't work."

"You should be a cabby," said Sandy.

"Thanks."

"No, I'm serious."

"I'm serious too."

"But don't they have to do that . . . what's it called? The Knowledge. The examiner asks them how to get from, I don't know, Banbury Cross to the Emirates Stadium and they have to describe it street by street."

"I don't think Banbury Cross is a real place."

"But you can do that. And they have special brains, don't they, cabbies?"

"The ones I meet don't seem to have particularly special brains."

"But they do," said Sandy.

"They have an enlargement in their mid-posterior hippocampus," said Frieda, "due to the enhanced neural activity in the region. And we're finished. We can go home."

"That's my kind of walk," said Sandy. "The kind you don't need to get out of bed for. And you're done."

"Except that poor Beth Kersey and Dean Reeve are still out there. We're warm in bed and they're out in the world."

"They're not your problem," said Sandy.
"They're being dealt with."

# 51

During the next morning, Frieda was perfectly able to play the role of a therapist. She leaned forward in her chair, she asked appropriate questions, she took a tissue from the box and handed it to a weeping woman. She rearranged appointments. At the end of each session, she took accurate notes and made brief plans for the future.

But all the time her mind was elsewhere. She had the feeling, which almost took her over, that something, somewhere was wrong. Her first thought was that it was within her own mind. Working with Karlsson and the police had been a sort of drug to her, and now that it had been snatched away, she was experiencing withdrawal symptoms. Was it all vanity? Was she missing the excitement and the attention? She remembered Thelma Scott, who had come to see her and offered her help, left her card. Frieda thought it might be time to start seeing a therapist again.

And she thought of Sandy. He was in London for work, but it was just a few weeks. In a month he would be back in New York. What, really, were the reasons that had made it seem impossible for her to go with him? "We're all afraid to acknowledge the freedom we really have." Someone had said that to her once. Was it Reuben? Or had she read it? Was she afraid to face up to her own freedom?

But mainly she thought of other things. Or, rather, she was aware of them. They were like strange noises outside in the darkness. She didn't know whether they were calling her or coming for her. She felt an urge that she could hardly define but that was telling her just to get away, to go anywhere. At twelve o'clock, after the last session of the day, she went into the tiny bathroom she had next to the consulting room, poured herself a glass of water, and drank it straight down, then another. After, she sat and finished her notes on the session.

She walked slowly back to her house. She didn't feel hungry; she felt she needed to lie down, get some sleep. Pushing her front door open, she saw the normal pile of letters. She picked it up. It was mostly junk mail; there was a gas bill, an invitation to a conference, and finally, a letter with no stamp, which must have been delivered by hand. There was nothing written on the envelope except her name in a vaguely familiar hand. Yes, Josef. She wondered why Josef would post a letter through her door instead of coming to see her. Had she been pushing him away? Him, too? Well, yes. She remembered their hasty words at Sasha's party. There was something he had wanted to tell her and she had rebuffed him. She tore the envelope open and read the letter:

Dear Frieda,
Sorry. You are cross I know. Sorry for that. I try to talk to you. Here is paper from Mrs. Orton. She want to burn it. I say I show to you. Sorry. I see you soon maybe.

Your best,<br>Josef

Frieda looked at Mary Orton's will. For just a few seconds she stood in furious thought, staring at the wall.

"Oh, my God," she said suddenly, ran through to the living room, found her notebook, and flicked through the pages. She found Mary Orton's number and dialed it. The phone rang ten times, fifteen times. She hung up and just stood in her room for almost a minute, paralyzed with indecision. She pushed the notebook into her pocket and ran out of the house. She hailed a taxi in Cavendish Street and gave the driver Mary Orton's address. He pulled a face.

"Bloody hell," he said. "What way shall we go, do you reckon?"

"I'm not the taxi driver," Frieda said. "What about Park Lane, Victoria, and then south of the river? Everywhere'll be jammed this time of day anyway."

"All right, love," said the driver, and pulled away.

Frieda dialed another number. She'd wanted Karlsson, but Yvette answered.

"I'm sorry about what happened," she said.

"That's fine. Is Karlsson there?"

"He's not available."

"I need to speak to him. It's really, really important."

"I can get a message to him."

Frieda contemplated her phone. She felt like banging it on the floor of the taxi. "Perhaps you can help," she said, forcing herself to speak calmly. "I just got a message from Josef, my friend, a builder, who was helping Mary Orton with her house.

Mary Orton made another will. She left a third of everything to Robert Poole." There was a silence. "Yvette, are you there?"

"Sorry, Frieda, didn't you get the memo? You're not working with us anymore."

"That doesn't matter. Don't you see? This will changes everything. I think it's likely that Poole was going to kill Mary Orton, once he knew that he would inherit hundreds of thousands of pounds at her death."

"Well, it's lucky he's dead instead, then."

"But Beth Kersey isn't."

"It's all right, Frieda. We're guarding the parents."

"The parents were never in danger. I talked to Lorna Kersey. Beth never threatened them. She tries to do things for people, what she thinks they want. It's when she does that, or when people try to stop her, that she turns violent. Very violent. You need to arrange protection for Mary Orton."

"That only meant something when Poole was alive."

"No. Don't you see? She would try to carry out his wishes. And if he wished Mary Orton dead — Yvette, will you tell Karlsson what I've told you?"

There was another pause. "I'll pass on your concern. But, Frieda, can't you just give this a rest? We've been shafted by that bastard Newton and we're trying to pick up the pieces. The case is over. Please. I'm sorry it happened this way, but we've got our own problems."

"Just tell Karlsson," Frieda said.

But the phone had gone dead. She tried Mary Orton's number again but, as before, it rang and rang. Who else was there to ring? Was it possible that Josef was still working there? Or nearby? She rang him and went straight to voice mail. She stared out of the window. The traffic wasn't as bad as it might have been. As they crossed the river, she rang Yvette again.

"Have you called Karlsson yet?" she said.

"I've told you, I'll contact him when I can. Now, please . . ."

The phone went dead again. Frieda stared at it. At first she felt dazed. There was nothing she could do. And then she thought of one thing she could do. What did it matter now anyway? She dialed 999.

"Emergency services. Which service, please?"

"Police."

There was a click and a whirr, then another female voice. "Hello, police. What is the nature of the emergency?"

Frieda gave Mary Orton's address. "I've seen an intruder."

624

"When was this?"

"A couple of minutes ago."

"Can you give any description?"

"No . . . Yes, I saw a knife. That's all."

"We'll arrange to send a car. Name, please."

Frieda imagined what Karlsson or Yvette would think of this. She felt as if she had cut the last fraying bit of thread that attached her to them. But it was the things you didn't do that mattered more than the things you did.

As the taxi turned into Mary Orton's road, Frieda expected to see brightly colored cars, flashing lights, but there was nothing. Jake Newton was right, she thought. Bloody hopeless. She handed a twenty-pound note to the driver.

"I haven't got any change," he said.

"Just keep it."

She walked toward the house. She hadn't planned for this moment. She moved to press the bell, then saw that the door wasn't quite shut. She pushed at it and it opened. Had a policeman on the beat arrived? Was Josef working there? She stepped inside.

"Mary?" she shouted. "Mrs. Orton?"

There was no reply. She felt her heart beating too strongly; she felt it in her neck and in her chest. There was a sour taste in her mouth. It was lactic acid, caused by the breakdown of oxygen. You got it when you ran fast or when . . . She called again. What to do? She couldn't phone the police. She'd already done that. Where the hell were they? Some false alarm somewhere probably. This was probably a false alarm. She walked through to the kitchen, her footsteps sounding horribly loud, as if they were telling her she was somewhere she wasn't meant to be.

The kitchen was empty. There was a mug on the table half filled with tea or coffee, an open newspaper. Frieda leaned over and touched the mug. It was warm. Not hot like tea that had just been made, but warmer than the ambient temperature. Mary Orton could have gone out, forgotten to shut the door. She turned and left the kitchen. Was there any point in looking round the house? She opened the door to the front room and stepped inside. She felt an immediate lurching, gulping shock. Mary Orton was lying on the carpet by the bookcase across the room from the door. Frieda knew about these things, and she felt her cognitive faculties close and narrow. She was looking at Mary Orton as if through a long tube. Frieda's first thought was that she'd fallen, like people of Mary Orton's age so often do. They fall and break a hip, and sometimes they can't get up and nobody finds them and they die. Then, almost dully and slowly, Frieda saw that what she had taken for a shadow on the cream carpet was actually blood. Mary Orton's blood. She ran across to her, trying to remember the pressure points. Anatomy had been such a long time ago.

Mary Orton was lying sprawled as if she had tried to roll over onto her back and failed.

"Mary," Frieda said coaxingly. "Mary, I'm here." Frieda looked into her eyes. She saw the tiniest flicker of something, a glimmer that puzzled her.

"Mary," said Frieda, and saw once again a minuscule movement in her eyes. And then Frieda realized what the movement signified. Barely alive, Mary Orton was not looking at Frieda but past her, over her shoulder, and Frieda thought, Oh, no. Oh, no. She felt a punch, hard and hot in her back, to one side, and from then on everything happened with great foggy slowness. So she had time to think, How slow everything is. And she was punched again, and now it was in her stomach. And she had time to think, Why am I being punched? After that, she was able to remember, quite calmly, that she had read of how being stabbed didn't feel at all like being stabbed. It didn't feel sharp. It felt blunt, like being hit by a fist in a boxing glove. Frieda raised her arms in some kind of defense but the next punch came on her leg and quite suddenly it was wet and warm. Frieda knew that she couldn't stand up anymore but she didn't fall. She stayed where she was, and Mary Orton's cream carpet came up to meet her. She lay face down on it. She could feel the rough threads on her lips and she was now very, very tired. All she wanted was to sleep. She realized that this was what it was like to die and that she mustn't die, so she made the most terrible, horrible effort to raise herself.

She saw a face, a girl's face. She had found Beth; Beth had found her. It seemed to be far away, like a dream. Then, from being slow, everything speeded up. There was a rush of sensations, noises, movement. She felt movement, she was moving herself, and then everything slowed down once more and became dark and first very warm and then very cold, and she felt her head fall back and then her leg started to hurt and then really hurt, so that she cried out and she almost did see something and someone, but it was too much effort and the pain faded, and she fell deeply, gratefully asleep.

# 52

It wasn't like waking. It was too patchy and painful and messy. She woke in fragments and flashes: a dirty white ceiling, faces leaning over her, faces saying things she didn't understand, the smell of soap and wetness on her body, being turned over, muttered conversations. Faces she recognized: Sandy, Sasha, Josef, Reuben, Jack, Karlsson, Olivia, Chloë, even Yvette. Some of them cried, some of them smiled. They came close and laid their hands on her shoulder, her face, and she couldn't tell them that she knew they were there. They talked to her. They talked about her in whispers. Josef sang Ukrainian lullabies between sobs, and Sasha read her poetry. Outside in the corridor she heard Chloë shouting at someone, her voice hoarse with fury, and she wished she could tell her angry, clumsy niece that it didn't matter, nothing mattered so very much, but she was unable to move her lips. Inside, a part of her found something funny. The Frieda Klein reunion party. She couldn't turn over. Sometimes she felt she was choking. Mostly she slept.

And then one day a voice said to her, "Frieda, can you hear me? Blink if you can hear." She blinked. "I'm going to count to three, then we'll pull the tube out and you should cough and breathe. All right, one, two, three."

Frieda felt like her insides were being pulled out through her mouth, as if she were vomiting them, and then she coughed and coughed.

"That's a good girl," said the voice.

"I'm not a girl," Frieda said huskily, and she started to say that she wasn't good, but it didn't feel worth the effort. There was more sleep, with occasional vague flashes. Was that Sasha in a chair by the bed reading a book?

There she was again, a hand on hers, looking down at her. This time she spoke to her, in her low and kindly voice: "Can you hear me, Frieda?"

She couldn't hear what she said back. She leaned closer and closer until she was whispering in her ear. "Water," she said.

Sasha lifted her head so gently and tipped the glass. The water was warm and stale and delicious.

"Frieda?" Sasha said. "The doctor's going to see you tomorrow. If you're up to it."

"You said I could tell you."

"What?"

It was very hard to form the words. "When I needed to talk."

She tried to find words, holding on to Sasha's slim cool hand while the machine behind her bleeped.

"It's all right," said Sasha, kissing her cheek. "We can talk later."

"One day," said Frieda, sinking back beneath dark waters.

The next day was different. Frieda woke, and was properly awake. She sat up and saw the ward she was in: three beds opposite, and two between her and the window. A woman across the way was complaining to a nurse, and behind a screen next to her she could hear the voice of an old woman saying the same word — "teacher" — over and over again. The day was gray and she felt awful. Her throat was ragged and almost the whole of her body ached. A trolley arrived with breakfast, some kind of porridge, milky tea, orange juice, all of it disgusting.

A nurse bustled across and said to Frieda, "He's here."

There, standing at the end of the bed, was a very distinguished-looking middle-aged man in a pin-striped suit and a bow tie. Through her bleary consciousness, Frieda managed to feel irritated. Why do consultants still wear bow ties even when they know it's a cliché?

He smiled down at her. "How's our phenomenon?" he said.

It took an effort, but Frieda could speak now. Even to herself, she sounded hoarse and halting, like someone who had just learned to speak. "I don't know what you mean."

He sat on the edge of the bed, still smiling. "I'm Dr. Khan," he said. "Your surgeon. I saved your life. But you saved it first. I've never seen anything like it. You have a medical degree, yes?" Frieda nodded. "Even so. Quite remarkable."

"I'm sorry," said Frieda. "What's remarkable?"

"You don't remember?" said Dr. Khan. Frieda shook her head. "It's understandable in the circumstances. One of the stab wounds resulted in a penetrating trauma that sliced a femoral artery. As you clearly realized, you would have bled out in a minute or two. Before you passed out, you managed to apply a tourniquet to your own leg."

"I didn't," said Frieda.

"You were in a state of severe shock," said Dr. Khan. "I have to say that tourniquets are no longer recommended. You risk necrotic damage but not in this case. We got you to the operating room in under an hour." He was about to pat her leg but stopped himself. "You were lucky with the stab wounds to the back and abdomen, if I can put it like that. Neither of them struck an organ. But, as they say, it only takes one. We worried about your leg at first, but you'll be fine. You may have to delay your triple-jump training until the Olympics after next, but apart from that . . ."

"Mary Orton," said Frieda.

"What?"

"What about Mary Orton?" said Frieda.

Dr. Khan's smile faded. "A friend of yours is here," he said. "He'll answer any questions. If you're strong enough, that is."

"Yes," said Frieda. "I am." She lay back on the pillow and saw Karlsson's face appear above her. She thought of a cloud floating overhead, or a zeppelin. Maybe it was the painkillers.

"You look terrible," she said.

"We can do this another time," he said.

"The nurse said you needed to rest."

"Now," said Frieda. "Mary Orton."

Karlsson looked to the side, as if he were waiting for someone else to speak. "She was pronounced dead at the scene," he said. "I think she'd been dead for some time."

"No," said Frieda. "She was alive. I remember her eyes. They were moving."

"They said she'd lost a lot of blood. I'm so sorry."

Frieda felt tears hot on her face. Karlsson reached for a tissue and dabbed them away.

"We let her down," said Frieda. "We failed her."

"The paramedics had enough on their hands with you. The other two were beyond help."

"The other two?"

"Mary Orton and Beth Kersey."

"What?" said Frieda, trying to raise herself from the pillow. "What do you mean?"

"Easy, easy," said Karlsson, as if he were soothing a restless child. "Don't worry. There won't be any trouble."

"What do you mean, trouble?"

"There's no problem at all," said Karlsson. "Quite the opposite. You'll probably get a medal."

"What do you mean?" said Frieda. "I don't remember anything."

"You don't?"

Frieda shook her head. She tried to think. It all seemed dim and far away.

"I was stabbed first from behind," she said. "I didn't even see her. Or at least — I barely remember. But there's something. I was losing blood, a lot of blood, and I passed out. I remember hearing something. That's all."

"I see this all the time," said Karlsson. "You'll probably never recover the memory. But it was easy to reconstruct what happened when we saw the scene. Christ, there was blood everywhere. Sorry, you don't need to hear this."

"But what happened?"

"We can save this for later, Frieda."

"Now," said Frieda. "Tell me."

"All right, all right," said Karlsson. "It's clear what must have happened. You acted out of self-preservation. After you were stabbed, you must have fought over the knife while you were bleeding yourself. You got hold of the knife and stabbed her in self-defense."

"How?"

"What?"

"How did I stab her?"

"She died of blood loss from a laceration to her throat."

"I cut her throat."

"Yes, and then you took her belt and tied it around your leg. The doctors say that if you hadn't done that you would have bled out in a couple of minutes."

Frieda gestured to the glass of water. Karlsson brought it to her lips. It hurt to swallow it.

"Sleep now," he said. "It'll all be fine."

"All right," Frieda said. Speaking seemed the hardest thing in the world just now. "But one thing."

He leaned close to her. "What?"

"I didn't do it."

"I've told you," Karlsson said. "You won't be in trouble. It was pure self-defense."

"No," said Frieda. "I didn't. I couldn't have. Besides . . ." Frieda made herself think of the moments before she had passed out. She tried to separate it from all that had followed, the oblivion, the nightmares, the fragments of waiting. "I heard something. But I know anyway. It was him."

Karlsson looked puzzled and then alarmed.

"What do you mean 'him'?"

"You know who I mean."

"Don't say that," hissed Karlsson. "Don't even think it."

# 53

Sandy parked the car near the western gate of Waterlow Park. On the steep drive up Swains Lane, Frieda had felt as if they were taking off and leaving London behind them.

"I think the park's open this time," Sandy said, with a smile that was full of pain.

Frieda winced as she got out of the car. She still felt sore, especially when she'd been sitting down.

"Are you up for this?" said Sandy.

Frieda had hated the pain, the treatment, the medication, the continuing hospital visits, but even worse was the sympathy, the attention, the concern, the look that came into people's eyes when they saw her, the way they worried about the right thing to say. She walked slowly and stiffly through the gate. A yellow dazzle of daffodils swaying in the wind.

"It really looks like spring now," said Sandy. "For the first time."

Frieda took his arm to support herself. "If you don't talk about spring and how it represents revival and new life, I won't say it's the cruelest month."

"Isn't April the cruelest month?"

"March is pretty cruel as well."

"All right," said Sandy. "I'll keep quiet about what a beautiful day this is and how the daffodils are out and how Waterlow Park has this wonderful position overlooking London. We could go next door to the cemetery, if that suits your mood more."

"You know me," said Frieda. "I like cemeteries. But this is good for today. I love this park. I don't know how Sir Thomas Waterlow earned his money. He probably stole it from someone or inherited it undeservedly. But he gave this park to London and I'm grateful to him for it. And I'm grateful to you."

"Well, gratitude isn't exactly —"

"Shhh. I know what you've gone through, Sandy, and what you can't say to me. You're too much of a gentleman, aren't you? You came back here and we met again and it was good. No, it was lovely. This should have been the time for us to think about our lives, make decisions, take pleasure in each other. Instead — well, you get to sit beside a hospital bed day after day, watching me sip thin chicken soup out of a straw or pee into a bowl."

"Thinking you might die."

"That too."

"When I thought you were going to die —"

"I know."

They made their way toward the pond. The park was busy and families were scattered along the path. Children were feeding ducks and pigeons and squirrels with nuts and stale bread.

"Look at that," said Sandy.

A small boy was throwing peanuts to a large rat that had emerged onto the grass from beneath a rhododendron bush.

"If you're going to feed pigeons," said Frieda, "you might as well feed rats too."

"Shall we walk up higher?" said Sandy. "There's a better view."

"In a minute," said Frieda.

"I wanted to come here for symbolic reasons. I didn't expect you to turn up at the wedding. I thought you'd cut me out of your life. I was very, very happy when I saw you."

"Yes," said Frieda. "Yes, I was happy too." It felt such a very long time ago.

A duck walked along, followed by a line of extremely small ducklings.

"Normally I would say that was very sweet," said Sandy. "But I won't." He turned and put his hands on her shoulders. "Frieda, I don't know how to put this, but I know it's been appalling beyond words for you, and if you ever want to talk . . ."

Frieda wrinkled her nose. "Do you want me to say that I'm traumatized?"

"Anyone would be."

"I don't know. We'll see. Right now, what I mainly feel is sad about Mary Orton. When I close my eyes, I can clearly see her looking up at me. She was looking at me in the last moments of her life, and I suppose she was thinking, But you said you were going to protect me. You said it would be all right. I can't think what else I could have done. I told the police. I dialed the emergency services. I went to her house."

"You did all you could."

"She had two sons who abandoned her. She was cheated and she turned to me for help and then she was murdered. Anyway, her two sons have got her money now, so at least someone's happy."

"This isn't you talking, Frieda. This isn't what you'd say to one of your patients."

"If I said to my patients what I say to myself, most of them would go off and kill themselves."

"It isn't what you say to Josef, when he blames himself for Mary Orton's death."

"No." Her face softened. "I tell Josef he did what he could and I should have listened."

"So it's one rule for everyone else and a different one for you."

"Yes."

"Why?"

"What do you mean?"

"Anyone would be affected by what you've been through. But it's not the being stabbed, the nearly dying, is it? When you talk about what happened to you, which isn't often, it's Mary Orton you dwell on, and Janet Ferris, even Beth Kersey, who would have killed you — indeed she almost did. And then there's Alan Dekker and Kathy Ripon. All the people who are gone. And it occurs to me that you feel — how can I put this? — too much about it, or too personally." Sandy stopped and looked at Frieda's fiercely glowing eyes. "What are you thinking?"

"Wait," she said. She turned away from him, looking out over the park.

When she turned back, her face was paler than ever, her eyes even brighter.

"I have something to tell you."

"Go on."

"I have never said this to anyone." She took a deep breath. "When I was fifteen years old, my father killed himself." She held up a hand to stop Sandy from saying anything, or coming closer. "He hanged himself in the attic of our house."

"I'm so sorry, Frieda."

"I found him. I cut him down but, of course, he was already dead. He had been very depressed, but I thought I could rescue him. I thought I could make him better. I still have a dream where I get to him in time. Over and over again." Her large eyes stared at him. "I didn't get to him in time, though," she said. "Or to Mary Orton. Or Janet Ferris. Or Kathy Ripon. Or poor Alan. People who trusted me and I let them down."

"No, my darling."

"I feel I carry a curse. You shouldn't come too close to me."

"You can't keep me away."

"Oh," said Frieda. For one moment, Sandy thought she would cry. She stepped forward and put one hand against his cheek, staring at him. "What are we going to do, Sandy?"

"We're going to give ourselves time."

"Are we?"

"Yes."

"So you'll still go back to the States, and I'll still be here?"

"Yes. But it won't be the same."

"Why?"

"Because of Waterlow Park. Because of our nighttime river walk. Because you've shown me how water can flow underground without drying up and disappearing. Because I know you."

"Yes," said Frieda very softly. "You know me."

"Hello!"

Sandy and Frieda both looked around. A little girl was standing next to Frieda, clutching a small bunch of daffodils with her two hands. She offered them to Frieda, stretching her arms out and standing on tiptoe. Frieda took them. "Thank you so much," she said. Even though the movement hurt her, she bent over so that her face was closer to the child's. "They're beautiful."

"It wasn't your time," said the little girl.

"What?" said Frieda. "What do you mean?"

"It wasn't your time." The little girl frowned with concentration, as if she was standing in front of her class at school. "It. Wasn't. Your. Time."

"What does that mean?"

She looked alarmed. Frieda thought she might run away. Sandy knelt down and spoke to her in a soft voice. "What's your name?" he said.

"Ginny."

"That's a nice name. Ginny, why did you say that?"

"Cause he told me to."

"Who?" said Sandy.

"The man."

Sandy looked up at Frieda, then back at the little girl. "Can you point to him?"

She looked around. "No," she said.

"What did he say?"

"He said, 'Give that woman these flowers and say . . .' " She paused. "I forgot."

"Ginny!" a voice called. "Ginny!"

The little girl ran back along the path to her mother.

"Well, what was that about?" said Sandy.

"He's watching me," said Frieda, in a voice hardly louder than a whisper.

"Who?"

"Dean," she said. "Dean Reeve. He's here. He's been here all along. I've felt him. It was him. I know it was." She turned to Sandy with a fierce expression. "I couldn't have cut Beth's throat. I couldn't have ripped her belt off to tie it round my leg. He saved me. Dean Reeve saved my life."

She waited for him to tell her she was paranoid, crazy, but he didn't. "Why?" he asked.

"Because he wants to be the person who has the power to destroy me."

"What are we going to do?"

She shrugged. "What can I do?"

"I said, 'we.' "

"I know. Thank you."

Sandy put his arms around her and she leaned against him. For a moment they didn't speak.

"So, shall we walk up the hill together?"

Frieda shook her head. "We should leave now," she said. "It's getting dark. The day's gone."

# ABOUT THE AUTHOR

**Nicci French** is the pseudonym for the internationally bestselling writing partnership of suspense writers Nicci Gerrard and Sean French. They are married and live in Suffolk and London, England. Visit nicci frenchbooks.com.

The employees of Thorndike Press hope you have enjoyed this Large Print book. All our Thorndike, Wheeler, and Kennebec Large Print titles are designed for easy reading, and all our books are made to last. Other Thorndike Press Large Print books are available at your library, through selected bookstores, or directly from us.

For information about titles, please call:
   (800) 223-1244

or visit our Web site at:
   http://gale.cengage.com/thorndike

To share your comments, please write:
Publisher
Thorndike Press
10 Water St., Suite 310
Waterville, ME 04901